THE SINS OF THE FATHER!

"What a cunning system you have there," Entreri said. "You and all the other self-proclaimed royalty of Faerûn. By your conditions, you alone are kings and queens and lords and ladies of court. You alone matter, while the peasant grovels and kneels in the mud, and since you are 'rightful' in the eyes of this god or that, then the peasant cannot complain. He must accept his muddy lot in life and revel in his misery, all in the knowledge that he serves the rightful king."

Gareth's jaw tightened, and he ground his teeth as he continued to stare unblinking at Entreri.

"You should have had Kane kill me," Entreri continued, "back at the castle."

"I am not your judge," the king said.

"Just my executioner," replied the assassin.

R.A. SALVATORE

TRANSITIONS
The Orc King
October 2007
The Pirate King
October 2008
The Ghost King
October 2009

THE LEGEND OF DRIZZT
Homeland
Exile
Sojourn
The Crystal Shard
Streams of Silver
The Halfling's Gem
The Legacy
Starless Night
Siege of Darkness
Passage to Dawn
The Silent Blade
The Spine of the World
Sea of Swords

THE HUNTER'S BLADES TRILOGY
The Thousand Orcs
The Lone Drow
The Two Swords

THE CLERIC QUINTET
Canticle
In Sylvan Shadows
Night Masks
The Fallen Fortress
The Chaos Curse

R.A. SALVATORE
ROAD OF THE PATRIARCH

THE SELLSWORDS

BOOK III

The Sellswords, Book III
ROAD OF THE PATRIARCH

©2007 Wizards of the Coast, Inc.

Cover art by Todd Lockwood
Map by Todd Gamble
Original Hardcover Edition First Printing: October 2006
First Paperback Printing: July 2007

9 8 7 6 5 4 3

ISBN: 978-0-7869-4277-0
620-95943740-001-EN

U.S., CANADA,
ASIA, PACIFIC, & LATIN AMERICA
Wizards of the Coast, Inc.
P.O. Box 707
Renton, WA 98057-0707
+1-800-324-6496

EUROPEAN HEADQUARTERS
Hasbro UK Ltd
Caswell Way
Newport, Gwent NP9 0YH
GREAT BRITAIN
Save this address for your records.

Visit our web site at www.wizards.com

PRELUDE

Yes, she is beautiful, Artemis Entreri thought as he watched the naked Calihye walk from the bed to the clothing rack to retrieve her breeches and shirt. She moved with the grace of a skilled warrior, one leg flowing effortlessly in front of the other, the soft pads of the balls of her feet coming down lightly and cushioning her step. She was of medium height, lithe but strong, and the few scars on her body did not detract from the graceful image of the tight cords of muscle. She was a creature of paradox, Entreri realized as he watched her, a being of fire and fluidity. She could be ferocious or tender, and she seemed to understand how to move between the two to the greatest effect when they were making love.

And no doubt she did the same on the battlefield. Calihye wasn't just a fighter; she was a warrior, a thinker. She knew her own strengths and weaknesses as well as any, but measured her opponent's better than most. Entreri had no doubt that the woman often used her feminine charms on unwitting opponents, throwing them off guard before eviscerating them.

He respected that; the image brought a smile to his often-scowling face.

It was a short-lived grin, though, as the man considered his own situation. On a peg near the clothes rack where Calihye dressed hung his small-brimmed black hat, the one Jarlaxle had given him. Entreri had found that the cap, like his drow companion, was much more than it seemed. It held many beneficial properties, magical and mechanical, including the ability to chill his body to better help him

1

hide from eyes that sensed heat instead of light, and a wire inset into the band, easily retractable, that allowed the hat to fit so snugly that even a fall from a horse wouldn't dislodge it.

More than it seemed, Entreri thought. Wasn't everything?

He had slept soundly after his encounter with Calihye the previous night. Too soundly? Calihye could have killed him, he realized, and the thought flickered through his mind that perhaps the woman was using her charms on him. She had put him into more vulnerable a position than he had ever known.

No, he assured himself. Her feelings for me are genuine. This is no game.

Except, he noted, wouldn't that have been Calihye's strategy, to put him so completely off his guard that she could risk an attack upon him?

Entreri dropped his head into his hands and rubbed his bleary eyes. He shook his head as he did, and was glad that his hands covered his helpless chuckle. He would drive himself mad with such thoughts.

"Are you coming with me, then?" Calihye asked, drawing him from his reverie.

He lifted his head and looked at her again as she stood by the rack. She was still nude, though his eyes did not roam her body, but rather settled upon her face. By all measures, Calihye had once been a strikingly beautiful woman, with startling eyes that sometimes showed reflections of gray amidst their blue. At other times, depending on the background—the lighting, her clothing—those eyes glowed an exquisite shade of medium blue, and either way they always seemed striking because of their contrast with her raven-dark hair. Her face was symmetrical, her bone structure impeccable.

But that scar. It ran across her right cheek to her nose, then down through her lips to the middle of her chin. It was an angry scar, often inflamed and red. Calihye hid behind it, Entreri knew, as if in denial of her feminine beauty.

When she flashed her smile, though, so mischievous and dangerous, Entreri hardly noticed the tear in her lips. To Artemis Entreri, she remained beautiful, and other than to consider her motivations for keeping the scar and the deeper meaning it seemed to hold to her, he hardly noticed it. It did not detract in the least for him, so lost was he in the mysteries that simmered in her eyes. She shook her head and her thick hair rolled over her shoulders, and Entreri wanted to leap over and bury his face in that warm, soft mane.

"We agreed to eat," Calihye reminded him. She gave a sigh and began pulling on her shirt. "I would have thought you'd worked up a great and growling hunger."

As her head came up through her collar her eyes set on her lover, and Calihye's smile disappeared.

That flash of a frown clued Entreri in to his own expression. He was scowling. He didn't know why. There wasn't a singular thought in his mind that might bring a scowl to his face just then. Calihye wouldn't elicit such a thought from him, after all, for he considered her a bright spot in his miserable life. But he was indeed scowling, as her reflective frown revealed.

He wore that dour expression often of late—or had it been forever?—and usually for no apparent reason at all. Except, of course, that he was often angry—at everything and nothing all at once.

"We do not have to eat," the woman said.

"No, no, of course we should go and get some food. The morning is late already."

"What troubles you?"

"Nothing."

"Did I not please you last night?"

Entreri nearly snorted aloud at that absurdity, and he couldn't suppress a smile as he considered Calihye and recognized that she was simply goading him for a compliment.

"You have pleased me many nights. Greatly. And last night was among those," he offered to her, and he was glad to see her apparent relief.

"Then what troubles you?"

"I told you that I am not troubled." Entreri reached down and gathered up his pants and began pulling them over his feet. He stopped when he felt Calihye's hand on his shoulder. He looked up at her, staring down at him, a look of concern on her face.

"Your words do not match your expression," she said. "Tell me. Can you not trust me? What is it that so upsets the humors of Artemis Entreri? What is it about you? What happened to you, to ignite this inner fire?"

"You speak in foolish riddles of your own imagination." He bent down again to pull his pants on, but Calihye gripped him more tightly, forcing him to look back at her.

"What is it?" she pressed. "How is a warrior of such perfection as Artemis Entreri created? What history did this to you?"

Entreri looked away from her, looked down at his own feet. But he didn't really see them. In his mind's eye, Artemis Entreri was a boy again, barely more than a child, in the dusty streets of a desert port city that was full of the smell of brine or filled with stinging sand, depending upon which way the wind was blowing.

The wagons creaked even though they were not moving, as the sandy breeze sizzled against their wooden sides. A couple of the horses nickered uncomfortably and one even reared up as far as its heavy, tight harness would allow. The driver, a thin and sinewy man of harsh, angular features who reminded the boy of his father, wasted no time in putting the whip savagely to the frightened creature.

Yes, just like his father.

The fat spice dealer seated on one wagon stared at him for a long time. Those heavy-lidded eyes seemed to invite him to slumber, as mesmerizing as a swaying serpent. There was something there, he knew, some magic behind that gaze, some method of control that had allowed the pathetic, slovenly beast to rise to prominence among the troupe gathered for their seasonal caravan out of Memnon. The others all deferred to that one, he could see, though he was just a boy and knew little about the world or about the hierarchy of the merchant class.

But that one was the boss, to be sure, and the boy flushed, flattered that the leader of so many would spend time with him and his mother. That prideful flush became an open-jawed, wide-eyed stare of disbelief as the fat man handed over coins—gold coins! *Gold* coins! The boy had heard of them, had heard of golden coins, but had never seen any. He had seen silver once, handed by some stranger to his father, Belrigger, before the stranger went behind the curtain with his mother.

But never gold. His mother was holding gold!

How thrilling it had been, but briefly. Then Shanali, his mother, grabbed him roughly by the shoulder and pushed him to the fat man's waiting grasp. He wriggled and fought the hold. He tried to tug away from the sweaty arms, at least so that he could get some answers from his mother.

But when he finally managed to face her, she had already turned and started away.

He called out to her. He pleaded with her. He asked her what it all meant.

"Where are you going?

"Why am I still here?

"Why is he holding me?

"Mama-hal!"

And she did glance back, only once and only for a moment. Just long enough for him to see her sunken, sad eyes one last time.

"Artemis?"

He shook his memories away and looked at Calihye. She seemed amused and concerned all at once. Strangely so.

"Are you to sit there with a flute in your hands and your breeches about your ankles all morning?"

The question shook him, and only then did Entreri realize that he was indeed holding Idalia's flute, the magical instrument the dragon sisters had given to him. And yes, as Calihye had noted, his breeches were still rumpled around his ankles. He placed the flute down beside him on his bed—or started to, but found he couldn't quite let it go just then. With that realization came a sudden strength, and he dropped the flute, quickly stood, and pulled up his pants.

"So what is it?" Calihye asked him, and he looked at her with curiosity. "What is it that creates a perfect warrior such as Artemis Entreri?" she clarified.

His mind flashed back again to Memnon. An image of Belrigger flashed before him and he felt himself jerk.

He realized that he was holding the flute again.

Tosso-pash's one-toothed leer flickered before him, and he threw the flute down on the bed.

"Training? Discipline?" Calihye asked.

Entreri snatched his shirt up from the chair and moved past her.

"Anger," he said, and in such a tone that no further questioning would likely be forthcoming.

It stood as just another clay-stone rectangle in a sea of similar houses, an unremarkable structure a dozen feet across and half a dozen front-to-back. It had an awning, like all of its neighbors, facing the sea breeze that usually offered the only relief from Memnon's unrelenting heat. There were no walls partitioning the house. A single threadbare curtain sectioned off a sleeping area, where his mother and father, Shanali and Belrigger—or Shanali and someone who had paid Belrigger—slept. For the boy there was just the floor of the common room. Once, when too many bugs had crawled around him, the boy had climbed on the table to sleep, but Belrigger had found him there and had beaten him severely for the infraction.

Most of the beatings had blended together in the haze of passing time, but that particular one, Artemis remembered clearly. Drunker than usual, Belrigger had taken to his back and rump with a rotted old board, and the battering had left several splinters in Artemis's backside that had become infected and oozed white and greenish pus for days.

Shanali had come to him with a wet cloth to wipe those wounds. He remembered that. She had rubbed his backside gently, with motherly love, and though she had uttered a few scolding words, calling him foolish for not remembering Belrigger's rules, even those had come tinged with sympathy.

Was that the last time Shanali had treated him kindly? Was that the last gentle memory he had of his mother?

The woman who had handed him over to the merchant caravan a few months later hardly seemed like the same creature. She had even physically changed by that fateful day at the merchant's, had grown pale and sunken, and she couldn't speak a full sentence without pausing to catch her breath.

His mind recoiled from the image of that day, rushing back

to Belrigger and Tosso-pash, the toothless and bristle-faced idiot who spent more time under Belrigger's awning than did Belrigger himself.

Tosso-pash came to him in flashing images—leering, always leering, and always leaning over him, always reaching for him. Even the man's words flashed in phrases Artemis had heard far too many times.

"I'm yer Papa-hal's brother.

"Ye call me Uncle Tosso.

"I can make ye feel good, boy."

Entreri's mind recoiled from those images, from those words, even more so than from the last image of his mother.

Belrigger had never done that, at least, had never chased him around the alleyways until his legs ached from the exertion, had never lain down beside him when he was trying to sleep, had never tried to kiss him or touch him. Belrigger hardly ever even acknowledged his existence, unless it was to administer another beating, or to lash out at him with a string of insults and curses.

He could only imagine that he had been a great disappointment to his father. What else could bring the man to such anger against him? Belrigger was embarrassed by the frail Artemis—ashamed and angry that he had to feed the boy, even if all he ever gave to Artemis was the stale crust of his bread or other morsels left over after he was done with his meal.

And even his mother had turned away from him, had taken the gold . . .

The fat merchant's flabby arms provided no warmth and no comfort.

Entreri woke in darkness. He felt the cold sweat all over his naked form; the blankets clung wetly to him.

The moment of panic subsided somewhat when he heard Calihye's steady breathing beside him. He moved to sit up, and was surprised to find that magical flute of Idalia lying across his waist.

Entreri picked it up and brought it before his eyes, though he could barely see it in the dim starlight slipping in through the room's single window. From its feel, both physically in his hands and in the emotional connection he had attained with it in his mind, he was certain that it was the same magical flute.

He paused for a moment to consider where he had placed the flute when he had gone to bed—on the lip of the wooden bed frame beside him, he recalled, and within easy reach.

So he had apparently scooped it up during his sleep, and it had brought him to those memories again.

Or were they even memories? Entreri had to wonder. Were the images flashing so clearly through his mind an accurate recounting of his childhood days in Memnon? Or were they some devilish manipulation by the always-surprising flute?

He remembered clearly that day with the caravan, though, and knew his flute-enhanced images of it were indeed correct. That memory of Memnon, the final and absolute betrayal by his mother, had followed Artemis Entreri for thirty years.

"Are you all right?" Calihye asked softly as he sat on the edge of the bed. He heard her shift behind him, then felt her against his back, leaning on him, her arm coming around to rub his chest and hold him close.

"Are you all right?" she asked again.

His fingers moving along the smooth curves of Idalia's flute, Entreri wasn't sure.

"You are tense," Calihye noted, and she kissed him on the side of the neck.

His reflexive movement showed her that he wasn't in the mood for any of that, though.

"Is it your anger?" the woman prodded. "Are you still thinking of that? The anger that created Artemis Entreri?"

"You know nothing," Entreri assured her, and shot her a look that even in the darkness she could sense warned her that she was walking on ground uninvited.

"Anger at who?" she asked anyway. "At what?"

"No, not anger," Entreri corrected, and he was talking to himself more than to her. "Disgust."

"At?"

"Yes," Entreri answered, and he pulled away and stood up.

He turned to Calihye. She shook her head and slowly slid off the

bed to move to stand at Entreri's side. She gently draped her arm behind his neck and leaned in close.

"Do I disgust you?" she whispered in his ear.

Not yet, Entreri thought, but did not say. But if you ever do, I will put a sword through your heart.

He forced that notion from his thoughts and put his hand over Calihye's, then glanced sidelong at her and offered a comforting smile.

PART  1

T I G H T R O P E

*A*re they still together, walking side by side, hands ever near the hilts of their weapons—to defend against each other, I would guess, as much as from other enemies?

Many times I think of them, Artemis Entreri and Jarlaxle. Even with the coming of King Obould and his orc hordes, even amidst the war and the threat to Mithral Hall, I find my thoughts often wandering the miles of distance and time to find in my mind's eye a reckoning of the unlikely pair.

Why do I care?

For Jarlaxle, there is the ever-present notion that he once knew my father, that he once wandered the ways of Menzoberranzan beside Zaknafein, perhaps much as he now wanders the ways of the World Above beside Artemis Entreri. I have always known that there was a complexity to this strange creature that defied the easy expectations one might have of a drow—even that one drow might have for another. I find comfort in the complexity of Jarlaxle, for it serves as a reminder of individualism. Given my dark heritage, oftentimes it is only the belief in individualism that allows me to retain my sanity. I am not trapped by my heritage, by my elf's ears and my coal-colored skin. While I often find myself a victim of the expectations of others, they cannot define me, limit me, or control me as long as I understand that there is no racial truth, that their perceptions of who I must be are irrelevant to the truth of who I am.

Jarlaxle reinforces that reality, as blunt a reminder as anyone could ever be that there resides in each of us a personality that defies external limitations. He is a unique one, to be sure, and a good thing that is, I believe, for the world could not survive too many of his ilk.

I would be a liar indeed if I pretended that my interest in Artemis Entreri only went so far as his connection to the affirmation that is Jarlaxle. Even if Jarlaxle had returned to the Underdark, abandoning the assassin to his lonely existence, I admit that I would regularly turn my thoughts to him. I do not pity him, and I would not befriend him. I do not expect his redemption or salvation, or repentance for, or alteration of, the extreme selfishness that defines his existence. In the past I have considered that Jarlaxle will affect him in positive ways, at least to the extent that he will likely show Entreri the emptiness of his existence.

But that is not the impetus of my thoughts for the assassin. It is not in hope that I so often turn my thoughts to him, but in dread.

I do not fear that he will seek me out that we might do battle yet again. Will that happen? Perhaps, but it is nothing I fear, from which I shy, or of which I worry. If he seeks me, if he finds me, if he draws a weapon upon me, then so be it. It will be another fight in a life of battle—for us both, it seems.

But no, the reason Artemis Entreri became a staple in my thoughts, and with dread, is that he serves as a reminder to me of who I might have been. I walked a line in the darkness of Menzoberranzan, a tightrope of optimism and despair, a path that bordered hope even as it bordered nihilism. Had I succumbed to the latter, had I become yet another helpless victim of crushing drow society, I would have loosed my blades in fury instead of in the cause of righteousness—or so I hope and pray that such is indeed the purpose of my fight—in those times of greatest stress, as when I believed my friends lost to me, I find that rage of despair. I abandon my heart. I lose my soul.

Artemis Entreri abandoned his heart many years ago. He succumbed to his despair, 'tis obvious. How different is he than Zaknafein, I have to ask—though doing so is surely painful. It almost seems to me as if I am being disrespectful of my beloved father by offering such a comparison. Both Entreri and Zaknafein loose the fury of their blades without remorse, because both believe that they are surrounded by a world not worthy of any element of their mercy. I make the case in differentiating between the two that Zaknafein's antipathy was rightly placed, where Entreri is blind to aspects of his world deserving of empathy and undeserving of the harsh and final judgment of steel.

But Entreri does not differentiate. He sees his environs as Zaknafein viewed Menzoberranzan, with the same bitter distaste, the same sense of hopelessness, and thus, the same lack of remorse for waging battle against that world.

He is wrong, I know, but it is not hard for me to recognize the source of his ruthlessness. I have seen it before, and in a man I hold in the highest esteem. Indeed, in a man to whom I owe my very life.

We are all creatures of ambition, even if that ambition is to free ourselves of responsibility. The desire to escape ambition is, in and of itself, ambition, and thus ambition is an inescapable truth of rational existence.

Like Zaknafein, Artemis Entreri has internalized his goals. His ambition is based in the improvement of the self. He seeks perfection of the body and the arts martial, not for any desire to use that perfection toward a greater goal, but rather to use it for survival. He seeks to swim above the muck and mire for the sake of his own clean breath.

Jarlaxle's ambition is quite the opposite, as is my own—though our purposes, I fear, are not of the same ilk. Jarlaxle seeks to control not himself, but his environment. Where Entreri may spend hours building the muscle memory for a single maneuver, Jarlaxle spends his time in coercing and manipulating those around him to create an environment that fulfills his needs. I do not pretend to understand those needs where Jarlaxle is concerned. They are internal ambitions, I believe, and not to do with the greater needs of society or any sense of the common good. If I were to wager a guess based on my limited experience with that most unusual drow, I would say that Jarlaxle creates tension and conflict for the sake of entertainment. He finds personal gain in his machinations—no doubt orchestrating the fight between myself and Artemis Entreri in the replica of Crenshinibon was a maneuver designed to bring the valuable asset of Entreri more fully into his fold. But I expect that Jarlaxle would cause trouble even without the lure of treasure or personal gain.

Perhaps he is bored with too many centuries of existence, where the mundane has become to him representative of death itself. He creates excitement for the sake of excitement. That he does so with callous disregard to those who become unwitting principles in his often deadly game is a testament to the same sort of negative resignation that long ago infected Artemis Entreri, and Zaknafein. When I think of Jarlaxle and Zaknafein side by side in Menzoberranzan, I have to wonder if they did not sweep through the streets like some terrible monsoon, leaving a wake of destruction along with a multitude of confused dark elves scratching their heads at the receding laughter of the wild pair.

Perhaps in Entreri, Jarlaxle has found another partner in his private storm.

But Artemis Entreri, for all their similarities, is no Zaknafein.

The variance of method, and more importantly, of purpose, between Entreri and Jarlaxle will prove a constant tug between them, I expect—if it has not already torn them asunder and left one or both dead in the gutter.

Zaknafein, as Entreri, might have found despair, but he never lost his soul within it. He never surrendered to it.

That is a white flag Artemis Entreri long ago raised, and it is one not easily torn down.

—Drizzt Do'Urden

CHAPTER

1

It wasn't much of a door, actually, just a few planks thrown together and tied with frayed rope, old cloth, and vines. So when the ferocious dwarf hit it in full charge, it exploded into its component parts. Wood, rope, and vine went flying into the small cave, trailed by ribbons of cloth.

No fury summoned from the Nine Hells could have brought more tumult and chaos in the instants that followed. The dwarf, thick black hair flying wildly, long beard parted in the middle into two long braids flopping across his chest and shoulders, lunged at the poor goblins, twin morningstars spinning with deadly precision.

The dwarf veered for the largest group, a collection of four of the goblins. He barreled into their midst without heed for the crude weapons they brandished, blowing past their defenses, kicking, stomping, and smashing away with his devastating morningstars, their spiked metal heads whipping at the ends of adamantine chains. He hit one goblin square in the chest, crushing its lungs and lifting it into a ten-foot flight. A turn and duck put him under the thrust of a spear that was no more than a pointed stick, and as he rolled around, the dwarf brought his trailing arm up and across, hooking the goblin's arm and throwing it aside. The dwarf squared before the goblin, and two overhead swings crushed its shoulder and its skull. He kicked the creature hard under the chin as it dropped to the stone, shattering its jaw, though it was already so far gone from life that it didn't even scream.

The dwarf's braids whipped as he leaped and turned to face the

17

two remaining goblins. They could not match that ferocity, could not seem to even comprehend it, and they hesitated just an instant.

An instant more than the dwarf needed.

Forward he raced, and each arm struck at the goblins. One hit squarely, the other a glancing blow, but even that second goblin stumbled under the weight of the assault. The dwarf rolled over the goblin, driving it down with kicks and chops.

He rushed past and broke for the door, leaping into a sidelong spin and coming around with a double swing that took one goblin in the back as it tried to retreat through the door and back to the mountain slopes. Indeed, it got through the door, and much more quickly than it ever would have believed possible if it had been thinking of such things.

Its shattered spine took precedence, though, and as it crumbled to the dirt and stone, it felt . . . nothing.

The dwarf landed in front of the door, feet wide and steady. He went into a defensive crouch, eyes wild, braids bouncing, and arms out to his sides with the morningstar's heads dropping down low.

There had been at least ten of the creatures in the cave, he was certain, but with five down, he found only two facing him.

Well, at least one was facing him. The other banged frantically on a second door at the back of the cave, one more substantial and made of iron-bound hardwood.

The second goblin shrank against its companion, not daring to take its gaze from the furious intruder.

"Ah, but ye got yerself a safer room," the dwarf said, and took a step forward.

The goblin recoiled, small and pathetic sounds escaping its chattering teeth. The other pounded more furiously.

"Come on, then," the dwarf chided. "Pick up a stick and fight back. Don't ya be takin' all the fun out of it!"

The goblin straightened just a little bit, and the dwarf had seen enough of battle to catch the clue. He whirled around, launching a high-flying backhand that got nowhere close to hitting the sneaky goblin that slipped in the blasted door behind him. But it wasn't supposed to hit the creature, of course, merely distract it.

So it did, and as the dwarf strode forward and came around with his second swing, he found a clean opening. The goblin's face shattered under the weight of the morningstar, and the creature would have flown far indeed had not the jamb of the door caught it.

When the dwarf turned back, both goblins were pounding on the unyielding door with desperate abandon.

The dwarf sighed and relaxed, shaking his head in dismay. He walked across the room, and one, two, caved in the backs of the creatures' skulls.

He took up his morningstars in one hand and grabbed one of the fallen creatures by the back of the neck with his other. With the strength of a giant, he flung that goblin aside, throwing it the ten feet to the side wall with ease. The second then went for a similar flight.

The dwarf adjusted his girdle, a thick leather enchanted affair that bestowed upon him that great strength—even more than his powerful frame carried on its own.

"Nice work," he remarked, studying the craftsmanship of the portal.

No goblin doors those; the creatures had likely pillaged them from the ruins of some castle or another in the bogs of Vaasa. He had to give the goblins credit, though, for they had fit the portal quite well into the wall.

The dwarf knocked, and called out in the goblin tongue, in which he was quite fluent, *"Hey there, ye flat-headed walking snot balls. Now ye don't be wantin' me to ruin such a fine door as this, do ye? So just open it up and make it easy. I might even let ye live, though I'm suren to be takin' yer ears."*

He put his own ear to the door as he finished, and heard a quiet whimper, followed by a louder *"Shhhh!"*

He sighed and knocked again. *"Come on, then. Last chance for ye."*

As he spoke, he stepped back and rolled his fingers around the leather-wrapped handles of the twin morningstars, willing forth their magic. Liquid oozed from the spikes of each ball, clear and oily on the right hand one, and reddish and chalky on the other. He sized up the door, recognizing the center cross of perpendicular metal bands as the most important structural point.

He counted to three—he had to give the goblins an honest chance, didn't he?—then launched into a ferocious leap and swing, left morningstar leading, and connecting precisely at the juncture of those two critical iron bands. The dwarf kept jumping and turning and building momentum with his right-hand weapon, though he did whack at the door a couple of times with the left, denting wood and metal and leaving behind that reddish residue.

It was the ichor of a rust monster, a devilish creature that made every knight in shining armor wet himself. For within moments, those solid iron bands began to turn the color of the liquid, rusting away.

When he was convinced that the integrity of the iron bands had been fully compromised, the dwarf jumped into his greatest leap of all, turning as he went so that he brought all of his weight and all of his strength to bear as he finally unloaded his right-hand morningstar at the same exact spot. Likely his great might and impeccable form would have cracked the door anyway, but there was no doubt at all as the liquid on that second head, oil of impact by name, exploded on contact.

Sundered in two, both the door and the locking bar in place behind it, the portal fell open, half flopping in to the dwarf's right, still held awkwardly by one hinge, while the left side tumbled to the floor.

There stood a trio of goblins, wearing ill-fitted, plundered armor—one had gone so far as to don an open-faced metal helm—and holding various weapons, a short sword for one, a glaive for the second, and a battle-axe for the third. That might have given younger adventurers pause, of course, but the dwarf had spent four centuries fighting worse, and a mere glance told him that none of the three knew how to handle the weapons they brandished.

"Well, if ye're wantin' to give me yer ears, then I'll be lettin' ye walk out o' here," the dwarf said in heavily-accented Goblin. *"I'm not for givin' the snot of a flat-headed orc one way or th'other whether ye live or whether ye die, but I'm takin' yer ears to be sure."* As he finished, he produced a small knife, and spun it to stick into the floor before the feet of the middle of the trio. *"Ye give me yer left ears, and give me back the knife, and I'm lettin' ye walk on yer way. Ye don't, and I'm takin' them from yer corpses. Yers to choose."*

The goblin on the dwarf's right lifted its glaive, howled, and charged.

Just the answer Athrogate was hoping for.

ROAD OF THE PATRIARCH

Artemis Entreri slipped behind a dressing screen when he heard the dwarf pushing through the door. Never an admirer of Athrogate, and never quite trusting him, the assassin was glad for the opportunity to eavesdrop.

"Ah, there ye be, ye elf-skinny pretender to me throne," Athrogate bellowed as he pushed into Calihye's room.

The woman looked at him with a sidelong glance, seeming unconcerned—and a big part of that confidence, Entreri knew, came from the fact that he was within striking distance.

"So ye're thinking that ye got yerself a title here, are ye?"

"What are you talking about?"

"Lady Calihye, leading the board," Athrogate replied, and Calihye and Entreri nodded in recognition.

At the Vaasan Gate, a contest of sorts was being run by the many adventurers striking out into the wilderness. A price had been put on the ears of the various monsters roaming the wasteland, and to add to the enjoyment, the gate's commanders had put up a peg board listing the rankings of the bounty hunters. Almost from the start, Athrogate's name had topped that board, a position he had held until only a few months previous, when Calihye had claimed the title. Her fighting companion, Parissus, had been only a few kills back of the dwarf.

"Ye think I'm caring?" the dwarf asked.

"More than I am, obviously," replied the half-elf.

Behind the screen, Entreri nodded again, pleased with the response from the warrior who had become so dear to him.

Athrogate harrumphed and snorted, and roared, "Well, ye ain't for staying there!"

Entreri paid close attention to every inflection. Was the dwarf threatening Calihye?

The assassin's hands instinctively went to his weapon, and he dared move a bit farther behind the screen so that he could peek around the edge closest to the door, the angle of attack that would bring him in at the powerful dwarf's flank, if it came to that.

He relaxed as Athrogate brought one hand forward holding a small, bulging sack—and Entreri knew well what might be in there.

"Ye'll be looking at me rump again, half-elf," Athrogate remarked, and gave the bag a shake. "Fourteen goblins, a pair o' stupid orcs, and an ogre for good measure."

Calihye shrugged as if she didn't care.

"Ye best be winter huntin', if ye got enough dwarf in ye," Athrogate said. "Meself, I'll be goin' south to drink through the snows, so if ye're having some good luck, ye might get back on top—not that ye'll stay there more than a few days once the melt's on."

Athrogate paused there, and a wry smile showed between the bushy black hair of his beard. "Course, ye ain't got yer hunting partner no more, now do ye? Unless ye're to convince the sneak to go out with ye, and I'm not thinking that one's much for snowy trails!"

Entreri was too distracted to take offense at that last remark, however honest, for Calihye's wince had not been slight when Athrogate had referred to Parissus. The wound was still raw, he knew. Calihye and Parissus had been fighting side-by-side for years, and Parissus was dead, killed on the road to Palishchuk after she fell from the wagon Entreri drove from a horde of winged, snakelike monsters.

"I have little desire to go out and hunt goblins, good dwarf," Calihye said, her voice steady—though with some effort, Entreri noted.

The dwarf snorted at her. "Do as ye will or do as ye won't," he replied. "I'm not for carin', for I'll be takin' me title in the spring, from yerself or anyone else who's thinkin' to best me. Don't ye doubt!"

"Not to doubt and not to care," Calihye said, taking some of his bluster.

Indeed, Athrogate hardly seemed to have an answer for that. He just nodded and made an indecipherable sound, and shook the bag of ears at Calihye. Then he nodded again, said, "Yeah," and turned and walked out the door.

Entreri didn't note the movement at all, for he stayed focused on Calihye, who held her composure well though the weight of the dwarf's remarks surely sat heavily on her delicate shoulders.

CHAPTER

2

The companions could not have appeared more disparate. Jarlaxle rode a tall, lean mare, seventeen hands at least. He was dressed all in finery—silk clothing, a great sweeping cloak, and a huge wide-brimmed purple hat, adorned with the gigantic feather of a diatryma bird. He seemed impervious to the dust of the road, as not a smudge or stain showed on his clothing. He was lean and graceful, sitting perfectly upright, appearing as a noble of great stature and breeding. One could easily imagine him as a prince of drow society, a dark emissary skilled in the ways of diplomacy.

The dwarf riding next to him, on a donkey no less, could never have been accused of such delicacies. Stocky and brutish, many might have confused Athrogate for the source of the road's dirt. To the obvious irritation of the poor donkey, he wore a suit of armor, part leather, part plated, and covered with a myriad of buckles and straps. He hadn't bothered with a saddle, but just clamped his legs tightly around the unfortunate beast, which poked along stiff-legged, giving the dwarf a jolting and popping ride. His weapons, a pair of gray, glassteel morningstars, rose up in an **X** from his back, their spiked heads bouncing with each of the donkey's jarring steps.

And of course, Athrogate's considerable hair, too, was so unlike the clean-shaven drow, whose head shone smooth and black beneath the rim of his great hat—and indeed, those occasions when Jarlaxle lifted the hat showed him to be completely devoid of hair on his head, save a pair of thin, angled eyebrows. Athrogate wore his mane like a proud lion. Black hair, lots of it, lifted wildly from his head in every direction, blending with an abundance coming out of his ears, and he had once more braided his great beard, with its customary part in the middle, each braid secured with ties that featured blue gemstones.

"Ah, but ain't we the big heroes," Athrogate said to his traveling companion.

Ahead of them on the trail rode Artemis Entreri and Calihye, with a couple of soldiers leading the way. Behind the drow and the dwarf came more soldiers, leading a caisson that held the body of Commander Ellery, the young and once-promising knight, niece of King Gareth Dragonsbane and an officer in the Army of Bloodstone. The people of the Bloodstone Lands mourned Ellery's loss. The heroine had been cut down in the strange castle that had appeared in the bog lands of Vaasa, north of the half-orc city of Palishchuk.

Jarlaxle was glad that no one other than he and Entreri knew the truth of her death, that it had come at Entreri's hand during a fight between Ellery and Jarlaxle.

"Heroes, indeed," the drow finally replied. "I prophesied as much to you when I pulled you out of that hole. Holding fast to your anger about Canthan's unfortunate demise would have been a rather silly attitude when so much glory was there for our taking."

"Who said I was angry?" Athrogate huffed. "Just didn't want to have to eat the fool."

"It was more than that, good dwarf."

"Bwahaha!"

"Your allegiances were torn—legitimately so," Jarlaxle said, and glanced at Athrogate to try to measure the dwarf's reaction.

Athrogate had been engaged in a fight to the death with Entreri when Jarlaxle had intervened. Using one of his many, many magical items, Jarlaxle had opened a ten-foot-deep magical hole at the surprised dwarf's feet, into which Athrogate had tumbled. Grumbling and complaining, the helplessly trapped Athrogate had been unwilling to join in and see the error of his ways—until Entreri had dropped the corpse of the dwarf's wizard associate into the hole beside him.

"Ye're not for knowing Knellict the way I'm for knowing Knellict," Athrogate leaned over and whispered. Again Jarlaxle was taken aback by the tremor that came into the normally fearless dwarf's voice when he mentioned the name of Knellict, who at that time was either the primary assistant of Timoshenko, the Grandfather of Assassins in the prominent murderers' guild in Damara, or—so hinted the whispers—who had assumed the mantle of grandfather himself. "Seen him turn a dwarf into a frog once, then another into a hungry snake," Athrogate went on, and he sat straight again and shuddered. "Halfway through dinner, he turned 'em back."

The level of cruelty certainly didn't surprise or unnerve Jarlaxle, third son of House Baenre, who, as a newborn, had been stabbed in the chest by his own mother—a sacrifice to the vile goddess who ruled the world of the drow. Jarlaxle had spent centuries in Menzoberranzan, living and breathing the unending cruelty and viciousness of his malevolent race. Nothing Athrogate had told him, nothing Athrogate *could* tell him, could elicit a shudder such as the one the dwarf had offered during his recounting.

And Jarlaxle had suspected as much about Knellict, anyway. Knellict was the darker background in an organization built in the shadows, the dreaded Citadel of Assassins. Jarlaxle knew from his own experience as leader of the mercenary band Bregan D'aerthe, that in such organizations the leader—in the case of the citadel, reputedly Timoshenko—played a softer, more politic hand, while his lieutenants, such as Knellict, were quite often the barbarians behind the throne, the vicious enforcers who made followers and potential enemies alike take some measure of hope in the leader's infrequent but not unknown smiles.

On top of that, Knellict was a wizard, and Jarlaxle had always found that type to be capable of the greatest cruelties. Perhaps it was their superior intellect that so divorced them from the visceral agony resulting from their actions. Perhaps it was the arrogance that often accompanied such great intellect that so allowed them to disassociate themselves from the common folk, as an ordinary man might step on a cockroach without remorse. Or perhaps it was because wizards usually attacked from a distance. Unlike the warrior, whose killing strike often soaked his arm in the warmth of his enemy's blood, a wizard might throw a spell from afar and watch its destructive effects divorced from their immediacy.

They were a complicated and dangerous bunch, spellcasters, aloof and ultimately cruel. In Bregan D'aerthe, Jarlaxle had often elevated wizards to lieutenant or higher posts for just those reasons.

And the dwarf beside him, the drow reminded himself, was not to be taken lightly either. For all his jovial and foolish banter, Athrogate remained a potentially dangerous and capable enemy, one who had put Artemis Entreri back on his heels in their battle within the Zhengyian construct. Athrogate was as pure an instrument of destruction as any assassin's guild—or any army, for that matter—could ever hope to employ. He had gained quite the reputation at the Vaasan Gate, bringing in the ears of bounty creatures by the sackload. And for all his passion, his bluster, and his raucousness, Jarlaxle saw a significant gulf in Athrogate's personality. However Athrogate might befriend Jarlaxle and Entreri, if the order came from on high to kill them, Athrogate would likely shrug and take on the task. It would be just business for him, much as it had been for Entreri for all those years he served the Pashas in Calimport.

"Is yer friend understandin' the honor he's gettin'?" Athrogate asked, nodding his chin toward Entreri. "Knight of the Order—ain't no small thing in the Bloodstone Lands these days, what with Gareth bein' the king and all."

"I am sure he does not, and will not," the drow replied, and he gave a little laugh as he considered Entreri's obstinacy. With the exception of the two half-orcs, Arrayan and Olgerkhan, who had remained in Palishchuk, the survivors of the battle with Urshula the dracolich and the other minions of the magically animated castle were being hailed as heroes in Bloodstone Village on the morrow. Even Calihye, who had not gone into the castle, and Davis Eng, a soldier of the Army of Bloodstone who had been wounded on the road out from the Vaasan Gate, were to be honored. Those two and Athrogate would be recognized as Citizens of Good Standing in Damara and Vaasa, a title that would grant them discounts from merchants, free lodging in any inn, and—most important for Athrogate—free first drinks in any tavern. Jarlaxle could easily picture the dwarf running from tavern to tavern in Heliogabalus, swilling down a multitude of first drinks.

For his part, recognized for a more important role, Jarlaxle was to be given a slightly higher title, that of Bloodstone Hero, which conveyed all the benefits of the lower medal, and also allowed Jarlaxle free passage throughout the burgeoning kingdom and granted the guarantee of Gareth's protection wherever it might be needed. While

Jarlaxle agreed that his own role in the victory had been paramount, he had been a bit perplexed at first by the discrepancies in the honors, particularly between himself and Athrogate, who had battled the dracolich valiantly. At first he had presumed it to be the result of Athrogate's rather extensive and less-than-stellar public record, but after hearing of the honors to be given to Entreri, the actual slayer of the beast, Jarlaxle had come to see the truth of it. These degrees of honor had been quietly suggested, whispered through appropriate and legitimate channels, by Knellict and the Citadel of Assassins. Knellict had already explained to Jarlaxle that his value to the guild would, in no small part, be due to his ability to fill the void left by the death of Commander Ellery, distant niece of King Gareth, who was also tied in with the citadel.

For Entreri, that one blow—luring the beast to thrust its head under the trap he had set in a side tunnel off the main lair—had changed the world. Entreri was the hero of the day, and accordingly, King Gareth would bestow upon him the title of Apprentice Knight of the Order.

Artemis Entreri, a knight in a paladin king's army . . . it was more than Jarlaxle could take, and he burst out laughing.

"Bwahaha!" Athrogate joined in, though he hadn't any idea what had set the drow off. Apparently catching on to that reality, Athrogate bit off his chortle and said, "So what's got ye titterin', coalskin?"

Low clouds in the west dulled the late afternoon sun, and the cool breeze comfortably tickled Master Kane. He sat cross-legged, hands on his thighs with his palms facing up. He kept his eyes closed, allowing his mind to focus inward as he consciously relaxed his body, using his rhythmic breathing as a cadence for his complete concentration.

One would not normally fly upon a magical carpet with his eyes closed, but Kane, former Grandmaster of Flowers at the Monastery of the Yellow Rose, was not concerned by trivial matters such as steering the thing. Every so often, he opened his eyes and adjusted accordingly, but he figured that unless a dragon happened to be soaring through the skies over Bloodstone Valley, he was safe enough.

So perfect was his mental count that he opened his eyes just as Bloodstone Village came into view far below him. He spotted all of the major buildings, of course, but they didn't impress him, not even the grand palace of his dear friend, Gareth Dragonsbane.

Nothing man-made could hold much of an impact over Kane, who had known the decorated corridors of the Monastery of the Yellow Rose, but the White Tree. . . .

As soon as the monk spotted it in the grand garden on the shores of Lake Midai his heart filled with serenity and the contentment that could only come from accepting oneself as a part of something larger, of something eternal. The seed for that tree, the Tree-Gem, had been given to Kane and his fellow heroes by Bahamut, the platinum dragon, the greatest wyrm of all, as a tribute to their efforts in defeating the Witch-King and his demonic associates and destroying the Wand of Orcus.

The White Tree stood as a symbol of that victory, and more than that, it served as a magical ward preventing creatures of the Abyssal planes from walking across the Bloodstone Lands. That tree showed Kane that their efforts had created not just a temporary victory, but a lasting blessing on the land he called home.

As he looked upon it, Kane reached to his side and picked up his walking stick, which had been fashioned from a branch of that magical tree. Smooth as polished stone and as white as the day he had taken it from the tree, for the dirt of no road could gray it, the jo staff was as hard and solid as adamantine, and in Kane's skilled hands, it could shatter stone.

With a thought, Kane veered the magic carpet toward the tree, gliding in to a smooth landing on the ground before its trunk. He stayed in his seated position, legs crossed, hands on his upturned thighs, the jo stick laid across his lap, as he offered prayers to the tree, and thanks to Bahamut, Lord of Goodly Dragons, for his wondrous gift.

"Well, by the blessings of the drunken god's double visions!" came a roar, drawing the monk from his meditation. He rose and turned, not surprised at all when Friar Dugald, nearly four hundred pounds of man-flesh, barreled into him.

Kane didn't move an inch against that press, which would have sent mighty warriors flying backward.

Dugald wrapped his meaty arms around the monk and slapped him hard on the back. Then he moved Kane back to arm's length—or rather, as he extended his arms, he moved himself back to arm's length—for again, the monk proved immovable.

"It has been too long!" Dugald proclaimed. "My friend, you spend all of your days wandering the land, or in the monastery to the south, and forget your friends here in Bloodstone Village."

"I carry you with me," Kane replied. "You travel in my prayers and thoughts. Never are any of you forgotten."

Dugald's flabby, bald head bobbed enthusiastically at that, and Kane could tell from the way he exaggerated his motions, and from the smell of him, that the friar had been consuming the blood of the vine. Dugald had found a kindred spirit within the Order of the God Ilmater in the study and patronage of St. Dionysus, the patron of such spirits, and Dugald was quite the loyal disciple.

Kane reminded himself that his own vows of discipline against such potent drink had been his conscious choice. He must not judge others based on his personal standards.

He turned away from Dugald to regard the tree, its spreading limbs framed by the quiet lake behind it. It had grown quite a bit in the two years since Kane's last visit to Bloodstone Village, and though the tree was only twelve years old, it already stood more than thirty feet, with branches wide and strong—branches it occasionally offered to the heroes that they might fashion items of power from the magical wood.

"Too long you've been gone," Dugald remarked.

"It is my way."

"Well, how am I to argue with that?" the friar asked.

Kane merely shrugged.

"You have come for the ceremony?"

"To speak with Gareth, yes."

Dugald eyed him with suspicion and asked, "What do you know?"

"I know that his choice of hanging a medal about the neck of a drow is something other than expected."

"More than Kane have said as much," Dugald said. "And this

drow's a strange one, even by the standards of his lot, so they're saying. Do you know anything of him? Gareth knows only the stories coming from the wall."

"And yet he will offer this one the title of Bloodstone Hero, and award his companion status as a Knight of the Order?"

"Apprentice Knight," Dugald corrected.

"A temporary equivocation."

Dugald conceded the point with a nod. No one who had attained the title of apprentice knight had not then gone on, within two years, to full knight status—except of course for Sir Liam of Halfling Downs, who had gone missing, and was presumed slain, on the road home after attending his ceremony of honor.

"You have reason to believe that this drow is not worthy, my friend?" Dugald asked.

"He is a dark elf."

Dugald sighed and assumed a pensive, almost accusing stare.

"Yes, we have the sisters of Eilistraee as evidence," Kane replied. "It is a precept of the Monastery of the Yellow Rose to judge the actions and not the heritage of any person. But he is a drow, who arrived here only recently. His history is unknown and I have not heard a single whisper that he serves Eilistraee."

"General Dannaway of the Vaasan Gate is meeting with the king and Lady Christine even now," Dugald replied. "He speaks well of the exploits of this Jarlaxle character and the soon-to-be-apprentice knight."

"Formidable warriors."

"So it seems."

"Skill with the blade is the least important asset for a knight of the order," Kane said.

"Every knight can lay waste to his share," Dugald countered.

"Purity of purpose, adherence to conscience, and the discipline to strike or to hold in the best interests of Bloodstone," Kane came right back, citing the crux of the Bloodstone knight's pledge. "Honorable General Dannaway will attest to their feats in killing monsters beyond the Vaasan Gate, no doubt, but he knows little of the character of these two."

Dugald looked at his friend curiously. "I'll be guessing that Kane does, then?"

The monk shrugged. Before his journey to Bloodstone Village, he had spoken to Hobart Bracegirdle, the halfling leader of the war gang the Kneebreakers, who had been operating from the Vaasan Gate in recent days. Hobart had offered a few clues to the intriguing duo, Jarlaxle and Entreri, but nothing substantial enough for Kane to yet draw any conclusions. In truth, the monk had no reason to believe that the two were anything less than their actions at the gate and in the battle outside of Palishchuk seemed to indicate. But he knew, too, that those actions had not been definitive.

"I fear King Gareth's choice regarding these newcomers is premature, that is all," he said.

The friar nodded his concession of that point, then turned and swept his arm out to the north, where stood the grand palace of Gareth and Christine. Still under construction after a decade of work, the palace was comprised of the original Tranth home, the residence of the Baron of Bloodstone, expanded in width and with perpendicular wings running forward on either end. Most of the continuing work on the palace involved the minor details, the finishing touches, the decorative parapets and stained-glass windows. The people of Bloodstone Village—indeed, the people and artisans of the entire region known as the Bloodstone Lands—wanted the palace of their king to be reflective of his deeds and reputation. With Gareth Dragonsbane, that would prove a tall order indeed, and one that would take all the artisans of the land years to fulfill.

Side by side, the two went to see their friends. They entered without questions, past guards who bowed in deference at the appearance of the ragged-looking man. Anyone who did not know the reputation of Grandmaster Kane would have no way of looking at the man and suspecting any such thing. He was past middle age, thin, even skinny, with fraying white hair and beard. He wore rags and no visible jewelry other than a pair of magical rings. His belt was a simple length of rough rope, his sandals worn and threadbare. Only his walking stick, white like the wood of the tree from which it was made, seemed somewhat remarkable, and that alone would not be enough to clue anyone in to the truth of the shabby-looking creature.

For Kane, a simple wanderer, had been the one to strike the fatal blow and free the Bloodstone Lands from the grip of the Witch-King Zhengyi.

The guards knew him, bowed as he passed, and whispered excitedly to one another when he had gone by.

As the pair came upon the decorated white wooden doors— another gift of the White Tree—of Gareth's audience chamber, the guards posted there scrambling to open them, they discovered that another of their former adventuring band had come calling. The animated and always-excited ramblings of Celedon Kierney charged out through the doors as soon as they were cracked open.

"Gareth has put out the call to Spysong, then," Kane remarked to Dugald. "That is good."

"Isn't that what brought you here?" Dugald asked, for Kane, like Celedon, was part of the Bloodstone scouting network known as Spysong, with the monk serving as its principle agent in Vaasa.

Kane shook his head. "No formal call summoned me, no. I thought it prudent."

The doors swung wider and the pair stepped through the threshold. All conversation in the room stopped. A wide smile erupted on the handsome face of King Gareth. Dugald had been expected, of course, but Kane's arrival was obviously a rather pleasant surprise.

Beautiful Lady Christine, too, offered a smile, though she remained less animated than her passionate husband, as always.

Celedon offered Kane the raised back of his right hand, fingers stiffened, thumb straight up. He held it there for a moment, then turned his hand so that his thumb tapped his heart, the greeting of Spysong.

Kane acknowledged it with a nod, and moved forward beside Dugald to stand before the dais that held the thrones of Gareth and Christine. He immediately noticed the weariness in Gareth's blue eyes. The man seemed very fit for his forties. He wore a sleeveless black tunic, his bare, muscled arms showing no weakness. His hair was still much more black than gray, though a bit of the salt had crept in. His jaw line remained firm and sharp.

But his eyes . . .

The blue still showed its youthful luster, but Kane looked past the shine to the increased heaviness of Gareth's eyelids and the slight discoloration of the skin around his eyes. The weight of ruling the land had settled upon his strong shoulders, and wore at him despite his disposition and despite the love showered on him always by almost everyone in Damara.

Leadership with consequence would do that to a man, Kane knew. To any man. There was no escaping such a burden.

Court etiquette demanded that King Gareth speak first, officially greeting his newest guests, but Celedon Kierney moved in between the guests and the royals.

"A-a drow!" he yammered, waving his arms in disbelief. "Surely that is what brought Master Kane to court . . . his surprise—nay, astonishment—that you are doing such a thing."

Gareth sighed and shot a plaintive look Kane's way.

Kane, though, found his attention stolen by the crinkled nose of General Dannaway, who stared at him with obvious disgust. The monk, dressed in his dirty rags, was not unaccustomed to such expressions, of course, nor did they concern him.

Still, he met the man's gaze with an intense look, one so unnerving that Dannaway actually took a step backward.

"I—I must be going, my king," Dannaway stammered, and bowed repeatedly.

"Of course," Gareth replied. "You are dismissed."

Dannaway moved at once for the exit, crinkling his nose again as he passed near an uncaring Kane.

But Dugald, smile wide, was not so generous. He put a hand on Dannaway's elbow to halt the man and make him turn, then whispered—but loudly enough for all to hear, "He could insert his hand into your chest, pull forth your heart, hold it beating before your disbelieving eyes, then put it back before your body ever missed it." He ended with an exaggerated wink and the unnerved Dannaway stumbled away and nearly to the ground.

He rushed ahead so quickly that he overbalanced, and had not the guard at the white doors swung them wide at his approach, he no doubt would have barreled into them head-first.

"Dugald. . . ." Lady Christine warned.

"Oh, he should know," the fat friar replied, and he laughed, and so did Celedon. Gareth soon joined in, and even Christine could not completely hide her giggle. Kane, though, showed little emotion.

It was just the five friends, then, and all pretense and protocol could not hold against the bonds of their shared experiences.

"A drow?" Kane asked after the titters died away.

"Dannaway speaks highly of him, and of the drow's friend," Gareth replied.

"Dannaway sees it as a source of glory for his work at the wall," Celedon put in. "And a mitigation of the great losses incurred in the journey he instigated to the replica of Castle Perilous."

"Not much of a replica if these vagabonds so easily defeated it," Dugald scoffed.

"We do not know their worth," Kane said. "And I remind all that a great ranger fell at that castle. We know not its true nature, nor the depth of its powers. To that end, Spysong has dispatched Riordan to Palishchuk to begin a more thorough investigation."

The mention of Riordan Parnell brought nods all around. Another member of the band of seven who had defeated Zhengyi, the bard still served the land well with his uncanny ability to coax the truth from reluctant witnesses.

"Other investigations will be needed, of course," Kane said. "I suggest that our responses be kept to a minimum until they are completed."

"Never a moment to relax, eh, my friend?" asked Gareth.

"Riordan went at the request of the Duke of Soravia," the monk replied, referring to still another of the seven heroes, Olwen Forest-friend, a bear of a man whose laughter would often shake the walls of a tavern. "Olwen did not receive the news of Mariabronne's demise well."

"His protégé," Dugald remarked, nodding. "Mariabronne studied under him for so many years, and has lately spent much time at Olwen's side." He gave a sigh and shook his head. "I must offer Olwen comfort."

"The Duke of Soravia will not attend tomorrow's ceremony," Gareth said, nodding in agreement.

"He believes it to be premature, no doubt," said Kane.

"We have visiting dignitaries who wished to witness the event," Lady Christine said. "Baroness Sylvia of Ostel—"

"We cannot deny the accomplishments of this group," Gareth interrupted, but Kane continued to look at Christine.

"The Baroness of Ostel," the monk said. "Whose closest ally is . . . ?"

"The Baron of Morov," said Celedon. "Dimian Ree."

Gareth rubbed his chin. "Ree is an unseemly character, I agree. But he is, first and foremost, a baron of Damara." Celedon started to interrupt, but Gareth held up his hand to stop him. "I know the rumors of his relationship with Timoshenko," the king said. "And I do not doubt them, though none of us have found any solid evidence of corroboration between Morov and the Citadel of Assassins. But even if it were true, I cannot move against Dimian Ree. Heliogabalus is his domain, and it remains the principle city of Damara, whether I am there or here."

Gareth's point was well taken by all in the room. The Sister Baronies, as Morov and Ostel were often called, commanded the center of Damara, and Baron Ree and Baroness Sylvia had the unquestioning loyalty of more than sixty thousand Damarans, nearly half the population of the kingdom. Gareth was king and had the love of all, so it seemed, but everyone in the room understood the tentative nature of Gareth's ascent. For in unifying Damara under one ruler, he had reduced the power of several long-entrenched baronies. And in trying to bring Vaasa into his realm to create the greater Kingdom of Bloodstone, he was rattling the nerves of many Damarans, who had known untamed Vaasa as a source of naught but misery for all of their lives.

More talk went on outside of Bloodstone Village than within, Gareth and everyone else in the room knew well, and not all of that talk favored the creation of a greater Kingdom of Bloodstone, or even the continued unification of the previously independent baronies.

Though Baroness Sylvia and Lady Christine had forged something of a friendship over the past few years, no one in the room thought highly of Baron Dimian Ree of Morov, considering him to be the consummate self-serving politician. But none in the room dared underestimate him, either, given the volatile political climate, and so Gareth's words put a block in the path of the debate.

"The drow and his friend approach Bloodstone Village in the company of a dwarf," Kane said.

"Athrogate, by name," said Gareth. "A most unpleasant fellow, but a fine warrior, by all accounts. A second dwarf died in the castle, and will be honored posthumously."

"Athrogate is a known associate of Timoshenko and Knellict," said Kane. "As was the wizard, Canthan, who also fell in the castle."

"Master Kane, you have quite a conspiracy envisioned," said Christine.

Kane took the jab with good nature, and bowed to the Queen of Bloodstone. "No, milady," he corrected. "It is my duty to serve Gareth's throne and King Gareth, and so I do. The web of a potential conspiracy appears faintly visible if the light is just right, but it could be a trick of the sun, I know."

"Wherever we have seen a filament of a web, we have found a spider," Celedon interjected, rather loudly. "It is not right, I say. There is more here than we know, and we should not be offering such honors as apprentice knight of the order until the questions are answered beyond all doubt. I'll not—"

Kane stopped him with an upraised hand, right before Gareth could tell him to shut up. "The drow, his human companion, and the dwarf," the monk said in a quiet voice. "Be they friends, we have gained worthy allies. Be they enemies, and we have put them under our eye, clearly so. To know your enemy is a warrior's greatest asset. If you wish to remain as king, Gareth my friend, and hope to expand beyond the gate fortress north of here, then you need to know Athrogate and the creatures of the shadows who work his strings."

"And if these three, this drow, the dwarf, and the man on whom I will tomorrow bestow knighthood, are truly aligned with the Citadel of Assassins?" Gareth asked, though his grin betrayed the fact that he already knew well the answer.

Kane shrugged as if it did not matter. "We will reward them and honor them, and never allow them free passage to any place or position where they might do us harm."

Even Celedon calmed at that assurance, for when Kane offered such words, he always delivered on his promise.

Soon after, Celedon, Dugald, and Kane took their leave, promising to return later that evening for a feast in their honor.

"You're hoping to lure Olwen here with a grand table," Christine said to Gareth when they were alone—alone except for the guards, who had become such a fixture of their lives that they were all but invisible to the couple.

"Olwen can smell an orc from a hundred yards, so it is said," Gareth replied. "And so it is also said that he can smell a meal from a hundred miles."

"It is more than a hundred miles to Kinbrace," Christine reminded, referring to the seat of Soravia's power, where Olwen dwelt. "Even with his enchanted boots, even with his growling stomach urging him on, Olwen could not cover that distance in time for your feast."

"I was thinking that another might enjoy the reunion of the seven," Gareth slyly replied.

Christine rolled her blue eyes, for she knew of whom her husband spoke, and she wasn't thrilled at the prospect of entertaining Emelyn the Gray. The oldest of the band who had defeated Zhengyi, past his seventieth birthday, Emelyn's understanding of "civility" often tried Lady Christine's patience. Glad she was those years ago when the wizard announced that he would return to the Warrenwood ten miles southeast of Bloodstone Village, and happier still was she when it became apparent that he would rarely return for a visit.

Gareth moved out of the audience chamber to a side corridor that led to his private rooms. He entered a small anteroom to his bedchamber and moved to a desk set against the side wall, near his bedroom door. The back of the desk rose high above the writing table, and was draped with a silken cloth. Gareth pulled the drape free, revealing a mirror, framed in gold that was molded into exotic runes and symbols. From the side of the mirror, the king slid forth a six-inch red ball set in a golden base. He positioned it right before the mirror and lifted his hand as if to cover it.

"There is no other way?" Christine asked from the doorway behind him.

Gareth glanced back at her and offered a grin as she rolled her eyes yet again. He knew that she was only half-serious, for Emelyn was indeed a trial, and in all truth, Gareth had not been sorry at the wizard's announcement of his "retirement" with the centaurs of Warrenwood.

"We may be needing Emelyn's services soon enough," Gareth replied, and he placed his hand on top of the red ball and closed his eyes, picturing his old friend in his thoughts.

A few moments later, he looked into the mirror, and instead of seeing his own reflection, he saw a separate room. It was full of vials and skulls, books and trinkets, statues small and large, and a grand and ornate desk that seemed as alive as the white tree from which it had been fashioned.

At the desk with his back to Gareth sat an old man in satiny gray robes. His white hair, long and unkempt, hung down nearly to the desk—in fact its end strands showed that they had dipped into the inkwell more than once—as he hunched over his parchment.

"Emelyn?" Gareth asked, then more insistently, "Emelyn!"

The wizard straightened, glanced left, then right, then turned around to look behind him and across the room at the sister mirror set in his wall.

"Peering in uninvited, are we?" he said in a nasal and scratchy voice. "Hoping to catch a view of Gabrielle, no doubt." He ended with a cackle of delight.

Gareth just shook his head, and wondered again why such a beautiful young woman as Gabrielle had agreed to marry the old kook.

"Oh, I know your game!" Emelyn accused, wagging a gnarled old finger Gareth's way and flashing a yellow, gap-toothed smile.

"One you perfected, no doubt," Gareth dryly replied, "which is why I keep a shroud over my mirror."

The wizard's smile disappeared. "Never were you one to share, Gareth."

Behind the king, Lady Christine made her presence known by clearing her throat, loudly. Of course, that only made Emelyn cackle all the more.

"I was looking for you, my friend, though Lady Gabrielle is surely a more welcome sight before my eyes," said Gareth.

"She is in Heliogabalus, seeking components and potions."

"A pity, then, for I have come with an invitation."

"To see a drow honored?" Emelyn replied. "Bah!"

Gareth accepted that with a nod. He knew, of course, that Emelyn would have heard about the morning's ceremony. Surely the word was general all about Bloodstone Valley.

"Kane and Celedon have arrived in Bloodstone Village," Gareth explained. "I think it a good time for old friends to eat and drink, and speak of adventures past."

Emelyn started to respond, apparently in the negative, but

stopped short and chewed his lip. A moment later, he rose from his chair and faced Gareth directly. "There is little I can do until Gabrielle's return, in any case," he said.

The mirror filled with smoke.

And so did the room, and both Gareth and Christine gave a shout and fell back.

The smoke cleared, revealing a sputtering Emelyn, waving his hands before his face to chase the fumes away.

"Never used to . . . create such combustion," Emelyn explained, coughing repeatedly as he spoke. At last he straightened and smoothed his robes. He looked alternately into the blank stares of Gareth and Christine, then back to Gareth. "So when do we eat?"

"I was hoping that perhaps you could retrieve Olwen before the meal," Gareth explained.

"Olwen?"

"The Duke of Soravia," Christine clarified, and Emelyn snapped a stare over her.

"How might we locate him?" Emelyn asked. "He is never near the six castles of Kinbrace of late. Always out and about."

"We could look," Gareth said. He stepped aside and waved his arm back at the scrying mirror.

"More than a meal?" Emelyn asked.

"You have heard of the goings-on in Vaasa?"

"I have heard that you mean to honor a drow, and that there is apparently a knight-in-waiting."

"A Zhengyian construct appeared north of Palishchuk," Gareth explained.

"They seem to be more common of late. There was a tower outside of Heliogabalus—"

"Mariabronne the Rover fell within the walls of this one."

That set Emelyn back on his heels.

"It was said to be a replica of Castle Perilous," Lady Christine interjected. "Alive with gargoyles, and ruled by a dracolich."

Emelyn's eyes, gray like his robes, widened with every proclamation. "And this drow and the others defeated the menace?"

Gareth nodded. "But the construct remains."

"And you wish me to fly to the north to see what I might learn," Emelyn reasoned.

"That would seem prudent."

"And Olwen?" Emelyn asked, but before Gareth or Christine could respond, the old wizard gasped and held up his hand. "Ah, Mariabronne!" he said. "I'd not considered Olwen's love for that one."

"Find him?" Gareth bade Emelyn, and again he indicated the mirror.

Emelyn nodded and stepped forward.

No one in Faerûn was better at preparing a banquet than Christine Dragonsbane. She was the daughter of Baron Tranth, the former ruler of the region known as Bloodstone Valley, which included Bloodstone Village. Growing up in the time of Zhengyi, in the noble House that controlled the sole pass between Vaasa and Damara, Christine had witnessed scores of feasts prepared for visiting dignitaries, both from the duchies and baronies of Damara and from Zhengyi's court. In the years before open warfare, much of the duplicity that had lured Damara into a position vulnerable to Zhengyi's imperialistic designs had occurred right there in Bloodstone Village, at the table of Baron Tranth.

The meal planned for that night held no such potential for intrigue, of course. The guests were the friends of Gareth, honest and true companions who had fought beside him in the desperate struggle against the Witch-King. Riordan Parnell wouldn't be there, as he was off to Palishchuk, which complicated things for Christine a bit. Had he been in attendance, Riordan, an extraordinary bard, would have provided much of the entertainment. And entertainment was paramount on Gareth's mind.

"This is a meal for solidarity of purpose and agreement of how we should proceed," he told Christine not long after Emelyn had magically flown out to Soravia. "But most of all it is for Olwen. He has lost a child, in effect."

"And we have both lost a niece," Christine reminded.

Gareth nodded, but neither of them were truly devastated by the death of Commander Ellery. She had been a relative, but a distant one, and one that neither Gareth nor Christine had known very well. Gareth had seen her only a few times and had spoken to her only once, on the occasion of her appointment to the Army of Bloodstone.

"This night is for Olwen," Christine agreed, and took her leave.

Soon after, though, they found out that they were both incorrect. Emelyn the Gray returned from Soravia, appearing in Gareth's audience chamber amidst a cloud of smoke. Coughing and waving his hands, more with annoyance than with any expectation that he would clear the cloud, Emelyn stood alone, shaking his head.

"Olwen is not in his castle," the old wizard explained. "Nor is he anywhere in the city, or in Kinnery or Steppenhall. He went out soon after the news of Mariabronne's fall reached Kinbrace, along with several of his rangerly ilk. Who knows what silliness they are up to."

" 'Rangerly'?" Gareth asked.

"Druidic, then?" Emelyn offered. "How am I to properly describe men who dance about the trees and offer prayers of gratitude to beautiful and benevolent creatures right before and right after they kill them?"

" 'Rangerly' will suffice," the king conceded, and Emelyn wagged his wrinkled old head.

"Do you have any notion of where they went?" Gareth asked.

"Somewhere in the northeast—some grove they have deemed sacred, no doubt."

"A funeral?"

Emelyn shrugged.

"And there was no way to find him?" Gareth asked.

Emelyn's look became less accommodating, his expression telling Gareth in no uncertain terms that if he could have found the man, Olwen would be standing beside him.

"Olwen has been an adventurer for most of his life," Emelyn reminded. "He has known loss as often as victory and has buried many friends."

"As have we all."

"He will overcome his grief," said the wizard. "Better, perhaps, that he is not here in the morning when you celebrate those who survived the trip to this Zhengyian construct. Olwen would have strong questions for them, do not doubt, particularly for the drow."

41

"We all have questions, my friend," Gareth said.

Emelyn eyed him with open suspicion, and Gareth couldn't hold back his smile from his ever-perceptive old companion.

"How could we not?" the king asked. "We had an unusual party travel north on our behalf, unbeknownst to us, and we are now left an unusual band of victorious survivors. We have a construct of unknown origin—"

Emelyn held up his hand to stop his friend. "I detest Palishchuk," he remarked.

Gareth's grin widened. "I could trust no other with this most important investigation. Riordan is already there, doing that which Riordan does best—interrogating people without them even realizing it—but he has no practical understanding of such creation magic as this."

"I am not fond of Riordan, either," grumped Emelyn, and Gareth couldn't contain a chuckle. "But he is a bard, is he not? Are bards not especially skilled at determining the origins and history of places and dweomers?"

"Emelyn. . . ." Gareth said.

The old wizard huffed. "Palishchuk. Oh joy of joys. To be surrounded by half-orcs and their unparalleled wit and wisdom."

"One of the heroes who defeated the castle's guardians was a half-orc wizard," said Gareth, and that seemed to pique Emelyn's curiosity for a moment.

A brief moment. "And I know a dwarf who dances gracefully," came the sarcastic reply. "For a dwarf. Which means that the area clerics need only repair a few broken toes among the spectators after each performance. Could a half-orc wizard be any more promising?"

"When the survivors returned to the Vaasan Gate, they reported that Wingham was in Palishchuk."

That did interest Emelyn, obviously so.

"Enough, my king," he surrendered. "You wish me to go, and so I go, but it will not be as brief a journey as my trip to Soravia, a land that I know well and can thus teleport to and from quickly. Expect me to be gone a tenday, and that only if the riddles presented by the Zhengyian construct are not too tightly wound. Am I to leave at once, or might I partake of the feast you promised in order to lure me here in the first place?"

"Eat, and eat well," said Gareth, smiling, then he paused and took on a more serious visage. "I trust that your magic is powerful enough to lift you and transport you when your belly is full?"

"If you were not the king, I'd offer a demonstration."

"Ah, but if I were not the king, then Zhengyi would not likely allow it."

Emelyn just shook his head and walked off to the guest rooms where he could clean up and prepare for Christine's table.

It was a night of toasts to old friends and old times. The five adventuring companions lifted their glasses to Olwen, most of all, and to Mariabronne, who had held such promise. They reiterated their goal of unifying the Bloodstone Lands, Damara and Vaasa, into a singular kingdom, and of defeating any and all remnants of the tyrant Zhengyi.

They talked of the next morning's ceremony, sharing what little they knew of the man who would be granted knighthood and of his strange, ebon-skinned companion. Celedon Kierney promised that they would know much more of the pair soon enough, a vow he made with a nod of approval from Kane. There was no disagreement at that table among the friends who had struggled hand-in-hand for more than a decade. They saw the challenges before them, the potential trouble, and the mystery of the newcomers, and they methodically set out their plans.

In the morning, after Friar Dugald offered a blessing for them all, Emelyn departed for Palishchuk and Celedon set out for Helio-gabalus. Celedon asked Kane to accompany him, or to fly him part of the way on the magical carpet, but Kane declined. He wanted to witness the day's events.

And so as King Gareth and Queen Christine prepared for their ceremony, they knew that they were well flanked by powerful friends.

CHAPTER

3

She exited the front door of her modest mercantile, a shop specializing in trinkets, around sunset, as she did every evening, handing the keys over to her trusted assistant. The sign over her head as she walked from her porch read Tazmikella's Bag of Silver, and true to the moniker, most of the items within, candlesticks and paperweights, decorative orbs and pieces of jewelry, were crafted of that precious metal.

Tazmikella herself had earned quite a handsome reputation among the merchant class of the circular road called Wall's Around in Heliogabalus, a cul-de-sac off the more major route, Wall Way, so named because of its proximity to the city's high defensive encirclement. The woman was rather ordinary looking and dressed simply. Her hair showed some of its former strawberry blond luster, but was mostly soft gray, and her shoulders appeared just a bit too wide in support of her smallish head. But she always had a kind word for her fellow merchants, and always a disarming smile, and if she had ever fleeced a customer, none had ever complained.

Unassuming and simple, with few needs and plain tastes, Tazmikella did not have a fancy coach awaiting her departure. She walked, every night, the same route out of the city and to an unremarkable cabin set on the side of a hillock.

The woman coming out of Ilnezhara's Gold Coins across the street from her could not have appeared more contrary. She stood straight, tall, and thin, with a shock of thick, copper-colored hair and huge blue eyes. She was dressed in the finest of threads, and a handsome coach driven by a team of shining horses awaited her.

"Can I offer you a ride, poor dear?" Ilnezhara asked her counterpart, as she did every evening—much to the amusement of the other merchants, who often whispered and chortled about the pair and their rivalry.

"I was given legs for a purpose," Tazmikella responded on cue.

"To the city gates, at least?" Ilnezhara continued, to which Tazmikella merely waved her hand and walked on by, as she did every night.

Any witnesses watching more closely that night might have seen something a bit out of the ordinary, though, for as Tazmikella passed by Ilnezhara's coach, she turned her head slightly and offered the tall woman the slightest of nods, and received one in return.

Tazmikella was out of the city in short order, moving far from the torchlit wall toward the lonely hill where she kept her modest home. At the base of that hill, in nearly complete darkness, she surveyed all the land around her, ensuring that she was alone. She moved to a wide clearing beyond a shielding line of thick pines. In the middle, she closed her eyes and slipped out of her clothes. Tazmikella hated wearing clothes, and could never understand the need of humans to hide their natural forms. She always thought that level of shame and modesty to be reflective of a race that could not elevate itself above its apparent limitations, a race that insisted on subjugating itself to more powerful beings instead of standing as their own gods in proud self-determination.

Tazmikella was possessed of no such modesty. She stood naked in that unnatural form, basking in the feel of the night breezes. The change came subtly, for she had long ago perfected the art of transformation. Her wings and tail began to grow first, for they were the least painful—additions were always easier than transformations, which included cracking and reshaping bone structure.

The trees around her seemed to shrink. Her perspective shifted as she grew to enormous proportions, for Tazmikella was no human. She had crawled from her egg centuries before beside her sister and sole sibling in the great deserts of Calimshan, far to the southwest.

Tazmikella the copper dragon lifted into the night air. She gained altitude quickly, flying away from the human city. The leaders of the land knew who she was, and accepted her, but the commonfolk would never comprehend, of course. If she revealed herself to them, King Gareth and his friends would be left with no choice but to evict her from the Bloodstone Lands. And she really didn't want a fight with that company.

She moved directly north, across the least populated expanse of Morov and into the even less densely populated Duchy of Soravia. She flew between the Goliad and the Galena Snake, the two parallel rivers running south from the Galena Mountains. And she continued to climb, for the thin air and the cold did not bother Tazmikella at all. A person on the ground might catch a fleeting glimpse of her, but would that person know her to be a dragon flying high, or think her a night bird, or a bat, flying low?

She was not concerned. She was naked in the night air, above such concerns. She was free.

Tazmikella crossed the mountains easily, weaving in and out of the towering peaks, enjoying the play of the multidirectional air flows and the stark contrast between the dark stones and moonlit snow. She entered Vaasa just to the west of Palishchuk, and turned east as she came out of the mountains. Within moments, she noted the lights of the half-orc city.

The dragon stayed up high as she overflew the city, for she knew that the half-orcs, living amidst the Vaasan wilds for so many years, knew how to protect themselves from any threat. If they saw the form of a dragon over-flying their city at night, they wouldn't pause to consider the color of the wyrm—nor would they be able to determine that in any case, under the light of the half-moon and stars alone.

Tazmikella used her extraordinary eyesight to scrutinize the city as she passed. It was late, but many torches burned and the town's largest tavern was bright and noisy. They still celebrated the victory over the Zhengyian castle, she realized.

She banked right, to the north, and began her descent, confident that none of Palishchuk's citizens would be out and about. Almost immediately, she saw the dark and dead structure, an immense fortress, a replica of Castle Perilous, only a few miles to the north of the city.

She came down in a straight line, too intrigued to pause and take a survey of the area. As she alighted, she changed back into a human form, thinking that anyone who subsequently spied her wouldn't feel threatened by the sight of a naked, middle-aged woman. Of course, if any lurking onlookers had watched her more closely, that image would have created more confusion than comfort, for she strode up to the huge portcullis that barred the front of the structure without pause. She considered the patchwork grate that had been chained over the break in the gate, where Jarlaxle and his companions had apparently entered. She could have removed that patch easily enough, but that would have meant stooping to crawl under.

Instead, the woman slipped her arms between two of the thick portcullis spikes, then pushed outward with both, easily bending the metal so that she could simply step through.

Unconcerned, Tazmikella strode right through the gatehouses and across the courtyard of torn, broken ground, littered with the shattered forms of many, many skeletons.

She found the great doors of the main keep repaired and secured by a heavy chain—one that she grabbed with one hand and easily snapped.

She found what she was looking for in the main room just beyond the doors. A pedestal stood intact, though blackened by fire near its top. The remnants of a large book, pages torn and burned, lay scattered about. Her expression growing more sour, Tazmikella went up to the ruined tome and lifted the black binding. Most of it was destroyed, but she saw enough of the cover to recognize the images of dragons stamped there.

She knew the nature of the book, a tome of creation and of enslavement.

"Damn you, Zhengyi," the dragon whispered.

The clues of Jarlaxle and Entreri's progress through the place were easy enough to follow, and Tazmikella soon entered a huge chamber far below the structure, where lay the bones of a long-past battle, and the debris of a more recent struggle. One look at the dracolich confirmed everything Tazmikella and her sister Ilnezhara had feared.

The dragon arrived back on the hillside outside of Heliogabalus shortly before the dawn. She dressed and rubbed her weary eyes, but she did not return to her home. Rather, she moved south to a singular tower, the home of her sister. She didn't bother knocking, for she was expected.

"It was that easily discerned that you did not even need a full day at the site?" the taller, copper-haired Ilnezhara said as soon as Tazmikella entered.

"It was exactly as we feared."

"A Zhengyian tome, animated by the captured soul of a dead dragon?"

"Urshula, I think."

"The black?"

"The same."

"And the book?"

"Destroyed. Torn and burned. The work of Jarlaxle, I would expect. That one is too clever to allow such a treasure to escape his greedy hands. He saw the truth of Zhengyian tomes when he destroyed Herminicle's tower."

"And we offered him too many clues," Ilnezhara added.

They both paused and considered the scenario unfolding before them. Ilnezhara and Tazmikella had been approached by Zhengyi those years before with a tempting offer. If they served beside his conquering armies, he would reward them each with an enchanted phylactery, waiting to rescue their spirits when they died. Zhengyi had offered the sisters immortality in the form of lichdom.

But the price was too high, they had agreed, and while the prospect of surviving as a dracolich might be better than death, it was anything but appealing.

"Jarlaxle understood exactly what was buried within the pages of Zhengyi's book, so we can only assume that he has Urshula now, safely tucked away in a pocket," Tazmikella said after a long while.

"This drow plays dangerous games," said Ilnezhara. "If he knows the power of the phylactery, does he also understand the magic behind it? Will Jarlaxle begin tempting dragons to his side, as did Zhengyi?"

"If he walks into Heliogabalus and offers us a dark pact toward lichdom, I will bite him in half," Tazmikella promised.

Ilnezhara put on a pouting expression. "Could you not just chain him and hand him to me, that I might use him as I please for a few centuries?"

"Sister. . . ." Tazmikella warned.

Ilnezhara simply laughed in response, but it was a chuckle edged with nervous tension. For both of them were beginning to understand that Jarlaxle, a creature they considered a minion, was not to be taken lightly.

"Jarlaxle and Entreri defeated a dracolich," Tazmikella stated, and there was no further laughter. "And Urshula the Black was no minor wyrm in life or death."

"And now he is in Jarlaxle's pocket, figuratively and literally."

"We should talk to those two."

Ilnezhara nodded her agreement.

Every so often in his life, the fiercely independent Artemis Entreri found himself in a time and place not of his choosing, and from which he could not immediately escape. It had been so for months in Menzoberranzan, when Jarlaxle had rescued him from a disastrous fight with Drizzt Do'Urden outside of Mithral Hall and had taken him back with the dark elves on their retreat from the dwarf lands.

It had been so quite often in his younger days, serving the dangerous Basadoni Guild in Calimport. In those early phases of his career, Artemis Entreri had done what he was told, when he was told. On those occasions when his assignment was not to his liking, the younger Entreri had just shrugged and accepted it—what else was he to do?

As he got older, more experienced and with a reputation that made even the Pashas nervous, Entreri accepted the assignments of his choosing, and no one else's. Still, every so often, he found himself in a place where he did not wish to be, as it was that morning in Bloodstone Village.

He watched the ceremony with a strange detachment, as if he sat in the crowd that had gathered before the raised platform in front of King Gareth's palace. With some amusement, he watched Davis Eng go forward and accept his honor. The man hadn't even made it to Palishchuk of his own accord. He had been downed on the road and had been carried in, a liability and not an asset, in the back of a wagon.

Some people will celebrate anything, Entreri mused. Even mediocrity.

Back on the streets of Calimport, a man who had performed as pathetically as Eng would have been given one chance to redeem himself, if that.

Calihye was called forward next, and Entreri watched that presentation more carefully, and with less judgment. The half-elf had refused to go into the castle, though she had agreed to stay with the wounded Davis Eng. She had broken her agreement with Commander Ellery, her vow of servitude to the mission, and still she was being rewarded.

Entreri merely smirked at that one and let the negative thoughts filter away, his personal feelings for the half-elf overruling his pervasive cynicism for the moment.

Still, it amazed him how liberal the king seemed to be with his accolades—because it was all for show, Entreri understood. The ceremony wasn't about Davis Eng or Calihye. It wasn't about the annoying Athrogate, who hopped forward next to receive his honor. It wasn't even about Jarlaxle and Entreri. It was about the people watching, the commonfolk of Bloodstone. It was all about creating heroes for the morale of the peasants, to keep them bowing and praising their leaders so that they wouldn't notice their own troubles. Half of them went to bed hungry most nights, while those they loved so, the paladin king and his court, would never know such hardship.

In the end, cynicism won over, and so when Entreri was called forward—the second time, for he had been too turned inward to even hear the first summons—he stepped briskly and didn't even hide his scowl.

He heard Jarlaxle's laugh behind him as he moved to stand before Gareth, and he knew that his companion was enjoying the spectacle. He managed one glance back at the drow, just to glare. And of course, Jarlaxle laughed all the more.

"Artemis Entreri," Gareth said, turning the man back to face him. "You are new to this land, and yet you have already proven your worth. With your actions at the Vaasan Gate, and in the north against the construct of Zhengyi, you have distinguished yourself above so many others. For your defeat of the dracolich, Artemis Entreri, I bestow upon you the title of Apprentice Knight of the Order."

A man dressed in dirty robes stepped up to the bald, fat priest at Gareth's side. The priest, Friar Dugald, offered a quick blessing over the sword then handed it to Gareth.

But as he did, the ragged man looked not at the king, but at Entreri. And though Gareth's complimentary words had been full of all the right notes, Entreri saw clearly that this man—a dear friend of the king's, apparently—was not viewing Entreri in the same complimentary light.

Artemis Entreri had survived the vicious streets of Calimport with his skill at arms, but even more importantly, he had survived due to his ability to measure friends and enemies at a glance.

That man, slightly older than he, and no commoner despite his ragged dress, was no friend.

Gareth took the sword and lifted it high with both hands.

"Please kneel," Queen Christine instructed Entreri, who was still regarding the man in rags.

Entreri turned his head slowly to consider the queen, then gave a slight nod and dropped to his knees. Gareth laid the sword on his left shoulder, and proclaimed him an apprentice knight of the order. The fat priest began to recite all of the honors and benefits such a title bestowed, but Entreri was hardly listening. He thought of the man in rags, of the look that had passed between them.

He thought about how Jarlaxle was wrangling them both into places where they did not belong.

⊹━┉━⊹

Far to the north of Bloodstone Village, the celebration in Palishchuk lasted long into the night, and Riordan Parnell continued to lead the way. Whenever things seemed to be quieting, the bard took up a rousing song about Palishchuk and its many heroes.

And glasses were lifted in toast.

Most of the town had turned out in the common room of the Weary Wanderer that night to honor—yet again—Arrayan and

Olgerkhan, their brave kinfolk who had ventured into the castle. Several of the citizens had been killed and many more injured in the battle with the castle's gargoyles, who had flown through the dark sky to assault the town. To a man and woman, the half-orcs recognized that had Arrayan, Olgerkhan, and the others not proven victorious over the dracolich and its vile minions, their beloved city would likely have been abandoned, with refugees streaming south for the safety of the Vaasan Gate.

So the half-orcs were more than willing to celebrate, and when Riordan Parnell, the legendary bard and a charter member of King Gareth's court, had arrived in Palishchuk, the revelry had taken on new heights.

Seeing that his reputation had preceded him, Riordan was determined not to disappoint. He sang and played on his fine lute, backed by some fairly good musicians from Wingham's traveling merchant band, who—as good luck would have it, for Wingham and Riordan were old friends—happened to be in town.

Riordan sang and everyone drank. He sang some more, and they drank some more. Riordan graciously treated many of the dignitaries, including the two guests of honor, from his seemingly endless pouch of coins—for in his generosity, the bard could cleverly determine how much each was drinking. Initially, he had thought to keep Arrayan and Olgerkhan semi-lucid, for there was much more to that particular evening's celebration than merely the bard showing off his musical talents. Drunken people talked more freely, after all, and Riordan had gone there for information.

After seeing the pair of heroes, though, the bard had slightly altered his plans. One look at Arrayan's beautiful face had convinced him to make sure that Olgerkhan was getting the most potent of drinks, all the night long. Truly, Arrayan had caught Riordan off his guard—and that was not a common occurrence for the brash and charming rake. It wasn't that she was spectacularly beautiful, for Riordan had bedded many of the most alluring women in the Bloodstone Lands. No, what had so surprised the bard was that he found himself attracted to Arrayan at all. Her face was flat and round, but very pleasantly so, her hair lustrous, and her teeth straight and clean, so unlike the crooked and protruding tusks so prevalent in her orc heritage. Indeed, had he seen Arrayan walking the streets of Heliogabalus or Bloodstone Village, Riordan would never have guessed that a drop of orc blood coursed her veins.

Knowing the truth of it, though, the bard could see bits of that heritage here and there on the woman. Her ears were a bit small, and her forehead just a little sloped, up from a brow that was a hair too thick.

But none of it mattered to the whole, for the woman was pretty, and pleasant and smiling, and Riordan was intrigued, and because of that, surprised.

So he made sure, with a wink at the barmaid and an extra coin on her tray, that Arrayan's escort and fellow hero, the brutish Olgerkhan, was amply sauced. Soon enough, Olgerkhan fell off his chair and out of the picture entirely, snoring contentedly on the floor to the howls and cheers of the other patrons.

Riordan picked his time carefully. He knew that he couldn't outmaneuver Wingham, for the old half-orc was far too crafty to be taken in by a man of Riordan's well-earned reputation, and he saw that Wingham took quite the interest in Arrayan, who, Riordan had learned, was his niece. When he judged that an ample number of patrons were falling by the wayside, the bard changed the tempo of his songs. It was early in the morning by then, and so he began to wind things down . . . slowly.

He also began slipping a bit more enchantment into his tunes, using the magic of his voice, the gift of the true bards, to manipulate the mood of the slightly inebriated Arrayan. He put her at ease. He charmed her with subtle flattery. The background magic of his songs convinced her that he was her friend, to be trusted, who could offer comfort and advice.

More than once, Riordan noticed Wingham glancing his way with obvious suspicion. He pressed on, though, continuing his quiet manipulation while trying to find a plan to be rid of the too-smart old half-orc.

Even clever Riordan realized that he was out of his league, though. There was no way he was going to distract Wingham. During one of his rare pauses from song, the bard gathered a pair of drinks from the tavernkeeper and moved to Wingham's side. He was not surprised when Wingham dismissed the other three merchants who had been sitting at his table.

"You sing well," the old half-orc said.

Riordan slipped one of the drinks over to him then lifted the other in an appreciative toast. Wingham tapped one glass to the other and took a deep swallow.

"You know Nyungy?" he asked before he had even replaced his glass on the table.

Riordan looked at him curiously for just a moment. "The bard? Of course. Who of my heritage and training would not know the name of the greatest bard to ever walk the Bloodstone Lands?"

"The greatest *half-orc* bard," Wingham clarified.

"I would not put such limitations on the reputation of Nyungy."

"He would tell you that the exploits of Riordan Parnell outshone his own." Wingham lifted his glass to lead the toast, and Riordan, grinning, tapped his glass to Wingham's.

"I think you flatter me too greatly," the bard said before he drank. After the sip, he added, "I played a small role, one man among many, in the defeat of the Witch-King."

"Curse his name," said Wingham, and Riordan nodded. "I stand by my comment, for I have heard those very words from Nyungy, and recently."

"He is still alive, then? Fine news! Nyungy has not been heard from for years now, and many assumed that he had passed on from this life, to a reward that we all know must be just."

"Alive and well, if a bit crotchety and sore in the joints," Wingham confirmed. "In fact, he warned me to be wary of Riordan Parnell when we learned that you were coming to Palishchuk, only two days ago."

Riordan paused and cocked his head, studying his companion.

"Yes, my friend, Nyungy lives right here in Palishchuk," Wingham confirmed. "Of course he does. Indeed, it was he who deciphered that Arrayan had unwittingly begun the cycle of magic of the Zhengyian construct. His wisdom helped guide me to the understanding that ultimately allowed Commander Ellery's group to defeat the construct and its hellish minions."

Riordan sat staring at the old half-orc through it all, neither blinking or nodding.

"Yes, you would do well to pay Nyungy a visit before you leave, since you have come to discern the complete truth of this construct and its defeat."

Riordan swallowed a bit too hard. "I have come to honor the exploits of Arrayan and Olgerkhan," he said, "and to share in the joy and celebration until King Gareth arrives from Bloodstone Village to formally honor them."

"And truly, what a fine honor it is that the king would even travel the muddy expanse of Vaasa to pay such a tribute, rather than demanding the couple travel to him in his seat of power."

"They are worthy of the honor."

"No doubt," Wingham agreed. "But that is far from the extent of it—for their visit and for your own."

Riordan didn't bother to deny anything.

"King Gareth is right to worry," Wingham went on. "This castle was formidable."

"The loss of Mariabronne, and Gareth's relative, Ellery, would attest to that."

"To say nothing of Canthan, a high-ranking wizard in the Citadel of Assassins."

The blunt statement gave Riordan pause.

"Surely you suspected as much," said Wingham.

"There were rumors."

"And they are true. Yes, my singing friend, there is much more for us—for you—to unravel here than the simple defeat of yet another Zhengyian construct. Fear not, for I will not hinder you. Far from it, for the sake of Palishchuk and all of Vaasa, my hopes lie with Riordan and King Gareth."

"We have always considered Wingham a valuable ally and friend."

"You flatter me. But our goals are the same, I assure you." Wingham paused and looked at Riordan slyly. "Some of our goals, at least."

At that surprising comment, Riordan let Wingham steer his gaze across the way to Arrayan.

Riordan gave a laugh. "She is beautiful, I admit," he said.

"She is in love, and with a man deserving of her."

Riordan glanced at Olgerkhan, who lay under the table curled up like a baby, and laughed again. "A man too fond of the liquor this night, it would seem."

"With the help of a few well-placed coins and better-placed compliments," said Wingham.

Riordan sat back and smiled at the perceptive half-orc. "You fear for Arrayan's reputation."

"A charming hero from King Gareth's Court . . ."

"Has come to speak with her, as a friend," Riordan finished.

"Your reputation suggests a bit more."

"Fair enough," the bard said, and he lifted his glass in salute to Wingham. "On my word, then, friend Wingham," he said. "Arrayan is a beautiful woman, and I would be a liar if I said otherwise to you."

"You are a bard, after all," came the dry reply, and Riordan could only shrug and accept the barb.

"My intentions for her are honorable," Riordan said. "Well, except that, yes, I have indeed played it so that she is . . . less inhibited. I have many questions to ask her this night, and I would have her honest replies, without fear of consequence."

He noted that Wingham stiffened at that.

"She has done nothing wrong," said the half-orc.

"That I do not doubt."

"She was unwittingly trapped by the magic of the tome—a book that I gave to her," Wingham said, and a bit of desperation seemed to be creeping into his voice.

"I am less concerned with her, and with Olgerkhan, than with their other companions, those who made it out alive and those who did not," the bard assured the half-orc.

"I will tell you the entire story of the book and the creation," Wingham replied. "I would prefer that you do not revisit that painful experience on Arrayan, this night or any other. Besides, since she was in the thrall of powerful and manipulative magic, my observations will prove more accurate and enlightening."

Riordan thought it over for a moment then nodded. "But you were not with them inside the construct."

"True enough."

Riordan set his glass down on the table, and slid his chair back. "I will be gentle," he promised as he stood up.

Wingham didn't seem overly pleased by it all, but he nodded his agreement. He didn't have much of a choice, after all. Riordan Parnell, cousin of Celedon Kierney, friend of Gareth and all the others, was one of the seven who had brought Zhengyi down and had rescued the Bloodstone Lands from the hellish nightmare of the Witch-King.

The celebration was fine that night in Bloodstone Village, as well. Though many had little idea of what had transpired in Vaasa to warrant such a ceremony, or a knighting, the folk of the long-beleaguered land seemed always ready for a celebration. King Gareth told them to eat, drink, and make merry, so make merry they did.

A huge open air pavilion was set up on the front grounds of Castle Dragonsbane, to the side of the Palace of the White Tree. A few tents had been set about, but most of the people preferred to dance and sing under the stars that clear, dark night. They knew they wouldn't have many such evenings left before the onset of winter's cold winds.

For his part, Jarlaxle wandered in small circles around the table where Entreri, the hero of the day, sat with Calihye and some of the lesser lords and ladies of King Gareth's court. Every so often, Friar Dugald would wander by, offering a mug in toast, before staggering off into the crowd.

Many, of course, showed great interest in the drow as he glided about the perimeter, and he found himself tipping his hat almost non-stop. It was a practiced gesture, and one that served well to hide the truth of Jarlaxle's attention. For with a wave of his hand and a call to a small silver cone he held tight in his palm, the drow had created an area of amplified sensibilities, from himself to Entreri and the half-elf. People strode up before Jarlaxle and addressed him directly, even loudly, but he just nodded and smiled and moved along, hearing not a word from them.

But hearing everything said between Entreri and Calihye.

"I have no desire to winter in the tight confines of the Vaasan Gate," Entreri said to her, and from his tone, Jarlaxle could tell that he had spoken those very words several times already. "I will find work in Heliogabalus, if it suits me to work, and enjoy fine food and drink if not."

"And fine women?" Calihye asked.

"If you would accompany me, then yes," Entreri replied without hesitation.

Jarlaxle chortled upon hearing that, then realized that he had just confused, and likely insulted, a pair of young women who had approached him.

With an offer, perhaps?

He had to find out, so he abandoned Entreri's conversation just long enough to recognize that the moment had passed.

"Your pardon," he managed to say as the pair turned their backs and rushed away.

With a shrug, Jarlaxle summoned the cone again and tuned in.

". . . Parissus has unfinished affairs," Calihye was saying, referring to her dear friend who had been killed on the road to Palishchuk—a death that she had initially blamed on Artemis Entreri, and for which she had vowed revenge. It seemed that she had entertained a change of heart, Jarlaxle thought, unless she planned to love the man to death.

Jarlaxle smiled and nodded at that rather discordant thought. For some reason, he found himself thinking of Ilnezhara, his dragon lover.

"I am bound to her by years of friendship," Calihye continued. "You cannot deny me my responsibilities to see that her final wishes are carried out as she desired."

"I deny you no road. Your path is your own to decide."

"But you won't come with me?"

Jarlaxle couldn't help but smirk as he regarded that distant exchange, how Calihye gently placed her hand on Entreri's forearm as she spoke.

Ah, the manipulation of human women, Jarlaxle thought.

"Jarlaxle has been my friend for years, as well," Entreri replied. "We have business in Heliogabalus."

"Jarlaxle is not capable of handling your affairs alone?"

Entreri gave a chuckle. "You would have me trust him?"

Jarlaxle nodded his approval at that.

"I thought you were friends," Calihye said.

Entreri merely shrugged and looked back to his drink, set on the table before him.

Jarlaxle noted Calihye's expression, a bit of a frown showing around the edges of her mouth. As Entreri turned back to her, that frown disappeared in the blink of a drow's eye, upturning into a calming, assured smile.

"Interesting," the drow muttered under his breath.

"What is?" came a question before him, one that had him nearly jumping out of his boots. Before him stood a group of young men, boys actually, all of them staring at him, sizing him up from head to toe.

All of those stares reminded Jarlaxle keenly that he was out of his element, that he was among a suspicious throng of lesser creatures. He was a novelty, and though that was a position he had long coveted among the drow, among the surface races, it was both a blessing and a curse, an opportunity and a shackle.

"A good evening to you," he said to them, tipping his outrageous hat.

"They're saying ye killed a dragon," the same boy who had spoken before offered.

"Many," Jarlaxle replied with a wink.

"Tell us!" another of the group exclaimed.

"Ah, so many stories . . ." the drow began, and he started off for a nearby table, herding the boys before him.

He glanced back at Entreri and Calihye as he went, to see his friend with both hands wrapped around his mug, his head down. At his side, Calihye held his arm and stared at him, and try as he might, Jarlaxle could not read her expression.

⊶⊷

Arrayan was thoroughly enjoying herself. All guilt had washed from her, finally. Even the defeat of the "living" castle had not allowed the woman to truly relax, for several people had died in battling that construct—a creation of her unwitting actions.

That was all behind her, though, for one night at least. The music, the drink, the cheers . . . had it all, just possibly, been worth it?

Sitting beside her, face down on the table—and that after clawing his way up from the floor—Olgerkhan snored contentedly. Dear Olgerkhan. He had been her truest friend when they had entered the castle, and had become her lover since they had left it. Soon they were to be married, and it was a day that could not come quickly enough for Arrayan. She had known the brutish half-orc for all of her life, but not until the crisis within the construct, when she had

59

watched Olgerkhan sacrifice so much for her benefit, had she come to understand the truth of his feelings for her—and hers for him.

She reached over and tousled his hair, but he was too drunk to even respond. She had never seen Olgerkhan drunk before, for neither of them often partook of potent liquor. For herself, Arrayan had begun sipping her drinks more carefully hours before. She wasn't much of a drinker, and it hadn't taken a lot to set her head spinning. She was only just coming back to clarity, somewhat.

She was glad of that indeed when she noted the handsome and heroic bard striding her way, a huge smile on his face. Behind him, she caught a glimpse of her uncle Wingham, but the concern clearly stamped on his old face did not register with the tipsy woman.

"Milady Arrayan," Riordan Parnell said as he moved near to her. He dipped a graceful, arm-sweeping bow. "I feel that the warmth of the night has almost overcome me. I wish to take a short walk in the cool air outside, and would be honored if you would join me."

A flash of concern crossed Arrayan's face, and she was hardly aware of the movement as she looked to Olgerkhan.

"Ah, milady, I assure you that my intentions are nothing but honorable," Riordan said. "Your love for Olgerkhan is well known, and so appropriate, given the status that you two have rightly earned. You will be the most celebrated couple in Palishchuk, perhaps in all of Vaasa."

"Help me to rouse him, then," Arrayan replied, and she blushed as she realized that she slurred her words a bit. She reached over to grab Olgerkhan, but Riordan took her by the wrist.

"Just we two," he bade her. He glanced back over his shoulder, leading her gaze to Wingham.

The old half-orc still wore that grave look, but he nodded in response to Arrayan's questioning expression.

With a fair amount of potent liquor clouding Arrayan's thoughts, it was not hard for the powerful Riordan to weave a magical enchantment over her as they walked out of the tavern. By the time they'd moved only a block from the place, Arrayan had come to fully trust the handsome man from Damara.

In such a situation, it didn't take Riordan long to learn what he needed. He had heard of Mariabronne's demise already—that the ranger had been killed not by the dracolich, but by shadowy demons beforehand when he had been out scouting. Yet, strangely, Mariabronne's corpse had been found at the scene of the dracolich battle, bitten in half.

Riordan got the complete picture, including when three of the already dead companions—Mariabronne, Canthan, and Ellery—had walked past Arrayan to join in the fight. They had been animated by someone or something. Canthan had thrown spells in the dracolich fight, and the animated warrior and ranger had battled fiercely.

The magic that had brought their physical bodies to animation had been powerful, Riordan understood.

He listened intently as Arrayan lowered her voice and admitted the truth of Canthan's demise: that the man and the dwarf had turned on her and Olgerkhan, and had been stopped by Entreri and Jarlaxle. She lowered her voice even more as she recounted the last moments of Canthan's life, when Entreri's horrible, vampiric dagger had drawn forth his remaining life-force and transferred it to Olgerkhan.

Riordan's head spun. There was so much more to the whole business than anyone had understood. And what had happened to Ellery, Gareth's niece, a Commander of the Bloodstone Army? Even Arrayan didn't know, for the woman had remained behind the group with Jarlaxle, studying the tome, and had not returned with the mysterious drow to the room where Entreri had finished off Canthan.

And so Riordan's interrogation, for all the answers it provided, had only led him to so many more, and more intriguing, questions.

They were questions to which he would find no answers from either Arrayan or Olgerkhan, or anyone else in Palishchuk.

With so much to report, he escorted the woman back to the tavern and didn't even stay the night, collecting his mount from the stable and riding out into the darkness, galloping hard to the south.

At the same time, not far to the west, Emelyn the Gray, in the form of a night bird, sped the other way. The grumpy wizard had no intention of going into Palishchuk, so he skirted around the town to the west and veered back to the northeast. He found the castle easily enough and flew over the outer wall, reverting to his human form as he settled before the doors of the main keep. He took a moment to consider the broken chain on the doors.

"Hmm," he said, a sound he would repeat many times that night and the next morning, as he made his way through the Zhengyian construct.

CHAPTER

4

Y ou should put the dragon statuette back," Jarlaxle remarked as he and Entreri arrived at the door to their apartment in Heliogabalus, a modest affair set on the second story of an unremarkable wooden building. Modest from outward appearances, at least, for inside lay the spoils of the pair's successful ventures before their trip north to Vaasa. Entreri and Jarlaxle were very good at gathering coin, and Jarlaxle in particular was very good at spending it.

"I left it in the castle," Entreri replied, an obvious lie that brought a grin to the drow. Never would Entreri leave behind such a powerful tool as the statuette, which had proven instrumental in defeating the dracolich. That tiny, silvery item could be set as a trap, bringing forth the various breath forms of the deadly chromatic dragons.

"Perhaps I can persuade Tazmikella and Ilnezhara to provide us with another one," Jarlaxle said.

"And what else might you coerce from the dragon sisters?"

Jarlaxle feigned a wounded look.

"Now that you have proffered a bargaining chip, I mean," Entreri clarified.

Jarlaxle's expression shifted to one of confusion—again, obviously feigned.

"Immortality was the prize Zhengyi offered to the dragons," Entreri said. "The gem you took from the book—the second one, not the one from Herminicle's tower—would prove intriguing for our dragon friends, would it not?"

63

"Perhaps," the drow agreed. "Or perhaps they will find it revolting. Perhaps they will kill me if I even mention it, or if I reveal it but do not turn it over to them."

"Jarlaxle is nothing if not daring."

The drow shrugged and grinned. "Our dragon friends sent us to Vaasa to find just such a tome, and just such a phylactery. I am duty-bound to report to them in full."

"And to turn over the spoils?"

"The phylactery?" The drow scoffed. "I made no such agreement."

"They are dragons."

"And one is a fine lover. That changes nothing."

Entreri shuddered at the thought, which of course only made Jarlaxle smile all the wider.

"We were not sent to retrieve anything more than information, and so information I shall offer," said Jarlaxle. "Nothing less."

"And if they demand the phylactery?"

"It belongs to Urshula. I am simply holding it for him."

"And if they demand the phylactery?" Entreri asked again.

"They need not know—"

"They already know! They are dragons. They have lived in this region for centuries. They remember well the time of Zhengyi—perhaps they even fought beside him, or against him."

"Presumptions."

"They are dragons," Entreri said yet again. "Why do you not seem to understand that? You live through manipulation—never have I seen anyone better at playing the emotions of those around him. But these are *dragons*. They are not serving wenches or even human kings or queens. You play with a force you do not understand."

"I have played with greater, and won."

Entreri shook his head, certain then that they were doomed.

"Ever the worrier," said Jarlaxle. He had just hung his cloak on a hook, but took it back. "I will settle this, and calm your churning gut. Tazmikella and Ilnezhara are dragons—yes, my friend, I understand this—but they are *copper* dragons. Formidable in battle, of course, but not so much in the realm of the mind."

"You forget how they enlisted us in the first place," said Entreri.

Indeed, the dragon sisters had created an elaborate ruse to entwine the pair and to determine their intentions. Tazmikella had hired them, secretly and from afar, and when they had discovered the riddle of the woman—not that she was a dragon, but merely that she was the one who had hired them to acquire a certain candlestick—she had created a second ruse, claiming that Ilnezhara was her bitter and hated rival and that the woman was in possession of something that rightfully belonged to Tazmikella: Idalia's flute, the same magical instrument that had later been given to Entreri.

But the deception hadn't ended there, with a simple theft, for during that attempted robbery, Entreri and Jarlaxle had been shown the awful truth of Ilnezhara, revealed to them in her dragon form. Then she had wound a third level of intrigue, and yet another secret test, offering them their lives only on condition that they return to their former employer, Tazmikella, and kill her.

By any measure, even that of Entreri and Jarlaxle, the dragon sisters had played them for fools, and repeatedly.

Jarlaxle shrugged at the painful reminder and admitted, "A decent enough game they played, but one, no doubt, they had spent years perfecting. In Menzoberranzan, a ruse within a ruse within a ruse is an everyday affair, and usually spontaneously generated."

"And yet you were tripped up by theirs."

"Only because I did not expect—"

"You underestimated them."

"Because I believed them to be humans, of course, and it would be hard to underestimate a human."

"I am truly glad you feel that way."

Jarlaxle laughed. "I know they are dragons now."

"This woman you take as a lover," Entreri added dryly.

That gave Jarlaxle pause. "Because I love you as a brother, I pray that you will one day fathom the truth of it all, my friend."

"They're dragons," Entreri muttered. "And I know how drow love their brothers."

Jarlaxle sighed at his friend's unrelenting ignorance, then offered a salute embedded in a resigned sigh and slung his cloak over his shoulders. "I will return after sunset. Perhaps you would do well to run back to Vaasa and the castle and retrieve the statuette. And if you do, pray use the powers of white or blue. The fiery breath of a red dragon would not be wisely placed over our door—too much wood, of course."

◄│═══╪═│►

The drow found his "employers" at Ilnezhara's tower. They always met there, rather than at the modest abode of Tazmikella. Perhaps that was an indication of Ilnezhara's haughtiness, her refusal to lower herself and venture to the hovel. Jarlaxle, of course, saw it a bit differently. Tazmikella's willingness to go to Ilnezhara's fabulous abode betrayed her true feelings, he believed. She pretended to care little for the niceties, but as with so many others who did likewise, it was a deception—a self-deception. So many people derided the materialistic tendencies of dragons, drow, humans, and dwarves . . . claiming that their own hearts were purer, their own designs more lofty and important, when in truth, they were merely deriding that which they believed they could not attain. Or if they could attain such things, they still used their "lofty" aspirations in the same manner the wealthy merchant used his gilded coach: to elevate themselves above other people.

That personal elevation was the true occupation of rational beings, even long-living creatures such as dragons.

"It was as we expected," Ilnezhara remarked after the initial greetings.

That it was she who had initiated the conversation and not the more typically forthcoming Tazmikella revealed the anxiety felt by both of the sisters.

"Your predictions that Zhengyi's library had been unearthed seem validated, yes," he answered. "You said there would be more constructs, and alas, that is what we found."

"One to dwarf Herminicle's tower," said Tazmikella, and the drow nodded.

"As a dragon might dwarf a human, in size and in strength," Ilnezhara added.

Jarlaxle didn't miss her point. The sisters knew that Zhengyi had enslaved dragons like Urshula the Black. They understood the magic that had created Herminicle's tower, and they had expected similar magic to reach to greater heights when fueled by a dragon.

So it was.

"The book was destroyed," Ilnezhara added.

"Unfortunately," said the drow.

"By Jarlaxle," the tall copper-haired creature said, and that put Jarlaxle back a step. "Or one like him," she quickly equivocated, "fast with the blade and with the spell."

Jarlaxle started to protest, but Tazmikella cut him short. "I went there," she said. "I ventured into the castle and found the podium in the main keep. I found the remnants of the book of creation, torn and burned."

Jarlaxle started to argue, then to deny, but he smiled instead, dipped a bow of congratulations to the deductive dragon, and said, "It had to be destroyed, of course."

"And the phylactery contained within?" asked Ilnezhara.

Jarlaxle's eyes shifted to take in the delicate creature, his lover, and his hand casually slipped near to the belt pouch on his right hip, wherein he kept a small orb that could blink him away from any threatening situation. Crushing that ceramic orb would throw him through the multiverse—to where, to which plane of existence even, he could not predict.

In that moment, he figured that there were few places in the multiverse more adverse than in the den of a pair of angry dragons.

"Zhengyi created many such phylacteries," Tazmikella explained. "He tempted every dragon in the Bloodstone Lands with his promises, we two included. Our guess is that the castle north of Palishchuk contained the phylactery of the dracolich Urshula the Black."

Jarlaxle shrugged. "The acidic breath of the creature we battled was consistent with that."

"And the dracolich was destroyed?"

"With help from the statuette you wisely gave to me."

"And the phylactery was removed," Ilnezhara said.

Jarlaxle held his free hand out to the side as if he did not understand.

"The phylactery that was embedded in the tome of creation, which was shredded by Jarlaxle, was, therefore, removed," the dragon clarified.

"By you," her sister added.

The drow stepped back and brought his hand away from his pouch and up to his chin. "And if what you say is true?" he asked.

"Then you possess something you do not understand," Ilnezhara replied. "You have made your way by playing your wits against those you encounter. Now you are playing with dragons—with dead dragons. That seems not a healthy course."

"Your concern is touching."

"This is no game, Jarlaxle," Tazmikella said. "Zhengyi wove a complicated web. His temptations were . . ." She looked to her sister.

"Potent," Ilnezhara finished for her. "Who would not wish immortality?"

"There are phylacteries for Tazmikella and Ilnezhara?" Jarlaxle asked, catching on to their anxiety, finally.

"We did not ally with Zhengyi," Ilnezhara stated.

"Not by the time of his demise," the drow replied. "I would guess that many of your kind refused the Witch-King, until . . ."

He let that hang in the air.

"Until?" Tazmikella's tone showed that she was in no mood for cryptic games.

"Until the moment of truth," Jarlaxle explained. "Until the moment when the choice between oblivion and lichdom was laid bare."

"You are a clever one," said Ilnezhara. "But not so if you think this a game to be manipulated."

"You demand the phylactery of Urshula the Black? You presume that I have it, and demand it of me?"

The sisters exchanged looks again. "We want you to understand that with which you play," Tazmikella said.

"We care nothing for Urshula, alive or dead," Ilnezhara added. "Never was he an ally, surely."

"You fear that I am unlocking Zhengyi's secrets," said the drow.

He paused for a moment, certain of his guess, and considered the fact that he was still alive. Obviously the sisters wanted something from him. He looked at Tazmikella, then over to his lover, and he realized that the dragons weren't going to kill him anytime soon. They knew he would come to a point of understanding—they *needed* him to come to a point of understanding—though it was a dangerous place for them.

"Zhengyi created phylacteries for you both," the drow said again, with more confidence. "He tempted you, and you refused him."

He paused, but neither dragon began to argue.

"But the phylacteries remain, and you want them," Jarlaxle reasoned.

"And we will kill anyone who happens upon them and does not turn them over immediately," Ilnezhara said with cold calm.

The drow considered the promise for a moment, and knew Ilnezhara well enough to realize that she was deadly serious.

"You would control your own destiny," he said.

"We will not allow another to control it," said Tazmikella. "A minor differentiation. The results will prove the same for any who hold the items."

"You sent me to Vaasa in the hope that I would learn that which I have learned," Jarlaxle reasoned. "You would have me find the rest of Zhengyi's still-hidden treasures, to return to you that which is rightfully yours."

They didn't disagree.

"And for me?"

"You get to tell others that you met two dragons and survived," said Ilnezhara.

Jarlaxle grinned, then laughed aloud. "Might I tell them of the more intimate encounters?"

The woman's return smile was genuine, and warm, and gave Jarlaxle great relief.

"And of Urshula the Black?" he dared ask after a few moments.

"We said we care nothing for that one, alive or dead," Ilnezhara replied. "But be warned and be wary, my black-skinned friend," she added, and she sidled up to the drow and stroked the back of her hand across his cheek. "King Gareth and his friends will not suffer a second Zhengyi. He is not one to underestimate."

Jarlaxle was nodding as she finished, but that disappeared in the blink of an eye as the dragon clamped her hand on the back of his cloak and shirt and effortlessly lifted him into the air, turning him as she did to face her directly.

"Nor would we suffer another tyrant," she warned. "I know that you do not underestimate me."

Hanging in the air as he was, feeling the sheer strength of the dragon as she held him aloft as easily as if he were made of feathers, the drow could only tip his great hat to her.

Entreri turned up the side of his collar as he walked past Piter's bakery, not wanting anyone inside to recognize him and pull him in. He and Jarlaxle had rescued the man from some highwaymen who had indentured him as their private cook. Then Jarlaxle, so typical for the drow, had set Piter up in Heliogabalus in his own shop. Ever was the drow playing angles, trying to squeeze something from nothing, which annoyed Entreri no end.

Piter was a fine baker—even Entreri could appreciate that—but the assassin simply wasn't in the mood for the perpetually smiling and overly appreciative chef.

He moved swiftly past the storefront and turned down the next side street, heading for one of the many taverns that graced that section of the crowded city. He chose a new location, the Boar's Snout, instead of the haunts he and Jarlaxle often frequented. As with smiling Piter, Entreri wasn't in the mood for making conversation with the annoying dregs, nor was he hoping that Jarlaxle would find him. The drow had gone off to see the dragon sisters, and Entreri was enjoying his time alone—finally alone.

He had a lot to think about.

He moved through the half-empty tavern—the night was young—and pulled up a chair at a table in the far corner, sitting as always with his back to the wall and in full view of the door.

The barkeep called out to him, asking his pleasure, and he returned with, "Honey mead."

Then he sat back and considered the road that had brought him to that place. By the time the serving wench appeared with his drink, he had Idalia's flute in his hands, rolling it over and over, feeling the smoothness of the wood.

"If ye're thinking to play for yer drink, then ye should be asking Griney over there," he heard the wench say. He looked up at the woman, who was barely more than a girl. "I ain't for making no choosings about barter." She placed the mead down before him. "A pair o' silver and three coppers," she explained.

Entreri considered her for a moment, her impertinent look, as if she expected an argument. He matched her expression with a sour one of his own and drew out three silvers. He slapped them into her hand and waved her away.

Then he slid his drink to the side, for he wasn't really thirsty, and went back to considering the flute and his last journey—truly one of the strangest adventures of his life. Entreri's trip to Vaasa had also been a journey inside himself, for the first time in more years than he could remember. Because of the magic contained in the flute—and he knew for certain that it was indeed the instrument that had facilitated his inward journey—he had opened himself to emotions long buried. He had seen beauty—in Ellery, in Arrayan, and in Calihye. He had felt attraction, mostly to Arrayan at first, and so strongly that it had led him to make mistakes, nearly getting him killed at the hands of that wretched creature Athrogate.

He had found compassion, and had done things for Arrayan's benefit, and for the benefit of her beloved Olgerkhan.

He had risked his life to save a brutish half-orc.

One hand still worked the flute, but Entreri brought his other up to rub his face. It occurred to him that he should shove this magical flute down Jarlaxle's throat, that he should use it to throttle the drow before its magic led him to his own demise.

But the flute had brought him to Calihye. He couldn't dismiss that. The magic of the flute had given him permission to love the half-elf, had brought him to a place where he never expected and never intended to be. And he enjoyed that place. He couldn't deny that.

But it is going to get me killed, he thought, and he nearly jumped out of his seat to see that a man sat at his table, across from him, waiting for him to look up.

No reminder that the flute was putting him off his normally keen guard could have been more clear to the assassin.

"I have allowed you to walk over unimpeded and unchallenged," Entreri bluffed, and looked back down at the flute. "State your business and be gone."

"Or you will leave me dead on the floor?" the man asked, and Entreri slowly lifted his eyes to lock his opponent's gaze.

He let his stare be his answer, the same look that so many in Calimport had experienced as the last thing they had ever seen.

The man squirmed just a bit, and Entreri could see that he was unsure if indeed he had been "allowed" to come over and sit down, and hadn't really caught Entreri by surprise as it had seemed.

"Knellict would take exception," the man whispered.

It took every bit of control Artemis Entreri could manage to not reach over the table and murder the man then and there, for even mentioning that cursed name.

"You put your threats away and you keep them away," the man went on, seeming to gain courage from the mention of the powerful archmage. He even shifted as if to point his finger Entreri's way, but Entreri's stare defeated that movement before it really got going. "I'm here for him, I am," the man said. "For Knellict. Ye thinking ye're in the mood for a fight with Knellict?"

Entreri just stared.

"Well? Ye got no answer for that, do ye?"

Entreri managed an amused grin at how badly the man was reading him.

The stranger sat up straighter and leaned forward, confidence growing. "Course ye got no answer," he said. "Ain't none wanting a fight with Knellict." Entreri nodded, his amusement growing as the fool's voice continued to mount in volume. "Not even King Gareth, himself!" the man ended, and he reached up and snapped his fingers before Entreri's face—or tried to, for the assassin, far quicker, grabbed the man by the wrist and slammed his hand down hard on the table, palm up.

Before the fool could begin to squirm, the assassin's other hand came up over the table, holding the jeweled dagger. Entreri flipped it and slammed it down hard, driving it into the wood of the table right between the fumbling fool's fingers.

"Raise your voice again, and I will cut out your tongue," Entreri assured him. "Your patron will appreciate that, I assure you. He might even offer me a bounty for taking the wagging tongue of an idiot."

The man was breathing so heavily, in such gasps, that Entreri half-expected him to faint onto the floor. Even when Entreri put his dagger away, the fool kept on panting.

"I believe that you have some information to relay," Entreri said after a long while.

"A-a job," the man stammered. "For yerself and just yerself,

Apprentice Knight. There's a merchant, Beneghast, who's come afoul o' Knellict."

Entreri's thoughts began to spin. Had they arranged for him to attain a position of trust within the kingdom only to waste the gain for the sake of a simple merchant? However, the perceptive Entreri lost his surprise as the fool went on, clarifying the plan.

"Beneghast's got a highwayman laying in wait. Ye're to rush to Beneghast's rescue from our men."

"But of course I won't get there quite in time."

"Oh, ye're to get there soon enough to kill the merchant," the fool explained, and he grinned widely, showing a few rotten teeth in a mouth that was more discolored gum than tooth. "But we'll be blaming the thief."

"And I am the hero for apprehending the murderer," Entreri reasoned, for it was a ruse he had heard many times in his life.

"And ye just turn him over to the city guards, who'll come rushing yer way."

"Guards paid well, no doubt."

The man laughed.

Entreri nodded. He walked his thoughts through the too-familiar, and too-complicated scenario. Why not have the highwayman just kill the man and be done with it? Or have the guards "find" the body of Beneghast, right where they placed it after killing him?

Because it wasn't about Beneghast at all, Entreri understood. It wasn't payback for any wrong done Knellict. It was a test for Entreri, plain and simple. Knellict wanted to see if Entreri would kill, indiscriminately and without question, out of loyalty to the Citadel of Assassins.

How many times had Artemis Entreri facilitated something very much like this back in Calimport when he had served as Pasha Basadoni's principle assassin? How many new prospects had he similarly tested?

And how many had he killed for failing the test?

The fool sat there, wagging his head and showing that repulsive grin, and rather than dismissing him, Entreri stood and took his leave, shoving past and heading for the door.

"Wall's Around," the man called after him, referring to a section of the city the assassin knew well. Entreri could only shake his head at the courier's stupidity and lack of discretion.

The assassin couldn't get out of that tavern fast enough.

He headed down the street, pointedly away from Wall's Around at first. With every step, he considered the test, considered that Knellict would deign to test him at all.

With every step, he grew angrier.

CHAPTER

U N S H A C K L E D

5

To the outside world, even to Artemis Entreri, it was a simple bakery, the place where chef Piter worked his wonders. After the sun set over Heliogabalus, Piter and his workers went home and the doors were locked, not to be opened again until the pre-dawn hours each and every day.

Entreri likely understood that the place was a bit more than that, Jarlaxle realized. Its pretensions as a simple bakery served as a front, a token of legitimacy for Jarlaxle. How might Entreri react, the drow wondered, if he discovered that Piter's bakery was also a conduit to the Underdark?

It was after dark and the door was locked. Jarlaxle, of course, had a key. He walked past the storefront casually, his gaze sweeping the area and taking in his surroundings to be certain that no one was watching.

He walked past again a few moments later, after a second inspection of the area, and quietly entered and secured the portal behind him, both with his key and with a minor incantation. In the back room, the drow moved to the left-most of the three large ovens. He glanced over his shoulder one last time, then climbed almost completely into the oven. He reached up into the chimney, holding forth a small silver chime, and lightly tapped it against the brick.

Then he climbed back out and brushed the soot from his clothing—none of the soot was stubborn enough to cling to Jarlaxle's magical garb.

He waited patiently as the minutes slipped past, confident that his call had been heard. Finally, a form bubbled out of the oven's base, sliding effortlessly through the bricks. It grew and extended, seemed no more than a shadow, but gradually took on a humanoid shape.

Shadow became substance and Kimmuriel Oblodra, the psionicist who had been Jarlaxle's principle lieutenant in the mercenary band Bregan D'aerthe, blinked open his eyes.

"You keep me waiting," Jarlaxle remarked.

"You call at inconvenient times," Kimmuriel replied. "I have an organization to run."

Jarlaxle grinned and bowed in response. "And how fares Bregan D'aerthe, my old friend?"

"We thrive. Now that we have abandoned expansionist designs, that is. We are creatures of the Underdark, of Menzoberranzan, and there—"

"You thrive," Jarlaxle dryly finished. "Yes, I get the point."

"But it seems one that you stubbornly refuse to accept," Kimmuriel dared to argue. "You have not abandoned your designs for a kingdom in the World Above."

"A connection to greater treasures," Jarlaxle corrected, and Kimmuriel shrugged. "I will not repeat my errors perpetrated under the influence of Crenshinibon, but neither will I recoil from opportunity."

"Opportunity in the land of a paladin king?"

"Wherever it may be found."

Kimmuriel slowly shook his head.

"We are heroes of the crown, do you not know?" Jarlaxle said. "My companion is a knight of the Army of Bloodstone. Can a barony be far behind?"

"Underestimate Gareth and his friends at your peril," the psionicist warned. "I set spies to watch them from afar, as you instructed. They are not blind fools who accept your tales at face value. They have dispatched emissaries to Palishchuk and to the castle already, and they even now question their informants in Heliogabalus and in other cities, whose primary duties involve keeping track of the movements of the Citadel of Assassins."

"I would be disappointed if they were inept," Jarlaxle replied casually, as if it did not matter.

"I warn you, Jarlaxle. You will find Gareth and those adventurers who stand beside him to be the most formidable foes you have ever faced."

"I have faced the matron mothers of Menzoberranzan," the drow reminded him.

"Who were ever kept at bay by the edicts of Lady Lolth herself. Those matron mothers knew that they would displease the Spider Queen if they brought harm upon one she had so blessed as Jar—"

"I do not need you to recount my life's history to me."

"Do you not?"

The ever-confident Jarlaxle couldn't help but wince at that statement, for of course it was true. Jarlaxle had been blessed by the Spider Queen, had been ordained as one of her agents of tumult and chaos. Lady Lolth, the demon queen of chaos, had rejected Matron Baenre's sacrifice of her third-born son, as was drow tradition. Due to the work of one loyal to Lolth, Baenre's spider-shaped dagger had not penetrated the babe Jarlaxle's tender flesh, and when Lolth had magically granted Jarlaxle the memories of his infancy, of that fateful night in House Baenre, he had keenly felt his mother's desperation. How she had ground that spider-shaped dagger on his chest, terrified that the rejection of her sacrifice had portended doom for her supreme House.

"Matron Baenre learned centuries ago that her own fate was inextricably tied to that of Jarlaxle," Kimmuriel, one of only three living drow who knew the truth, went on. "Ever were her hands tied from retaliating against you, even on those many occasions she desperately wanted to cut out your heart."

"Lady Lolth spurned me long ago, my friend." Jarlaxle tried hard not to betray any emotions other than his typically flippant attitude, but it was difficult. On his mother's orders, the failure of the sacrificial ceremony had been buried beneath a swath of lies. She had ordered him declared dead, then wrapped in a shroud of silk and thrown into the lake known as Donigarten, as was customary for sacrificed third sons.

"But Baenre never knew of your betrayal of the Spider Queen, and her rejection of you as her favored drow," said Kimmuriel. "To Matron Baenre, to her dying breath, you were the untouchable one, the one whose flesh her dagger could not penetrate. The blessed child who, as a mere infant, utterly and completely destroyed his older brother."

"Do you suggest that I should have told the witch?"

"Hardly. I only remind you in the context of your present state," Kimmuriel said, and he offered his former master a low and respectful bow.

"Baenre found me, and Bregan D'aerthe, to be a powerful and necessary ally."

"And so Bregan D'aerthe remains an ally to House Baenre, and Matron Mother Triel, under the guidance of Kimmuriel," the psionicist said.

Jarlaxle nodded. "Kimmuriel is no fool, which is why I entrusted Bregan D'aerthe to you during my . . . my journey."

"Your relationship with the matron mothers was not akin to the one you now seem determined to forge in the Bloodstone Lands," Kimmuriel stated. "King Gareth will not suffer such treachery."

"You presume I will offer him a choice."

"You presume that you will hold the upper hand. Your predecessor in this adventure, a Witch-King of tremendous power, learned the error of his ways."

"And perhaps I have learned from Zhengyi's failure."

"But have you learned from your own?" Kimmuriel dared to say, and for just a brief instant, Jarlaxle's red eyes flared with anger. "You nearly brought ruin to Bregan D'aerthe," Kimmuriel pressed anyway.

"I was under the influence of a mighty artifact. My vision was clouded."

"Clouded only because the Crystal Shard offered you that which you greatly desired. Is the phylactery you now hold in your pocket offering you any less?"

Jarlaxle took a step back, surprised by Kimmuriel's forwardness. He let his anger play out to a state of grudging acceptance—that was exactly why he had given Bregan D'aerthe over to Kimmuriel, after all. Jarlaxle had chosen a road of adventure and personal growth, one that could have proven disastrous for Bregan D'aerthe had he dragged them along. But with the possibilities he had found in Vaasa and Damara, was he, perhaps, dragging them right back into the path of ruin?

No, Jarlaxle realized as he considered his dark elf counterpart, the intelligent and independent psionicist who dared to speak to him so bluntly.

A smile grew upon his face as he looked over his friend. "There are possibilities here I cannot ignore," he said.

"Intriguing, I agree."

"But not enough to bring Bregan D'aerthe to my side should I need them," Jarlaxle reasoned.

"Not enough to risk Bregan D'aerthe. That was our agreement, was it not? Did you not install me as leader for the very purpose of building a wall between that which you created and that which you would gamble?"

Jarlaxle laughed aloud at the truth in that.

"I am wiser than I know," he said, and Kimmuriel would have laughed with him, if Kimmuriel ever laughed.

"But you will continue to monitor, of course," Jarlaxle said, and Kimmuriel nodded. "I have another duty for you."

"My network is stretched thin."

Jarlaxle shook his head. "Not for your spies, but for yourself. There is a woman, Calihye. She did not travel south with me and Entreri, though she is his lover."

"That one is not possessed of the frailties that would allow for such unreasonable emotions," Kimmuriel corrected. "She is his partner for physical release, perhaps, but it could be no more with Artemis Entreri. It is the one thing about the fool that I applaud."

"Perhaps that is the reason I find comfort around him. His demeanor reminds me of home."

Kimmuriel didn't react at all, and Jarlaxle figured the psionicist, so cunning regarding the larger issues of life but so oblivious about the little truths of existence, hadn't even realized the comparison of himself to Entreri.

"I see no incongruity between her actions and her professed intent," Jarlaxle explained, a code he had often used with his invasive lieutenant.

Kimmuriel bowed, showing his understanding.

"You will continue to monitor?" Jarlaxle asked.

"And to inform," Kimmuriel assured him. "I do not abandon you, Jarlaxle. Never that."

"Never?"

"To date," Kimmuriel said, and despite himself, he did chortle a bit.

"It could get very dangerous here," Jarlaxle finally admitted.

"You play dangerous games with dangerous enemies."

"If it comes to war, I am well-prepared," said Jarlaxle. "The armies of the nether world await my call, and Zhengyi left behind constructs that are continually self-protecting."

"You will claim the castle."

"I already have. I own he who owns it. The dracolich is mine to command. As I said, I am well prepared. Better prepared if Bregan D'aerthe offered support. Quietly, of course."

"If it escalates, I will watch and I will judge what is best for Bregan D'aerthe," said Kimmuriel.

Jarlaxle grinned and bowed. "You will offer me an escape, of course."

"I will watch and I will judge," the psionicist said again.

Jarlaxle had to accept that. His deal with Kimmuriel precipitated on the fulcrum of Kimmuriel's independence. Kimmuriel, and not Jarlaxle, ruled Bregan D'aerthe, and would continue to until Jarlaxle returned to Menzoberranzan and formally retrieved his throne. That was as they had agreed upon after the destruction of the Crystal Shard. Neither held any illusions about that agreement, of course. Jarlaxle knew that if he stayed away from his homeland for too long, allowing Kimmuriel to make inroads into the supportive relationships Jarlaxle had built within the City of Spiders, then Kimmuriel would not relinquish control of Bregan D'aerthe without a fight.

Jarlaxle also knew that calling upon Kimmuriel in times of desperation was a risky prospect indeed, for if Kimmuriel allowed him to fall, the psionicist would stand unopposed as leader of the profitable mercenary band. But Jarlaxle understood well the drow who served as his steward. Kimmuriel had never coveted power over other drow, as had Rai-guy or Berg'inyon Baenre, or any of the other notables in the band. Kimmuriel's designs dwelt in the realm of the intellect. He was a psionicist, a creature of thought and introspection. Kimmuriel preferred intellectual sparring with illithids to bargaining for position with the wretched matron mothers of Menzoberranzan. He would rather spend his day destroying brain moles or visiting the Astral abodes of githyanki than reporting his findings to Matron Mother Triel or maneuvering Bregan D'aerthe's warriors to capitalize on any dramatic events in the nearly constant intra-House warfare.

"You try to build here," Kimmuriel remarked even as he started into the chimney and his magical road back to the Underdark. "You grasp to create something on the World Above, yet no matter your success, it could not rival that which awaits you in Menzoberranzan. I try to understand you, Jarlaxle, but even my brilliance is no match for your unpredictability. What is it you seek here that does not already await you in our homeland?"

Freedom, Jarlaxle thought, but did not say.

Of course, Kimmuriel was a psionicist, and a powerful one indeed, so Jarlaxle never really had to "say" anything to him to get his point across.

Kimmuriel stared at him for a few moments, then slowly nodded. "There is no freedom," he finally said. "There is only survival."

When Jarlaxle didn't immediately respond, the steward of Bregan D'aerthe slipped into the chimney and melted into the stone.

Jarlaxle stood staring into the oven for a long while, fearing that Kimmuriel was right.

The roadway formed a wide circle inside the sharp right angle of Heliogabalus's wall, a cul-de-sac of mercantiles. Ilnezhara's shop was nearby, as was Tazmikella's. Dozens of chandlers, cobblers, blacksmiths, weavers, tailors, wheelwrights, importers, bakers, and other craftsmen and tradesmen of every imaginable stripe made Wall's Around their working home.

A large, three-tiered fountain centered the cul-de-sac, water dribbling from top to bottom without much energy, more of a continual rolling overflow. As he had envisioned it during his approach, Entreri had thought to use the fountain as his base, his vantage point to watch the scripted attack play out around him. But as he came through another alley to gain his third angle on the fountain, he realized that Knellict's hired highwayman had beaten him to it. The man was cleverly curled inside the second bowl, and only the uneven drip of the water had clued the assassin in to the fact that something was amiss.

He considered the highwayman's dark form and sensed patience and discipline—he was no novice.

With a nod, Entreri faded back into the shadows of the alley, grabbed a rail, and scaled the side of one shop, propelling himself to the roof. Low at the edge, he studied the fountain again, though he couldn't see the would-be assailant from that angle. Silent as a shadow, he slipped from roof to roof, circling the cul-de-sac, taking in a full view of the layout.

And noting two more figures lurking in the darkness under the porch of a darkened emporium.

The assassin froze in place then slipped lower on the roof, his gaze never leaving the two silhouettes. Those were Knellict's men, he knew, the wizard's insurance that nothing went amiss. Entreri couldn't make out many details, for they were well-concealed, but their lack of movement as the moments slipped past again spoke to him of discipline and training.

The easy course—to slay the merchant Beneghast and be on his way in Knellict's good graces—called out to him.

But Artemis Entreri had never been fond of the easy course.

The moment of truth, the time that Entreri had to ready himself one way or the other, slipped past, and the assassin transitioned into an almost unthinking, instinctual state. He had to move fast, back around the cul-de-sac, to put the fountain directly between himself and the two men under the porch. Roof to roof he went, fading back to the far side of each building, his body bending and twisting with each stride so that he seemed a part of the landscape and nothing more, and moving so silently that people in the buildings below his running feet wouldn't think that so much as a squirrel was skittering across their rooftops.

He came back down to the ground with equal grace, sliding flat at the eave, hooking his hand on the lip of the roof, and rolling over to extend himself fully before gently dropping to the alleyway.

He hesitated at the front corner of the building, for someone exited the door just a couple of steps to his left. That oblivious figure walked right past without taking any note of him, and continued on out of the cul-de-sac.

When a second figure appeared across the way and to his right, Entreri crouched a bit more. It was Beneghast.

The highwayman in the fountain would have noticed the merchant, as well, Entreri realized, and so he used that split second of distraction. He exploded into motion, running low and silently, then diving into a forward roll that brought him up against the lowest bowl of the fountain.

The man watched Beneghast's approach; the merchant would cross right by the fountain on the side opposite Entreri. The highwayman tried to find Entreri then, staying low and slowly swerving his head to take in as much of Wall's Around as possible, briefly locking his stare on this alleyway and that in search of the shadowy figure of the assassin he'd been told to expect.

Entreri quietly counted it out. He had already taken a measure of Beneghast's distance from the fountain, and could easily approximate the walking speed of the bent little man with a sack thrown over his shoulder.

The man in the fountain up above him was skilled, he reminded himself, and that meant that he would continue his scan for Entreri until the last possible second. But as Beneghast approached, the highwayman would have to shift his focus to the merchant.

That one moment, after the highwayman stopped his scan to look back at the target, yet before the highwayman actually found Beneghast again and moved to intercept, was Entreri's time.

He rolled up to a standing position, thin behind the stem of the fountain. He didn't allow Beneghast's approach to occupy a moment of his thought, but simply leaped up to the rim of that bottom bowl, a vertical jump of three feet. While his feet set quietly and surely on the slick, rounded rim, his left hand went out against the second bowl to secure his balance and his right hand, dagger drawn, struck hard and sure.

He felt the blade slide through the highwayman's ribs, and as soon as he noted the pressure of the initial contact, he came forward with it, releasing his grip on the second bowl and snapping his hand against the highwayman's head instead, driving him down below the water so that his cry became a burst of bubbles and nothing more.

Entreri felt the warmth of the man's blood rushing over his forearm, but the angle of the stab was all wrong for a quick in-the-heart kill. That mattered not at all to Entreri, though, for he summoned the vampiric powers of his dagger, drawing the highwayman's life-force into the magical blade, leaving him limp and lifeless in the bowl in a matter of a few heartbeats.

How convenient that the highwayman was wearing a mask, he thought, as he slipped the cloth free and quickly set it over his own face.

A short pause, a quick breath, and Entreri moved again, swiftly and gracefully, barely making a splash in the bowl as he slipped up to the rim and sprang free, landing lightly in the street beyond the wider, lower level. Beneghast noted his approach, of course, but the assassin moved so fast that the poor merchant barely had the time to gasp.

Entreri was there with frightening speed, standing right before him, the tip of his dagger just below Beneghast's Adam's apple

He locked stares with the man, letting Beneghast see the intensity in his dark eyes, the promise of death. The merchant groaned and wobbled, as if his legs would simply give out beneath him—but of course, the dagger remained tight and held him upright. A slight grin appeared on Entreri's face, and he retracted the dagger just a bit.

"Oh, I am murdered!" the merchant squealed, and Entreri smiled wider and made no move to silence him. "Oh, fie, that my life should be taken by . . . by . . ."

"Ah, ah," Entreri warned, lifting one finger of his free hand up before Beneghast and wagging it back and forth.

The merchant fell silent, except for the short gasps of his breathing.

"Drop your sack behind you," Entreri instructed.

The satchel hit the ground.

Entreri paused, considering the two watching from under the porch. They were tense, he knew, on edge and ready to strike, and wondering where Entreri might be.

The assassin paced slowly around Beneghast, smoothly picking up the sack as he moved around behind the man. His eyes never left the merchant, but also, he looked past the man, noting movement behind the windows and open doors of several shops. A whistle in the distance told him that the city guard had been alerted. No doubt Knellict's paid stooges were fast approaching to arrest the murderous highwayman even then.

And no doubt, the two fools under the porch across the way were wringing their hands and cursing under their breath that Artemis Entreri had yet to make an appearance.

"If you want to live, you will do exactly as I instruct—and even then, I cannot guarantee that you will escape with your life," Entreri told Beneghast. The man yelped—or started to, before Entreri cut him short. "You have one chance. Do you understand?"

"Y-yes," the merchant stammered, nodding stupidly.

"A bit of discretion would go a long way toward keeping my dagger out of your heart," the assassin told him.

"Y-yes—yes—" Beneghast stammered, but then stopped and slapped a hand across his mouth.

"When I tell you to run, you will go straight ahead," Entreri explained. "Turn into the alley on this side of the emporium—do not pass the porch. Do you understand?"

The sound of shouting came to them, from down the straight road leading to Wall's Around.

"Run," said Entreri.

Beneghast leaped into motion, screaming and sprinting, stumbling like a fool and nearly falling onto his face. He veered out toward the center of the road and seemed as if in his panic he would run right past the porch—to his sudden demise, no doubt—but then he stumbled again at the last moment and came out of it running straight into the alley.

Whistles and shouts closed from behind, but Entreri didn't even glance that way. He watched the two forms rush out from under the porch, two men, one large, one small—or perhaps the small one was a woman. They both looked Entreri's way, to which he offered a simple shrug, then the large one charged down the alley behind Beneghast, while the smaller began gesturing as if casting a spell.

So intent was that one on the fleeing Beneghast, that she—for it was indeed a woman—never even noted Entreri's swift approach. Just as she was about to release her spell, a blade flashed down before her, trailing a line of magical ash that hung in the air, blocking her view.

"What—?" she gasped and fell back a step, turning to regard Entreri just as he pulled the mask down from his face.

"I just wanted you to see the truth," he said.

The woman's eyes popped open wide, and her jaw dropped.

Entreri stabbed her with his dagger—or tried to, for she had an enchantment about her that defeated the attack. It was as if he had struck the blade against solid stone.

The woman shrieked again and turned to flee, but Entreri smacked her with his sword, again to no avail, and kicked her trailing foot back over her leading ankle. She tripped up and fell flat, immediately rolling to her back and raising her hands defensively before her.

"Do not kill me!" she begged. "Please, I have wealth."

He hit her again, and again, and again. "How many will your shield stop?" he said as she thrashed helplessly below him.

Beneghast's cry echoed out of the alleyway.

Entreri kicked the female mage one more time, then leveled Charon's Claw at her, the magnificent red blade barely an inch from her wide eyes.

"Tell your master that I am not a pawn," he said.

The woman bobbed her head frantically, and Entreri nodded and ran off. He noted two guards passing the fountain in hot pursuit, but he outdistanced them, disappearing into the darkness of the alley. As he did, he threw the sack up to a roof and ran on. Past a pile of discarded boxes and a broken wagon, he came in sight of Beneghast, down against the wall and bleeding, one hand up before his face pitifully. Above him loomed the larger assassin from the porch, a warhammer raised for the kill.

Entreri's dagger flew down the alleyway, striking true in the side of the killer's chest. The man staggered a step but did not go down. He turned and offered a defensive stance, though he couldn't help but lurch to the side from the pain.

Charon's Claw in both hands, Entreri went in with sudden and overwhelming fury. He swiped across, right to left, and the murderer, no novice to battle, blocked and disengaged quickly enough to keep his hammer in front of him.

"You're mad," he gasped, intercepting an overhand chop.

Entreri noted how forcefully that hammer came up to parry, and was not surprised in the least when the man moved forward underneath the angle of Charon's Claw. Nor did Entreri try to prevent that movement, nor did he twist aside. He simply loosened his grip on Charon's Claw and went forward as well, coming against the big man, who tried to overpower him and bull rush him to the ground.

Except Artemis Entreri was much stronger than he looked, and also had his hand clamped around the hilt of the jeweled dagger. A slight twist stopped the momentum of the large man as surely as any stone wall ever could. The killer looked down at Entreri, his hammer falling free to clang to the ground beside the fallen Charon's Claw. A look of absolute horror crossed his face, a look that never failed to bring a grin to Artemis Entreri's lips.

Entreri twisted the dagger again. He could have drawn the man's life-force out, utterly destroying his soul, but he found a moment of mercy. Instead of utter annihilation, he settled for the simple kill.

Entreri eased the dying man to the ground, and picked up Charon's Claw as he did.

"You . . . he saved me," Beneghast said, and the change in pronoun clued Entreri in to the fact that they were not alone. He came up fast and spun, facing the two guards—men he knew to be in Knellict's employ.

The expressions on the faces of the two guards revealed their utter confusion. Entreri hadn't followed the script.

"Saved you?" Entreri scoffed at Beneghast. "No amount of your gold will make me follow you down your road of lies! Take this man," Entreri ordered the guards. "He murdered the merchant Beneghast and left him dead in the fountain. His companion lies dead here, by my own hand, and he has promised me riches if I feign ignorance of his murderous ways."

The guards exchanged confused looks and Entreri was certain that he could have knocked them both over if he merely blew upon them. To the side, Beneghast stuttered and stammered, spitting all over himself.

Entreri silenced him with a look, then reached down and grabbed him by the front of his tunic. As he roughly pulled the merchant to his feet, purposely bringing a concealing grunt from the man, he whispered into his ear, "If you wish to live, play along."

He stood straight and shoved Beneghast into the arms of the confused guards.

"Be quick and escort him away. There may be more murderers hiding in the shadows."

They didn't know what to do—that much remained plain on their faces. They finally turned and started away, Beneghast in tow. The merchant managed to look back at Entreri, who nodded and winked, then put a finger to his pursed lips.

Did the guards fall for the ruse, Entreri wondered? Did they know Beneghast and the Citadel of Assassins's killers? He had seen no recognition on their faces in the moment before he had made his choice.

And even if he was wrong, even if they knew the truth of Beneghast's identity and subsequently killed him, what did Artemis Entreri care?

He tried to tell himself that, over and over, but he found himself back up on the rooftops. He moved to retrieve the merchant's sack—no reason he shouldn't collect some reward for his good deed, after all—then slipped along the tops of the buildings, shadowing the movements of the guards and their prisoner. As he expected, the corrupted soldiers didn't stay out in the street, but turned down another alleyway, one that opened out the back end, where they and their "prisoner" could easily escape.

"Go on, then," Entreri heard one tell Beneghast.

"Knellict's not to like losing one of his men," the other remarked.

"Not our affair," the other said. "That merchant fellow is dead and this one's to leave. That's all we were told to do."

On the roof above them, Entreri smiled. He watched Beneghast stumble out the back side of the alleyway, running as if his life depended on it—for surely it did.

The two guards followed slowly, chatting amongst themselves. One of them produced a small bag and jiggled it to show that it was full of coins.

Entreri looked at the sack he carried, then glanced back at the pair. For the first time since he had entered Wall's Around, the assassin paused to consider the ramifications of his course. He knew that he had just bought himself and Jarlaxle a lot of trouble from a very dangerous enemy. He could have gone along with Knellict's orders so easily.

But that would have meant accepting his fate, admitting that he was reverting to the life he had lived in Calimport, when he had been no more than a killing tool for Pasha Basadoni and so many others.

"No," he whispered and shook his head. He wasn't going back to that life, not ever, whatever the cost. He looked at the departing guards again.

He shrugged.

He dropped the sack.

He jumped down between the guards, weapons drawn.

He left soon after, a sack over one shoulder, and a bag of coins tied to his belt.

CHAPTER

6

The white cat dropped down from the windowsill and strode toward the disheveled merchant. Purring, the cat banged its head against Beneghast's leg.

"Ah, Mourtrue," the merchant said, sagging back against the wall and reaching down to pat his companion. "I thought I would never see you again. I thought I would never see anything again. Oh, but they were murderers, Mourtrue. Murderers, I say!"

"Do tell," the cat answered.

Beneghast froze in place, his words catching on the lump in his throat. He slowly lifted his hand away from the animal and shrank back against the wall.

Mourtrue began to grow.

"Please," the cat implored him, "do tell your tale. It is one that interests me greatly."

Beneghast gave a wail and flung himself aside—or tried to. A paw caught him and threw him back hard against the wall, the sharp claws shredding his good vest and overcoat in the process.

"I am not asking," the cat explained, grimacing as popping sounds erupted from all over its body. Bones broke and reformed, and skin stretched and twisted. The white fur shortened, became a bristly coat of fuzz, and disappeared.

Beneghast's knees went weak and he slumped to the floor. Knellict the wizard towered over him.

"You like cats," Knellict said. "That is a mark in your favor, for so do I."

"P-please, y-your magnificence," Beneghast stuttered, shaking his head so violently that his teeth chattered.

"You should be dead, of course."

"But . . ." Beneghast started, but he was too terrified to go on.

"But my men are dead instead," Knellict finished for him. "How is it that a foolish and flabby merchant could have done such a thing?"

"Oh, no, your magnificence!" Beneghast wailed. "Not that! Never! I struck no one. I did as I was told, and nothing more."

"You were told to kill my men?"

"No! Of course not, your superiorness. It was the masked man! Wicked with the blade, was he. He killed one in the alley that I saw. I know not of any oth—"

"The masked man?"

"The one with the red-bladed sword, and the dagger with the jeweled hilt. He caught me on the street and took my goods—your payment was in there. Oh please, your magnificence! I had your coin, and I wouldn't have been late but for the guards who came and took my gemstones. I tried to tell them that I needed the stones to—"

"You told city guards that you owed coin to Knellict?" the wizard interrupted, and his eyes flashed with the promise of death.

Beneghast got even smaller—Knellict didn't think that possible—and gave a strange squeaking sound.

"You killed my man in the fountain," Knellict accused, trying to break it down piece by piece to get a better sense of it all. Had his men provoked Entreri? Jailiana, who had survived, was just the type to have changed the plan, the impetuous little wench.

Beneghast shook his head violently. "There was no man in the fountain, except that the masked man came out of the fountain."

"The man with the red-bladed sword?"

"Yes," the merchant replied, bobbing his head.

"And that was when you were first accosted?"

"Yes."

Knellict pursed his lips. So, Entreri had betrayed him from the start.

"Please, magnificent sir," Beneghast whined. "I did nothing wrong."

"What of the two guards found at the other end of the alley?"

Beneghast's expression was all the answer Knellict needed, for the man obviously had no knowledge of that pair.

"You did nothing wrong?" Knellict asked. "Yet you were late in repayment."

"But . . . but . . ." Beneghast stammered, "but it's all here. All of it and more. And all for you."

"Get it."

The man moved fast, arms and legs flailing in all directions and ultimately doing little to get him out of the corner and off the floor. But then an invisible hand grabbed at him and hoisted him up, right off the ground.

"Where?" Knellict asked.

Hanging in midair, the terrified Beneghast lamely pointed at a dresser across the way. Knellict's telekinetic grip launched him that way, to crash into the drawers and crumble at the bureau's base. He only remained down for an instant, though, to his credit, and he yanked open a drawer so forcefully that it came right out of the dresser and fell at his feet. Clothes flew every which way and the merchant spun back, a large pouch in hand.

"All of it," he promised, "and more."

As Knellict reached out toward the merchant, a movement from the side caught both their attention. Into the room walked the real Mourtrue, looking exactly as Knellict had a moment before. The cat started for his master, but suddenly went up into the air, magically grasped, and flew fast to Knellict's waiting grasp.

"No!" the merchant wailed, lunging forward. "Please, not my Mourtrue."

"Commendable," said Knellict as he held and gently stroked the frightened cat. "You are loyal to your feline companion."

"Oh please, sir," said Beneghast, and he fell to his knees begging. "Anything but my Mourtrue."

"You love her?"

"As if she was my child."

"And does she return the love?"

"Oh yes, sir."

"Let us see, and if you are right, then I forgive your debt and your tardiness. In fact, if you have so garnered the loyalty of such a beautiful creature as this, I will return all of the coin in that purse tenfold."

Beneghast stared at him with confusion, not really knowing what to say.

"Fair?" Knellict asked.

Beneghast had no idea what to say, but he nodded despite himself.

Knellict began to cast a spell and Beneghast recoiled. It took some time for the wizard to complete the enchantment, finally waggling the fingers of one hand at the merchant, sending out waves of crackling energy.

Beneghast heard popping sounds—the sounds of his bones cracking and reshaping. The room got larger suddenly, impossibly huge, which confused poor Beneghast as much as did the fact that his breaking bones didn't really hurt.

He felt strange. His vision was black and white, and so many odors floated out at him they overwhelmed his sensibilities. He glanced left and right and saw white lines across his field of vision, as if he had . . . whiskers.

Mourtrue's growl turned his attention back to the wizard, who stood with gigantic, titanic even, proportions. In Knellict's arms, Mourtrue squirmed and twisted.

Beneghast started to question it all, but his voice came out as a chirp and nothing more.

Then he understood, and he glanced back to see his thin tail.

He was a mouse.

He snapped his gaze back to Knellict and Mourtrue.

"Shall we learn the depths of your cat's loyalty, then?" asked the smug mage.

He dropped Mourtrue to the floor, but it seemed to Beneghast as if the cat never even touched down, so graceful and fast was Mourtrue's leap.

"I guess not so deep," Knellict said.

Knellict left a short while later, the well-fed cat curled up against his shoulder, wondering what in the world he was going to do about this Artemis Entreri fellow.

Tazmikella knew who it was as soon as she saw the lean, late-middle-aged man walking slowly up the hill toward her front door. His threadbare and weather-beaten robes could have belonged to any of a thousand nomads who wandered the region, of course, but the walking stick, white as bone, belonged to one man alone.

A shudder coursed Tazmikella's spine and she couldn't help but wince at the sight of Master Kane. She hated the monk—irrationally so, she knew. She hated him because she feared him, and Tazmikella did not like "fearing" any human. But Kane was a monk, a grandmaster, and that meant that he could all too easily avoid the effects of her breath weapon, her greatest battle asset. Tazmikella didn't fear wizards, not even an archmage like Knellict. She didn't fear the paladin king, nor any of his heroic friends—not the ranger, priest, thief, or bard—save for one. The only humans—the only creatures of the lesser races, the drow included—who so unnerved the dragon were those strange ascetics who dedicated their lives to perfecting their bodies.

And Kane was no ordinary monk, even. In the martial sense, he was the greatest of the disciples in all the Bloodstone Lands and far beyond. So perfect was his understanding of and control over his body, that he could achieve a state of otherworldliness, it was said, where his physical form transcended its corporeal limitations to escape the very bonds of the Material Plane.

All of those rumors and whispers bounced about Tazmikella's thoughts as she watched the seemingly simple man's determined approach.

"Remember who you are," the dragon finally whispered to herself. She gave a quick shake of her head and her concerned look became a grimace.

"Master Kane," she said as the man neared her porch. "It has been far too long . . ." She meant to continue with an invitation for the monk to enter her home, but Kane didn't wait, walking right past her with only a slight nod of his head for acknowledgement.

Tazmikella paused at the door and didn't look back inside at the monk until she found the strength to wipe the sneer off her face. She reminded herself repeatedly that Kane was there at the request of King Gareth, no doubt.

"To what do I owe the honor of your presence?" she said, a bit too sweetly, as she turned and walked to her seat at the table opposite the monk. She noted his posture as she went, and that too only reminded her that the man was different. Kane did not sit with his feet on the floor, as others would. He had his legs folded tightly beneath him, feet under his buttocks, and with his back perfectly straight and balanced over the center of his form. He could move in a blink, Tazmikella realized, unfolding faster than any enemy, even a coiled snake, might strike.

"Your sister will join us presently," Kane replied.

"You expect Ilnezhara to arrive in a timely fashion?" Tazmikella asked, her tone light and sarcastic, and for effect, she rolled her eyes.

She might as well have rolled out of the chair and across the floor, for all the effect her humor had on Kane. He sat there, unblinking and unmoving. Not just unmoving, but utterly still, save the minor rise and fall of his breathing. The dragon paused, even shifted noisily a few times, leaning forward in anticipation, trying to prompt the monk to speak.

But he did not.

He just sat there.

Many moments slipped past, and he just sat there.

Tazmikella got up repeatedly and walked to the door, glancing out for any sign of her sister. Then she sat back down, offering both smiles and frowns. She asked a few questions—about the weather, about Vaasa, about King Gareth and Lady Christine, inquiring how they fared.

Kane just sat there.

Finally, after what felt like the whole of the morning to Tazmikella, but was in fact less than an hour, Ilnezhara arrived at the door. She came in and greeted her sister and the monk, who gave the slightest of nods in response.

"Do take care, good sister," Tazmikella dared to say, for she drew confidence with the arrival of a second dragon. "It would seem that my guest is not in good humor this morning."

"You were not at the ceremony honoring those returning from Vaasa," he said, addressing both.

"I did hear of that," Ilnezhara replied. "Those who investigated the latest Zhengyian construct, yes?"

Kane stared long and hard at her.

"Well of course, information travels slowly from Bloodstone Village to Heliogabalus, and we are not about to take wing."

"By order of King Gareth," Tazmikella added. "We would not wish to terrify half of Damara."

"Jarlaxle the drow and Artemis Entreri are known to you," Kane stated. "They were in your employ before their journey to Vaasa—a journey they took at your request, perhaps?"

"You presume much, Master Kane," said Ilnezhara.

"You deny little," Kane replied.

"We have had minor dealings with this drow and his friend," Tazmikella said. "You know our business. Who better to acquire goods than that pair?"

"You sent them to Vaasa," the monk said.

Ilnezhara scoffed, but Kane didn't blink, so Tazmikella remarked, "We suggested to Jarlaxle that his talents might serve him better in the wilderness, and that perhaps he would find adventure, reputation, and booty."

"There is an old saying that a dragon's suggestion is ever a demand," the monk remarked.

Tazmikella managed a weak grin, and looked to her sister. She noted the exchange of looks between Kane and Ilnezhara, bordering on threatening.

"We know Jarlaxle and Entreri," Tazmikella said bluntly. "They are not in our employ, but we have, on occasion, employed them. If you have come to question their bona fides, Master Kane, should you not have arrived before the ceremo—"

Kane stopped her with an upraised hand, a gesture that had the proud dragon fighting hard to suppress her anger.

"Your accommodations here are at the suffrage of King Gareth," Kane reminded her. "Never forget that. We are not enemies; we have welcomed both of you into the community of Bloodstone with open arms and trust."

"Your warning does not reek of trust, Grandmaster," said Ilnezhara.

"You repudiated Zhengyi's advances. That is not unnoticed."

"And now?" Ilnezhara prompted.

Kane unfolded suddenly, standing on the chair, and dipped a low bow. "I pray you understand that we are in dangerous times."

"You see the world from a human perspective," Ilnezhara cautioned. "You view disasters in the terms of years, at most, and not in terms of decades or centuries. It is understandable that you would utter such a silly statement."

Kane betrayed no anger at the statement as he sat again, but neither did he seem impressed. "The castle was no small matter, was perhaps the greatest manifestation of Zhengyi, curse his name, since his demise those years ago."

"Zhengyi himself was a small matter," Ilnezhara replied. "A temporary inconvenience and nothing more."

Even Tazmikella winced at the obvious and self-serving understatement. Both she and her sister had breathed much easier indeed when the Witch-King had fallen, and not since the time when Aspiraditus the red dragon and her three fiery offspring had flown into the mountains of western Damara four hundred years before had the dragon sisters been that concerned about anything.

"Perhaps we measure our catastrophes in the sense of tendays, or even years, good lady, because that is all we have," Kane countered. "Our time is short by your measures, but eternity by our own. I am not overly concerned about this latest Zhengyian construct, for it is dead now, and I am confident that whatever plagues the Witch-King left behind for us will be handled accordingly by Spysong and the Army of Bloodstone."

"And yet, you are here," reasoned Tazmikella.

"This is how we handle accordingly our catastrophes," Kane answered, and for the first time, a bit of emotion, a dry sarcasm, crept into his monotone voice.

"Then pray tell us of your catastrophe," Ilnezhara stated with a clear air of condescension.

Kane stared at her for a few moments but did not reply.

"Pray tell us why you have come to see us," Tazmikella intervened, guessing correctly that the monk wasn't willing to label the purpose of his visit as such.

"That this drow and human in your employ walked out of that castle, while King Gareth's niece, a knight of the order, did not, is worrying," the monk admitted. "That this drow and human walked out of that castle, while Mariabronne the Rover, a hero of the realm by all measures and a student of Olwen, did not, is worrying. I would be ill-serving my king and friend Gareth if I did not investigate the circumstances of his niece's death. And I would be ill-serving my friend Olwen if I did not investigate the circumstances of his student's death. It is no mystery why I have come."

The sisters looked at each other.

"Do you vouch for the character of the drow and human?" Kane asked.

"They have not disappointed us," Tazmikella said.

"Yet," added her sister.

Tazmikella looked from Ilnezhara to Kane, trying to judge the monk's response, but reading his emotions was like trying to find footprints on hard stone.

"We are not well acquainted with the pair, truth be told," Tazmikella offered.

"You were not responsible for importing them to Damara?"

"Certainly not," Tazmikella answered, and Ilnezhara echoed her words as she was speaking them. "We learned of them in Heliogabalus, and decided that we could put their talents to use. It is not so different from the methods of Spysong, and I am certain that if we had not hired the pair, your friend Celedon would have."

"They are talented at what they do," Ilnezhara added.

"Stealing?" asked Kane.

"Procurement," Tazmikella corrected.

Kane actually offered a bit of a smile at that equivocation. He snapped up to stand on the chair again, and dipped a low bow. Without another word, he turned and walked out of Tazmikella's house.

"Those two are going to get themselves killed," Tazmikella remarked when the monk was far away.

"At least," said her sister, with more concern than Tazmikella expected. She glanced over to see Ilnezhara staring at the open door and the back of the departing Kane.

Indeed, Tazmikella thought, few creatures in all the world could unnerve a dragon more than a grandmaster monk.

"You have heard about the fight at Great Fork Ford?" Ilnezhara said, obviously noticing Tazmikella's stare. "Two reds and a mighty white seemed about to rout one of Gareth's brigades."

"And Grandmaster Kane rushed in," Tazmikella continued. "He

dared their breath, fire and frost, and avoided it all."

"And even deceived the dragons into breathing upon each other," Ilnezhara added.

"The white—Glacialamacus, it is rumored—was severely burned, and none know if she has survived her wounds. And both reds were wounded, by the frost and by the blows of Kane, followed by the charge of Gareth's warriors."

"It is all rumor, you know," Tazmikella remarked.

"Perhaps, but a plausible rumor, no doubt."

After a long pause, digesting the implications, Tazmikella added, "I grow weary of those two."

"Jarlaxle troubles me," Ilnezhara agreed.

"Troubles?"

"But he is a fine lover," Ilnezhara went on unabated. "Perhaps I should keep him close."

Tazmikella just rolled her eyes at that, hardly surprised.

From the outside, the black hole in the mountainside seemed like just another of the many caves that dotted the region of towering stones and steep facings of the high peaks of the Galenas, east of the Vaasan Gate. Anyone who entered that particular cave, though, would find it to be much more, full of comforts and treasures, inviting aromas and magically lit walkways.

Of course, anyone who entered it uninvited would likely find himself dead.

Chased from Heliogabalus after the fall of Zhengyi, Timoshenko, the Grandfather of Assassins, and his mighty advisor Knellict, had moved the band to their remote, well-defended location. Suites of rooms went far back into the mountain, some carved by hired stone-masons and miners, and many others created by Knellict's magic. Timoshenko's band lived in comfort and security, but were not too remote from their dealings in Damara, for Knellict and his mage companions had also created and maintained a series of magical portals to strategic locations within Gareth's kingdom.

Through one of those portals, Jailiana, the mage who had survived Entreri's betrayal at Wall's Around, had arrived back at the citadel, trembling with outrage. She had delivered her report quickly, and had asked for support that she might go right back to Heliogabalus and slaughter the traitor. As angry as she was, however, Jailiana knew better than to act without the express permission of Knellict, and so when he had ordered her to stand down, she had quietly gone, sulking, to her chambers.

Knellict came out into the sunlight on the natural stone balcony of the cave, staring west along the northern foothills of the stony mountains. He still held Mourtrue, and had taken quite a liking to the purring cat, and was even considering creating a magical wizard-familiar bond with the animal.

It pleased Knellict to know that one of those who had tried to deceive him was making his way through this creature's intestines.

"Jailiana trembles with anger," came a voice behind him, one of his lieutenants, a dependable if unremarkable fellow named Coureese.

"I have a spell prepared that can cure that," Knellict absently replied. "Of course, it would freeze her solid in the process."

"She knows that she failed you," Coureese said.

"Failed?" Knellict turned, and Coureese looked at him, at the white cat, with obvious surprise. "She did not fail."

"She was to ensure the death of Beneghast."

"She was to witness the loyalty, or lack thereof, of Artemis Entreri," Knellict corrected. "She did not fail."

"But he got away, and two men were slain."

"Where can he run, I wonder? And we lose young recruits almost daily. There are always more to take their places, and if we did not lose so many, then how would we ever know which ones were worthy of our efforts to train them?"

Coureese's lips moved, but he didn't say anything, and Knellict smiled at the man's confusion.

"Perhaps I should go and tell Jailiana of your feelings," Coureese offered.

"Perhaps I should telekinese you over the cliff."

The man blanched and fell back a step.

"Let her stew in her anger," Knellict explained. "It is a fine motivator. And let us set an order of elimination on the head of dear Artemis Entreri. Perhaps our female friend would seek the coin."

"She would go after him for free," Coureese replied. "She would pay us for the opportunity."

"Well, that is her decision to make. She has seen this man at his craft. I would expect that a woman wise enough to dabble in the arcane ways would also be wise enough to recognize the difference between opportunity and suicide."

Coureese wagged his head for a few moments, digesting all of that. Finally, he asked, "The bounty?"

Knellict considered it for a moment, thinking it might be a good training exercise for the younger members, and a good way to truly measure the prowess of Artemis Entreri. "Fifty pieces of platinum," he replied.

Coureese licked his lips and nodded.

"Your thoughts?" Knellict prompted, seeing, and expecting, his discomfort. After all, a man of Entreri's reputation—even the little bit that was known in Damara, which was likely only a very minor piece of the intriguing killer's history—would normally bring a bounty of ten times that offering.

"Nothing, my lord Knellict. I will post the order of elimination." He bowed quickly and turned to leave. Before he reached the cave, however, the magical stone door slid out from its concealment at the side, sealing the entrance in a camouflaged manner that made it seem as if no cave existed there. Coureese spun back to face Knellict, for he knew that the archmage had closed that door with a minor spell.

"When I ask for your thoughts, you would do well to offer them," Knellict explained. "All of them."

"Your pardon, master," Coureese begged, bowing repeatedly and awkwardly. "I only . . ."

"Just speak them," the mage demanded.

"Fifty pieces of platinum?" Coureese blurted. "I had thought that I would try to collect this bounty myself, but to go after this Entreri—who walks beside a drow!—for such a price is not enticing."

"Because you are intelligent."

Coureese looked up at him.

"Only a fool would go after Artemis Entreri for this price, agreed. So let us see what fools we need to remove from our ranks. Or I should say, let us see what fools Entreri will eliminate for us. And in the process, perhaps he will leave a trail of bodies that King Gareth cannot ignore. We can only gain here."

"But Entreri will not likely be killed," Coureese dared to remark.

Knellict snorted as if that hardly mattered. "When I want him to die, he will die. Athrogate is close to him, do not forget, and the dwarf is loyal. Better to enrage Entreri—or should I call him 'Sir' Entreri?—and embarrass King Gareth. And perhaps one of those who seek him out will show unexpected promise and actually slay him. Or perhaps several will prove resourceful enough to work together to win the bounty."

Coureese began to nod, catching on to all the potential gains.

"Every so often, we must put such a test before our young recruits," Knellict explained and shrugged. "How else are we to know who is worthy and who should be dead?"

Coureese offered a final nod then, hearing the door magically sliding open behind him as Knellict simply waved a hand, he bowed and took his leave.

Knellict chuckled and stroked the purring Mourtrue. "Ah, cat, how am I ever to survive with such fools as that serving me? And he is one of the better ones of late!"

He went back to the ledge and stared out over southern Vaasa. He missed the days of glory when Zhengyi had occupied the trouble-some Gareth and the Citadel of Assassins had thrived.

He hated living in a cave—even one magically furnished.

CHAPTER

S H A D O W S

7

To a surface dweller, they were called shadows, patches of confusing darkness made all the harder to decipher because of the splotches of light beside them. But to Jarlaxle, who had spent centuries wandering the lightless abyss known as the Underdark, these "shadows" were really just dimmer areas of lightness. And so the drow had no trouble at all in discerning the man crouched beside a pile of debris in the alleyway beside the building where he and Entreri shared their second-story apartment. So painfully obvious was the fool that Jarlaxle had to work hard to keep from giggling at him as he walked past the alleyway to the wooden staircase that would take him to the outer door of his apartment.

At the foot of those stairs, the drow casually glanced all about. Sure enough, he spotted a second man, slipping along the rooftop of an adjoining building.

"What have you done, Artemis?" Jarlaxle whispered under his breath.

He started up the stairs, but stopped short and turned around, acting very much as if he had forgotten something. He even went so far in his deception as to snap his fingers in the air before starting off quickly back the way he had come. They were all watching him, he knew, and there were likely more than two.

But how could they question his decision to enter Piter's Bakery, given the sweet, sweet aroma emanating from its open door?

The drow's turnabout might have fooled the would-be ambushers, but it revealed much more to Artemis Entreri, who watched from his apartment, from the corner of the small window overlooking the street. He understood the significance of Jarlaxle's somewhat exaggerated movements: the finger snap and the feigned expression of forgetfulness.

Agents of the Citadel of Assassins were nearby, no doubt, and Jarlaxle had spied them.

After waiting a bit longer to see if anyone followed Jarlaxle's detour to Piter's shop—and no one did—the assassin moved back into the center of the room and considered his course. He was most certainly outnumbered, and the first rule when so outmanned was to never allow oneself to be cornered. He moved swiftly to the door, drew his sword and dagger, and kicked it open. He went through in a rush, speaking the command password, "White," so that the magic of his trap didn't kill him where he stood.

As he went under the arch of the door, he jumped up and hooked his dagger inside the looped silver chain that held a small statuette of a dragon rampant, its eyes shining like white moonstones. A flick of his wrist had the dragon safely dangling on the blade of his dagger, a second fluid twist dropped the figurine safely away in a pouch, and a third, executed with such precision and speed that it all seemed as one swipe, replaced the dagger in its scabbard with the fine chain from the statuette still looped around it.

Three running steps took Entreri down the hall, to the outer door, the balcony, then the stairway to the street. He thought to pause and inspect whether his uninvited guests had placed any traps on the door, but suspecting that he didn't have that much time, he just lowered his shoulder and crashed through. On the balcony, he cut fast to the left, to the stairs, and he started down—one, two, three strides. There, still more than halfway up, he slipped over the waist-high railing, catching it with his free hand, sliding down its angled decline for a moment, then dropping to the ground. He rolled as he landed to absorb the shock, and came back to his feet already into his run. As he ran across the street, he could feel the eyes of archers upon him.

A small two-wheeled cart of fruit had been placed across from Entreri's stair. The jovial vendor and his teenage son chatted easily with a young couple who were inspecting the wares—a scene very typical for the streets of Heliogabalus.

Or not so, Entreri realized as he approached, for he noted that the foursome were not fast to react to his sudden and unexpected appearance and his obvious urgency—or even to the fact that he held a red-bladed, fabulously designed sword in one hand. He locked stares with the bearded vendor, just for a moment, but that was enough for him to see a flicker of recognition in the man's dark eyes. Not the recognition of a common vendor who might have seen him pass by a dozen times, but the look of a man who had found what he was seeking.

Entreri broke into a charge just as he heard the click of a crossbow releasing from somewhere to the side—and he heard the bolt hum through the air right behind him. He drew his dagger back out as he went, but again kept the blade carefully tipped so that it did not allow the silver chain to slide off as he pulled the statuette free of the pouch.

The young couple next to the cart threw off their peasant cloaks and spun around, weapons at the ready, but Entreri charged through with a quick back-and-forth slash of his sword that had them both falling aside in opposite directions.

A leap brought Entreri to the edge of the cart. A second spring brought him past the "vendor" and the younger man, sailing through the entryway to the alley. Up snapped Entreri's dagger arm as he crossed just under a trellis beam that joined the buildings. He set his dagger into the wooden beam, the dragon statuette bouncing beneath it. He hit the ground in more of a dive than a run, for he understood how little time he had, how close came the pursuit.

And those pursuers, he knew, wouldn't utter the password, wouldn't properly identify the dragon.

He was still rolling and scrambling—anything to move down the alleyway—when the trap went off right behind him and he felt a blast of frost that chilled him to the bone and left a red burn on his trailing ankle. He tried to stand, but his leg had gone numb, and he quickly found himself face down on the cobblestones. He thrashed and rolled, sword slashing across, for he was certain that another of the killers would be fast upon him.

Pie in hand, Jarlaxle leaned casually on Piter's counter and watched the couple, a man and his petite and pretty lover, come through the door. They looked into each other's eyes, giggling all the while.

Jarlaxle knew a put-on when he saw one.

"Ah, young love!" he cried dramatically. "Good Piter, I will gladly pay for their sweets."

The two looked at Jarlaxle, expressions correctly confused. He tossed the pie to the man, but up high. When the man went to catch it, the movement lifted up the hem of his waistcoat, revealing a pair of well-worn dagger handles.

The second pie Jarlaxle threw came in harder, and was not meant to be caught—except by the man's surprised expression.

"What?" the woman yelled as the pie splattered across her lover's face, and he gave a yell, as well, but one of pain.

"Jarlaxle, what are you about?" Piter demanded.

"I am killed!" the surprised man cried. He slapped at his face, sending cream flying and eventually revealing a small dart that had been concealed within the pie, protruding from his cheek. He reached for it, hands trembling, but he couldn't quite seem to grasp it.

Beside him, the young girl screamed and cried.

Jarlaxle had his arms bent, hands by his shoulders, ready to thrust them down and call forth a pair of blades from the magical bracers set on his wrists. He could summon daggers with a thought, then elongate the magical weapons into long swords with a snap of his arms.

But he didn't, because at least the girl's reaction was all wrong. The man, predictably, slumped down to the floor, his eyes rolling back into his skull, froth spilling from his slack jaw.

"Jarlaxle!" Piter cried, scrambling out beside his investor. "What have you done? Oh, Clairelle! Oh, Mischa!"

Jarlaxle cleared his throat as Piter wobbled his way to help Clairelle support the limp form of her lover.

"You know them?" the drow asked.

A troubled Piter looked back at him. "This is Maringay's daughter and her husband-to-be! They live right next to you. They are to be wed in the spring, and I am . . . I was to bake . . . oh, what have you done?"

"I have put him to sleep, and nothing more," Jarlaxle explained as he moved past the trio to the door. "Keep them inside, for there are killers about."

Clairelle slapped at him, then grabbed his pant leg as he moved past.

"It was for his own good," the embarrassed drow lied. "Your gallant lover would wish to play the role of hero, no doubt, and now is not the time. Lock your door, Piter, and keep all inside. On pain of death, do not go out!"

Jarlaxle tugged his leg away, spent the time to tip his hat at the distressed young lady, then quickly took his leave. He burst onto the street, suddenly doubting all that he had seen and inferred.

But he heard the tumult a bit farther down, across from his apartment. A man staggered out of the alleyway, white—frosted—from head to toe and walking awkwardly, stiffly. He crashed into the fruit cart, and the jolt sent a pile of apples spilling onto the street.

Apples frozen so solid that some of them shattered like glass when they hit the cobblestones.

"Entreri," the drow whispered.

He slipped a ring onto his finger and clenched his fist, releasing its magic. Up he jumped, a dozen feet and more, to land lightly on the roof of Piter's shop, where he fast melted from sight.

Entreri staggered down to the end of the alley, which was blocked by a wall and fronted by a pile of broken crates and some old wooden furniture. He had thought to use the pile to go over the wall and sprint out across the street parallel to his own, but his legs were barely working, one of them shifting from complete numbness to a pervasive, burning pain. He looked back to see the phony vendor and his "son" lying very still on the ground, covered in frost. A third killer, one of the pair who had feigned shopping at the cart, leaned up against the alley wall, seeming frozen in place, eyes open and unseeing, eyelashes white with ice. His companion staggered back out in the street behind him then tripped over the partially frozen fruit cart and tumbled hard to the cobblestones where he lay shivering and helpless, likely dying.

But more were coming, Entreri realized as a pair of forms darted left to right across his field of vision, on the other side of the street.

Entreri knew that he was in trouble. He used the pile of debris to pull himself up, and he tried to walk, but his numb foot flopped forward and he tripped over his own toes. He kept his balance, though, and did not fall down. Instead he used the stumble to propel himself back behind some of the crates, turning as he went.

A dark form slipped in around the left-hand corner of the alley exit, hugging the wall and using it for support as he inched down across the icy surface. A second killer came in a bit faster, and skidded across the ice. When his feet hit dry ground, he jolted forward several steps.

Had his legs been capable, Entreri would have leaped out to intercept, laying the overbalanced fool low before he ever came out of that bent-over stumble.

But his legs were not capable, and and he could hardly stand, let alone move to attack.

The man regained his balance and straightened to face the assassin, a gleaming long sword in one hand, a small buckler strapped to his other arm. He stayed out of reach and remained in a defensive crouch, glancing back repeatedly at his slowly approaching companion.

"Hurry it on, then," he whispered harshly. "We got the rat cornered."

"The rat that spews like a dragon of white," the other replied.

"Yes, come and freeze," Entreri bluffed.

He angled himself so that he did not appear as if he was leaning quite so heavily on the wall, but in truth, had it not been for that solid barrier behind him, Entreri would have toppled over. He brought his impressive sword out in front of him, waving the red blade tantalizingly.

The nearer man straightened a bit and took a step away.

"It was a trap set in the alley, and nothing he's got to play again," the man closer to Entreri deduced, calling the assassin's bluff.

"As you wish," Entreri said with an evil little chuckle, and he waved the blade in invitation.

He held his sigh of relief when the man backed another half a step, for he felt the tell-tale tingling in his legs to indicate that the feeling was beginning to return, that his blood flowed once more. It took all of his training to hold back his grimace in the next few moments, but he knew that he couldn't let on how weak he still was.

If they attacked boldly, he was dead.

"Knellict sent you, of course," Entreri said. "He promised me that he would utilize me as a trainer, though he may decide, after the six of you lie dead, that I take my task far too seriously."

The two men exchanged nervous looks. More importantly to Entreri, they held their ground and did not advance.

But then one of them, the second who had come in, straightened and relaxed, and began to laugh a bit. "He thinks there's but six of us," he said, and he slapped his friend on the shoulder, and that fool, too, began to giggle stupidly.

Entreri got the meaning, and he lamented that he would die in such a way—struck from above, no doubt, and without any means to defend himself from that quarter.

⊰⊹⊱

Despite his speed, despite his stealth, despite the uneven grades and facings of the various rooftops, Jarlaxle kept his bearings. He knew exactly where he was at all times, and when he saw the two men standing overlooking one alleyway, one hunched over and with crossbow in hand, aiming down, he could well imagine the target.

The drow's hand came up fast and steady from under his cloak, holding a favored weapon of his race, a hand crossbow. He let fly and watched with satisfaction as the archer twitched from the sting of the tiny bolt. The other man looked at the archer in surprise, but the crossbowman couldn't answer, for he was already swaying from the sleep poison, leaning forward, sure to tumble.

The other man grabbed at him.

Jarlaxle reached into himself, summoning forth his innate dark elven magic in the form of a globe of absolute darkness that covered both would-be killers.

Jarlaxle heard the shuffling, the grunt, and the shout. He was quite pleased, but hardly surprised when he saw the movement over the lip of the ledge, just below his stationary globe, as the archer pitched forward, taking his grabbing companion with him.

"Entreri, what have you done?" Jarlaxle whispered.

The drow faded into the shadows of the jumble of jagged, multi-pitched rooftops, looking for a way to get a safe view of the alley below.

Entreri reacted on instinct when he caught movement out of the corner of his eye. He threw himself across to the opposite side of the narrow alleyway. He took care to stay on balance, though, for the pair of ruffians advanced. Apparently emboldened by the arrival of their reinforcement, they charged.

Entreri started forward, sword leading, in a sudden rush. The newcomers crashed down beside him. He pulled up short, though, for his attack was no more than a feint, an attempt to buy time so that he could take care of the newest threat. Had he been a lesser fighter, a desperate charge would have been the only course, an attempt to burst through the pair and run off.

But Entreri wasn't about to flee any fight.

He nearly fell over when he stopped so abruptly, though, for the feeling had not yet fully returned to one leg. Still, he covered the stumble, falling against the wall of the alley, and bouncing back to center balance.

He spun around, and nearly froze in confusion when he noted the tangle of the two newcomers, who had crashed through some of the debris. One lay perfectly still and limp and the other squirmed in pain, grabbing at his wrist, ankle, and knee alternately, having done serious damage to all three. Entreri understood a moment later, when he glanced up from where they had come, to see a globe of enchanted blackness hovering in the air.

Jarlaxle.

With the other pair coming on fast, Entreri leaped at the reinforcements and stabbed hard, driving Charon's Claw right through the top, unconscious man and into the fellow below him. The first made no sound, as though he was already dead, but the bottom man screamed and thrashed.

Entreri had no time to finish him off. He yanked Charon's Claw free, a gush of blood following its retraction, and spun around. His blade crossed just in time to bat aside a thrusting sword then force the other man's dagger arm up and out. The assassin pressed his advantage, shuffling ahead and stabbing repeatedly, not in any real hope of scoring a hit on his skilled opponents, but more to drive them back and give him some room to maneuver—and to react in case the man on the bottom of the pile had any fight left in him.

He turned his back foot perpendicular to both enemies and to his front foot. He brought it forward and tapped his heel, then planted and stepped ahead. Then again and again, quick-stepping in perfect balance and driving the two killers back. He still couldn't feel one foot, but his every plant was solid and certain, and bolstered by the coordination of foot against foot, using the leg he could feel to guide the leg he couldn't.

Finally, and just before they hit the still-slick area where the white dragon's breath had struck, the pair managed to coordinate a counter stance. They moved wider apart, each turning slightly to better their angles of attack.

Entreri recognized that his momentum had played out. He fell back in a defensive crouch, legs wide and balanced, though one remained a bit stiff and more immobile than he let on.

"Ah, but he killed Wyrt!" cried the knave on the right, the one with the sword.

"Shut your mouth, fool!" his companion snapped at him.

"You'll meet him again, and soon," Entreri promised. He wasn't fond of speaking to his opponents in battle, but he had to buy time. His leg tingled and burned, and it was all he could do to hide his winces.

The man with the dagger lunged, and Entreri slapped Charon's Claw out to intercept. The man was fast, though, and he retracted his arm inside the reach of the sword, and came ahead with a cunning second strike.

He didn't understand.

For even on one leg, even distracted by the pain and the numbness and off balance, Entreri easily brought his blade back in—indeed, it moved to such a position even as his opponent began to pull the dagger back.

And Entreri knew that feint wasn't all of it.

To the side came the other man, sword thrusting, but Charon's Claw slashed across smoothly, slapping the blade and driving him back.

Entreri brought all his weight over his numb left leg. He had to trust it, and he locked it in place, pivoting his right leg back with the coming of the anticipated second dagger thrust.

The knife came in short, its tip just brushing his backing hip.

To the attacker's credit, the man recognized his miss quickly enough to leap backward from any coming counter.

That, too, Entreri anticipated, and instead of pursuing, he brought Charon's Claw back across the other again. Calling forth the magic of the sword, he hung a line of opaque ash in the air to shield himself from the swordsman's sight.

He knew the man would instinctively straighten before he managed to shuffle his feet back. In that instant, Entreri dropped to one knee and slashed his sword across under the wall of ash.

The assassin felt the impact, then the tug of ligament and bone resisting the cruel cut, and the swordsman howled in agony.

Entreri came up in a complete spin, around left to right, that left him squared up to the man with the dagger. A crash to the side told him that the swordsman had fallen back hard, and was out of the fight for a little while at least.

Entreri instinctively brought his sword across to block, and sure enough, the dagger flew at him, clanging harmlessly off of Charon's Claw's blood-red—and bloody—blade.

The killer drew another dagger.

Entreri grinned.

The man turned and ran, howling for mercy with every step. He only got a couple of strides before he hit the ice and went sprawling to the ground. Crying, screaming, and scrambling, he continued away as if expecting the killing blow to fall at any moment. He finally got back to dry ground, and went flailing down the street.

Entreri just stood there, amused.

A sharp cry from behind, followed by a gurgle, had him turning around. There stood Jarlaxle, wiping the blood from a dagger, having finished off the bottom man.

The drow looked at Entreri for a long while, silently asking him what it was all about. Entreri just returned the stare, offering nothing. Finally, Jarlaxle looked away, just a bit.

"Oh lovely," the dark elf said.

Entreri followed the drow's gaze to the side, where the ash wall began to drift apart. There, right where the man had been standing, remained both of his feet, severed at the ankles. The rest was back from there, slumped against the wall, bloody hands in the air, trembling. He didn't even try to stem the flow any longer.

Jarlaxle walked up to him and looked him over. "You are bleeding to death," he calmly explained. "It will be slow, but no more painful than that which you experience now. You will get cold, however, and do not panic when the world goes dark before your eyes."

The man whimpered, shaking his head, hands up, pleading.

"Perhaps if you are willing to divulge . . ." Jarlaxle started, and the man wagged his head furiously—or started to, until Entreri stepped up beside his friend and plunged Charon's Claw into the fool's heart.

Entreri pulled the sword free, glanced at Jarlaxle only briefly, and offered nothing more as he started out of the alleyway to retrieve his dagger and the dragon statuette.

"You seek no answers because you know them already, I must presume," Jarlaxle said.

Entreri kept walking, and fortunately, the feeling in his leg had returned enough for him to manage his balance across the slick surface of the frozen alleyway.

CHAPTER

<small>TO SLEEP WITH DRAGONS</small>

8

Bwahaha, ye just keep the drink flowing," Athrogate howled.

He hoisted his foamy mug and gulped it down in one swallow—at least the contents of it that didn't pour all over his braided black beard. He dropped the mug back on the table and drew his sleeve across his beard, taking only a bit of the foam from the frothy mess.

Jarlaxle started to slide the next mug of ale across the table. "I know they were Knellict's men," he said, holding the ale just out of Athrogate's reach. "Else, he has a rival band operating right in Heliogabalus."

"Goblin snot. Any rival band'd be lying dead in a day's time," the dwarf blustered, and gave an exaggerated wink.

Jarlaxle slid the ale the rest of the way, and the mug never even stopped in its slide before it went up into the air and overturned into the dwarf's mouth.

"Bwahaha!" Athrogate howled as he slammed it back down, gave an enormous belch, and slapped his arm across his mouth yet again. As he moved to retract his arm, he noted that the cuff of his sleeve was sopping wet, so he put it in his mouth and sucked the ale out of the fabric.

Jarlaxle shook his head, looked at the lines of empty mugs covering more than half the large tavern table, and nodded to the serving girl who watched him from the bar. He'd known he'd have to get Athrogate drunk to get his tongue wagging, of course, but he hadn't quite realized how expensive a proposition that might be.

"Shall I order more?" he asked, and the dwarf howled at the absurdity of the question.

Jarlaxle chuckled and held up his open hand, indicating five more of the large mugs, then saluted the nodding serving girl with a tip of his wine glass—the only drink he had imbibed while Athrogate had gone through a dozen ales.

"So it was Knellict, and the target was Artemis Entreri," Jarlaxle remarked.

"Never said it was Knellict," Athrogate corrected, and he belched again.

"A rival within the Citadel of Assassins?"

"Never said it weren't Knellict," Athrogate added with an even louder burp.

The waitress began placing the full mugs on the table then, so Jarlaxle paused and offered a disarming smile. She cleared her tray and began scooping some of the empties, and the drow dropped a pair of shiny gold coins on the platter beside them, drawing a wide smile from her.

"Then say," he said to the dwarf as soon as the girl had gone. The drow kept his hand tight on a mug, holding it hostage.

"Entreri got himself a job to kill a merchant," Athrogate said, then he paused to stare at the mug. After a moment, Jarlaxle slid the ale over, and Athrogate wasted no time studying it.

"Knellict believes that Entreri kept the spoils from that job?" Jarlaxle reasoned. "He would have no reason. We are still fat on the bounties collected in Vaasa, and as a knight of the order, coin is hardly Artemis Entreri's concern."

"*Bwahaha,* knight of the order!" the dwarf howled.

"Apprentice knight, then."

"*Bwahaha!*"

"He would have no incentive to keep the booty from the slain merchant," Jarlaxle said.

"Weren't no slain merchant, so I'm hearing," Athrogate replied. He motioned to another mug. Jarlaxle slid one to his waiting grasp, but he didn't flip it right up to his mouth. "Not until Knellict caught up to the merchant, at least. Seems yer friend got his identities all crossed."

"He killed the wrong merchant?"

"He killed a couple o' Knellict's men, sent to watch his work." Athrogate finished by emptying the mug then offering a resounding belch.

Jarlaxle sat back, letting it all digest. What have you done, Artemis? he thought, but did not ask aloud. Certainly his companion, as professional and fine an assassin as had ever walked the streets of Heliogabalus or any other city, could not have made such a grievous error as that.

So it was no error on Entreri's part. It was a statement. Of what? Independence? Stupidity?

"Tell me, Athrogate," Jarlaxle quietly and calmly asked, "is the bounty offered for Entreri enough to entice those morningstars from your back?"

"Bwahaha!" howled the dwarf.

"Is that why you have returned to Heliogabalus, instead of taking the road to Vaasa?"

"Winter's coming, ye dolt. Got no thoughts o' riding out Vaasan blizzards. Work through the summer, drink through the winter—now there's a formula for dwarven success."

"But if some easy work is to be found in Heliogabalus . . ." Jarlaxle teased. "An unexpected windfall, perhaps."

"For yer Entreri? *Bwahaha!* Would hardly cover the drink ye bought me here and now."

Jarlaxle slid another mug across as he furrowed his brow in confusion. "Knellict underestimates—"

"He wouldn't give yer friend the respect of a decent bounty," the dwarf explained. "He's knowin' that many'd take up the hunt for Entreri, on the gain to their reputation alone. To kill a hero knight? Now there's a feather to rival that thing you keep in yer stupid hat!"

"For an upstart, perhaps," the drow reasoned.

"Or as an insult. Whatever."

"But when Knellict realizes his error, and runs out of upstarts, he will reconsider the remuneration."

"I'd be agreeing, or not, if I knew what in a pig's nose ye was talking about," said Athrogate. "Remuner-what?"

"The payment," Jarlaxle explained. "When all those who try for Entreri are slain, Knellict will recognize the truth of this enemy and will offer a larger reward."

"Or he'll kill yer friend himself—course, I still ain't telling ye it's Knellict at all, now am I?"

"No, of course not."

Athrogate howled, belched, and downed another mugful.

"And if the reward goes higher, might Athrogate be tempted to try?"

"Meself don't ever *try*, black skin. I do or I don't."

"And would you 'do'? If the price were right?"

"No more or less than yerself'd do it."

Jarlaxle started to reply, and sharply, but he recognized that he couldn't honestly disagree with the proposition, though of course the reward would have to be exceedingly high.

"I like yer friend," Athrogate admitted. "Nine Hells, I like ye both."

"But you like gold more."

Athrogate lifted the next mug up high before him in salute. "I'm liking what coin buys me. Got meself one life for living. Could be over next tenday, or in three hunnerd years. Either case, I'm thinking the more time I'm spending drunk and fat, the better a life I'm living. And don't ye never doubt me, black skin, the better life I'm living is th'only thing what's really mattering."

It was a philosophy that Jarlaxle found hard to contradict. He motioned to the waitress again, indicating that she should keep the drink coming, then he fished out some more gold coins and dropped them on the table.

"I like you as well, good dwarf," he said as he rose from his seat. "And so I tell you in all seriousness, whatever bounty Knellict—yes, yes, if it is Knellict," he added, seeing Athrogate about to interject. "Whatever bounty you find on Artemis Entreri's head, it is not enough to make the attempt worth your while."

"Bwahaha!"

"Simply consider all the years of drinking you will forfeit. Let that be your guide." Jarlaxle winked, gave a slight bow and walked away, passing by the serving girl who was coming over with another full tray. He gave her a little pat on the buttocks as he passed, and she offered a promising smile in return.

Yes, he could understand why Athrogate would shy from Vaasa when the weather turned cold. Certainly he, too, would like to weather the winter in the more hospitable city.

Unless, of course, Artemis Entreri had worn through that hospitality.

Jarlaxle exited the tavern. The rain had ended, the heavy clouds blown away by a cold northern wind to reveal the faint first stars of evening above. So quickly had the chill come through that the puddles left over from the day's rain steamed into the night air, rising in ghostly wisps. Jarlaxle spent a while looking both ways along the boulevard, examining those wisps and wondering if killers lurked behind their gray veils.

"What have you done, Artemis?" he asked quietly, then he bundled his cloak around his neck and started off for home. He reversed direction almost immediately, though, having no patience for the events swirling around him.

By the time he got to Wall's Around, twilight had fallen across the city. A bank of clouds hanging along the western horizon defeated the last, meager rays of the sun, ushering in an earlier and deeper darkness. Thus, several of the mercantiles had candles burning, for though it was dark, it was not yet time for them to close their doors.

So it was for Ilnezhara's Gold Coins, where a single, multi-armed candelabra danced in the large window. All around it, crystals sparkled in the uneven light.

The little bell set upon the door sang out when Jarlaxle entered. The place was nearly empty, with only one middle-aged woman and a young couple walking the length of the showcases, and a single figure behind the counter across the way.

Jarlaxle took pleasure in the blanch of the middle-aged woman when she finally noticed him. Even more delicious, the younger woman slid a step to the side, bringing her much closer to her male companion. She clutched the man's arm so urgently that she roused him from his shopping.

The man's jaw drooped, stiffened suddenly, and he puffed his chest out. He gave a quick glance around, and led his companion toward the exit, moving past Jarlaxle, who politely tipped his hat.

The young woman gave a little yelp at that, and being on the side closest the drow, she shrank even nearer to her protector.

"I do so enjoy the taste of human flesh," Jarlaxle whispered as they passed, and the woman gave another little yelp and her brave friend moved even more furiously to the door.

Jarlaxle didn't even bother to glance back at them as they departed. The sharp ring of the bell was enough to amuse him.

And to draw the attention of the other two in the shop. The middle-aged woman he did not know stared at him—a bit fearful, perhaps, but seemingly more intrigued than frightened.

Jarlaxle bowed to her and when he came up, he worked his fingers through a simple parlor trick and produced a single flower, a late summer purple alveedum, a rare and striking Bloodstone spectacle.

He held it out to the woman, but she did not take it. She slid past him instead, staring at him every step of the way.

Jarlaxle's fingers worked fast and the flower disappeared. He offered the woman a shrug.

She just kept staring, and her eyes roamed up and down, sizing him from head to toe.

Jarlaxle moved to a nearby case and pretended to inspect several pieces of golden jewelry. He did not glance the woman's way, nor toward the proprietor behind the counter, but he covertly kept careful track of both of them. Finally, he heard the bell on the door tinkle, and he glanced that way to lock a final stare with the obviously intrigued woman. She betrayed her thoughts with a wry smile as she exited the store.

"The wife of Yenthiele Sarmagon, the Chief Gaoler of Heliogabalus and a close personal friend of Baron Dimian Ree," Ilnezhara remarked as soon as the door closed behind the departing woman. "Take care if you bed that one."

"She seemed quite boring to me," Jarlaxle replied, never looking up from the necklace he rolled through his fingers, reveling in the weight of the precious metal.

"Most humans are," Ilnezhara said. "I suspect it is their state of always being close to death. They are confined by fears of what may come next, and so they cannot step outside of their caution."

"But of course, by that reasoning, a drow is a much better lover."

"And a dragon better still," Ilnezhara was quick to respond, and Jarlaxle didn't dare question that statement. He offered a grin and a tip of his hat.

"But even the companionship of a dragon cannot sate the appetite of Jarlaxle, it would seem," Ilnezhara went on.

Jarlaxle considered her words, and the somewhat sour look that had come over her fair features. She crossed her arms in front of her—a most unusual gesture from this one, he thought.

"You do not think me content?" the drow asked, a bit too innocently, he knew.

"I believe that you stir."

"My contentment, or lack thereof, is compartmentalized," Jarlaxle explained, thinking that it might be wise to assuage the dragon's ego. "In many ways, I am indeed content—quite happy, in fact. In other ways, less so."

"You live for excitement," Ilnezhara replied. "You are not content, never content, when the road is smooth and straight."

Jarlaxle mulled that over for a few moments, then grinned even wider. "And you would live out the rest of your life in the bliss of buying trinkets and reselling them for profit," came his sarcastic reply.

"Who says I buy them?" Ilnezhara answered without hesitation.

Jarlaxle tipped his hat and offered a quick smile that did not hold, for he would not release the dragon from the bite of his sarcasm so readily as that.

"Are you content, Ilnezhara?"

"I have found a life worth living, yes."

"But only because you measure it by the short lifespan of King Gareth and his friends, whom you fear. This is not your life, your existence, but merely a pause for position, a plateau from which Ilnezhara and Tazmikella can move along to their next pursuits."

"Or perhaps we dragons are not as anxious and agitated as drow," the dragon replied. "Might it be the little things—a drow lover this tenday, salvaging a destroyed merchant ship next—that suffice?"

"Should I be insulted?"

"Better that than consumed."

Jarlaxle paused again, trying to get a reading on his most curious of counterparts. He couldn't rightly tell where Ilnezhara's jokes ended and her threats began, and that was no place he wanted to be where a dragon was concerned.

"Perhaps it is the excitement I can provide extraneous to our . . . relationship, that so enthralls you," he offered somewhat hesitantly a moment later. He put on his best cavalier effect as he finished the thought, striking a pose that evoked the mischievous nature of a troublemaking young boy.

But Ilnezhara did not smile. Her jaw tightened and her eyes stared straight ahead, boring through him.

"So serious," he observed.

"The storm approaches."

Jarlaxle put on an innocent expression and posture, standing with his arms out wide.

"You survived the trials of the castle of the Witch-King," Ilnezhara explained. "And it is not in Jarlaxle's nature to merely survive. Nay, you seek to prosper from every experience, as you did with Herminicle's tower."

"I escaped with my life—barely."

"With your life and . . . ?"

"If we are both to speak in riddles, then neither will find an answer, milady."

"You believe that you have found advantage in the constructs of Zhengyi," the dragon stated. "You have discovered magic, and allies perhaps, and now you seek to parlay those into personal gain."

Jarlaxle started to shake his head, but Ilnezhara would not be so easily dismissed.

"To elevate your position within the current structure of Damara—to be named as apprentice knight of the order, then to climb to full knighthood—is one thing. To elevate your position without, to aspire to climb a ladder of your own making, in a kingdom where Gareth reigns the fields and farms and Timoshenko haunts the alleyways and shadows, is to invite disaster on no small scale."

"Unless my allies are more powerful than my potential enemies," Jarlaxle said.

"They are not," the dragon replied without pause. "You reveal a basic misunderstanding of those you seek to climb beside, or above. It is not a misunderstanding shared by myself or my sister, at any level, be assured. I met with Zhengyi in the days before the storm, as did my sister. His name is reviled throughout the land, of course, but there was a brief period when he was highly regarded, or absent that, when he was powerful enough to destroy any who openly defied him. He came to us not with threats, but with powerful temptation."

"He offered you immortality," Jarlaxle said. "Dracolichdom."

"Urshula the Black was not alone in Zhengyi's designs," the dragon confirmed. "A hundred dracoliches will rise in turn because of the legacy of the Witch-King. A month from now, perhaps, or a hundred years or a thousand years. They are out there, their spirits patient in phylacteries set within tomes of creation, immortal."

"And of Ilnezhara?"

"I chose my course, as did Tazmikella, and at a time when it seemed as if Zhengyi could not be stopped."

She paused there, staring hard, and Jarlaxle silently recited the next logical thought: if Zhengyi could not tempt the dragon sisters back in the day when he seemed to be the supreme and unchallenged power in the Bloodstone Lands, how might Jarlaxle hope to tempt them now?

"My sister and I expect that your services will not be required through the quiet winter months," Ilnezhara said. "Nor those of Entreri. If you wish to journey out of Heliogabalus, mayhaps to rest from your recent trials in the softer climate of the Moonsea, then go with our blessing."

A knowing smile widened on Jarlaxle's face.

"If a situation arises where your particular skills might be of value, and you two are still about Heliogabalus, we will seek you out," the dragon went on, in a tone that made it clear to the drow that she had no intention of doing any such thing. He was being dismissed.

More than that, Ilnezhara and Tazmikella were running from him, distancing themselves.

"Take care, Ilnezhara," Jarlaxle dared to warn. "Artemis Entreri and I uncovered much in the northland."

Ilnezhara narrowed her eyes, and for a moment, Jarlaxle feared that she would revert to her true dragon form and assault him. That threatening stare flashed away, though, and she calmly replied, "Enough to garner attention, of course."

That gave Jarlaxle pause.

"Whose attention?" he asked. "Your own?"

"You had that before you went north, of course."

Jarlaxle let that digest for a moment. She was torn, he could see, and there remained in her a wistfulness toward him. She had dismissed him—almost.

"Ah, perhaps we will travel south," he said. "Weaned in the Underdark, I have little tolerance for winter's cold bite."

"That may be wise."

"I expect that I, and particularly Artemis, would do well to report our departure to King Gareth," the drow reasoned. "Though the journey north to Bloodstone Village is not one I care to take. Already the wind blows cold up there. Still, as I see this as our responsibility, I should send word, and it is not a message I wish to entrust to a city guardsman."

"No, of course not," the dragon agreed, in an almost mocking tone that conveyed to the drow that she was catching on to his little game.

"Perhaps if any of Gareth's friends are in town. . . ." the drow mused aloud.

Ilnezhara hesitated, locking stares with him. She smiled, frowned, then slowly nodded, making it clear to him that *that* favor was the last he should expect, her expression reminding him of, and confirming, the earlier dismissal.

"I have heard that Grandmaster Kane has been seen about Heliogabalus," she said.

"A remarkable character of unique disposition, I would gather."

"A vagabond in weathered and dirty robes," Ilnezhara corrected. "And the most dangerous man in all of the Bloodstone Lands."

"Artemis Entreri is in the Bloodstone Lands."

"The most dangerous man in all of the Bloodstone Lands," the dragon reiterated, and with a surety that Jarlaxle did not lightly dismiss.

"Grandmaster Kane, then," he said. "He will deliver my message, I am certain."

"He does not fail King Gareth," Ilnezhara agreed, and warned: "Ever."

Jarlaxle sat there nodding for a few minutes. "Perhaps he will be interested in some information regarding Gareth's dead niece, as well." The dark elf rose and offered a disarming smile to the dragon. He tried very hard to appear appreciative of the information she had just shared, and tried even harder to keep his supreme disappointment hidden.

He turned to go, but stopped in his tracks when the dragon said from behind him, "You weave webs that entrap. It is the way of your existence, from your earliest days in Menzoberranzan, no doubt. You play intrigue with characters like Knellict and Timoshenko, and it is a game in which you excel. But hear me well, Jarlaxle. King Gareth and his friends ride hard and straight, and bother not with the meandering strands of webs. Your weave will never be strong enough to slow the charge of Kane."

Out in the street, Jarlaxle quickly regained the spring in his step. He had gone to Ilnezhara hoping to enlist both her and her sister in his plans. Certainly he had to adjust his thinking and his immediate aspirations regarding Vaasa. Absent the dragons, his position was severely compromised—and even more so when he considered the mischief Artemis Entreri had apparently begun.

Caution told him he might do well to go to ground, perhaps even to take that holiday Ilnezhara had offhandedly advised—step away and reassess his opportunities against the seemingly mounting obstacles.

Never did Jarlaxle laugh louder than when he was laughing at himself.

"Caution," he said, letting the word roll off his tongue so that it seemed as if it was ten syllables instead of two. Then he offered the same treatment to a word he considered synonymous: "Boredom."

Every sensible bone in Jarlaxle's body screamed out at him to heed the advice of Ilnezhara, to remove himself from the web of intrigue that grew ever more intricate in the Bloodstone Lands. Truly, Jarlaxle realized that the current tide was pushing against him, that shadows gathered at every corner. A wise man might cut his losses—or winnings, even—and run for safer ground. For such "wise" men, Jarlaxle reasoned, though they didn't know it, death was irrelevant, redundant.

The tide swelled dangerously, to be sure. When facing a losing combination in *sava*, the wise player sacrificed a piece or surrendered.

But Jarlaxle, above them all, moved boldly in a way that seemed incongruous, even foolish. He bluffed harder.

"'Let a roll of chance's dice alter the board,'" he recited, an old drow saying that exalted in chaos. When dangerous reality closed in, so went Lolth's edict, the goal was simply to alter the reality.

His heels clicked loudly on the cobblestones—as he willed his enchanted boots to do—as he made his way down the cul-de-sac, with one name rolling through his thoughts: Grandmaster Kane.

Jarlaxle slept with dragons.

⊰⊱

"Hang from the ceiling by yer toes, do ye?" Athrogate harrumphed. "Ye're bats!"

"They should not know?" the drow replied innocently.

"They shouldn't be knowing how Athrogate's knowing!"

"You believe that Spysong knew nothing of Canthan and his dwarf friend who accompanied him to the castle?"

Athrogate pursed his lips and seemed to shrink down in his seat. He alleviated his mounting fear with a mug of ale, dropped straight to the belly.

"Are you so naïve regarding your enemies?" Jarlaxle pressed.

"They ain't me enemies. Ain't done nothing against the crown, nor anyone else who didn't make me do it."

Jarlaxle smiled at the familiar words, spoken with Dwarvish flair but so similar to the claims of Entreri.

"The reckoning is coming fast," the drow warned. "Gareth's niece Ellery is dead."

"I'm still wondering how that might've happened."

"The details will matter not to Gareth's friends."

"Could say the same o' Knellict's friends if I'm doing what ye're asking me to be doing."

"The opposite, I would venture," said Jarlaxle. "The complicity of Ellery will mitigate the blow to Knellict. You will be doing him a favor."

Athrogate snorted, and a bit of ale spurted from his hairy nose.

"My little friend, you have thrived by remaining outside the web woven by your spidery friends."

"What in the Nine Hells are ye babbling about?"

"You are part of them, but removed from them," Jarlaxle explained. "You serve the Citadel of Assassins, but you do not plot with them. There is nothing in your past for which you will answer at the Court of King Gareth, else you would have been called to answer long ago."

"Would I, now?"

"Yes. You walk the edge of a coin, as do I, and now heads and tails are ready for a fight. How tight will our edge become when the blows begin to fall? Too narrow to tread, I expect, and if we must fall to one side or the other, which shall it be?"

"If ye're thinking Knellict's the tail, then yer friend's already jumped to the head," the dwarf reminded.

"This is not about Artemis Entreri," the drow replied. "It is about Jarlaxle, and Athrogate." He slid another mug Athrogate's way, and as per usual it never even stopped sliding before being scooped up and overturned into the dwarf's mouth.

Jarlaxle went on, "There is an old saying in my home, Menzoberranzan. *Pey ne nil ne-ne uraili.*"

"And here I'm thinking that ye looked funny. Next to the way ye talk . . ."

" 'In truth, the bonds are shed,' " the drow translated. "You feel the chains of worry now, my friend. Shed them."

"He won't be likin' the truth."

"But he is wise enough to lay blameless the messenger."

Athrogate took a deep breath then swallowed another ale. He slammed his hands on the edge of the table and pulled himself to his feet. "He's payin'," he said to the serving wench who turned his way, and he pointed to Jarlaxle.

"Pey ne nil ne-ne uraili," Jarlaxle whispered as Athrogate embarked on his mission to find Kane. His translation of the drow saying had been exact, if incomplete, for the bonds referenced were not the chains of worry, but the limiting boundaries of the flesh.

Announce yer arrival, Athrogate silently and repeatedly reminded himself. Surprising a grandmaster monk probably wasn't a wise choice. He placed the rickety wooden ladder before the wall of the inn and banged it loudly in place against the eave of the roof.

"Ye buy a room *in* the inn," he grumbled as he started up. "That's why they're callin' it an inn. Ye don't rent a bed *on* the durned inn. Ain't called an out!"

Every bootfall rang more loudly than the previous as the dwarf clumped his way up to peer over the edge.

A dozen feet from the lip, his back against the stone chimney, sat the monk. His legs were folded under him, his hands on thighs, palms upright. He sat with perfect posture and balance, and seemed more a fixture of the building, like the chimney, than a living creature.

Athrogate paused, expecting a response, but when the limit of his patience slipped past with no word or movement from the monk, the dwarf hauled himself up again, rolling his upper body awkwardly onto the slightly-sloping roof. He belched as his belly—grown more ample in just the few days he had been in Heliogabalus—wedged against the soffet.

"Are ye sleeping, then?" he asked as he pulled himself up to his hands and knees. One of the bouncing heads of his twin morning-stars swung in and bashed him off the side of his face, but he just blew out the side of his mouth as if to push it aside. "I'm thinking a friend o' King Gareth'd have himself a better bed. King ain't paying ye much these days?"

Kane opened one eye to regard the dwarf.

"And I'm surprised that ye got no guards," Athrogate dared to say. The dwarf managed to stand up, and when he did, he realized that the slate shingles all around him were loose—no, not just loose, but were a false set of extra shingles set upon the real ones!

"Oh, by Clangeddin's fartin' arse," he managed to say as his feet slid out from under him, dropping him hard to his belly then off the roof entirely. He crashed into the debris-filled alleyway all entangled with his ladder, arms and legs flailing helplessly, morningstar heads bouncing and slapping around him.

He sprang to his feet and hopped about, eyes darting to every shadow. If anybody had witnessed that humiliation, Athrogate would have to kill him, of course.

When he was satisfied that his unceremonious fall had gone unnoticed, he slapped his hands on his hips and looked back up at the roof.

"Durned monk," he muttered as he collected his morningstars, set them back in place across his back, and untangled the ladder. A couple of the steps had been knocked out, but it would still suffice, he decided, so he propped it back in place and began his careful climb, again taking care to announce his arrival.

When he came up to the edge of the roof, he reached out and tested the remaining slate.

"It is safe now, dwarf," Kane said. He remained in the same position, eyes still closed.

"Clever trap," Athrogate remarked, and he came up slowly, inch by inch, feeling every bit of ground before settling his weight onto it. "Couldn't ye just hire a few guards and leave the traps for stinky thieves?"

"I need no guards."

"Ye're up here all alone—and why ain't ye in a room?"

"I am in the grandest room in all the universe."

"Lookin' like the rains're coming. Think ye'll be singing that then?"

"I did not invite you here, dwarf," Kane replied. "I do not welcome company. If you have purpose, then speak it. Or be gone."

Athrogate narrowed his eyes and crossed his burly arms over his chest.

"Ye know who I be?" he asked.

"Athrogate," the monk replied.

"Ye know the things I done?"

No answer.

"Ain't none killed more at the wall," Athrogate declared.

"None who bothered to count, at least," came the quiet—and infuriating—reply.

"I went to the castle north o' Palishchuk!" the dwarf declared.

"And that is the only reason I allow you to bother me now," said Kane. "If you have come to speak with me of that adventure, then pray wag. If not, then pray leave."

Athrogate deflated just a bit. "Well, good enough then," he said. "Weren't for that trip, then I'd be having no business with ye anyway."

"None that you would wish," Kane calmly and confidently replied, and the dwarf shrank just a bit more.

"I come to talk about Ellery."

Kane opened his eyes and turned his head, suddenly seeming very interested. "You saw her fall?"

"Nope," the dwarf admitted. "I saw Canthan fall, though. Fell at me feet, killed to death by Artemis Entreri."

Kane didn't blink. "You accuse him?"

"Nope," the dwarf clarified. "Was a fight Canthan started. Stupid wizard was tryin' to kill them half-orcs." The dwarf paused and collected his thoughts. "Ye got to know that Canthan weren't one to follow the lead o' King Gareth."

"He had ulterior motives in traveling to the castle?"

"Don't know what an 'ulterior' might be, but he was looking out for Canthan, and for his masters—and ain't none o' them sitting by your king, for the sake o' yer king." He ended with an exaggerated wink, but Kane didn't blink and Athrogate issued a frustrated sigh.

"He was part o' the Citadel of Assassins," the dwarf explained.

"That much was suspected."

"And known," said Athrogate, "by yer own Commander Ellery. And she knowed it well before she picked him to go along to the north."

"Are you saying that Canthan killed Ellery?"

"Nah, ye dolt—" Athrogate bit the word back as it escaped his flapping lips, but again, Kane showed no reaction. "Nah, none o' that. I'm saying that Ellery, yer king's blood kin, picked Canthan to go because she was told to pick him to go. Ye might be thinking her a paladin o' yer order, but ye'd be thinking wrong."

"You are claiming that Ellery had connections with the Citadel of Assassins?"

"I'm adding two fingers and three fingers and making a fist to whack ye upside the head. If yerself can't count, that'd be yer own problem."

"Spysong counts more proficiently than you can imagine, good dwarf. The strands of the citadel entwine many, it would seem, to varying degrees."

The level of threat in that statement was not lost on Athrogate, a sobering reminder of who he was dealing with, and of his own complicity—at least in the eyes of King Gareth's court.

"Well, I was just thinking ye should know," he said then backed to the ladder and eased one foot onto the top step. He didn't turn as he climbed down, though, preferring to keep his gaze squarely on Kane.

The monk didn't move, didn't stand, didn't react at all.

When he was back in the alley, walking briskly away, Athrogate puzzled over the wisdom of that meeting, and of betraying Knellict.

"Damned drow," he muttered, and suddenly every shadow seemed darker and more ominous. "Damned drink."

Those last words rang in his head, nettling his sensibilities.

"Think I'll go get me some," Athrogate added, compelled to offer a formal apology to his beloved ale.

CHAPTER

9

Bah, ye're listenin' to the way I babble and ye're thinking I'm a stupid one, ain't ye, elf?"

"I?" Jarlaxle replied with mock innocence. He grabbed Athrogate's arm as the dwarf reached his hand into a pocket and produced some coin for the waiting serving girl.

Athrogate looked down at the drow's hand, tight around his wrist, then lifted his gaze to consider Jarlaxle eye-to-eye.

"Ye're asking me to go, ain't ye?"

"It is an offer of adventure."

Athrogate snorted. "Yer friend's tied Knellict's butt hairs in a knot and now yerself's flicking yer finger under the nose o' Kane hisself. Adventure, ye say? I'm thinking ye built yerself two walls o' iron, Jarlaxle, and now they're both to fall atop ye. Only question is, which'll flatten ye first?"

"Ah, but if they fall together, might they not impede each other's progress?" He held his hands up before him, fingers together and skyward, then dropped them in toward each other until the fingers tapped together, forming an inverted **V**. "There is room left between them, is there not?"

"Ye're bats."

Jarlaxle could only laugh at that observation, and really, when he thought about it, there wasn't much point in disagreeing.

"Ain't far enough in all the world to run from them," Athrogate said more solemnly, preempting the drow's forthcoming repeat of the offer. "So ye're to run from Heliogabalus, and a good choice that'll

131

be—best ye got, anyway, though I'm not saying much in that!"

"Come with us."

"Ah, but ye're a stubborn one." The dwarf planted his hands on his hips, paused for just a moment, then shook his hairy head. "Can't be doing that."

Jarlaxle knew that he was beaten, and he couldn't rightly blame the pragmatic dwarf. "Well, then," he said, patting Athrogate's strong shoulder. "Take heart in my assurance that your tab here is paid the winter through." He turned to the tavernkeeper standing behind the bar and the man nodded, having obviously overheard. "Drink yourself into oblivion until the snows have receded and you return to the Vaasan Gate. Compliments of Jarlaxle. And visit baker Piter as you wish. Your coin will not be welcomed there, but your appetite surely will."

Athrogate pursed his lips and nodded his appreciation. Whether he wanted to get entangled with Jarlaxle or not, the dwarf wasn't about to turn down those offers!

"Eat well and drink well, good Athrogate, my friend," Jarlaxle finished, and he bowed.

Athrogate grabbed him hard by the arm before he could straighten, though, and pulled his ear close. "Don't ye be calling me that, ye durned elf. Least not when ears're perked our way."

Satisfied that they understood each other, Jarlaxle straightened, nodded in deference to the dwarf's demands, and left the tavern. He didn't look back because he didn't want Athrogate to see the sting of disappointment on his face.

He went out into the street and spent a moment surveying his surroundings. He tried to remain confident in his decisions even in the face of Athrogate's doubts. The dwarf knew the region well, of course, but Jarlaxle brushed it off as the dwarf underestimating him.

At least, he tried to tell himself that.

"You heard?" the drow asked the shadows, using the language of his Underdark home.

"Of course," came a reply in the same strange tongue.

"It is as I told you."

"As dangerous as I told you," the voice of Kimmuriel Oblodra replied.

"As promising as I told you."

No answer drifted to Jarlaxle's ears.

"One enemy is manageable," Jarlaxle whispered. *"The other need not be our enemy."*

"We shall see," was all Kimmuriel would offer.

"You are ready when the opportunity presents itself?"

"I am always ready, Jarlaxle. Is that not why you appointed me?"

Jarlaxle smiled and took comfort in those confident words. Kimmuriel was thinking ahead, of course. The brilliant psionicist had thrived on the treachery of Menzoberranzan, and so to him the games of humans were child's play. Entreri and Jarlaxle had become targets of the Citadel of Assassins and curiosities of Spysong. Those two groups would battle around the duo as much or more than they would battle *with* the duo. And that would present opportunities. The citadel was the less formidable, by far, and so it followed that they could be used to keep Spysong at bay.

Jarlaxle sensed that Kimmuriel was gone—preparing the battlefield, no doubt—so Jarlaxle made his way through Heliogabalus's streets. Lights burned on many corners, but they flickered in the wind and were dulled by the fog that had come up, so typical of that time of the year, where the temperature varied so greatly day to night. The drow pulled his cloak tighter and willed his magical boots to silence. Perhaps it was better that he blend in with his surroundings just then.

Perfectly silent, nearly invisible in his drow cloak, Jarlaxle had little trouble not only getting back to the stairs leading to his apartment in the unremarkable building, but he managed to do a circuit or three of the surrounding area, noting others who did not notice him.

A tip of the right side of his great hat lifted Jarlaxle's feet off the ground and he glided up the rickety, creaky staircase silently. He went inside, into the hallway, and moved up to his door in complete darkness.

Complete darkness for a surface dweller, but not for Jarlaxle. Still, he could barely make out the little dragon statuette trap set above the apartment door. He couldn't tell the color of its eyes, though.

He had told Entreri to keep it set at white, but was he to trust that?

Not wanting to bring up any light to alert the many suspicious characters he had noted outside, the drow reached into his hat and pulled forth from under its top a disk of black felt. A couple of roundabout swings elongated it enough and Jarlaxle tossed it against the wall beside the door.

It stuck, and its magic created a hole in the wall, revealing dim candlelight from within.

Jarlaxle stepped through to see Entreri standing in the shadows of the corner, at an angle that allowed him to peer out through the narrow slot between the dark shade and the window's wooden edge.

Entreri acknowledged him with a nod, but never took his eyes off the street outside.

"We have visitors gathering," the assassin whispered.

"More than you know," Jarlaxle replied. He reached up and pulled his disk through, eliminating the hole and leaving the wall as it had been before.

"Are you going to berate me again for angering Knellict? Are you going to ask me again what I have done?"

"Some of our visitors are Knellict's men, no doubt."

"Some?"

"Spysong has taken an interest," Jarlaxle explained.

"Spysong? King Gareth's group?"

"I suspect they've deduced that the fights with the gargoyles and the dracolich were not the only battles at the castle. After all, of the four who fell, two were to the same blade."

"So again, I am to blame?"

Jarlaxle laughed. "Hardly. If there is even blame to be had, by Gareth's reckoning."

Entreri moved closer to the window, slipped the tip of his dagger under the edge of the shade and dared to retract it just a bit to widen the viewing space.

"I do not like this," the assassin said. "They know we're in here, and could strike—"

"Then let us not be in here," Jarlaxle interrupted.

Entreri let the shade slip back into place and stepped to the side of the window, eyeing his friend. "To the dragons?" he asked.

Jarlaxle shook his head. "They will have nothing to do with this. Gareth's friends unnerve them, I think."

"Wonderful."

"Bah, they are only dragons."

Entreri crinkled his face at that, but wasn't about to ask for clarification. "Where, then?"

"Nowhere in the city will be safe. Indeed, I expect that we will find strong tendrils of both our enemies throughout all of Damara."

Entreri's face grew tight. He knew, obviously, what the drow had in mind.

"There is a castle where we might find welcome," Jarlaxle confirmed.

"Welcome? Or refuge?"

"One man's prison is another man's home."

"Another drow's home," Entreri corrected, eliciting a burst of laughter from Jarlaxle.

"Lead on," the assassin bade his black-skinned companion a moment later, when a sound from outside reminded them that it might not be the time for philosophical rambling.

Jarlaxle turned for the door. "White as we agreed?" he asked.

"Yes."

The drow opened the door then paused and glanced back. Holding the door wide, he stepped aside and motioned for Entreri to go first into the hallway.

Entreri walked by, over the threshold. "Blue," he said, and reached up to retrieve the dragon statuette.

Jarlaxle laughed all the louder.

"It's Gareth's boys, I tell ya," Bosun Bruiseberry said to his companion. An incredibly thin and wiry little rat, Bosun seemed to move through the tightest of alleyways and partitions as easily as if they were broad avenues—which of course only frustrated his hunting partner, Remilar the Bold, a young wizard whose regard for himself greatly exceeded that of his peers and masters at the citadel of Assassins.

"So Spysong, too, has taken an interest in this Artemis Entreri creature," Remilar replied. He bit the words off short, nearly tripping as his rich blue robes caught on the jagged edge of a loose board on the side of Entreri's apartment building.

"Or an interest in us," Bosun said. "Seems that group across the street're watching Burgey's boys in the back alley off to the left."

"Competing interests," Remilar answered in a disinterested drawl. "Very well then, let us be quick about our task, and about our departure. I did not interrupt my all-important research to leave without that bounty."

"This one's dangerous, by all accounts, and his drow friend's worse."

Remilar gave a disgusted sigh and brushed past his cautious companion. He moved to the end of the alley, the front corner of the building, and glanced out at the street beyond.

Bosun moved up very close behind, even put a hand on Remilar's back, which made the mage straighten and offer another heavy and disgusted sigh.

"Quickly, then," he said to the young assassin.

"I can slip in and get behind the rat Entreri," Bosun offered. "Yerself'll distract them and me blades'll do the dirty task. I'll be taking his ear for proof."

If Remilar was impressed, his expression certainly didn't show it. "We've no time for your legendary stealth," he replied, and had Bosun been a brighter chap, he'd have caught the sarcastic tone in the adjective. "You are the decoy in this one. Right in through the front door you go. Draw him out—or them, if the drow is at home—and show him your blades. You need keep his thoughts and actions occupied for but a few seconds and I will lay him low with a blast of lightning and a burst of missiles to still his twitching. Be sharp and fast with your blade to retrieve the trophy—his head, if you will—and with a snap of my fingers, we will depart this place, teleporting back to the hills outside the citadel."

Bosun wore a stupid look as he digested all of that. He began to question the plan, but Remilar grabbed him by the front of the tunic and pulled him past, out into the street.

"You wish to do battle with Spysong, or to lose Entreri to other bounty-claimers?" the wizard asked.

A yell went up from a nearby building, and the pair knew they were out of time for their planning. Bosun stumbled to the door and reached up for the handle.

But the door exploded before his surprised face, torn from its hinges as out charged Entreri astride a tall, gaunt black stallion that snorted ebon smoke and wore cuffs of orange fire around its thundering hooves. The mount, a hellish nightmare, apparently didn't distinguish between barriers, for it treated the frozen-with-surprise Bosun in the exact same manner as it had the door.

Down he went under a sudden and vicious barrage of hooves. He hit the ground and squirmed, and good fortune turned him inside the thundering back hooves as the nightmare charged over him. That good fortune didn't hold, however, as the second nightmare exited the building, the dark elf astride. Poor Bosun lifted his head just enough to get it clipped, and to get his scalp torn away, by the fiery hooves of the second mount.

To the side, still in the shadows of the alley, Remilar the More-Smart-Than-Bold improvised, casting the third of his planned spells first.

Her hands trembled as she opened the small chest, for it was the first time she had dared to lift that cover since returning from Palishchuk. She had kept herself busy during her short stopover before going to Bloodstone Village for the ceremony, and mostly so that she could avoid that very thing. The task, necessary and painful, was something that Calihye could hardly bear.

Inside the small chest were trinkets and a necklace, and a rolled-up parchment with a sketch done by one of the merchants of a caravan that had spent some time on the Fugue. The artist had done a sketch of Calihye and Parissus, arm-in-arm. She looked at it and felt tears welling behind her blue eyes. The likeness was strong enough to elicit memories of her dear Parissus.

Calihye ran the fingers of one hand gently over the image. The pose was so natural for the pair, so typical. The taller Parissus stood firm, with Calihye's head resting on her shoulder. Calihye lifted a scarf with her free hand and brought it to her face. She closed her eyes, the image in the sketch firmly rooted in her thoughts, and breathed deeply, taking in the scent of her lost companion.

Her shoulders bobbed with sobs, tears wetted the scarf.

A few moments later, Calihye sorted herself out with a deep and steadying breath. Her lips grew very tight as she put both scarf and sketch off to the side. More trinkets came out: some jewelry, a pair of medals given to the duo by one of the former undercommanders at the Vaasan Gate, and a necklace of varied gemstones. The woman paused then pulled forth a fake beard and a cap of brown leather, a disguise that Parissus had often worn when she and Calihye had gone out tavern-hopping. Parissus impersonated a man quite well, Calihye thought, and she heard in her mind the husky voice her friend could assume at will. How they had played with the sensibilities of folks across the Bloodstone Lands and beyond!

The woman finally arrived at the item she had gone there to retrieve: a small crystal vial filled with blood: Calihye's and Parissus's, mixed and mingled, a reminder of their shared pledge.

"In life and beyond," she recited quietly. She looked at her dagger, which she had placed on a small table to the side, and continued as if addressing it, "Not yet."

Calihye produced a small silver chain from her pouch, an item she had purchased in Bloodstone Village upon her departure. She held the vial up before her eyes, turning it slowly so that she could see the tiny golden eyelet set in the back. With the fingers of an accomplished thief, Calihye threaded the chain through the eyelet then brought it up and set the unusual necklace around her delicate elf's neck.

She lifted her hand to cover the crystal vial then touched the scarf to her face once more and inhaled the scent of Parissus.

She did not cry again and when she removed the scarf, her face was devoid emotion.

⊷══⊶

Remilar nearly lost his train of thought, and his spell, when he noted Bosun crawling his way, blood streaming down his forehead. The garishly wounded man reached out a trembling hand Remilar's way, his look plaintive, confused, dazed.

In the midst of the spell, and unwilling to let it go, Remilar nodded furiously at the man, bidding him to hurry.

Somehow Bosun found a burst of energy, scrambling along, but he wouldn't get there in time, Remilar knew.

Across the street, agents of the Citadel of Assassins came out of the shadows to give chase and fire arrows and spells at the retreating duo. But to Remilar's horror, others came out of the shadows as well, and it only took the mage a moment to understand the identity of the second force.

Spysong!

Had the Citadel of Assassins been baited with Entreri and Jarlaxle? Had Entreri's treachery been nothing more than a ruse to lure the network into Spysong's deadly sights?

Remilar shook the thoughts from his head, and realized that he had lost his spell, as well. He motioned more vigorously to the crawling Bosun and began casting again.

Bosun got there in time, falling at Remilar's feet and hooking his arms around the mage's ankles. Remilar even reached down and grabbed the man's shoulder as his spell released, transporting them across space to a rocky hillside in southern Vaasa, a score of miles east of the Vaasan Gate.

"Come along, then," Remilar said to his prone companion. "It's two hundred yards uphill to the citadel, and I'm not about to carry you." He reached down and tugged at the man, and shook his head when he looked into Bosun's eyes, for the man seemed hardly conscious of his surroundings.

And indeed, Bosun was not even there behind that vacant gaze. He was lost in a swirl of gray mists and flashing, sharp lights, the confusion of the psionicist's mind attack as Kimmuriel Oblodra possessed his corporeal body.

The nightmares pounded down the cobblestones, smoke and gouts of flame flying from their otherworldly hooves. Jarlaxle led Entreri around one tight corner—too tight!—and his coal black, hellish steed brushed a cart of fresh fish. Patrons ran every which way and the vendor threw his arms defensively over the open cart. The look upon the middle-aged man's bloodless, open-jawed, wide-eyed face was one Artemis Entreri would not forget for many tendays to come.

The market parted before the charging pair, people scrambling, tripping, calling out for one god or another, even crying in terror. Mothers grabbed their children and hugged them close, rocking and cooing as if Death himself had arrived on the street that day.

Jarlaxle seemed to be enjoying it all, Entreri noted. The drow even pulled off his hat at one point and waved it around, all the while expertly weaving his mount through the dodging crowds.

Entreri spurred his steed past the drow and took the lead, then led Jarlaxle down a sharp corner to a quieter street.

"The peasants are cover for our escape!" Jarlaxle protested.

Entreri didn't answer. He just put his head down and spurred his nightmare on faster. They crossed several blocks, turning often and fast, frightening every horse and every person who viewed their fiery-hoofed nightmares. Pursuit rang out behind them, from the back and the sides, but they were moving too quickly and too erratically, and they had left too much confusion back at the initial scene, for anyone to properly organize to cut them off.

"We've got to make it through the gate," Entreri said as Jarlaxle pulled up even with him on one wide and nearly deserted avenue.

"And then my own," Jarlaxle replied.

Entreri glanced at him curiously, not understanding. He hadn't the time to contemplate it then, however, for as they came around the next corner, leaning hard and turning harder, they came in sight of Heliogabalus's northern gate. It was open, as always, but more than a few guards were already turning their way.

The reactions of those guards, sudden frantic running and screaming, led both riders to guess that the massive portcullis would soon lower, and the heavy iron gates would begin their swing.

Jarlaxle put his head down and kicked hard at the nightmare's sides, and the coal black horse accelerated, its hooves crackling sparks off the cobblestones. Rather than pace his friend, Entreri fell into line behind him, and similarly spurred on his mount. Jarlaxle waved his arms, and a globe of darkness appeared on the sheltered parapet above the open gates. The drow's arm went out to the side and Entreri saw that Jarlaxle held a thin wand.

"Wonderful," the assassin muttered, expecting that his reckless friend would set off a fireball or some other destructive magic that would bring a retaliatory hail of arrows down upon them.

Jarlaxle leveled the wand and spoke a command word. A glob of green goo burst forth from the item's tip and leaped out ahead of the riders, soaring toward a man who worked a crank at the side of the gate. Jarlaxle adjusted his sights and launched a second glob at the gates themselves, then spurred his nightmare on even faster.

The man working the crank fell back and cried out, pulling free the crank's setting pin as he went. The crank began to spin, and the portcullis started to drop.

But the magical glob slapped hard against the mechanism, filling the gears with the sticky substance. The spin became a crawl and the crank creaked to a halt, leaving the portcullis only slightly closed, with enough room for the ducking riders to get through.

The second glob struck its target as well, slapping into place at the hinge of the right-hand gate, filling the wedge and holding back the guards who tried to pull the gates closed. One of them turned for the glob, but then all of them cried out and scrambled aside as the riders and their hellish steeds bore down upon them.

Jarlaxle was far from finished, and Entreri was reminded quite clearly why he still followed that unusual dark elf. The wand went away and the drow switched the reins to his right hand. He brought his left hand out with a snap, and a golden hoop bracelet appeared from beneath the cuff on the sleeve of his fine shirt. That hoop went right over his palm, and he grabbed it and brought it in before his face.

An arrow arced out at the pair, follow by a second.

Jarlaxle blew through the hoop, and its magic magnified his puff a thousand-thousand times over, creating a barrier of wind before him that sent the arrows flying harmlessly wide.

"Stay right on my tail!" the drow shouted to Entreri, and to Entreri's horror, Jarlaxle summoned a second globe of darkness in the clearing between the narrowly opened gates.

Jarlaxle put his head down, and three powerful strides brought him under the creaking portcullis, straining against the strength of the goo. He plunged into the darkness, and Entreri, teeth gritted in abject horror, rushed in behind.

Then it was light again, or relatively so, as the normal night was as compared to Jarlaxle's summoned globes, and the pair galloped off down the road north of Heliogabalus. A couple of arrows reached for them from behind—one even managed to clip Entreri's horse—but the nightmares were not slowed, carrying their riders far, far away.

Some time later, the city lost in the foggy night behind them, Jarlaxle pulled up short and clip-clopped his nightmare off the road.

"We've no time for your games," Entreri chastised him.

"You would ride straight to the Vaasan Gate?"

"To anywhere that is not here."

"And Knellict, or one of Gareth's wizards, or perhaps both, will enact a spell and land before us, as happened on the road south of Palishchuk upon our return from the castle."

The drow dismounted, and as soon as he hit the ground he dismissed his nightmare then reached down and picked up the obsidian statuette and placed it safely in his pouch.

Entreri sat astride his horse, making no move to follow suit.

Seemingly unperturbed, Jarlaxle drew another wand out of a loop inside his cloak, one of several wands set in a line there. He held it up before him and offered a questioning look at his companion. "Are you meaning to join me?"

Entreri looked around at the drizzly, dark night, then sighed and dropped from his saddle. He spoke the command, reducing his nightmare to a tiny statuette, then scooped it up and shuffled toward the drow.

Jarlaxle held out his free hand and Entreri took it, and a moment later, colorful swirls began to fill the air around the pair. Streaks of yellow and shocks of blinding blue flashed all around, followed by a sudden and disorienting distortion of visual perception, as if all the light, stars and moon, began to warp and bend.

A sudden blackness fell over the pair, a thump of nothingness as profound as the moment of death itself.

Gradually, Entreri reoriented himself to his new surroundings, the nook where a great, man-made wall joined a natural wall of towering mountain stone. They had arrived at the westernmost edge of the Vaasan Gate, he realized as he got his bearings and noticed the tent city set upon the plain known as the Fugue.

"Why didn't you do that from the beginning?" the flustered assassin asked.

"It would not have been as dramatic."

Entreri started to respond, but bit it back, recognizing the pragmatism behind Jarlaxle's decision. Had the drow used his magic wand to whisk them out of the city, the remnants of the spell would have been recognized by their enemies, who might have quickly surmised the destination. Riding out of town so visibly, they might have bought themselves at least a little time.

"We should ride out to the north with all speed," Jarlaxle informed him.

"To hide in the castle?"

"You forget the powers of Zhengyi's construct. We won't be hiding, I assure you."

"You sound as if you've already put things in motion," Entreri remarked, and he knew, of course, that that was indeed the case. "I need some time here."

"Will you bring the half-elf along?" Jarlaxle asked, catching Entreri off his guard. "She might lack the common sense of Athrogate, after all, and out of misplaced loyalty to you decide that she should join us."

"And you think that would be foolish? Does that mean that you're not as confident as you pretend?"

Jarlaxle laughed at him. "She is not implicated in any of this. Not by Knellict and not by Gareth, whatever either side might know of your relationship with her. We would do well to put her at arms' length for a short time. Once we are established in the northland, Calihye can ride in openly. Until that time, she might prove more valuable to us, and will certainly remain safer, if there is distance between you two. Of course, I am presuming that you can suffer the pain in your loins. . . ."

Entreri narrowed his eyes and tightened his jaw, and Jarlaxle merely chuckled again.

"As you will," the drow said with a great flourish, and he walked off along the wall.

Entreri remained there in the shadows for a short time, considering his options. He knew where he would find Calihye, and soon enough, he decided on what he would say to her.

Her fingers trembled as she traced the delicate outline of Parissus's face in the precious portrait. Calihye closed her eyes and could feel again the smoothness of Parissus's cheeks, the softness of her skin above the hard and strong tension of her muscles.

She would never replace that feel, Calihye knew, and moistness came into her blue eyes once more.

She sniffed it away, dropped the portrait, and spun when her door opened. Artemis Entreri stepped into the room.

"I knocked," the man explained. "I did not mean to surprise you."

Calihye, so skilled and clear-thinking, forced herself up quickly and closed the ground to her lover. "I did not expect you," she said, hoping she hadn't too obviously exaggerated her excitement. She wrapped her arms around the man's neck and kissed him deeply.

Entreri was more than glad to reciprocate. "My plans have changed," he said after lingering about the woman's lips for a long while. "Again I find myself at the center of a storm named Jarlaxle."

"You were chased out of Heliogabalus?"

Entreri chuckled.

"By Knellict or Gareth?"

"Yes," Entreri replied, and he smiled widely and kissed Calihye again.

But the woman would have none of it. She pulled back to arms' length. "What will you do? Where will we go?"

"Not 'we,'" Entreri corrected. "I will go out to the north, straight-away. To the castle north of Palishchuk."

Calihye shook her head, her face crinkling with confusion.

"It will all sort out," Entreri promised her. "And quickly."

"Then I will go with you."

Entreri was shaking his head before she ever finished the thought. "No," he replied. "I need you here. It may well be that you will serve as my eyes, but that is not possible if you are known to be an associate."

"We have been seen together," the woman reminded him.

"Such liaisons are not uncommon, not unexpected, and not indicative of anything more."

"Is that how you feel?" the woman asked, a hard edge coming to her voice.

Entreri grinned at her. "How I feel isn't the point, is it? It is how we are, or will easily be, perceived, and that is all that matters. We engaged in a brief and intense affair, but we parted ways in Bloodstone Village and went on with our separate lives."

Calihye considered his words, considered all of it for a few moments, then shook her head. "Better that I come with you," she insisted, and she pulled away and turned for the rack that held her traveling gear.

"No," Entreri stated, his tone leaving no room for debate.

The woman was glad that her back was to him, else he would have seen her sudden scowl.

"It is not wise, and I'll not put you in such danger," Entreri explained. "Nor will I willingly relinquish the advantage I have with you as a secret ally."

"Advantage?" Calihye spat, turning to face him. "Is that the goal of your life, then? To seek advantage? You would forego pleasure for the sake of tactical advantage that you likely will not even need?"

"When you put it that way," Entreri replied, "yes."

Calihye straightened as if she had been struck.

"I'll not allow either my loins or my heart to bring us both to disaster," the assassin told her. "The road before me is dark, but I believe it is a short one." His voice changed, growing husky and serious, but no longer harsh and grave. "I'll not lead you to your doom out of selfishness," he explained. "We will not be apart for long—perhaps no longer than we had originally intended."

"Or you will die out in the northland, without me."

"In that instance, I would be doubly grateful that I did not allow you beside me."

Calihye tried to understand her own feelings well enough to respond. Should she be angry with him? Should she be insulted? Should she thank him for thinking of her above his own desires?

She felt like she was wrapping herself into winding webs, where even her emotions had to execute a feint within a feint.

"I did not come here to argue with you," Entreri said, his voice growing steady once more.

"Then why did you come? To have me one last time before you ride out of my life?"

"A pity, but I haven't the time," he answered. "And I am not riding out of your life. This is temporary. I owed it to you to keep you abreast of my travels."

"You owe it to me to tell me that you'll likely die by someone else's hand?" Calihye asked, and in a moment of particular wickedness, she wondered how Entreri might appear if he recognized the double meaning in her words.

He didn't, obviously, for he began shaking his head and slowly approached.

Calihye noted his belt and the dagger set there on his hip.

But the door opened then and Jarlaxle poked his head into the room. "Ah, good, you remain upright," he said with an exaggerated wink.

"You said I had time," a frustrated Entreri growled at him, turning to face him.

"I fear I underestimated the cleverness of our enemies," the drow admitted. "Kiss the girl farewell and let us be gone. Some time ago would have been preferable."

Entreri turned back to Calihye. He didn't kiss her again, but merely took her hands in his own and shrugged. "Not long," he promised, and he followed the dark elf.

Calihye stood there for a long time after the door had closed behind the departing pair, her emotions swirling from confusion to fear to anger and back again. She looked back at the portrait of her lost friend, then, and wondered if Entreri too would be lost to her in the Vaasan wasteland.

She found no options, though. She could only clench her fists and jaw in helpless frustration.

PART 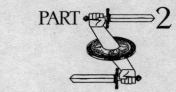 2

BY BLOOD OR BY DEED

I am not a king. Not in temperament, nor by desire, nor heritage, nor popular demand. I am a small player in the events of a small region in a large world. When my day is past, I will be remembered, I hope, by those whose lives I've touched. When my day is past, I will be remembered, I hope, fondly.

Perhaps those who have known me, or who have been affected by the battles I've waged and the work I've done, will tell the tales of Drizzt Do'Urden to their children. Perhaps not. But likely, beyond that possible second generation, my name and my deeds are destined to the dusty corners of forgotten history. That thought does not sadden me, for I measure my success in life by the added value my presence brought to those whom I loved, and who loved me. I am not suited for the fame of a king, or the grandiose reputation of a giant among men—like Elminster, who reshapes the world in ways that will affect generations yet to come.

Kings, like my friend Bruenor, add to their society in ways that define the lives of their descendants, and so one such as he will live on in name and deed for as long as Clan Battlehammer survives—for millennia, likely, and hopefully.

So, often do I ponder the ways of the king, the thoughts of the ruler, the pride and the magnanimity, the selfishness and the service.

There is a quality that separates a clan leader such as Bruenor from a man who presides over an entire kingdom. For Bruenor, surrounded by the dwarves who claim membership in his clan, kin and kind are one and the same. Bruenor holds a vested interest, truly a friendship, *with every dwarf, every human, every drow, every elf, every halfling, every gnome who resides in Mithral Hall. Their wounds are his wounds, their joys his joys. There isn't one he does not know by name, and not one he does not love as family.*

The same cannot be true for the king who rules a larger nation. However good his intent, however true his heart, for a king who presides over thousands, tens of thousands, there is an emotional distance of necessity, and the greater the number of his subjects, the greater the distance, and the more the subjects will be reduced to something less than people, to mere numbers.

Ten thousand live in this city, a king will know. Five thousand reside in that one, and only fifty in that village.

They are not family, nor friends, nor faces he would recognize. He cannot know their hopes and dreams in any particular way, and so, should he care, he must assume and pray that there are indeed common dreams and common needs and common hopes. A good king will understand this shared humanity and will work to uplift all in his wake. This ruler accepts the responsibilities of his position and follows the noble cause of service. Perhaps it is selfishness, the need to be loved and respected, that drives him, but the motivation matters not. A king who wishes to be remembered fondly by serving the best interests of his subjects rules wisely.

Conversely, the leader who rules by fear, whether it be of him or of some enemy he exaggerates to use as a weapon of control, is not a man or woman of good heart. Such was the case in Menzoberranzan, where the matron mothers kept their subjects in a continual state of tension and terror, both of them and their spider goddess, and of a multitude of enemies, some real, some purposefully constructed or nurtured for the sole reason of solidifying the matron mother's hold on the fearful. Who will ever remember a matron mother fondly, I wonder, except for those who were brought to power by such a vile creature?

In the matter of making war, the king will find his greatest legacy—and is this not a sadness that has plagued the reasoning races for all of time? In this, too, perhaps particularly in this, the worth of a king can be clearly measured. No king can feel the pain of a soldier's particular wound, but a good king will fear that wound, for it will sting him as profoundly as it stings the man upon whom it was inflicted.

In considering the "numbers" who are his subjects, a good king will never forget the most important number: one. *If a general cries victory and exclaims that only ten men died, the good king will temper his celebration with the sorrow for each, one alone repeated, one alone adding weight to his heart.*

Only then will he measure his future choices correctly. Only then will he understand the full weight of those choices, not just on the kingdom, but on the one, or ten, or five hundred, who will die or be maimed in his name and for his holdings and their common interest. A king who feels the pain of every man's wounds, or the hunger in every child's belly, or the sorrow in every destitute parent's soul, is one who will place country above crown and community above self. Absent that empathy, any king, even a man of previously stellar temperament, will prove to be no more than a tyrant.

Would that the people chose their kings! Would that they could measure the hearts of those who wish to lead them!

For if that choice was honest, if the representation of the would-be king was a clear and true portrayal of his hopes and dreams for the flock and not a pandering appeal to the worst instincts of those who would choose, then all the folk would grow with the kingdom, or share the pains and losses. Like family, or groups of true friends, or dwarf clans, the folk would celebrate their common hopes and dreams in their every action.

But the people do not choose anywhere that I know of in Faerûn. By blood or by deed, the lines are set, and so we hope, each in our own nation, that a man or woman of empathy will ascend, that whoever will come to rule us will do so with an understanding of the pain of a single soldier's wound.

There is beside Mithral Hall now a burgeoning kingdom of unusual composition. For this land, the Kingdom of Many-Arrows, is ruled by a single orc. Obould is his name, and he has crawled free of every cupboard of expectation that I, or Bruenor, or any of the others have tried to construct about him. Nay, not crawled, but has shattered the walls to kindling and strode forward as something beyond the limitations of his race.

Is that my guess or my observation, truly?

My hope, I must admit, for I cannot yet know.

And so my interpretation of Obould's actions to this point is limited by my vantage, and skewed by the risk of optimism. But Obould did not press the attack, as we all expected he certainly would, when doing so would have condemned thousands of his subjects to a grisly death.

Perhaps it was mere pragmatism; the orc king wisely recognized that his gains could not be compounded, and so he looked down and went into a defensive posture to secure those gains. Perhaps when he has done so, beyond any threat of invasion by the outlying kingdoms, he will regroup and press the attack again. I pray that this is not the case; I pray that the orc king is possessed of more empathy—or even of more selfishness in his need to be revered as well as feared—than would be typical of his warlike race. I can only hope that Obould's ambitions were tempered by a recognition of the price the commoner pays for the folly or false pride of the ruler.

I cannot know. And when I consider that such empathy would place this orc above many leaders of the goodly races, then I realize that I am being foolhardy in even entertaining these fantasies. I fear that Obould stopped simply because he knew that he could not continue, else he might well lose all that he had gained and more. Pragmatism, not empathy, ground Obould's war machine to a stop, it would seem.

If that is the case, then so be it. Even in that simple measure of practicality, this orc stands far beyond others of his heritage. If pragmatism alone forces the halt of invasion and the settling of a kingdom, then perhaps such pragmatism is the first step in moving the orcs toward civilization.

Is it all a process, then, a movement toward a better and better way that will lead to the highest form of kingdom? That is my hope. It will not be a straight-line ascent, to be sure. For every stride forward, as with Lady Alustriel's wondrous city of Silverymoon for example, there will be back-steps.

Perhaps the world will end before the goodly races enjoy the peace and prosperity of the perfect realm.

So be it, for it is the journey that matters most.

That is my hope, at least, but the flip of that hope is my fear that it is all a game, and one played most prominently by those who value self above community. The ascent to kingship is a road of battle, and not one walked by the gentle man or woman. The person who values community will oft be deceived and destroyed by the knave whose heart lies in selfish ambitions.

For those who walk that road to the end, for those who feel the weight of leadership upon their shoulders, the only hope lies in the realm of conscience.

Feel the pain of your soldiers, you kings.

Feel the sorrow of your subjects.

Nay, I am not a king. Not by temperament nor by desire. The death of a single subject soldier would slay the heart of King Drizzt Do'Urden. I do not envy the goodly rulers, but I do fear the ones who do not understand that their numbers have names, or that the greatest gain to the self lies in the cheers and the love fostered by the common good.

—Drizzt Do'Urden

CHAPTER

10

The day had been mild of that time of year, though it was gray and with a persistent, soaking drizzle. The clouds had broken right before sunset, blown away by a north wind that reached down from the Great Glacier like the cold, dead fingers of the Witch-King himself. That clearing had afforded the townsfolk of Palishchuk a brilliant red sunset, but by the time the stars had begun to twinkle above, the air had grown so cold that all but a few had been driven indoors to their peat-filled hearths.

Not so for Wingham and Arrayan, though. They stood side by side on Palishchuk's northern wall, staring out and wondering. Before them on the dark ground, puddles and rivulets shone silver in the moonlight, like the veins of a great sleeping beast, frozen, as was the ground below.

"Do you think they will thaw again before the first snows?" Arrayan asked her much-older uncle.

"I have known the freeze to come earlier in the year than this," Wingham replied. "One year, it never actually thawed!"

"1337," Arrayan recited, for she had heard the stories of the two-year freeze many times from Wingham. "The Year of the Wandering Maiden."

The old half-orc smiled at her overly-exasperated tone and the roll of her eyes. "They say a great white dragon was behind it all," Wingham teased, the beginning of one of the many, many folktales that had arisen from that unusually cold summer.

Arrayan rolled her eyes again, and Wingham laughed heartily and draped his arm around her.

"Perhaps this winter will be one of which I will spin yarns in the decades hence," the woman said at length, and with enough honest trepidation in her voice to take the grin from Wingham's wrinkled and weathered face.

He hugged her closer, and she tucked her arms and pulled her fur-lined cowl tighter around her frosty cheeks.

"It has been an eventful year already," Wingham replied. "And one with a happy endin' . . ." He paused when she tossed him a fearful look. "A happy *middle,*" he corrected.

For indeed, the adventure that they all had thought successfully concluded with the defeat of the dracolich had returned to them yet again with the arrival a few days earlier of Artemis Entreri and Jarlaxle. The pair had come riding in to Palishchuk on hellish steeds, coal black and with hooves pounding fire into the frozen tundra.

They had been welcomed warmly, as heroes, of course. They had earned the accolades for their work beside Arrayan and Olgerkhan, and they had been granted free room and board in Palishchuk at any time for the remainder of their lives. Indeed, when the pair had first arrived, several of the townsfolk had argued loudly over who would have the honor of boarding them for their stay.

How quickly things had changed from that initial meeting.

For the pair would not stay. They were merely passing through on their way to the conquered castle—Castle D'aerthe, Jarlaxle had named it. *Their* castle, the seat of their power, hub of the kingdom they planned to rule.

The kingdom they planned to rule.

A kingdom that by definition would surround or encompass Palishchuk.

There had been no answers forthcoming to the multitude of questions shot back at the surprising pair by the leaders of Palishchuk. Jarlaxle had nodded, and merely added, "We hold nothing but respect and admiration for Palishchuk, and we consider you great friends in this wondrous adventure upon which we now embark."

Then they had gone, the pair of them back on their impressive steeds, thundering out of Palishchuk's northern gate, and while some of the leaders had called for the pair to be detained and questioned, none had the courage to stand before them.

But they had returned, and the city's scouts had been filtering in and out with reports of shadowy figures moving about the castle's formidable walls, and of gargoyles taking flight only to crouch at another spot along the parapets and towers of the magical construct.

Arrayan glanced down the length of the wall, where a doubled number of guardsmen stood ready and nervous.

"Do you think they will come?" she asked.

"They?"

"The gargoyles. I have heard the tales of Palishchuk's fight while I was battling within the castle walls. Do you think this night, or tomorrow's, will bring another struggle to the city?"

Wingham looked back to the north and shrugged, but was shaking his head by the time his shoulders slumped back down. "The scouts have claimed sightings of gargoyles in the dark of night," he said. "I can imagine their fear as they crouched outside of that formidable place."

Arrayan looked at him at the same time he was turning to her.

"Even if it is true and Jarlaxle and Artemis Entreri have brought the castle back to life, I fear no attack from them," Wingham went on. "Why would they have bothered to stop in Palishchuk to proclaim their friendship if they meant to attack us?"

"To put us off our guard?"

With a nod, Wingham directed her attention back to the doubled sentries lining the wall. "Our guard would have been nonexistent had they just ridden by the city, to animate the castle and attack while we played under the delusion that our battle was successfully completed, I expect."

Arrayan spent a moment digesting that as she looked back to the north. She smiled when she met Wingham's gaze yet again. "Are you not curious, though?"

"More than you are," the old barker replied with a mischievous grin. "Fetch Olgerkhan, will you? I would appreciate his sturdy companionship as we venture to the home of our former allies."

"Former?"

"And present, we must believe."

"And hope."

Wingham smiled. "Castle D'aerthe," he mumbled as Arrayan

started for the ladder. Even more quietly, he added, "It can only portend trouble."

Two sets of eyes looked back in the direction of Wingham and Arrayan, from far away and with neither pair aware of the other. On the southern wall of the magical castle north of Palishchuk, Jarlaxle and Entreri did not huddle under heavy woolen cloaks—nothing that mundane for Jarlaxle, of course, who had taken out a small red globe, placed it on the stone between them, and uttered a command word. The stone glowed red, brightly for a moment, then dimmed and began to radiate heat comparable to that of a small campfire. The northern wind rushing off the Great Glacier still bit at them, for they were thirty feet up atop the wall, but the mediating warmth sufficed.

"What now?" Entreri asked, after they had been up there for many minutes, staring in silence across the miles to the dim glow of Palishchuk's nighttime fires.

"You started the fight," Jarlaxle replied.

"We ran from the Citadel. Better that we fight them in the streets of Heliogabalus, one alley at a time."

"It is a bigger fight than just the Citadel," Jarlaxle calmly explained—and indeed, it was that tone, so self-assured and reasonable, that had Entreri on his edge. Whenever Jarlaxle got comfortable about something, Entreri knew from experience, big trouble was usually brewing.

"We have stirred the nest," Entreri agreed, "between the king and Knellict. So now we must choose a side."

"And you would select?"

"Gareth."

"Conscience?"

"Practicality," Entreri countered. "If there is to be an open war between the Citadel of Assassins and King Gareth, Gareth will win. I've seen it before, in Calimport, and you've known this struggle in Menzoberranzan. When a guild pricks too sharply at the side of the open powers, they retaliate."

"So you believe that King Gareth will obliterate Knellict and the Citadel of Assassins? He will wipe them from the Bloodstone Lands?"

Entreri mulled that over for a few moments, then shook his head. "No. He will drive them from the streets and back into their remote hideouts. Some of those will likely fall, as well. Some of the Citadel's leaders will be killed or imprisoned. But Gareth will never truly be rid of them. That is never the way." He paused and considered his own words, then chortled, "He wouldn't wish to be completely rid of them."

Jarlaxle watched him out of the corner of his eyes, and Entreri noted the little grin spreading on the drow's face. "King Gareth is a paladin," the drow reminded. "Do you doubt his sincerity?"

"Does it matter? Having the Citadel of Assassins lurking in the shadows is good for Gareth and his friends, a reminder to the people of Damara of the alternative to their hero king.

"He is no Ellery, perhaps, in that he won't deal with the Citadel, but he uses them all the same. It is the nature of power."

"You have a cynical view of the world."

"It is well earned, I assure you. And it is accurate."

"I did not say it was not."

"Yet you seem to think Gareth above reproach because he is a paladin."

"No, I think him predictable because he is guided more by principle—ill-reasoned or not—than by pragmatism. Gareth's end plan is always known, is it not? He may be served well by the Citadel, but he is likely too blinded by dogma to see that truth."

"You still have not answered my question," said Entreri. "What now for us?"

"It seems obvious."

"Enlighten me."

"Always."

"Now."

Jarlaxle gave an exasperated sigh. "We declare our independence from King Gareth, of course," he replied.

Far below the pair, very near the room where the bones of Urshula the dracolich lay, Kimmuriel Oblodra conferred with his drow lieutenants, laying out plans for the defense of the castle, for assaults from the walls and gates, and most important of all, for orderly and swift retreat back to that very chamber. Not far from the drow, a magical portal glowed a light blue. Through it came more drow warriors of Bregan D'aerthe, driving mobs of goblins, kobolds, and orcs bearing supplies, armaments, and furniture, fashioned mostly of sturdy Underdark mushrooms.

A continual line passed through the gate, and other drow went through in the other direction, back to the corresponding magical portal set in the maze of tunnels along the great Clawrift in Menzoberranzan, the complex that Bregan D'aerthe called home.

"The sooner we are gone, the better," one of Kimmuriel's lieutenants remarked, and though others nodded their accord, Kimmuriel flashed the drow a dangerous look.

"Do say," the psionicist prompted.

"This place is uneasy," the drow replied. "It teems with an energy that I do not recognize."

"And thus, an energy you fear?"

"The portcullis on the front gate . . . grows," another soldier added. "It was damaged by unwanted entry, and now it repairs itself of its own accord. This is no inert construction, but a magical, living creature."

"Is this place any different than the towers of the Crystal Shard?" said the first lieutenant.

"Is Jarlaxle, you mean," Kimmuriel remarked, and neither of the pair disavowed him of that notion.

"I do not know," the psionicist answered honestly. "Though I believe that Jarlaxle is acting of his own volition and wisdom here. If I did not, I would not have marched us to this wretched place." He led their gazes to the portal, and another group of goblins trudging through, bearing several rolled tapestries and carpets. "He recognizes equivocation . . ."

"An easy egress," one of the others remarked.

Beside them, a quartet of goblins tripped and stumbled, spilling a mushroom-fashioned hutch across the floor. Drow drivers stepped up, cracking their whips against the flesh of the miserable creatures, who all fell to their hands and knees to try to collect the broken pieces.

The soldiers beside Kimmuriel nodded, recognizing the truth of it all, that they weren't bringing anything of real value to the castle, just utilitarian furniture and simple dressings.

And fodder, of course. Goblins, orcs, and kobolds, all as easily expendable to the dark elves as a cheap piece of mushroom furniture.

"Our independence?" Artemis Entreri answered after many stunned moments. "Could we not just leave the Bloodstone Lands?"

"And take this castle with us?"

Entreri went silent, finally understanding the drow's machinations. "You were serious when you warned Palishchuk to remain neutral?"

"We must pick a name for our kingdom," Jarlaxle said, ignoring the question and confirming it all at once. "Have you any suggestions?"

Entreri looked at him with complete incredulity.

"The gauntlet is down," Jarlaxle said. "You threw it at Knellict's feet when you did not kill the merchant."

Entreri looked away again, his lips going very tight.

"Was the man not worthy of your blade? Or was he not deserving of it?"

Entreri turned a hateful gaze the drow's way.

"I thought as much," Jarlaxle said. "You might have found a better moment to discover your conscience. But it does not matter, for it had to come to this in any event. Better now, I suppose, than when Knellict grew a better appreciation for what has truly come against him."

"And what might that be? A pair of impetuous fools, a small army of gargoyles and an undead dragon we can hardly control?"

"Look more closely," Jarlaxle said slyly, and he directed Entreri's attention to the watchtower off to the right of the gatehouse. A slender form moved there, silent as, and seeming no more substantial than, the shadows.

A drow.

Entreri snapped his gaze back over Jarlaxle. "Kimmuriel?"

"Bregan D'aerthe," Jarlaxle replied. "And ample slave fodder arrive regularly through magical gates. If you wish to start a war, my friend, you need an army."

"Start a war?"

"I had hoped that we could do this more easily, and more by proxy," Jarlaxle admitted. "I had hoped that we could get the two beasts—the king and the Grandfather of Assassins—to devour each other. You played our hand too quickly."

"And now you wish to start a war?"

"No," Jarlaxle corrected. "But it is not beyond the realm of possibility. If Knellict comes, we will drive him back."

"With the drow and Ursula and all the rest?"

"With everything at our disposal. Knellict is not one to be bargained with."

"Let us just leave."

That seemed to catch Jarlaxle off guard. He leaned on the wall, staring out at the south and the darkness that was interrupted only by the glow of a few fires burning in Palishchuk and the starlight. "No," he finally answered.

"There is a big world out there, where we might get lost—sufficiently so. It would seem that we have worn out our welcome."

"With Knellict."

"That is enough."

Jarlaxle shook his head. "We can leave whenever we wish, thanks to Kimmuriel. As of now, I do not desire to go. I like it here." He paused there and let his smile fall over Entreri until the man finally acknowledged it—with a derisive snort, of course. "Consider Calihye, my friend. Remind yourself that some things are worth fighting for."

"We make a stand where we need not. Calihye is not a plot of ground or a magically created castle. There is nothing to stop her from coming with us. Your analogy cannot hold."

Jarlaxle nodded, conceding the point. His smile told Entreri, however, that the point was moot. Jarlaxle liked it there; for the drow, apparently, that was enough.

Entreri looked over to the corner tower again, and though he saw no movement there, he knew that Jarlaxle's friends had come. He thought of Calimport and the catastrophe Bregan D'aerthe had wrought there, eliminating guilds that had stood for decades and altering the balance of power within the city with relative ease.

Would the same occur in the Bloodstone Lands?

Or was Jarlaxle's ambition even more ominous? A kingdom to rival Damara. A kingdom built on an army of drow and slave fodder, on undead servants and animated gargoyles, and forged in a bargain with a dracolich?

Entreri shuddered, and it was not from the cold northern wind.

"A gargoyle," Arrayan remarked, nodding toward the dark castle wall where a humanoid, winged creature had taken flight, moving from one guard tower to another. "The castle is alive."

"Curse them," Olgerkhan grunted, while Wingham only sighed.

"We should have known better than to trust a drow," Arrayan said.

"How often have I heard those words about our own half-orc race," Wingham was quick to answer, drawing surprised looks from both of his companions.

"The castle is alive," Olgerkhan reiterated.

"And Palishchuk has not been threatened," said Wingham. "As Jarlaxle promised."

"You would trust the word of a drow?" Olgerkhan asked.

Wingham's answer came in the form of a shrug and the simple reply of, "Have we a choice?"

"We beat the castle once," Olgerkhan growled in defiance, and he held a clenched fist up before him, the muscles in his arm bulging and knotting.

"You beat an unthinking animation," Wingham corrected. "This time, it has a brain."

"And one who has marched several steps ahead of us," Arrayan agreed. "Even inside, when they saved me from Canthan. When they brought you back to life through the vampirism of Entreri's dagger," she said to Olgerkhan, stealing much of his bluster. "Jarlaxle understood it all where I, and the wizard Canthan, did not. I wonder if even then his goal was not to destroy the construct, but to control it."

"His castle stands here, alive and strong, and King Gareth's is to the south," Wingham remarked. "And Palishchuk is in between them."

"Again," Arrayan said with great resignation, "as it was with Zhengyi."

⊶═══╪═══⊷

"I am no longer surprised by the clumsiness of the surface races," Kimmuriel Oblodra said to Jarlaxle. The two were very near the same spot on the wall where Jarlaxle had held his conversation with Artemis Entreri a short while before, and as with then, they looked out to the south. Not to Palishchuk, though, for Kimmuriel had directed Jarlaxle's attention to a copse of leafless trees a bit to the right, in the shadow of a small hill. Neither drow could make out the forms that Kimmuriel had promised his former leader lurked in there, a trio of half-orcs.

"There is a wizard among them," Kimmuriel said. "She is of little consequence and no real power."

"Arrayan," Jarlaxle explained. "She has her uses, and is comfort to weary eyes—as much as any with orc heritage could be, of course."

"Your promises did not hold much sway in the town, it seems."

"They are being careful, and who can blame them?"

"They will know that the construct is awakening," said Kimmuriel. "The gargoyles fly about."

Jarlaxle nodded, making it obvious that they did so at his behest. "Have they seen any of your scouts? Are they aware of any drow about other than myself?"

Kimmuriel scoffed at the ridiculous notion. Drow were not seen by such pitiful creatures as these unless they wanted to be seen.

"Show them, then," Jarlaxle instructed.

Kimmuriel stared hard at him, to which Jarlaxle nodded a confirmation.

"You would use terror to hold them at bay?" Kimmuriel asked. "That speaks of diplomatic weakness."

"Palishchuk will have to choose eventually."

"Between Jarlaxle—"

"King Artemis the First," Jarlaxle corrected with a grin.

"Between *Jarlaxle,*" the stubborn Kimmuriel insisted, "and King Gareth?"

"I surely hope not—not for a long while, at least," Jarlaxle replied.

163

"I doubt that Gareth will be quick to charge to the north, but the Citadel of Assassins is likely already infiltrating Palishchuk. It is my hope that the half-orcs will think it unwise to provide aid to Knellict's vile crew."

"Because they will be more fearful of Jarlaxle and the dark elves?"

"Of course."

"Your fear tactics will work against you when King Gareth comes calling," Kimmuriel warned, and he knew that he had struck a chord there by Jarlaxle's long pause.

"By that time, I hope to have Knellict long dispatched," Jarlaxle explained. "We can then build a measure of trust to the half-orcs. Enough trust coupled with the fear that will force them to keep King Gareth at arm's length."

Kimmuriel was shaking his head as he looked back to the southwest.

"Show them," Jarlaxle said to him. "And allow them to go on their way."

Kimmuriel wasn't about to question Jarlaxle just then, for his words to his doubting lieutenants just a short while before had been spoken sincerely. It was Jarlaxle's scheme, and in truth, Kimmuriel, for all of his growing confidence, recognized that standing beside him was a drow who had survived the intrigue of Menzoberranzan and elsewhere for several centuries. With the notable exception of the near-disaster in Calimport, had Jarlaxle's schemes ever failed?

And that near-disaster, Kimmuriel pointedly reminded himself, had been caused in no small part by the corrupting influence of the artifact known as Crenshinibon.

The psionicist could not manage a reassuring expression to his companion, though. For all of the history of successful manipulations Jarlaxle brought to the table, Kimmuriel had familiarized himself quite extensively with the recent events in the region known as the Bloodstone Lands, and had come to understand well the power King Gareth Dragonsbane could wield.

Jarlaxle's own actions showed him clearly that he was not alone in his fears, he realized. Jarlaxle had not reclaimed control of Bregan D'aerthe, though he had bade Kimmuriel to garner all of their resources. For all of his outward confidence, Jarlaxle was hedging his bets by allowing Kimmuriel complete control. He was protecting himself from that very confidence.

Understanding the compliment that Jarlaxle was once again paying to him, Kimmuriel offered a salute before going on his way.

CHAPTER

THE LURE

11

Jureemo Pascadadle put his back against the wall just inside the door of the tavern and heaved a great sigh of relief. Out in the street, several of his companions lay dead or incapacitated, and several others had been dragged off by the thugs from Spysong.

Glad indeed was Jureemo that he had been given the rear guard position, watching the back of his Citadel crew as they had closed in on the dark elf and the assassin. "Spysong," he muttered under his breath, his throat filling with bile.

The door burst open beside him and the man fell back with a shriek. In stumbled Kiniquips the Short, a slender—by halfling standards— little rogue of great renown within the organization. Kiniquips was a master of disguise, actually serving as a trainer of such at the Citadel, and was often the point halfling on Citadel of Assassins operations in Heliogabalus. He had spent the better part of two years creating his waif alter-ego. Watching him stumble through the common room, though, Jureemo knew that the halfling's cover had been blown. His shirt was ripped and a bright line of blood showed across his left shoulder, and it looked like a substantial part of his dark brown hair had been torn away, as well.

He glanced at Jureemo and the man nearly fainted. But Kiniquips was too much the professional to betray an associate, even with a glance, and so the halfling looked away immediately and stumbled on.

The air erupted with a shrill whistling in Kiniquips's wake, though, and a most unusual missile, a trio of black iron balls

166

spinning at the ends of short lengths of rope flew past the startled Jureemo and caught the fleeing halfling around the waist and legs. The balls wrapped around the poor fellow and came crunching together with devastating efficiency, cracking bones and thoroughly tangling him up.

Kiniquips hit the floor in a heap, ending up on his side, writhing in pain and whimpering pitifully. Tables skidded every which way as the patrons of the tavern scrambled to get as far from him as possible.

For in came a pair of dangerous-looking characters, an elf and a human woman, both dressed in dark leather. The elf had thrown the bolos, obviously, and moved steadily to retrieve them, his fine sword set comfortably on his hip. The woman wore a pair of bandoliers set full of gleaming throwing knives and moved with the same grace as her companion, betraying a lifetime of training.

With brutal efficiency, the elf unwound and yanked the bolos free, and the halfling shrieked again in pain.

Jureemo looked away and headed for the open door. The woman called after him, but he put his head down and hurried around the open door, turning fast for the street.

And there he was blocked by a man in plain, dirty robes. Jureemo tried to push by, but with a single hand, the man stopped him fully.

Jureemo offered a confused expression and looked down at the hand.

With a subtle shift and short thrust, the man in robes sent Jureemo stumbling back into the room, uncomfortably close to the dangerous woman.

"Wh-what attack is this?" he stammered, looking plaintively about. His continuing protests stuck in his throat, though, as he locked stares with the woman.

"This one?" she asked, turning to the elf behind her.

In response, the elf leaned on the fallen Kiniquips's broken hip, and the halfling yelped.

"That one?" the elf asked Kiniquips.

The halfling grimaced and looked away, and grunted again as the elf pressed down on his hip.

"What is the meaning of this?" Jureemo demanded, and he

cautiously stepped back from the woman. Others in the tavern stirred at that display of brutality, and it occurred to Jureemo that he might garner some assistance after all.

The woman looked from him to the man in the robes. "This one, Master Kane?" she asked.

The stirring stopped immediately, and a palpable silence, almost a physical numbness, fell over the tavern.

Jureemo had to remind himself to breathe, then he gave up trying when Master Kane walked over to stand before him. The monk stared at him for a long time, and though Jureemo tried to look away, for some reason he could not. He felt naked in front of that legendary monk, as if Kane looked right through him, or right into his heart.

"You are of the Citadel of Assassins," Kane stated.

Jureemo babbled incoherently for a few moments, his head shaking and nodding all at once.

And Kane just stared.

The walls seemed to close in on the trembling assassin; he felt as if the floor was rushing up to swallow him, and he hoped it would! Panic bubbled through him. He knew that he had been discovered—Kane had stated the fact, not asked him. And those eyes! The monk didn't blink. The monk knew all of it!

Jureemo didn't reach for his own knife, set in his belt at the small of his back. He couldn't begin to imagine a fight with that monster. His sensibilities darted in every different direction, instincts replacing rational thought. He cried out suddenly and leaped for the door . . . or started to.

A white wooden walking stick flashed up before him, cracking him under the chin. He vaguely felt the sensation, the sweet and warm taste, of blood filling his mouth, and he sensed that walking stick sliding under his armpit. He didn't see Kane grab its free end, behind his shoulder-blade, but he did realize, briefly, that he was airborne, spinning head-over-heels, then falling free. He hit the floor flat on his back and immediately propped himself up on his elbows—

—right before the walking stick, that deadly jo stick, cracked him again across the forehead, dropping him flat to the floor.

"Take them both to the castle," Kane instructed his minions. "This one will require the attention of a priest, perhaps even

Friar Dugald," replied the elf standing over the halfling.

Kane shrugged as if it did not matter, which of course it did not. Certainly the priests would make the little one more comfortable.

Perhaps he would even be able to walk up the gallows steps under his own power.

The creature was well-dressed by the standards of Damaran nobles, let alone the expectations aroused by his obvious orc heritage. And he carried himself with an air of dignity and regal bearing, like a royal courier or a butler at one of the finer houses in Waterdeep. That fact was not lost on the half-orcs manning Palishchuk's northern wall as they watched the orc's graceful approach. He walked up as if without the slightest concern, though several arrows were trained upon him, and he dipped a polite bow as he stopped, swinging out one arm to reveal that he held a rolled scroll.

"Well met," he called in perfect Common, and with an accent very unlike anything the sentries might have expected. He seemed almost foppish, and his voice held a nasal quality, something quite uncommon in a race known for flat noses and wide nostrils. "I pray you grant me entrance to your fair city, or, if that is not to be, then I bid you to fetch your leadership."

"What business ye got here?" one of the sentries barked at him.

"Well, good sir, it is an announcement of course," the orc replied, holding forth his hand and the scroll. "And one I am instructed by my master to make once, and once only."

"Ye tell it to us and we might let ye in," the sentry replied. "Then again, we might not."

"Or we might be getting Wingham and the council," a second sentry explained.

"Then again, we might not," the first added.

The orc straightened and put one hand on his hip, standing with one foot flat and the other heel up. He made no move to unroll the scroll, or to do anything else.

"Well?" the first sentry prompted.

"I am instructed by my master to make the announcement once, and once only," the orc replied.

"Well then ye've got yerself some trouble," said the sentry. "For we aren't letting ye in, and aren't bothering our council until we know what ye're about."

"I will wait," the orc decided.

"Wait? Ack, fullblood, how long are ye to wait, then?"

The orc shrugged as if it did not matter.

"We'll leave ye to freeze dead on the path before the gate, ye fool."

"Better that than disobey my master," the orc replied without the slightest hesitation, and that made the sentries exchange curious, concerned looks. The orc pulled a rich, fur-lined cloak tightly around his shoulders and turned slightly to put his back to the wind.

"And who might yer master be, that ye're so willing to freeze?" the first sentry asked.

"King Artemis the First, of course," the orc replied.

The sentry mouthed the name silently, his eyes widening. He glanced at his companions, to see them similarly struggling to digest the words.

"Artemis Entreri sent ye?"

"Of course not, peasant," the orc replied. "I am not of sufficient significance to speak with King Artemis. I serve at the pleasure of First Citizen Jarlaxle."

The two lead sentries slipped back behind the wall. "Damned fools meant it," one said. "They built themselves a kingdom."

"There's a difference between building one and just saying ye built one," the first replied.

"Well, where'd they find the page?" the other asked. "And look at him, and listen to him. He isn't one to be found wandering about in a fullblood hunting party."

A third guard moved up to the huddled pair. "I'm going for Wingham and the councilors," he explained. "They'll be wanting to see this." He glanced out over the wall at their unexpected visitor. "And hear it."

In less than half an hour, Wingham, Arrayan, Olgerkhan, the leadership of Palishchuk, and most of the town's citizens were gathered at the northernmost square, watching the strange courier prance in through the gate.

"I almost expect to see flowers dropping in his wake," Wingham whispered to Arrayan, and the mage giggled despite the obvious gravity of the situation.

Taking no apparent notice of any of the many titters filtering about the crowd, the fullblood orc moved to the center of the gathering, and with great dramatic flourish, an exaggerated flip of his wrist, he unrolled the scroll before him, holding it up in both hands.

"Hear ye! Hear ye!" he called. "And hear ye well, O good citizens of Palishchuk, in the land formerly known as Vaasa."

That started some stirring.

"Formerly?" Wingham whispered.

"Never trust a drow," Olgerkhan added, leaning past Arrayan, who was no longer giggling, to address Wingham.

"King Artemis the First doth proclaim full and unfettered rights to Palishchuk and the people therein," the orc went on. "His Greatness makes no claim over your fair city, nor a demand of tithing, nor does he deny any of you any passage over any road, bridge, or open land in the entirety of D'aerthe."

"D'aerthe?" Wingham echoed with a shake of his head. "Drow name."

"Excepting, of course, those roads, bridges, and open land within Castle D'aerthe itself," the orc added. "And even in there, Palishchukians are welcome . . . by specific grant of entrance, of course.

"King Artemis sees no enemy when he looks your way, and it is his fondest wish that his reign will be marked with fair trade and prosperity for D'aerthian and Palishchukian alike."

"What is he talking about?" Olgerkhan whispered to Wingham.

"War, I expect," the wizened and worldly old half-orc replied.

"This is insanity," Arrayan said.

"Never trust a drow," Olgerkhan lectured.

Arrayan looked to Wingham, who merely shrugged as the fullblood finished his reading, mostly reciting titles and adjectives—excellence, magnificent, wondrous—to accompany the name of King Artemis the First of D'aerthe.

As he finished, the orc flicked his wrist and let go with his bottom hand, and the formed parchment rolled up tight. With a swift and graceful movement, the orc tucked it under one arm, and stood again, hand on hip.

Wingham glanced across the way to a group of three of the town's leading councilors, and waited for them to nod deferentially for him to lead the response—a not surprising invitation, for the half-orcs of Palishchuk often looked to the worldly Wingham for guidance in matters outside of their secluded gates. At least, for matters that did not entail the immediate threat of battle, as was usually the case.

"And what is your name, good sir?" Wingham addressed the courier.

"I am of no consequence," came the reply.

"Would you have me speak to you as fullblood, orc, or D'aerthian Courier, perhaps?" Wingham asked as he stepped out from the gathering, trying to get a better take on the odd creature.

"Speak to me as you would to King Artemis the First," said the orc. "For I am but the ears and mouth of His Greatness."

Wingham looked to the town councilors, who had no insight to offer other than smirks and shrugs.

"We beg you look past our obvious surprise . . . King Artemis," Wingham said. "Such an announcement is hardly expected, of course."

"You were told as much less than two tendays ago, when King Artemis and the first citizen rode through your fair city."

"But still . . ."

"You did not accept his word?"

Wingham paused, not wanting to cross any unseen lines. He remembered well the battle Palishchuk had fought with the castle construct's gargoyles, and neither he nor any of the others wanted to replay that deadly night.

"You must admit that the claim of Vaasa—"

"D'aerthe," the orc interrupted. "Vaasa is to be used only when speaking of what was, not of what is."

"The claim of a kingdom here, by a king and a first citizen until recently unknown to all in the Bloodstone Lands, is unprecedented, you must agree," Wingham said, avoiding any overt concurrence or disagreement. "And yes, we are surprised, for there is another king who has claimed this land."

"King Gareth rules in Damara," the orc replied. "He has made no formal claim on the land once known as Vaasa, excepting his insistence that the land be 'cleansed' of vermin, including one race that you claim as half your heritage, good sir, in case you had not noticed."

That ruffled some feathers among the gathered half-orcs, and more than a few harsh whispers filtered about the uneasy crowd.

"But yes, of course, and your surprise was not unforeseen," the orc went on. "And it is a minor reaction compared to that which the first citizen expects will greet your courier when he travels to the D'aerthian, formerly the Vaasan, Gate and through Bloodstone Pass to the village of the same name." He snapped his arm out, handing Wingham a second scroll, sealed with a wax mark.

"All that King Artemis the First bids you, and of course it is in your own interest as well, is that you send a courier forthwith to King Gareth to deliver news of the birth of D'aerthe. It would do well for King Gareth to cease his murderous activities within the borders of D'aerthe at once, for the sake of peace between our lands.

"And truly," the orc finished with a great and sweeping bow, "such harmony is all that King Artemis the First desires."

Wingham hardly had an answer to that; how could he? He took the rolled parchment, glanced again at the strange seal, which was formed of some green wax that he did not recognize, and glanced again at the puzzled councilors.

By the time he looked back, the orc was already swaggering well on his way to the city's northern gate.

And no one made a move to intercept him.

"You enjoyed that," Jarlaxle said with a wry grin that was not matched by his psionicist counterpart.

"I will itch for a tenday from wearing the shell of an orc," Kimmuriel replied.

"You wore it well."

Kimmuriel scowled at him, a most unusual show of emotion from the intellectually-locked dark elf.

"News will travel fast to Damara," Jarlaxle predicted. "Likely Wingham will send Arrayan or some other magic-user to deliver the announcement before the way is sealed by deep snows."

"Then why did you not wait until the snows began?" asked

Kimmuriel. "You will grant Gareth the time to facilitate passage."

"Grant him?" Jarlaxle asked, leaning forward on his castle parapet. "My friend, I am counting on it. I do not desire to have the fool Knellict here uncontested, and I expect that King Gareth will be more reasonable than the betrayed wizard of the Citadel of Assassins. With Gareth, it will be politics. With Knellict, it is already personal."

"Because you travel with a fool."

"I would not expect patience from a human," said Jarlaxle. "They do not live long enough. Entreri has moved the situation along, nothing more. Whether now before winter's onslaught, or in the cold rain of spring, Gareth will demand his answers. Better to pit him against Knellict outside our gates than to deal with each separately."

Athrogate's misery at being jailed was mitigated somewhat by the generous amounts of mead and ale his gaolers provided. And Athrogate never let it be said that he couldn't sublimate—well, he used the words, 'wash down,' since 'sublimate' was a bit beyond him—his misery with a few pounds of food and a few gallons of ale.

So he sat on his hard bed in his small but not totally uncomfortable cell, filling his mouth with bread and cake and washing it down with fast-overturned flagons of liquid, golden and brown alternately. And to pass the time, between bites and gulps and burps and farts, he sang his favorite dwarven ditties, like "Skipping Threesies with an Orc's Entrails" and "Grow Your Beard Long, Woman, or Winter'll Freeze yer Nipples."

He saved the latter for those times when a female elf or a human woman was set as guard outside his door, and he took special care to raise his voice to a thunderous level whenever he happened upon the refrain about "shakin' them by the ankles, so ye're seein' up their skirts."

For all of his bluster and belch-filled outward joviality, though, Athrogate could not truly ignore the continual hammering outside of his cell's small, high window. Late one moonlit night, when the lone guard outside his cell door breathed in the smooth rhythms of sleep, the dwarf had propped his angled cot against the wall and managed to get up high enough to peek out.

They were building a gallows, with a long trap door and no less than seven noose-arms.

Athrogate had been told his crime against King Gareth, and he knew well the penalty for treason. And though he was cooperating, and had surrendered several of Knellict's spies placed in Heliogabalus—men he had never really liked anyway—none of Gareth's representatives had given him any hint that his sentence might be put aside or even reduced.

But he had ale and mead and plenty of food. He figured he might as well be fat if the door dropped out beneath him so that his neck would get a clean break and he wouldn't be flailing about and peeing himself in front of all the spectators. He had seen that a few times, and decided it would not be a fitting end for one of so many accomplishments as he.

Perhaps he could even bargain to have his name kept on the plaque at the Vaasan Gate. . . .

He had that very thought in mind late one afternoon when his cell door swung open and a familiar figure strode into the room.

"Ah, Athrogate, it will take more than a Bloodstone winter to make you lean for the spring," said Celedon Kierney.

"Lean's for elfs," the dwarf grunted at the charming rogue who had more than a bit of elf blood in him. "For them who're needin' to twist and turn to get out o' the hammer's way."

"You don't think that wise?"

"Bah!" Athrogate blustered and puffed out his chest, smacking his balled fist against it.

"And what if that hammer was instead a fine elven sword?"

"I'd grab it and snap it, then take yer hand and pull ye close for a fine Athrogate hug."

Celedon grinned widely.

"Ye're not for believin' me, then? Well go and get yer fine elven blade. And bring a bow, and not the shooting kind, when ye do. I'll bend yer sword over and play ye a tune that'll put ye in a dancing mood afore I give ye the big hug."

"I do not doubt that you could do just that, Athrogate," Celedon replied, and the dwarf looked at him with complete puzzlement.

"Your exploits in Vaasa have been sung across all the Bloodstone Lands. A pity it is, as I'm sure King Gareth will agree when he arrives this very night, that one so accomplished as Athrogate chose to collude with the likes of Timoshenko."

"The Grandpappy? Bah, never met him."

"Knellict then, and voice no denials."

"Bah!" Athrogate snorted again. "Ye got no course to hang me."

"Hang you?" Celedon Kierney replied with exaggerated incredulity—the animated rogue was good at that particular ploy, Athrogate recognized. "Why, good dwarf, we would never deign to do such a thing. Nay, we intend to celebrate you, in public, to honor you for your aid in capturing so many criminals of the dreaded Citadel of Assassins."

Athrogate stared hatefully at the man, at the threat that made hanging seem quite pleasant by comparison. The mere thought of an angry Knellict in that moment sent a shiver coursing up the dwarf's sturdy spine.

"There may even be a knighthood in it for Athrogate, hero of Vaasa, and now hero of the crown in Heliogabalus."

The dwarf spat on the floor. "Ye're a wretched one, ain't ye."

Celedon laughed at him, and walked out of the small cell. He paused at the door and turned back to the dwarf. "I will have a ladder brought with your breakfast," he said, glancing at the window. "Better than a leaning cot. We have prepared a ceremony for King Gareth, of course, as is right and just."

"Pleasure for ye, elf?"

"Practicality, good dwarf, and grim resolve. We've not enough cells, nor are they really called for on this occasion." He gave a wink and half-turned, before adding, "They attacked a knight of the order—an apprentice knight, to be honest. The case is clear enough, is it not?"

"Ye know it's more muddled than that," said Athrogate. "Ye know what happened at that castle, and what allegiances yer own king's niece struck on her own."

"I know of no such thing," Celedon replied. "I know only that order must be maintained, and that the Citadel of Assassins has brought this fate upon itself."

"And yer Lady Ellery's still dead."

176

"And Gareth is still the king."

On that definitive note, Celedon Kierney exited the room, banging the door closed behind him.

True to his word, Celedon had a ladder delivered to Athrogate that morning, along with his voluminous breakfast. The dwarf munched his food loudly, trying to drown out the ceremony playing outside his window, trying to ignore the reading of charges and the demands for confession, many of which were offered in pathetic, whining tones.

"Bah, just go with yer dignity, ye dolts," Athrogate muttered more than once, and he chomped down all the harder on his crusty cake.

Like a moth to the flame, though, the dwarf could not deny his curiosity, and he managed to set and climb the ladder just in time to see seven of the Citadel's men drop from the platform and sway at the end of a rope. Most died right away, Jureemo Pascadadle among them, and two, including a halfling Athrogate knew as Kiniquips the Short—*Master* Kiniquips—struggled and kicked for some time before finally going still.

Master Kiniquips, Athrogate thought as he climbed back down to his remaining portions.

Master of the Citadel.

Athrogate winced as he considered Celedon's threats.

Suddenly, and for perhaps the first time in his life, the dwarf didn't feel the desire to eat.

CHAPTER

12

W hat do I do?" the nervous woman asked the great mage.

Knellict eyed her sternly and she shrank away from him. It was not her place to ask such questions. Her duties at the Vaasan Gate were simple enough, and hadn't changed in five years, after all.

The woman chewed on her lower lip as she summoned the courage to press on—and she knew that if she did not, the danger to her would be greater than that of invoking the anger of the mage. "Pardon, sir," she said, working her way around the damaging words. "But people are hanging by their necks, o' course. Spysong's all about . . . here, too. They're finding our like and turning them on others, and them that don't turn're getting the hemp collar in the south, so it's said."

Knellict's returned stare was utterly cold, devoid of emotion. The woman, despite her fears, couldn't hold firm under that gaze and she lowered her eyes and assumed a submissive and contrite posture, and managed to whisper, "Beggin' yer pardon, sir."

"Consider that it is good that you know of no one here against whom you might turn," Knellict said to her. He reached over and cupped her chin in his hand and gently tilted her head up.

The woman's knees wobbled when she looked into the archmage's cruel face.

"Because of course nothing that Spysong might do to you would approach the exquisite agony you would suffer at my vengeful hands. Do not ever forget that. And if you find the noose about your slender neck, will yourself to sleep, to relax completely when the trap door falls out beneath you. The clean break is better, I am told."

"B-but sir . . ." The poor woman stammered. She trembled so badly that had it not been for Knellict's hand against her chin, she would have wobbled across the room.

Knellict stopped her by placing the index finger of his free hand over her lips. "You have served me well again today," he said, and no words ever sounded more like a condemnation to the fitful and terrified tavern girl. "As you have since you *chose* to enter my employ those years ago," he added, emphasizing her complicity.

"A little extra this time," the mage went on, smiling now—and that seemed even more cruel. He let the woman go and reached to his belt, producing a small pouch that rattled with coins. "All of it gold."

For a brief moment, the woman's eyes flashed eagerly. Then she swallowed hard, though, considering how she might explain such a treasure if Spysong came calling.

Still, she took the pouch.

A cloud of smoke and the sound of coughing told King Gareth and his friends that Emelyn the Gray had at last arrived in Heliogabalus. Surprisingly, the old wizard had chosen to teleport to the king's audience hall in the city's Crown Palace, rather than in the safer—for teleportation purposes—wizard's guild on the other side of the city. And even more surprisingly, Emelyn was not alone.

All eyes—Gareth, Celedon, Kane, Friar Dugald, and Baron Dimian Ree—turned to the pair, the old wizard and a pretty young woman with a round, flat face and fiery red hair.

"Well met, troublesome one," Celedon remarked dryly. "As always, your timing nears the point of perfection."

"I did not ask for your advice, and that alone would make any of my actions less than perfect in your self-centered thinking," Emelyn countered. "If all the world obeyed only Master Kierney, then all the world would be . . . perfect."

"He's learning, now isn't he?" Celedon asked the others, turning back to Gareth.

Emelyn grumbled and waved his hands at the rogue, and coughed again.

"In truth, I find your timing quite favorable," Gareth said. He looked from Emelyn to his guest, the Baron of Heliogabalus, who had long been a quiet adversary. For Dimian Ree, who led Damara's most populous and important barony, was rumored to be in league with the Citadel of Assassins to some extent, and so it didn't surprise Gareth and his friends to find the agitated man banging on their door that morning to complain vociferously about the multiple hangings that Gareth's men were carrying out in his fair city.

"Baron Ree," Emelyn said, rather coldly, and he did not dip a bow.

"Gray one," Ree responded.

"Our friend the barom has come to protest the justice we have brought to his city," Friar Dugald explained.

"I only just arrived," Emelyn prompted.

"Spysong has encountered many agents of the Citadel of Assassins," King Gareth explained. "They brazenly attacked an apprentice knight of the order."

"That Entreri creature?"

"Precisely him," said Gareth. "But our enemies overplayed their hand this time. They did not know that Master Kane and Celedon were about, along with many allies."

"And you're hanging them? Well, good! And what of this matter might Baron Ree find objectionable, I must ask? Are any of his former lovers swinging by their necks?"

"You would do well to weigh carefully your words before uttering them, gray one," Dimian Ree said, drawing a dismissive scoff from the archmage.

"And you would do better to remember that the only reason I did not utterly destroy you with the fall of Zhengyi was because of the mercy of that man sitting on the throne before you," Emelyn countered, beside him the woman shuffled and glanced about, nervous.

"Enough, Emelyn," commanded King Gareth. "And the rest of you." He looked at them all alternately and sternly, letting his gaze fall at last over the angry baron. "Baron Ree, Heliogabalus is your city, to be sure. But your city lies within my kingdom. I do not ask for your permission to enter."

"And you would always be welcomed as my guest, my king."

"I am not your guest when I come to Heliogabalus," Gareth answered. "That is your basic misunderstanding here. When your king comes to Heliogabalus, *you* are *his* guest."

That brought a widening of eyes all around the room, and Dimian Ree began stepping nervously from foot to foot, like a fox caught against a stone wall with dogs fast approaching.

"And when I offer my resources, as with Spysong, to aid you in keeping your fair city safe, you would do well to express your appreciation."

Dimian Ree swallowed hard and didn't blink.

But Gareth didn't blink, either. "Pray do so and be gone," he said.

Ree glanced about, mostly at Kane then Emelyn, the two members of Gareth's band most antagonistic toward him—openly at least.

"The king is waiting for you, fool," came a booming voice from the back of the hall, and all turned to see the bearlike figure of Olwen Forest-friend and the lithe Riordan Parnell, the missing two of Gareth's band of seven, standing by the door.

"Go on, then," Olwen commanded, coming forward with great, long strides, and seeming even more ominous because he carried his mighty axe Treefeller in one of his large hands. "Tell your king how grateful you be, and how all your city will dance the streets tonight knowing they are more safe because of his arrival."

Dimian Ree turned on Gareth. "Of course, my king. I only wish I had been invited to the hangings, or that my city guards had been informed of the many battles before they were waged about our streets."

"And they'd be flipping gold pieces to see what side to join," Emelyn muttered to the woman at his side, but loud enough for the others to hear, drawing muted chuckles from all—except for Gareth, and Dimian Ree, of course, who glared at him.

"And it would have been even more interesting to see how many of the doomed prisoners looked to their baron for clemency," Emelyn said, taking up the dare of that look.

"Enough," Gareth demanded. "Good Baron Ree, I pray you be on your way, and I thank you for your . . . advice. Your complaints are duly noted."

"And discarded," said Emelyn, and Gareth glared at him.

"And how long might Heliogabalus be honored by your presence, my king?" Dimian Ree asked too sweetly.

Gareth looked to Kane, who nodded. "Our time here is nearly ended, I expect," Gareth answered.

"Indeed," Emelyn added, turning Gareth his way yet again. The mage tilted his head to indicate the woman at his side, and Gareth got the message. "Baron," he said, and he stood and motioned toward the door.

Dimian Ree paused for just a moment, then bowed, turned, and walked from the hall. Before he had even departed, all of the friends descended on Olwen, patting him on the back and offering their condolences over the loss of Mariabronne the Rover, the ranger who had been as a son to him.

"I will know Mariabronne's final tale, in full," Olwen promised.

"And I have brought with me one who might tell you some of that tale," said Emelyn, and he led the others to look at the woman, who still stood off to the side. "I give you Lady Arrayan of Palishchuk."

"That's a half-orc?" Olwen blurted, and he cleared his throat and coughed repeatedly to cover his rather blunt observation.

"Arrayan?" said Gareth. "Ah, good lady, please approach. You are most welcome here. I had hoped to be in Palishchuk by now to present you with your well-deserved honors, but the situation here intervened, I fear."

Arrayan skittishly moved toward the imposing group, though she relaxed visibly when Riordan offered her a confident wink.

"We had been told that you would not be journeying south to the gates," Gareth said.

"And so I was not, good king," Arrayan replied, her voice barely above a whisper. She bowed, then curtsied, halfway at least, before turning it into another uncomfortable bow.

"Pray be at rest, fair lady," said Gareth. "We are honored by your presence." He turned to Dugald and Kane and added, "Surprised, but honored nonetheless."

Arrayan's glance at Emelyn, one full of nervousness, clued in Gareth and the others that she wasn't there merely as a courtesy.

"I did as you bade and traveled to the gates to see if our friends Jarlaxle and Artemis Entreri were there," Emelyn explained. "I found them."

"At the gate?" Gareth asked.

"Nay, they had already passed through, within hours of the skirmish here in Heliogabalus, so it seems."

"There is more magic about that pair than we know," Friar Dugald remarked, and no one disagreed.

"North?" Gareth and Celedon asked together.

"To Palishchuk?" Gareth added.

"Beyond," said Emelyn, and he looked to Arrayan.

When she hesitated, the old mage put his arm around her shoulders and practically shoved her forward to stand directly before the throne. Arrayan took a long moment to collect her wits then produced a parchment from a loop under a fold of her robes.

"I was bid travel here and read this to you, my king," she said in an uncharacteristically quiet voice. "But I do not wish to speak the words." As she finished, she reached out with the parchment.

Gareth took it from her and unrolled it, arching his thick eyebrows curiously and looking briefly to his friends. He silently read the proclamation of the Kingdom of D'aerthe and the rule of King Artemis the First, and his face grew dark.

"Well, what is it?" Olwen demanded of Emelyn.

The old wizard looked to King Gareth, who seemed to feel his gaze and at last lifted his eyes from the parchment. He regarded all of his six friends alternately and said, "Rouse the Army of Bloodstone, all major divisions. Within a fortnight, we march."

"March?" said a confused Olwen, perfectly echoing the thoughts of the others, other than Emelyn, who had seen the proclamation, and Kane, who, principal among them, was beginning to understand the complexity of the web.

Gareth handed the parchment to Dugald. "Read it to them. I go to pray."

⊷━━━⊶

"There is nowhere to run, I assure you," Knellict said to Calihye, after simply appearing before her in her private quarters. "And I would advise against going for the sword," he added when the woman's eyes betrayed her and glanced at her weapon, which lay against the far wall. "Or for the dagger you keep at the back of your belt. In fact, Lady

Calihye, if you make any movement against me at all, I can promise you the most exquisite of deaths. You know me, of course?"

Calihye had to force the words past the lump in her throat. "Yes, archmage," she said deferentially, and she only then remembered to avert her gaze to the floor.

"You wanted to kill Entreri for what he did to your friend," Knellict said matter-of-factly. "I share your feelings."

Calihye dared to look up.

"But of course, you buried that honest desire for vengeance, silly girl." The archmage gave a great and exaggerated sigh. "The flesh is too, too weak," he said, and he reached out to stroke the trembling woman's cheek.

Calihye instinctively recoiled—or tried to, but Knellict waggled his fingers and a wind came up behind her, pushing her back to his waiting hand. She didn't dare resist any more overtly.

"You have taken one of my mortal enemies for your lover," Knellict said, shaking his head, and he added a few mocking "tsks."

Calihye's mouth moved weirdly, trying vainly to form words.

"Perhaps I should simply incinerate you," Knellict mused. "A slow burning fire, carefully controlled, that you might feel your skin rolling up under the pressure of its heat. Oh, I have heard strong men reduced to whimpering fools under such duress. Crying for their mothers. Yes, it is a most enjoyable refrain.

"Or perhaps for such a one as pretty as you—well, as you once were before a blade reduced you to medusa-kin . . ." He paused and mocked her with laughter.

Calihye was too terrified to respond, to show any emotion at all. She knew enough of Knellict to understand that they were by no means idle threats.

"Still, you are a woman," Knellict went on. "So you are possessed of great vanity, no doubt. So for you, perhaps I will summon a thousand-thousand insects, that will bite at your tender flesh, and some that will break through. Yes, your eyes will reveal your terror no matter how stubbornly you choke back your screams when you see the bulge of beetles boring underneath your pretty skin."

It proved too much for the warrior woman. She exploded into action, leaping forward at Knellict with raking fingers aimed at his smug expression.

She went right through him and stumbled forward. Stunned, off balance, Calihye tried quickly to re-orient. She spun around, focusing on the image, which was even then fading to nothingness.

"It was so easy to fool you," came the wizard's voice, over by her sword. She looked that way, but he was not to be seen. "You were so terrified by the thought of my presence that a simple illusion and an even more simple ventriloquism had you feeling my touch."

Calihye licked her lips. She shifted her feet beneath her, setting her balance for a spring.

"Can you get to the sword, do you think?" Knellict's disembodied voice asked, and it still seemed to be coming from very near the weapon.

Before he had even finished the sentence, Calihye's hand reached behind her, grabbed the dagger, and whipped forward, launching the missile at the voice. It seemed to stutter in its progress for just a moment, before pressing on with a flash of bluish light. Then it hung there, in mid-air, hilt tilted down as if it had struck into some fabric or other flimsy material.

"Oh, and it is a magical dagger," Knellict said. "It defeated the weakest of my wards!"

His position confirmed, Calihye swallowed her fear and darted for her sword. Or tried to, for even as she started, the archmage materialized. Her dagger hung limply, caught in a fold of his layered robes. He extended his arm toward her, finger pointing, and from that digit came a green flash of light. A dart shot forth to strike the woman in the midsection.

"My dart is magical, as well," Knellict explained as Calihye doubled over and clutched at her belly. Her grimace became a loud groan, then a continual scream, as the dart began to pump forth acid.

"I have found gut wounds to be the most effective at neutralizing an enemy warrior," Knellict said with detached amusement. "Would you agree?"

The woman staggered forward a step.

"Oh please, do press on, valiant warrior woman," Knellict teased. He stepped aside, leaving the path to her sword clear and visible before her.

With a growl of defiance, Calihye grasped the dart and tore it free

of her belly with a bit of intestine, yellow-green acid, and bile dripping forth from the hole, followed by the bright red of blood. She
threw the dart to the ground and grabbed for her sword.

As soon as her fingers touched the blade, a jolt of lightning arced
from it and through her body, launching her back across the room
and to the floor. She tried to curl, but her spasms allowed her no control of her body. Her hair stood out wildly, dancing from the shock.
Her teeth chattered so violently that her mouth filled with blood,
and her joints jolted repeatedly and painfully. She wet her breeches,
as well, but was too agonized to even realize it.

"How did you ever survive the trials of Vaasa?" the archmage
taunted her, and the sound of his voice told her that he stood right
over her. "A first-year apprentice could destroy you."

The words faded along with Calihye's consciousness. She felt
Knellict reach down and grab her hair. She had the thought that he
would kill her conventionally—a knife across the throat, perhaps.

She hoped it would come that quickly, at least, and was relieved
indeed when darkness descended.

The heavy cavalry were the first to come through the open gates
into the frozen marshland of Vaasa. Four abreast they rode, breaking off two-by-two to the left and right, the plated armor of knight
and horse alike gleaming dully under the heavy gray sky. The clatter
of hooves continued for a long while, until a full square of cavalry,
seven ranks of seven, had formed at each flank of the gate. Forty-five
of the riders in each square were veteran warriors, trained in lance,
bow, spear, and sword, and tested in battle. But every other row,
one, three, five, and seven, was centered by a man in white robes,
which, like the chestplates of the warrior's metal armor, was embla-
zoned with the White Tree symbol of the king. They were Emelyn's
warriors, the wizards of the Army of Bloodstone, well-versed in
defensive magic and well-trained to keep the magical trickery of an
enemy at bay, while the superior warriors of Bloodstone won the day.
Well-respected by the armored warriors who surrounded them, the
wizards were affectionately known as the Disenchanters.

Behind the cavalry came the armored infantry, ten abreast,

marching in unison and presenting a deliberately ominous cadence by thumping their maces against their shields with every other step. They did not veer to either side, but continued their straightforward march, until fifty full ranks had cleared the gate. There too, the ranks were speckled with Disenchanters, and few wizards in all the region could hope to get a spell, even a sorely diminished spell, through the web of defensive magic protecting King Gareth's men-at-arms.

Then came more riders, the mounted guard of King Gareth Dragonsbane, encircling the paladin king and his entourage of six trusted advisors, including the greatest wizard of all in the Bloodstone Lands, Emelyn the Gray.

The rest of the heavy infantry, fifty more ranks of ten, the core of the Army of Bloodstone, followed in tight and disciplined formation, similarly playing the cadence of mace and shield. As they passed out onto the field, the cavalry began its march again, riding wide and stretching the line to aptly protect the flanks of the core group, eleven hundred men and women, many the children of warriors who had fought with Gareth against the Witch-King.

If the infantry was the backbone of the force, and the cavalry its arms, and King Gareth and his six friends its head, then next came the legs: a second cavalry force, less armored and with swifter mounts. They were Olwen's men, rangers and scouts trained to act more independently. And behind them came still more infantry, lightly armored spearmen, mostly, serving as protection for the batteries of longbowmen.

On and on it went. More light infantry, battalions of priests with carts full of bandages, caravans of supply wagons, lines of strong men carrying ladders, horses towing rams and beams for siege towers. . . .

Men and women lined the top of the wall, watching the procession as it issued forth from the Vaasan Gate for hours, and when at last those great gates swung closed, the sun was beginning its western descent and more than eight thousand soldiers, the heart and soul of the Army of Bloodstone, marched out to the north.

"It surprises me that Gareth moved so quickly and decisively on this," Riordan Parnell said to Olwen and Kane, the three of them bringing up the rear of Gareth's diamond set between the main ranks of heavy infantry.

"That has always been his strength, as Zhengyi learned," Kane replied.

"To his great dismay," Riordan agreed with a wide grin. "Zhengyi's, I mean," he added when he saw that his two companions were not similarly smiling.

While the others rode, Kane walked, his face as stoic as always, his eyes set with his typical grim determination. On the far side of Kane, on his lightly-armored but large horse, Olwen obviously stewed, and his great black beard was wet around his mouth from chewing his lip.

"Still," Riordan argued, "we have merely a simple piece of paper. It might mean little or nothing at all."

Kane motioned forward with his chin, directing Riordan's gaze to Gareth and Dugald, and the two wizards, Emelyn and Arrayan.

"The half-orc woman was very clear that the castle had returned to life," the monk reminded. "Our apprentice knight and his dark elf cohort meddle with the artifacts of Zhengyi. That is not 'nothing at all.'"

"True," Riordan admitted, "but is it sufficient to rouse the Army of Bloodstone and abandon Damara at a time when we have gone to open war against the Citadel of Assassins?"

"The Citadel has been dealt a severe blow—" Kane began to answer, but Olwen cut him short.

"It's worth it all just to get the answers on the death of Mariabronne," he said, a throaty growl behind every word, so that it seemed to his companions as if he might use some ranger magic and turn into a bear at that moment.

It occurred to Riordan that the ranger's horse might not enjoy that experience, but the bard kept the thought to himself—though he did begin composing a song about it.

"Those two were involved, I'm sure," Olwen went on.

"Our information says they were not," said Kane. "Mariabronne scouted forward of his own volition, and contrary to the orders of Ellery. It is a convincing tale, particularly given Mariabronne's reputation for risk-taking."

Olwen snorted and looked away, his meaty hands working the knuckles white by clenching at the reins.

"Well, they are two people, and foolish ones at that," Riordan quickly put in, trying to get the conversation away from a subject that was obviously too painful for his ranger friend. "Even if they are dabbling in Zhengyian magic, as this report from Palishchuk and the words of the dragon sisters might indicate, are they truly such a threat that we should open our flank and our kingdom to the retribution of Knellict and Timoshenko?"

"Nothing is open," Kane assured him. "Spysong's network is fully ready to repel any moves by the Citadel, and if we are needed Emelyn can get us back with a wave of a wand."

"Then why didn't Emelyn just take us six there, leaving Gareth and the soldiers in place?"

"Because this is the opportunity our king has been patiently awaiting, to fully reveal his influence in Vaasa," answered another voice, that of Celedon Kierney. The eavesdropper slowed his horse to bring him in line with the three. "Gareth's aim here is not the castle—or at least, not the castle alone."

Riordan paused and considered that for a moment, then said, "Palishchuk." He glanced at Kane, who nodded knowingly. Olwen gave no indication that he was even listening. "He's showing Palishchuk that they are vital to his designs, and that when they are threatened, he will take that as seriously as if it were Heliogabalus itself under the Zhengyian shadow," Riordan reasoned on the fly.

The looks from Celedon and Kane showed him that he had correctly sorted the puzzle.

"That's why he's the king," Riordan added with a self-deprecating chuckle.

"I expect that by the time we return through the Vaasan Gate, the Kingdom of Bloodstone will be whole, Vaasa and Damara united under the banner of Gareth Dragonsbane," said Celedon.

Suddenly, to Riordan, the day seemed just a bit brighter.

CHAPTER

A BET HEDGED

13

The half-orc city was on edge. And why not? Word had reached Jarlaxle, and so it had reached Palishchuk as well, that King Gareth was on the march, his formidable army rolling northward across the Vaasan bog to challenge the claim of King Artemis the First. The news had surprised Jarlaxle—who didn't much like being surprised. He hadn't thought Gareth would move so decisively, or so boldly. Winter was coming on, which alone could destroy an army in Vaasa, and Gareth was dealing with drow, after all. Gareth had no idea what Jarlaxle had arrayed against him—how could he? And yet he had marched out at once, and in force.

Jarlaxle's respect for the man had multiplied with the news. Rarely had he encountered humans with such confidence and determination.

He made certain his boots clicked loudly even on the slick, rain-soaked stones on the side of the hill. He did not want a fight with Wingham, and did not want to startle any of the nervous sentries surrounding the half-orc.

Wingham stood near a small fire at the center of the hillock's flat top, with another, larger half-orc—Olgerkhan, Jarlaxle realized—close beside him. They noticed Jarlaxle's noisy approach and turned to greet him.

As he neared the pair, Jarlaxle recognized the anxiety in their expressions. A bit of fear, a bit of anger, all very clearly revealed in the way they, particularly Olgerkhan, kept glancing around them. Olgerkhan even had his burly arms crossed over his chest, as sure a sign of resistance as could be offered. The differences in racial habits occurred to Jarlaxle at that moment. In Menzoberranzan, when a drow male crossed his arms over his chest, it was a sign of obedience and respect. On the World Above, though, and as with the drow matrons, it was a signal of steadfast defiance, or at least defensiveness.

"Master Wingham," he greeted sweetly. "I am honored that you answered my call."

"You knew I would come out," Wingham replied, his tone less diplomatic than usual. "How could I not, with the winds of war stirring about my beloved Palishchuk?"

"War?"

"You know that King Gareth has marched."

"To celebrate the coronation of King Artemis the First, of course."

Wingham put on a sour expression that seemed even more exaggerated in the dancing shadows of the small fire.

"Well, we shall learn of his intent soon enough," Jarlaxle offered. "Let us both hope that King Gareth is as wise as his reputation indicates."

"Why have you done this?"

"I serve the king."

"You challenge the rightful king," Olgerkhan interjected.

From under the great brow of his ostentatious hat, Jarlaxle narrowed his red-glowing eyes and thinned his lips, locking Olgerkhan in a stare that surely reminded the burly warrior of his recent adventure beside the drow. Olgerkhan's crossed arms slipped down to his side and he even stepped back a bit, the aggressiveness melting from his posture. With that one look, Jarlaxle had reminded him of Canthan, to be sure.

"The Bloodstone Lands were opened to you and Artemis Entreri both," Wingham said, forcing the drow to look back his way. "Opportunity awaited you. With respect and song, and the appreciation of all the people, you and Entreri could have had much of what you desire without this confrontation. Would King Gareth have denied you the castle?"

"I doubt he would approve of the magic it offers," the drow replied.

"Even without it! A knight of the order can lay claim to a barony that is as yet unclaimed and untamed. Negotiations with Gareth would have handed the castle to you, and would have earned you the allegiance of Palishchuk, as well, a friendship we were all too willing to extend. Likely, King Gareth would have been grateful to have such worthy warriors helping him to tame the northern wilderness."

"And why should we help Gareth extend his claim? Are you so willing to kneel, Wingham?"

Both half-orcs stiffened at the insult, but Wingham didn't back away. "Kneel?"

"If King Gareth tells Wingham to kneel, his knees will soil, no doubt."

"It is respect freely given."

Jarlaxle laughed at him. "It is the obedience of resignation."

Olgerkhan grumbled something indecipherable, shaking his head, and Jarlaxle wasn't really surprised that he had confused that one. Wingham, though, just continued to stare, his expression showing clearly that he wasn't buying the premise one bit.

"Ah well, it is a sad state, is it not?" Jarlaxle asked. "It is the way. The way it has been for millennia uncounted, and the way it will be until the end of time."

"And you accuse *me* of resignation?"

Jarlaxle laughed again. "I accept the truisms of ambition," he explained. "What is resignation to you is relished by me." He looked down and pulled his fine *piwafwi* open a bit to reveal his black leather trousers. "I do not dirty my fine clothes. Not for any man. Not for any king."

"King Gareth will tarnish them with your own blood!" Olgerkhan promised.

Jarlaxle shrugged as if it did not matter.

"You called us out here," said Wingham. "Is there more a point to it than this banter? When you came through Palishchuk, you asked nothing of us, and we were glad to offer you the same."

"But now King Gareth marches," Jarlaxle replied. "The situation is changed, of course. Palishchuk finds herself caught between the breaking waves of possibility. To remain between them as they crest is to be crushed by both. It is time to swim, Wingham."

Olgerkhan stood with his tusky jaw hanging open, a look upon his ugly face so perfectly blank that Jarlaxle nearly laughed out loud. Wingham, though, nodded as he grasped the analogy and its dire implications all too clearly.

"You would have us war with King Gareth, who saved us from the Witch-King and has been a great friend to us?" the worldly old half-orc asked.

Jarlaxle grinned knowingly as he weighed the determination in Wingham's words—a resolve that he knew he would not weaken however great the threat of Kimmuriel's drow armies. In fact, it was a resolve that he had counted on since he had learned of Gareth's bold initiative against the new King of Vaasa.

"Palishchuk will not betray King Gareth," Wingham stated, and the drow knew that he was speaking truth.

"We do not forget the time of Zhengyi," Wingham went on, and his need to justify his position amused Jarlaxle. "We remember well the darkness of the Witch-King and the light named Gareth who risked all, who risked his life, his friends, and all of Damara to ensure that we were not out here all alone against a foe we could not defeat."

"It is a fine tale," the drow agreed.

"We will not betray King Gareth," Wingham said again.

"I never said that you should," Jarlaxle replied, and Wingham's steely gaze melted into one of confusion. "The Army of Bloodstone has marched, with their fine glittering weapons and shining armor. A most impressive sight, to be sure. They come armed and armored, and with wizards and priests aplenty.

"And yet, on the other side, you are faced with the unknown," Jarlaxle continued. "Other than the reputation of my kin and what you so painfully learned of the powers of the Zhengyian castle. I do not make your choice for you, my friend. I only seek to explain to you that the waves are closing and you must swim into one or the other or be destroyed. The time of neutrality has passed. I had not thought it would come to this—not so quickly, at least—but it has, and I would be remiss as a friend if I did not help you to understand."

"A friend?" Olgerkhan roared. "A friend who brings war to Palishchuk's door?"

"My army is not marching," Jarlaxle remarked, and at his reference to an army, he noted Wingham's eyebrows arching just a bit.

"But you come with threats," said Olgerkhan.

"Nay, far from it," Jarlaxle was quick to reply. "King Artemis is a man of peace. Look to the south for the winds of war, not to the north." He turned from the brutish Olgerkhan to Wingham's doubting expression, and added, "It would seem that King Gareth is not a man who shares."

"With thieves?" Wingham dared to ask. "Who take that which is not theirs? Who lay claim to a kingdom without cause of blood or deed?"

"Deed?" Jarlaxle replied as if wounded. "We conquered the castle, did we not? It was King Artemis who slew the dracolich, after all. Your friend beside you can testify to that, though he lay on the ground helplessly when Artemis struck the fateful blow."

Olgerkhan bristled and seemed stung by the simple truth, but did not reply.

"So claim the castle, and bargain with King Gareth for a barony," Wingham suggested. "Avert the war, for the sake of all."

"A contract that would entail our fealty to Gareth, no doubt," the drow said.

"And did you not promise exactly that when you accepted the honors bestowed upon you at King Gareth's court?"

"A moment of duress."

Wingham's expression soured. "You have no claim."

Jarlaxle shrugged, again as if it did not matter. "Perhaps you will be proven correct. Perhaps not. Ultimately, the claim goes to the strongest, does it not? In the final sort of things, I mean. He who remains alive, remains alive to write the histories in a light favorable to him and his cause. Surely as worldly as you are, you know well the histories of the world, Master Wingham. Surely you recognize that armies carrying banners are almost always thieves—until they win."

Wingham didn't flinch, and Jarlaxle knew enough about him, about people in general, to understand that he clutched at the rather pitiful—from Jarlaxle's perspective—ideal of a higher justice, of a universal truism of right and wrong. No man could be more broken, after all, than he who at last must face the truth that his king, his living god, is flawed.

"Look forward, good Wingham," Jarlaxle offered. "The outcome is not known to you, but the result after the battle is indeed. The victor will determine which king rules the land of Vaasa. One wave will overtake the other, and will flatten all the water under its weight. That is the truth facing Palishchuk, however we might feel about it. And in that light, I would caution you to withhold your judgment about who rightfully—and more importantly, who practically—will rule in Vaasa."

Wingham seemed to blanch for just a moment, but he squared his shoulders and firmed his jaw, his round, flat face tightening with admirable determination. "Palishchuk will not battle against King Gareth," he stated.

"Neutrality, then?" asked the drow, and he let his expression sour. "Rarely is the course of the coward rewarded, I fear. But perhaps King Artemis will forgive—"

"No," Wingham interrupted. "You are right in one thing, Jarlaxle. Palishchuk must not let the events around her bury her under their weight. Not without a fight. We have survived by the sword for all of our history, and so it will be again. Kill me now if you will. Kill us all if you are so thirsty for blood, but understand that if King Gareth's horn calls out for allegiance, the warriors of Palishchuk will answer that call."

Jarlaxle's sudden smile took the half-orc off his guard, and the drow dipped a sincere and respectful bow. "I never said that you should not," Jarlaxle offered, and he turned and walked off into the night

He knew that the half-orc would misinterpret him, would think that his carefree attitude regarding any alliance Palishchuk might choose was a sign of supreme confidence.

Jarlaxle loved irony.

"King Gareth has reached Palishchuk," Kimmuriel informed Jarlaxle the following afternoon in large and airy foyer of the main keep of Castle D'aerthe. The room had become his audience chamber, in effect, though Artemis Entreri, the man Jarlaxle had named as king, hardly spent any time in the place. He was always out along the walls, in some odd corner with a stone wall sheltering him from the increasingly cold north wind. Jarlaxle understood that his human friend was trying to keep as far away as possible from Kimmuriel and the scores of other dark elves who had come in through the magical gate the psionicist and the wizards of Bregan D'aerthe had created.

The king's absence had not deterred Jarlaxle from playing the games of court fashion, however. Bregan D'aerthe had brought in furnishings that soon adorned every room of the keep. Jarlaxle sat on Entreri's throne, a purple and blue affair fashioned of a giant mushroom stalk and with the cap used as a fanlike backdrop. Other smaller chairs were set about, including the one directly before the throne, in which sat Kimmuriel.

All around them, dark elves tacked tapestries up on the walls, both to defeat the intrusion of stinging daylight and to steal some of the bluster of the biting breeze. Those tapestries showed no murals to the onlookers, however, just fine black cloth, for they were folded in half, their bottom hem tacked up with the top, Kimmuriel's expression, and those of the other dark elves, reminded Jarlaxle keenly that he was asking quite a bit of his former band in making them come up to such an inhospitable environment.

"He has made good time, given the size of his force," Jarlaxle replied. "It would seem that our little announcement made an impression."

"You waved a wounded rothé before a hungry displacer beast," Kimmuriel remarked, an old Menzoberranyr saying. "This human, Gareth, strikes with the surety of a matron mother. Most unusual for his race."

"He is a paladin king," Jarlaxle explained. "He is no less fanatical to his god than my mother, Lolth torment her soul eternally, was to the Spider Queen. More so than the dedication one might expect out of fallen House Oblodra, of course."

Kimmuriel nodded and said, "Thank you."

Jarlaxle laughed aloud.

"You anticipated this move by Gareth, then," Kimmuriel reasoned, and there was an edge to his tone. "Yet you allowed me to expend great resources in opening the many gates to this abysmal place? The price of the cloth will come out of your fortune, Jarlaxle. Beyond that, I have only a minimal crew operating in

Menzoberranzan at the height of the trading season, and almost all of my wizards have been fully engaged in transporting goods, warriors, and fodder for your expedition."

"I did not know that he would march, no," Jarlaxle explained. "I suspected that it could come to this, though the speed of Gareth's response has surprised me, I must admit. I expected this decisive encounter to occur no earlier than next spring, if at all."

Kimmuriel stroked his smooth, narrow black chin and looked away. After a moment of mulling it over, the psionicist offered a deferential nod to his former master.

"There was great potential gain, and nothing to lose," Jarlaxle added.

Kimmuriel didn't disagree. "Yet again I am reminded of why Bregan D'aerthe has not seen fit to kill you," he said.

"Though you have come to see me as an annoyance?"

Kimmuriel smiled—one of the very few expressions Jarlaxle had ever seen on the soulless face of that one. "This will rank as no more than a minor inconvenience, with perhaps some gain yet to be found. Whenever Jarlaxle has an idea, it seems, Bregan D'aerthe is stretched."

"Dice have six sides for a reason, my friend. There is no thrill in surety."

"But the win must come from more than one in six," said Kimmuriel. "The Jarlaxle I knew in Menzoberranzan would not wager unless four of the sides brought a profit."

"Do you think I have so changed my ways, or my odds?"

"There was the matter of Calimport."

Jarlaxle conceded that point with a nod.

"But of course, you were caught in the thrall of a mighty artifact," said Kimmuriel. "You cannot be blamed."

"You are most generous."

"And, as always, Jarlaxle won out in the end."

"It is a good habit."

"And he chose wisely," said Kimmuriel.

"You have a high opinion of yourself."

"Little of what I say or think is opinion."

True enough, Jarlaxle silently conceded. Which was exactly why he had made certain that Rai-guy, the temperamental and unpredictable wizard, was dead and Kimmuriel was still alive and in charge of Bregan D'aerthe during Jarlaxle's sabbatical.

"And I must admit that your recent scheme has intrigued me," Kimmuriel said. "Though I know not why you insist on even visiting this Lolth-forsaken wilderness." He wrapped his arms around him as he spoke and cast a disparaging glance to the side, at a tapestry that lifted out from the wall under the weight of the howling wind rushing in through the cracks in the stone.

"It was a good chance," Jarlaxle said.

"It always is, when there is nothing truly to lose."

Jarlaxle sensed the hesitance in his voice, almost as if Kimmuriel was expecting a confrontation, or an unpleasant surprise. The psionicist feared, of course, that Jarlaxle meant to challenge him and order Bregan D'aerthe into battle against King Gareth.

"There are ways around Gareth's unexpectedly bold move," he said to reassure his former, and likely future, lieutenant.

"There are ways through them, as well," Kimmuriel replied. "Of course."

"The point of this wager is not to place too much on the table. I'll not lose a drow soldier here—and though I do believe that our fodder serve us well by charging into the chewing maw of Gareth's able army, in even that endeavor we must be stingy. I am not Matron Baenre, obsessed with the conquest of Mithral Hall. I do not seek a fight here—far from it."

"Gareth will grant you nothing in a parlay," said Kimmuriel. "You say that he is acting boldly, but no less so than you did when you sent word of the rise of King Artemis."

"He will not parlay," Jarlaxle agreed, "because we have nothing to offer to him. We will remedy that, in time."

"So what will you say to him now?"

"Not even farewell," Jarlaxle answered with a grin.

Kimmuriel nodded with contentment. He glanced again at the waving tapestry, and squeezed his arms just a bit more tightly around himself, but Jarlaxle knew him well enough to realize that he was at peace.

A few miles to the south of the castle, on a field outside of Palishchuk, another warrior was anything but at peace. Olwen Forest-friend stalked about the encampment, speaking encouragement to the men and women of the Army of Bloodstone. His forest-green cloak whipped out behind him as he strode briskly from campfire to campfire. His face flushed with passion and eagerness and his legendary war axe gleamed in the firelight. For many years, his favorite weapon had been the bow, but as his agility had decreased with age, he found that running along the fringes of the battlefield no longer suited him. It hadn't taken long for Olwen to discover the thrill of close combat, nor to perfect the technique.

"We press the walls tomorrow," he promised one group of young soldiers, who stared up at him in awe. "We'll be home through the Galenas in a matter of days."

Their eager and grateful responses followed Olwen as he moved on to the next group, dragging a second, far thinner and more graceful figure in his wake.

Riordan Parnell was usually charged with maintaining morale. Often in the calm before battle, the bard would entertain with stirring tales of heroic deeds and darkness shattered. But his planned performance had been sidetracked by the overwhelming presence of his ranger friend.

He caught up to Olwen before the ranger reached the next group in line, and even dared tug on the man's sleeve to halt him, or slow him at least. That brought a warning glare, Olwen locking his bright eyes on Riordan's grasping hand then slowly lifting his gaze to meet that of the bard.

"We have much yet to learn," Riordan said as he gently pulled away.

"I've not the time or the desire to read the history of King Artemis."

"It is all vague."

"They're for taking King Gareth's hard-won land," said Olwen. "They locked themselves in a castle, and we'll knock that castle down. I see nothing vague here. But don't you worry, bard. I'll give you a song or two to write." As he made the promise, Olwen brought his war axe over his shoulder and held it firmly before him. With a nod, the ranger turned to go.

But Riordan caught him again by the sleeve. "Olwen," he said.

The ranger cocked his head to consider the man.

"We do not know all of the details of Mariabronne's death," said Riordan.

Olwen's expression hardened. "Why are you bringing Mariabronne into this?"

"Because he fell in that castle, and you know that well. Nothing you do in there tomorrow will change that sad reality."

Olwen turned to face Riordan squarely, his muscular chest puffed out. He slipped the axe down at the end of one arm, but the movement did little to diminish his imposing posture. "I march to King Gareth's call, and not that of a ghost," he said, "to defeat a pretender named Artemis Entreri."

"Emelyn has been inside the castle," said Riordan. "And I have spoken with Arrayan and Olgerkhan of Palishchuk, and with Wingham. All of the indications and all of the stories—consistent tales, one and all—do not indicate treachery, but misjudgment, in the death of Mariabronne the Rover. We believe that he was felled by a monster's blow, and not due in any way to the actions, or even the inactions, of Artemis Entreri or the drow Jarlaxle."

"And of course, it wouldn't be the way of a dark elf to create any mischief."

It was hard for Riordan to hold his stance against that simple logic.

"Nor for the Witch-King," the bard finally managed to counter. "From all that we have learned, Mariabronne was slain by the enduring and dastardly legacy of Zhengyi."

"Speak not that name!" Olwen ground his teeth and the considerable muscles on his arms twisted as he rolled tight the fingers of his hands, one fist clenched on his right, the knuckles of his other hand whitening as they clamped on the axe handle.

Riordan offered a sympathetic look, but Olwen scowled all the more.

"And it might be that the dastardly and enduring legacy of Zhengyi is now in the hands of King Artemis," Olwen said and he brought his axe up before him to catch it again in both hands. He pulled it back a bit and slapped it hard into his right mitt for effect. "I've grown weary of that legacy."

As much as he wanted to argue that point, Riordan Parnell found himself without an answer. Olwen nodded gruffly and spun away, then launched into another rousing cheer as he approached the next group of soldiers in line, all of whom lifted their flagons to the legendary ranger and shouted out in unison, "For Mariabronne the Rover!"

Riordan watched his friend for a moment, but sensed the approach of another and turned to greet his cousin, Celedon Kierney.

"It is a cheer that will rush us to bloodshed," Celedon remarked. "Olwen will be in no mood for delay when we reach this Castle D'aerthe on the morrow."

"I cannot imagine his pain," said Riordan. "To lose a man who was as a son to him."

"I wish Gareth had bid him stay in Damara," Celedon replied. "He is as fine a warrior as I have ever known, but he is in no humor for this."

"You fear his judgment?"

"As I would fear yours, or my own, if I had just lost a son. And Mariabronne was exactly that to Olwen. When word reached his ears, he cast about like a lion on the rampage, so the story claims. He went to the druids of Olean's Grove outside of Kinnery and bade them to reveal the tale in full, and even, it is rumored, to inquire about the possibilities of reincarnation."

Riordan blanched, but was not really surprised. "And he was refused, of course."

"I do not know," said Celedon, "but I trust that the Great Druid of Olean's would not entertain such a notion."

"So he will assuage his pain with his axe instead," said the bard. "I hope that King Artemis has not grown too fond of his title."

"Or his head."

The next morning, Entreri and Jarlaxle stood on the southern wall of Castle D'aerthe, near the western tower that flanked the castle's main, south-facing gate. Behind and below them in the courtyard that had once teemed with undead monsters that had risen against their initial incursion into the castle, three hundred goblins and kobolds shifted nervously. None dared speak out, for around them stood merciless dark elf guards bearing long canes and drow priests with their trademark whips, the heads of which were living, biting snakes. Any kobold or goblin who shuffled too far out of line felt the sting of those bites, then squirmed and writhed in horrible, screaming agony on the ground before sweet death finally took it.

Entreri and Jarlaxle hardly paid any attention to the spectacle behind them, however, for before them came the Army of Bloodstone. The main infantry marched in tight ranks in the center, flanked by heavy cavalry to either side and with batteries of longbowmen grouped behind the front ranks. The many pennants of Damara, of the Church of Ilmater, and of King Gareth waved in the brisk morning breeze, and the cadence played out on the shields of the warriors, as they had drummed when leaving the Vaasan Gate less than a tenday earlier.

A mere fifty yards out from the castle, the procession stopped, and with remarkable precision, they moved into their defensive formations. Shields turned crisply and the front ranks fanned left and right, streaming in thin lines, then thickening again into defensive squares. Wizards danced about as if they were jesters in a court procession, waving their arms and enacting all sorts of wards and shields to deflect and defeat any incoming evocative magic. Just inside the infantry square, the archers formed their ranks, every bow with arrow ready. As the center of the line fully separated, the companions on the wall were treated to a view of the king himself, all splendid in his shining silver armor, and flanked by his powerful friends.

"Do you think they have come for a banquet in my honor?" Entreri asked.

"That would be my guess. Friar Dugald is dressed in finery, you see, and of course, the king shines as if the sun itself has settled upon him."

"And yet that one," said Entreri, nodding to indicate the man standing to Gareth's right, "seems ill-dressed for anything other than the ruts of a cattle trail."

"Master Kane," Jarlaxle agreed. "He truly is an embarrassment. One would think that the King of Damara would find someone to infuse some fashion sense into that fool."

Entreri smirked, remembering all the days on the road with Jarlaxle, when his companion had set out fine shirts for him. He thought of the night when Jarlaxle had returned with a new belt and scabbard for Charon's Claw and Entreri's jeweled dagger. That belt was a magnificent black leather affair, and as fine in design as in appearance, for it held a pair of small throwing knives, fully concealed, within its back length.

"Perhaps Gareth will hire you to instruct the monk," Entreri said.

Jarlaxle hesitated for a moment before responding, "He could do worse."

Six riders and Master Kane came forward from the line. The monk walked in front of Gareth, who was centered by Celedon Kierney and Olwen Forest-friend. Directly behind Gareth rode Riordan Parnell, the bard, strumming a lute and singing. Flanking the bard were Dugald and Emelyn, both quietly spellcasting, building defensive walls.

The group closed half the distance to Castle D'aerthe then stopped, and Riordan came out around his king and galloped the short expanse to pull up before the great gates. He noted Jarlaxle and Entreri and trotted his mount off to the side, to sit directly below them.

"Master Jarlaxle and Artemis Entreri, Apprentice Knight of the Order" he began.

"*King* Artemis," Jarlaxle corrected, loudly enough so that Gareth and his friends heard, and bristled—which brought a smile to the drow's face.

"Good subjects—" Riordan began again.

"We are not."

The bard stared hard at the obstinate drow. "You pair of fools, then," he said. "King Gareth Dragonsbane, he who defeated Zhengyi, who cast the Wand of Orcus across the planes of existence, who—"

"Spare us," Jarlaxle interrupted. "It is cold, and we have heard this litany before—in Gareth's own court, and not so long ago."

"Then your folly should be obvious to you."

"Someday I will tell you my own litany of deeds, good bard," Jarlaxle called down. "Then indeed will your friends label you as long-winded."

"King Gareth demands audience," Riordan called out. "If you refuse, then war is upon you." He looked to the east, and motioned with his right arm. Following that, the pair saw a light cavalry force flanking Castle D'aerthe, and a light infantry taking up defensive positions in its wake.

Riordan then motioned west, and the pair saw a similar scene unfolding in that direction.

"To grant audience or to accept a siege," Riordan said. "The choice seems quite obvious."

"Why would we not grant free and friendly passage to King Gareth of Damara," Jarlaxle asked him, "our sister kingdom, after all, and no enemy to the throne of Artemis? You need not come to us so formally, and with threats. King Gareth is ever allowed free and welcomed passage through our lands—though if he intends to be accompanied by so large a contingent, who will tramp down our flora and fauna, I do fear that I might have to impose a toll."

"A toll?"

"For smoothing the bog after your passage, of course. Simple upkeep."

Riordan sat perfectly still for a long while, clearly not amused. "Will you grant the audience?"

"Of cour—" Jarlaxle started to answer, but Entreri grasped his shoulder and shifted in front.

"Tell King Gareth that we do not enjoy the spectacle of an army at our doorstep unannounced," Entreri called down to Riordan, and again loud enough for Gareth, and perhaps even some of those in the ranks of the main force, to hear. Keeping his tone polite, and his voice loud, he continued, "But even so, Gareth may enter my home. We have many tall towers here, as you can see. Please tell Gareth, from me, that he is most welcomed to dive headlong off of any of them."

Riordan sat a moment, as if digesting the words. He even glanced at one of the towers. "You are besieged!" he declared. "Know that war has come to your door!" He expertly turned his mount and galloped it back to his group, who were already turning for the main force.

"That wasn't the wisest thing you've ever done," Jarlaxle remarked to his friend.

"Isn't this what you wanted?" Entreri replied. "War with King Gareth?"

"Hardly."

Entreri's face screwed up with doubt. "You thought to parlay our good deeds to an independent kingdom for Jarlaxle?"

"For King Artemis," the dark elf corrected.

"You believe that Gareth would allow a drow to rule a kingdom within that which he now calls his own kingdom?" Entreri went on, disregarding the correction. "You are a bigger fool than I once thought you—and on that previous occasion, you had the excuse of the lure of Crenshinibon. What is your excuse now beyond abject stupidity?"

Jarlaxle eyed him for a long while, his thin drow lips curling into a smile. He half-turned and looked to the courtyard below, then lifted his hand and clenched his fist.

The drivers snapped into action, cracking their whips and setting the fodder into a frenzy. A great crank creaked, chain rattling in protest, and the massive portcullis that blocked Castle D'aerthe's main gate lifted.

"I was shown two roads," Jarlaxle explained to Entreri. "One would lead me to operate in the shadows, much as I have always done. To find my niche here in the Bloodstone Lands in comfort behind the powers that be—perhaps to serve the Citadel of Assassins, though in a sense far removed from that which Knellict envisioned. Perhaps I would then convince Kimmuriel that this land was worth his efforts, and he and I would lead Bregan D'aerthe to grab at absolute leadership in the underworld of the Bloodstone Lands, similar to what we achieved back in Calimport for a short while, and certainly as we have created in the darkness of Menzoberranzan for nearly two centuries." He ended with a laugh, as he finished with, "It would be worth the effort, perhaps, merely to see Knellict beg for his eternal soul."

Jarlaxle stopped and stood staring at his friend. Beneath them, the gates of the castle swung open and the three hundred goblins and kobolds, the unfortunate shock troops who had only death and pain behind them and a waiting army before them, flooded out onto the field in full charge.

"And the other road?" Entreri finally, and impatiently, prompted.

"The one we have walked," Jarlaxle explained. "Autonomy. The Kingdom of D'aerthe, presented to King Gareth and the other powers of the Bloodstone Lands, aboveboard and with all legitimacy. A sister and allied kingdom to Damara's north, living in harmony with Damara, and with Palishchuk."

"They would accept a kingdom of drow?" Entreri made no effort to keep the incredulity out of his voice, which elicited a smirk from Jarlaxle.

"It was worth a try, as I found the other option . . . boring. Would you disagree?"

"You wanted it, not I."

Jarlaxle looked at him as if wounded.

"You led our adventures here," Entreri said. "You put us in the service of a pair of dragon sisters, and tricked me to Vaasa, knowing well, all the while, the destination of this road we walk and the inevitable ending."

"I could not have known that such an opportunity as Urshula would present itself so readily," Jarlaxle argued, but he stopped short and threw up his hands in defeat. "As you will," he said. "In any event, our time here is at its end."

"Beware the ruse!" Friar Dugald and his clerics shouted out the length of the line, using magic to enhance their shouts.

Before the heavy priest, King Gareth and the others coordinated the response to the monstrous charge. Left and right, great longbows bent back and volleys of arrows flew at the goblins and kobolds, the shots spaced properly so that a falling, dying target would not intercept a second arrow.

Emelyn the Gray and his wizards held back as the monstrous ranks thinned under the rain of arrows. "Minor spells only!" the archmage instructed his forces. "Keep your power in reserve. They are trying to exhaust us!"

"And to lessen the burden on their foodstuffs, perhaps," Kane quietly added. He was between Gareth and Emelyn when he spoke, and both caught his meaning well. "They expect a siege, we can conclude, and believe that they can outlast us with winter fast approaching."

Before them, those monsters who had somehow managed to avoid the arrows came on fast, and were met by a barrage of minor spells. Missiles of wizardly energy—blue, green, and red—shot out and swerved of their own accord, it seemed, unerringly blasting into the targeted creatures. When a pair of ambitious goblins drew too near, Emelyn waved away his charges and stepped forward personally. He touched the tips of his thumbs together, fingers spread wide before him, and spoke a simple command.

The goblins, more confused and terrified than bloodthirsty, could not pull up in time, and burst into flame as a wave of fire erupted from the wizard's hands, fanning out before them.

"Archers fire a volley over the wall!" Gareth called, and the order echoed down the line. Indeed, with the monstrous ranks so depleted, there was no need for another, point-blank barrage.

Out rode Gareth with Celedon, Olwen and Riordan beside him, and, amazingly, the monk Kane sprinted before the charging horses and was the first to engage. He leaped and fell straight out, feet leading, as he neared a goblin and kobold duo, taking the smaller, doglike kobold with a snap kick to the face and slamming the five-foot goblin with a solid hit to the chest.

Both shot back as surely as if a horse had kicked them.

Kane landed on his back, but moved so quickly and fluidly that many onlookers blinked and shook their heads. For he was up again, in perfect balance, almost as soon as the trailing folds of his dirty robes touched the ground. He stomped on the downed kobold's neck for good measure, then leaped ahead and to the side, spinning as he landed beside a surprised goblin. The creature took an awkward swing with its mace, one that Kane easily pushed up into the air as he came around. Not breaking the momentum of his turn, the monk snapped his arm back to the right angle and followed through with a jarring elbow, catching the goblin right below the chin and fully crushing its windpipe.

"He does steal all the fun," Celedon remarked to Gareth.

Gareth began to reply that there were plenty of enemies to be found, but he didn't bother. The infantry came on hard, and Emelyn's wizards continued their devastation, and the paladin realized that he would have to be quick if he intended to stain his brilliant sword, Crusader the Holy Avenger, in that initial battle. A quick glance at his friend Kane told him to veer in a different direction if he hoped to find a target.

Gasping for breath from the perfectly aimed, driving elbow, the goblin fell away, and before it had even hit the ground, Kane had already engaged another, his hands working furiously in the air before him, like great sweeping fans.

And it was all a ruse, designed to get the goblin leaning forward, to get its weapon shifted out just a bit to the side. As soon as that happened, Kane sprang forward, high and turning a somersault as he went. He hooked his leading forearm under the goblin's chin then planted his shoulder against the goblin's back as he came around and over. The monk landed on his feet back-to-back with the dizzy goblin, and as he continued forward, he pulled his arm up and over the goblin, forcing its head back and up.

Hearing the snap of the creature's neck bone, Kane quickly released, let the limp thing fall dead to the ground, and charged on.

The battle, the slaughter, was over in minutes, with the charge stalled and crushed, the goblins and kobolds lying dead or dying, other than a few who knelt on the ground, their arms up in the air, pleading for their lives.

Across the field, the portcullis had already fallen back in place and the gates had swung closed.

"Beware the following wave!" Dugald and others cried out. "Beware the gargoyles!"

But there were none. Nothing. The castle sat before them, enormous and deathly quiet. Goblin statues set along the wall leered out, but merely as unmoving, unthreatening stone. No figures moved behind them.

Another volley of arrows went over that wall, then a second, but if they hit anything other than the interior walls or the empty ground, no confirming cries of alarm or agony indicated it.

"Hold fire!" Gareth called as he and the other warriors turned back to reform their previous ranks. The paladin king cast a disparaging glance at the castle of King Artemis the First as he rode, thinking that Kane's observation had been quite on the mark.

But knowing as well that he had neither the patience nor the supplies to support such a siege.

ROAD OF THE PATRIARCH

Entreri and Jarlaxle heard the arrows cracking on the front door of the main keep, and the assassin was glad that he had thought to close the repaired portal behind him as he had entered.

Inside the main room of the ground level, Kimmuriel and several other dark elves waited for the pair, and Entreri couldn't contain a sour expression at the sight of the hated creatures.

"They will not wait long," Kimmuriel told Jarlaxle in the drow tongue, and it bothered Entreri that he still understood that paradoxically lyrical language. How could creatures so vile sound so melodious? *"Gareth will show no patience with the winter winds blowing. As soon as they come to believe that our assault was not merely a diversion for a greater attack, expect that they will come on. They've dragged war engines across the miles, and they will not let the catapults remain silent."*

"We are well prepared, of course."

"We are the last," Kimmuriel replied. *"The gate is held fast in the lower chamber. It is time to choose, Jarlaxle."*

"Choose what?" Entreri asked his companion, using the common tongue of the surface world.

That didn't exclude the fluent Kimmuriel in the least. "Choose between flight and awakening the full power of the castle," he said in the same language, his inflection perfect. He seamlessly went back to the drow tongue as he added to Jarlaxle, *"Will you awaken Urshula?"*

Jarlaxle thought on that for a short while. Another volley of arrows streamed into the castle, some cracking against the keep's doors.

"We might fight a great battle here," Jarlaxle said. "With Urshula and the gargoyles, with the undead who will come to my call, we could inflict great misery on our enemy. And with Bregan D'aerthe's full power, there is no doubt that we would win the day."

"The gain would be temporary, and not worth the price," said Kimmuriel. "We have no reinforcements, yet Damara is a country of King Gareth's minions, who will not sit idly by. And Gareth likely has many treaties that would bring other nations against us in time."

Jarlaxle looked to Entreri. "What say you?"

"I say that I have traveled with an idiot," the assassin replied, and Jarlaxle merely laughed.

"Many dead dark elves have said the same," Kimmuriel warned, and Entreri shot him a threatening look.

But Jarlaxle's laughter defeated all of the tension. "It was a good attempt," he decided. "But now that we've seen the response, it is time to take our leave of King Gareth and his Bloodstone Lands."

He motioned for Kimmuriel and the others to lead the way into the tunnels, then waited for Entreri to walk up beside him before following. As they passed the mushroom throne, Jarlaxle tossed a rolled scroll, bound with two strings of gold, onto its seat.

Entreri turned as if to retrieve it, but Jarlaxle put a hand on his shoulder and guided him along.

They moved through the tunnels, to the room where Mari-abronne had fallen to the daemons, then farther down the winding way. Dust fell from the ceiling as the bombardment began above in full. Finally they entered the chamber of Urshula, the scars of the battle bringing that deadly encounter clearly back into Entreri's thoughts.

And reminding him that, in his darkest hour, Jarlaxle had abandoned him.

At the back of the huge chamber, beyond the sprawled, bony corpse of the dracolich, its head and neck blackened from the fire of Entreri's killing trap, an ornate portal, a glowing blue doorway, loomed. While the walls of the chamber could be seen all around its edges, within the frame of the jamb there was only blackness.

One after another, the dark elf soldiers of Bregan D'aerthe walked through and disappeared.

Soon there were only three left, and Kimmuriel nodded to Jarlaxle then stepped through.

"After you," Jarlaxle invited Entreri.

"Where?"

"Why, in there, of course."

"Not that where," Entreri growled. "Where does it lead?"

"Where does it look like?"

"A place I do not wish to go." As he spoke the words, the truth of them assaulted the human assassin. It was time to leave Gareth and the Bloodstone Lands, so Jarlaxle had said, and that was a sentiment Entreri shared. But to leave with Kimmuriel and the Bregan D'aerthe soldiers implied something entirely different than what he had in mind.

"But the choice has been made," said Jarlaxle.

"No. That is the Underdark."

"Of course."

"I will not return there."

"You act as if there's an option to be found."

"No," Entreri said again, staring at the portal as if it was the gateway to the Nine Hells. His memories of Menzoberranzan, of his subjugation to twenty thousand cruel drow, of his understanding that he was no more than *iblith,* offal, and that anything he might do, anyone he might kill, would be completely irrelevant in altering that recognition of his worth, flooded back to him at that terrible moment.

And he thought of Calihye, the first woman he had loved both emotionally and physically, the first woman with whom the bond had become complete. How could he desert her?

But what choice did he have?

He took a step toward the doorway, and paused as he saw its lines waver, as he saw that the magic was fast diminishing.

During that pause came a second wave of memory, of pain, of regret, of anger.

The doorway wavered again.

"No," said Entreri, and he put his hand on Jarlaxle's shoulder and guided his companion. "Go quickly. The magic is fading."

"Be not a fool," Jarlaxle warned.

Entreri sighed and seemed to deflate before the obvious indictment. He looked at Jarlaxle and nodded—just enough to get the drow to relax his guard.

In the blink of an eye, Entreri had the red blade of his sword up high, held in both hands over his front shoulder. He gave a growl and went into a sudden spin, bringing the blade around at waist height, an even slice that would have cut Jarlaxle in half.

The drow had no way to defend.

He offered a sneer as he fell away the only way he could, tumbling more than running into the gate. Jarlaxle winked away just ahead of the cutting blade.

Entreri stood there staring at the shimmering extraplanar opening for a few moments longer, but even had its magic not then dissipated, there was no way Artemis Entreri was returning to the Underdark, to Menzoberranzan.

Not even to save his life.

CHAPTER

14

As the castle fell quiet, the horns on the field began to blare and a great cheer swept through the line. "King Gareth!" the enthusiastic soldiers chanted, and nowhere was that cry more energetic and grateful than among the contingent from Palishchuk.

As heartwarming as it was, though, Gareth Dragonsbane was not amused. They had not lost a single man, and hundreds of monsters lay dead on the field, almost all of them felled before combat had even been engaged.

"That was not an assault, it was mass suicide," Emelyn the Gray commented, and none of the friends could disagree.

"It accomplished nothing, but to wipe a bit of the stain of goblins and kobolds from the world," Riordan said.

"And to strengthen our resolve and cohesion," Friar Dugald added. "A free moment of practice before a joust? Are our enemies so inept?"

"Where is the second assault?" Gareth asked, as much to himself as to the others. "They should have struck hard at the moment of our greatest diversion."

"Which was never so great at all, now was it?" asked Emelyn. "I expect that Kane was correct in his assessment—they were clearing out fodder to preserve their supplies."

Gareth looked at his wise friend and shook his head.

They waited impatiently as the moments slipped past, and the castle only seemed more inert, more dead. Nothing stirred behind the high walls. Not a pennant flew, not a door banged open or closed.

"We know that Artemis Entreri and Jarlaxle are in there," Celedon Kierney remarked after a long while had passed. "What other forces have they at their disposal? Where are the gargoyles that so threatened Palishchuk when first the castle awakened? Gargoyles that regenerate themselves quickly, so it was reported. An inexhaustible supply."

"Perhaps it was all merely a bluff," Friar Dugald offered. "Perhaps the castle could not be reanimated."

"Wingham, Arrayan, and Olgerkhan saw the gargoyles fluttering about the walls just days ago," Celedon replied. "Tazmikella and Ilnezhara clearly warned us that Jarlaxle has Urshula the Black, a mighty dracolich, handy at his summons. Is the conniving drow trying to draw us in now, where his magical minions will prove more deadly?"

"We cannot know," King Gareth admitted.

"We can," said Kane, and all eyes turned his way. The monk squared himself to Gareth and offered a slow and reverential bow. "We have been in situations like this many times before, my old friend," he said. "Perhaps this will be a matter for our army, perhaps not. Let us forget who we are for a moment and remember who we once were."

"You cannot expose the king," Friar Dugald warned.

Beside him, Olwen Forest-friend snorted in derision, though whether at Kane or Dugald, the others could not yet discern.

"If Jarlaxle is as wise as we fear, then our caution is his ally," said Kane. "To play the games of intrigue with a drow is to invite disaster." He turned to face the castle, compelling them all to look that way with his set and stern expression.

"We have been in this situation before," Kane said again. "We knew how to defeat it, once. And so we shall again unless we have become timid and old."

Friar Dugald began to argue, but a smile widened on King Gareth's face, a smile from a different time, a decade and more past, when the weight of all the Bloodstone Lands was not sitting squarely on his strong shoulders. A smile of adventure and danger that wiped away the typical frown of politics.

"Kane," he said, and the sly edge in his voice had half his friends grinning and the other half holding their breath, "do you think you could get over that wall without being seen?"

"I know my place," the monk replied.

"As do I," Celedon quickly added, but Gareth cut him short with an upraised hand.

"Not yet," the king said. He nodded to Kane and the monk closed his eyes in a moment of meditation. He opened them and gently swiveled his head, taking in the whole scene before him, absorbing all of the angles and calculating the lines of sight from any hidden sentries on the castle walls. He dropped his face into his hands and took a long and steady breath, and when he exhaled, he seemed to shrink, as if his entire body had become somehow smaller and less substantial.

He held up one hand, revealing a small jewel that glowed with an inner, magical fire, one that could flash to light at the wielder's desire. It was their old signal flare, a clear indication of Kane's intent and instructions, and the monk went off in a trot.

The friends watched him, but whenever any of them turned his gaze aside, even for a moment, he could not then relocate the elusive figure.

Sooner than anyone could have expected, even those six men who had spent years beside the Grandmaster, Kane signaled back to them with the lighted jewel from the base of the castle wall.

Kane moved like a spider, hands sweeping up to find holds, legs turning at all angles to propel him upward, even sometimes reaching above his shoulder, his toes hooking into the tiniest jags in the wall. In a matter of a few heartbeats, the monk went over the wall and disappeared from view.

"He makes you feel silly for using your climbing tools, doesn't he?" Emelyn the Gray said to Celedon, and the man just laughed.

"As Kane would make Emelyn feel rather silly and more than a little inept as he avoided all of your magical lightning bolts and fireballs and sprays of all colors of the prism," Riordan was quick to leap to Celedon's defense.

"That strange one mocks us all," Dugald agreed. "But he's too tight to down a belt of brandy, and too absorbed to bed a woman. You have to wonder when it's simply not worth the concentration anymore!"

That brought laughter from all the friends, and all those nearby.

Except from Olwen. The ranger stared at the spot where Kane had disappeared, unblinking, his hands tight on his war axe, his beard wet from chewing his lips.

Two flashes from the monk's jewel, atop the wall, signaled that the way was clear.

"Emelyn and Celedon," Gareth instructed, for that was the usual course this group would take, with the wizard magically depositing the stealthy Celedon to join up with Kane. "A quick perusal and raise the portcullis—"

"I'm going," Olwen interrupted, and stepped before Celedon as the rogue made his way toward the waiting Emelyn. "You take me," the ranger instructed Emelyn.

"It has always been my place," Celedon replied.

"I'm going this time," Olwen said, and there was no compromise to be found in his steady, baritone voice. He looked past Celedon to Gareth. "You grant me this," he said. "For all the years I followed you, for all the fights we've shared, you owe me this much."

The proclamation didn't seem to please any of the friends, and Friar Dugald in particular put on a sour expression, even shook his head.

But Gareth couldn't ignore the stare of his old friend. Olwen was asking Gareth to trust him, and what sort of friend might Gareth be if he would not?

"Take Olwen," Gareth said to Emelyn. "But again, Olwen, your duty is to quickly ensure that the immediate area about the court-yard is secure then raise that portcullis and open those gates. We will all be together when we face Artemis Entreri and Jarlaxle, and whatever minions they have hidden inside their castle."

Olwen grunted—as much of a confirmation as Gareth would get—and moved to Emelyn, who, after a concerned look Gareth's way, launched into his spellcasting. Olwen grabbed onto the wizard's shoulder and a moment later, with a flash of purple light, the pair disappeared, stepping through a dimensional doorway to the spot on the wall where Master Kane waited.

In the tunnels of the upper Underdark, far below the construct Jarlaxle had named Castle D'aerthe, the soldiers of Bregan D'aerthe set their camp, along with those fortunate slaves who had not been forced onto the field to face the might of King Gareth. Off to one side of the main group, in a short, dead-end corridor, Kimmuriel and a pair of wizards had already enacted a scrying pool, and by the time Jarlaxle caught up to them, they looked in on various parts of the castle.

Jarlaxle smiled and nodded as the image of Entreri moved through the dark waters of the pool. The assassin had traveled up from the dracolich's lair, back into the upper tunnels, near where he had battled Canthan the wizard.

"He tried to kill you," Kimmuriel said. "We cannot go back immediately, but if he somehow escapes this time, I promise you that Artemis Entreri will fall to a drow blade, or to drow magic."

Jarlaxle was shaking his head throughout the speech. "If he had wanted to kill me, he would have used his wicked little dagger and not his cumbersome sword. He was making a statement—perhaps even one of complete rejection—but I assure you, my old friend, that if Artemis Entreri had truly tried to slay me before the portal, he would now lie dead on the floor."

Kimmuriel cast a doubting, even disappointed look at his associate, but let it go. A wave of his hand over the pool brought a different, brighter image into focus, and the four dark elf onlookers watched the movements of three men.

"It is a moot point anyway," the psionicist said. "I warned you of these enemies."

"Kane," Jarlaxle said. "He is a monk of great renown." One of the drow wizards cast him a confused look. "He fights in the manner of the kuo-toa," Jarlaxle explained. "His weapon is his body, and a formidable weapon it is."

"The second one is the most dangerous," Kimmuriel said, speaking of Emelyn the Gray. "Even by the standards of Menzoberranzan, his magic would be considered powerful."

"As great as Archmage Gromph?" one of the drow wizards asked.

"Do not be a fool," said Kimmuriel. "He is just a human."

Jarlaxle hardly heard it, for his gaze had settled on the third of the group, a man he did not know. While Kane and Emelyn appeared to be searching about cautiously, the other was far more agitated. He held his large axe in both hands before him, and it was quite obvious to Jarlaxle that he desperately wanted to plant it somewhere fleshy. And while Kane and Emelyn kept looking toward, and moving in the direction of, the front gates, the third man's attention had been fully grabbed by the central keep across the courtyard.

Kimmuriel waved his black hand over the pool again, and the image shifted back to Entreri. He was in a chamber Jarlaxle did not recognize, with his back to the wall just beside an upward-sloping tunnel. He had not yet drawn his weapons, but he seemed uneasy, his dark eyes darting about the torchlit tunnels, his hands resting comfortably close to his weapon hilts.

He gave a sudden laugh and shook his head.

"He knows we are watching him," one of the wizards surmised.

"Perhaps he thinks we will come to his aid," remarked the other.

"Not that one," said Jarlaxle. "He saw his choices clearly, and accepted the consequences of his decision." He looked at Kimmuriel. "I told you Entreri was a man of integrity."

"You confuse integrity with idiocy," the psionicist replied. "Integrity is the course of protecting one's own needs for survival, first and foremost. It is the ultimate goal of all wise people."

Jarlaxle nodded, not in agreement, but in the predictability of the response. For that was the way of the drow, of course, where the personal trumped the communal, where selfishness was a virtue and generosity a weakness to be exploited. "Some would consider simple survival the penultimate goal, not the ultimate."

"Those who would are all dead, or soon to be," Kimmuriel replied without hesitation, and Jarlaxle merely continued to nod.

"We cannot get back to help him without great cost," Kimmuriel added, and from his tone alone, Jarlaxle understood that return was not an option in Kimmuriel's mind. The psionicist was not willing to bring Bregan D'aerthe back into the fray, clearly, and from his inflection—and perhaps he had added a telepathic addendum to his statement; Jarlaxle could never be certain with that one!—it was clear to Jarlaxle that if he tried to use the opportunity to assume the mantle of leadership over Bregan D'aerthe once more, and order a return to Entreri's defense, he would be in for a fight.

But Jarlaxle had no such intention. He accepted fate's turn, even if he was not pleased by it.

The courtyard remained visible in the scrying pool, but the three figures had moved out of view. Then movement at the side of the pool revealed one, the anxious man with the axe, as he briefly showed himself. He moved fast, from cover to cover, and given the angle in which he moved out of view again, it was clear that he was making his way fast for the door of the keep.

"Farewell, my friend," Jarlaxle said, and he reached forward and tapped his hand on the still water of the pool. Ripples distorted the image before it blacked out entirely.

"You will return to Menzoberranzan with us?" Kimmuriel asked.

Jarlaxle looked at his former lieutenant and gave a resigned sigh.

◆━━━◆

No one in all the Bloodstone Lands was better able to discern movements and patterns better than Olwen Forest-friend. The ranger could track a bird flying over stone, so it was said, and no one who had ever seen Olwen's deductive powers at work ever really argued the point.

"They've got a gate," Olwen said to Kane and Emelyn when they came down from the wall into the main open courtyard of the castle. The tracks of the goblin and kobold army were clear enough to all three, the ground torn under their sudden, confused—and forced, Olwen assured his friends—charge.

The ranger nodded back toward the main keep of the place, a squat, solid building set in the center of the wall that separated the upper and lower baileys. "Or they've found tunnels below the keep where the monsters made their home," he said.

"No tracks coming in?" Emelyn asked.

"The goblins and kobolds came out that door," Olwen assured the others, pointing at the keep. "But they never went in it. And three hundred of them would have pressed the castle to breaking."

"There are many tunnels underneath it," replied Emelyn, who had been through the place before.

"Finite?" Olwen asked.

"Yes."

"You're certain?"

"I used a Gem of Seeing, silly deer hunter," the wizard huffed. "Do you think I would allow something as miniscule as a secret door to evade my inspection?"

"Then they have a gate," Olwen reasoned.

"Two-way, apparently," said Kane.

The ranger looked around at the emptiness of the place, and paused a moment to consider the silence, then nodded.

"Well, let us throw the place open wide, and inspect it top to bottom," said Emelyn. "King Artemis and his dark-skinned, fiendish friend will not so easily evade us."

Emelyn and Kane turned to the gates and portcullis, and to the room open along the base of the right-hand guard tower, where a great crank could be seen. But Olwen kept his gaze focused on the keep, and while his friends moved toward the front of the castle, he went deeper in.

He could move with the stealth of a seasoned city thief, and his abilities to find shelter in the shadows were greatly enhanced by his cloak and boots, both woven by elf hands and elven magic. He disappeared so completely into the background scenery that any onlookers would think he had simply vanished, and his steps fell without a whisper of noise. In fact, it wasn't until they noticed the keep's door ajar that Kane and Emelyn—who stood near the crank, trying to figure out how to reattach the broken chain—even realized that Olwen had moved so far from them.

"His grief moves him to recklessness," Kane remarked, and started that way.

Emelyn caught the monk by the shoulder. "Olwen blazes his own trails, and always has," he reminded. "He prefers the company of Olwen alone. No doubt his training of Mariabronne incited similar feelings in that one."

"Which got Mariabronne killed, by all reports," said Kane.

Emelyn nodded. "And Olwen likely realizes that."

"Guilt and grief are not a healthy combination," the monk replied. He glanced back behind them. "Fix the chain and bring our friends," he instructed, and he started off after Olwen.

The furniture and half-folded tapestries in the audience chamber didn't slow Olwen. He moved right to the multiple corridor openings on the far side of the room, all of them bending down and around. He crouched low and moved across them, finally discerning the one that had seen the most, and probably most recent, traffic.

Axe in hand, Olwen jogged along. He came through a series of rooms, slowly and deliberately, and the repetition did nothing to take him off his guard, to bring any carelessness to his step. Nor did the multitude of side passages distress him, for though there were few tracks to follow, he suspected that they were all connected. If he misstepped, he could easily regain the pursuit in the next room, or the one beyond that. Silent and smooth went the ranger, down another corridor that ended at an open portal, spilling into a candlelit room beyond. As he neared the doorway, along the right-hand wall, the ranger noted the fast cut of the tracks to the right, just inside the door.

Olwen crept up. Barely a foot from the opening, he held his breath and leaned out, just enough to see the tip of an elbow.

He looked back at the floor—one set of tracks.

With grace and speed that mocked his large form, Olwen leaped forward and spun, bringing his two-handed axe across for a strike that the surprised sneak couldn't begin to block. Satisfaction surged through the ranger as his perfectly-balanced, enchanted blade swiped cleanly through the air with no defense coming. It drove hard into the sneak's chest; there was no way for the fool to defend!

Off to the side of the portal where Olwen had abruptly and aggressively entered, in the shadows of another corridor, Artemis Entreri watched with little amusement as the ranger's weapon blew apart the chest of the mummy Entreri had propped next to the opening.

The weapon went right through, as Entreri had planned, to slice the securing rope set behind the perserved corpse, before finally ringing off the stone.

Across from the mummy, on the other side of the intruder, a glaive, released by the severing of the rope, swung down.

Entreri figured he had a kill, and that there was no turning back because of it.

But the burly intruder surprised him, for as soon as the ring of stone sounded, almost as soon as he had cut through the rope, the man was moving, and fast, diving into a sidelong roll. He tumbled deeper into the room, just ahead of the swinging glaive, and came back to his feet with such balance and grace that he was up and crouched before Entreri had even fully exited the side corridor.

And even though Entreri moved with unmatched silence, Olwen apparently heard him, or sensed him, for he leaped about, axe swiping across, and it was all Entreri could do to flip Charon's Claw up and over to avoid getting it torn from his hand.

Olwen cut his swing short, re-angling the axe with uncanny strength and coordination, then stabbing straight out with it, its pointed crown jabbing for the assassin's throat.

Entreri let his legs buckle at the knees, falling back as Olwen came on. He finally got Charon's Claw out before him, forcing the ranger to halt, but by that point he was so overbalanced that he couldn't hope to hold his ground. He just twisted and let himself fall instead, his dagger hand planting against the ground.

Olwen's roar signaled another charge, but Entreri was already moving, using those planted knuckles as a pivot and throwing himself out to the left over his secured hand, twisting and tucking his shoulder to turn a sidelong roll into a head-over somersault. He was up and turning before Olwen could close, coming around much as the ranger had done in dodging the glaive trap, with Charon's Claw humming through the air before him as he spun.

"Oh, but you're a clever killer, aren't you?" Olwen asked.

"Isn't that the difference between the killer and the deceased?"

"And Mariabronne wasn't so clever?"

"Mariabronne?" Entreri echoed, caught by surprise.

"Don't you feed your lies to my ears," Olwen said. "You saw the threat of the man—the honest man."

He finished with a sudden leap forward, his axe slicing the air in a downward diagonal chop, right to left. Olwen let go with his top hand, his right hand, as the axe swung down, and he didn't slow its momentum at all, turning his left arm over to bring it sailing back up, catching it again in his right with a reversed grip, then executing a cross-handed chop the other way.

Entreri couldn't begin to parry that powerful strike, so he simply backed out of reach. He planted his back foot securely as the axe came past, thinking to dart in behind it. As Olwen let go with his left hand, the axe swinging out to the right, his right hand gripping it at mid-handle, Entreri saw his opening. With the shortened grip, Olwen couldn't hope to stop him.

Artemis Entreri got his first taste of the true powers of the Bloodstone Lands then, the powers of the friends of King Gareth.

Olwen sent his right arm to full extension to the right, and loosened his grip on the axe so that it slid out to full extension. The ranger's freed left hand grabbed up a hand axe set in his belt, just behind his left hip, and as Entreri came on, a flick of Olwen's wrist sent the smaller weapon spinning out.

Entreri ducked and threw Charon's Claw up desperately, just nicking the spinning hand axe, defeating its deadly spin if not entirely its angle. He still got clipped, across the side of his head, but at least the weapon hadn't planted in his face!

Worse for Entreri, though, was Olwen's mighty one-handed chop, his powerful axe soaring back across with frightening speed and strength.

The only defense for Entreri was to go under that blow, turning as he went to absorb the impact.

For any other fighter, it would have been no more than a desperate and defensive turn, but Entreri improvised, flipping his weapons as he went. His left arm caught Charon's Claw, and his right hand deftly snagged and redirected his jeweled dagger. Even as he slowed the axe, Entreri was into the counter, stabbing ahead for Olwen's ample belly.

But Olwen's free hand came across to slap hard against Entreri's leading forearm, forcing the thrusting dagger to the side as the ranger turned away from the strike. With both his weapons to Olwen's right, and with the ranger turning, balanced, behind his shoulder, Entreri had no choice but to press forward even more forcefully, diving into a headlong roll and again coming to his feet in a sudden defensive spin.

He picked off another soaring hand axe, barely registering the silvery flickers of the blade, and he could hardly believe that Olwen had managed to square himself, pull another weapon and throw it with such deadly precision and fluidity.

"Akin to catching the greased piglet, I see," Olwen taunted.

"Which rarely gets caught, and oft makes a fool of the pursuers."

Olwen smiled confidently as he walked to the side, his battle-axe swinging easily at his right side, and retrieved the first hand axe he had thrown. "Oh, it takes a while to catch it," he said. "But the greater truth is that the piglet never wins."

"Those who rely on certainties are certain to be disappointed."

Olwen gave a belly laugh, and waved his hands at Entreri in an invitation. "Come along then, murdering dog, King Artemis the Stupid. Disappoint me."

Entreri stared at the man for a short while, watched him drop into a balanced defensive crouch, setting his axes, battle- and hand-, in fine position and with a comfort that showed he was not unused to two-handed fighting. The ranger apparently believed that Entreri had killed Mariabronne, a crime for which he was innocent.

He thought to protest that very point. He thought, fleetingly, of calming the fine warrior with—uncharacteristically—the truth.

But to what end? Entreri had to wonder. Jarlaxle had proclaimed him as King Artemis the First, a usurper of lands Gareth claimed as his own. That crime carried the same sentence the man was trying to exact, no doubt.

So what was the point?

Entreri glanced at his own weapon, the red blade of Charon's Claw, the glimmering jewels of a dagger that had gotten him through a thousand battles on the streets of Calimport and beyond.

"Oh, come on, then," his opponent teased. "I'm expecting more out of a king."

With a resigned shrug, an admission yet again that it was all just a silly and insanely random game, an admission and acceptance that, though he was for once being misjudged, there had been more than a few occasions when Olwen's verdict would have been quite fair, Artemis Entreri advanced.

The sounds of battle echoed up the corridors to the foyer, where Master Kane stood before the perplexing array of tunnel openings. Because of the design of the place, with all the tunnels curving the same way, there was no way for the monk to accurately discern which opening would lead him to the fight. Even the battle sounds clattered out of all the openings uniformly, as if they were joined by cross channels.

"You should have marked it, Olwen," he mumbled, shaking his head.

Kane tried to gauge the angle of the curve and the distance of the battle sounds. He moved to the second opening from the right. He paused for a moment, until he realized that his hesitation wouldn't grant him any more insight or any better guess. He reached into a pouch, produced a candle, and dropped it on the floor, marking the opening.

Down he ran, silently and swiftly.

Entreri thrust with his sword and Olwen's hand axe descended quickly to deflect it. The assassin retracted the blade, feinted with his dagger, and thrust again with the longer weapon. Olwen had to twist aside and bring his larger axe across from his right.

And again, Entreri retracted fast and shifted as if to bring his left foot forward and thrust with the dagger, which was again in his left hand. The ranger stopped in his twist and tried to re-align himself to the right, but Entreri came on with another thrust of Charon's Claw.

He thought the fight at its end—against a lesser opponent, it surely would have been—but then the assassin realized that Olwen had anticipated that very move, and that the ranger's twist back to the right had been no more than a feint of his own, one designed to line him up for a throw.

The hand axe spun at Entreri, and only the assassin's great agility allowed him to snap his jeweled dagger up fast enough to tip it up high as he ducked. Entreri kept his feet moving as he did, reshuffling fast so that as he went down low under the spinning missile, he also was able to dart forward, once again leading with Charon's Claw.

Olwen blocked it, but Entreri stepped right behind that parry—or so he thought—and thrust with the dagger.

For Olwen had to have parried with his larger axe, the assassin had believed, and so confusion enveloped him as his dagger thrust came up short, as Olwen, more squared to him than he had thought possible, managed to slide back a stride.

As it untangled, Entreri noted that the man had pulled a second hand axe, and that it, and not the larger weapon, had defeated his low thrust.

And he was too far forward and too low, his blades hitting nothing but air, and with Olwen recoiled, his large axe up high and back. Forward it came in a sudden and devastating rush.

Entreri fell flat to the floor, wincing as the air cracked above him. He planted his hands and shoved up with all his strength, and with a perfect tuck, tugging his legs back under him, he came up straight, his weapons circling in a cross down low before him and rising fast and precisely. The lifting Charon's Claw caught Olwen's following chop with the hand axe, the red blade locking under the curved axe head, and Entreri drove the ranger's arm up and out. Entreri dropped his left arm lower, to belt height, and thrust forth the dagger, pushing the ranger back, and forcing the man to drop his larger axe low to block.

That thrust only set up the real move, though, as Entreri hopped up and to the right, gathering leverage. With the better angle, he rolled Charon's Claw right over Olwen's small axe and stabbed it down, twisting the ranger's arm.

Olwen surprised him, by dropping the axe and punching out, clipping Entreri's chin.

He staggered back a step, but recovered quickly—and a good thing he did, for on came Olwen, chopping wildly with his battle-axe. Down it rushed, and around, a sudden backhand followed by another lightning-fast strike. Metal rang against metal, clanging and screeching as the axe head ran the length of Entreri's blades in rapid succession. And in the midst of that barrage, Olwen produced yet another hand axe and added to the fury, both hands chopping.

Entreri fought furiously to keep up, deflecting and parrying. For many moments, he found no opportunities to offer any sort of a counter, no openings for any strikes at all. It was all instinct, all a blur of movement—sword, dagger, and axes whipping to and fro.

And if Olwen was growing at all weary, he certainly didn't show it.

As he exited the tunnel where he had entered, Kane turned the candle to the side, so that it was parallel to the tunnel opening, a sign for Emelyn or anyone else who came in that he had explored the passage and was no longer within. He placed a second candle on the ground at the entrance to the next corridor in line, its wick pointing into the descending darkness, clearly marking his trail for his friennd, who knew how to read his signals.

He set off more speedily, both because he understood the general layout of the tunnel, given the other, and because he was certain that it was the one that would take him to Olwen and the fight.

And judging from the frenetic pace of the ringing metal, the tempo of that battle had increased greatly.

He knew the instant his red-bladed sword cut nothing but air that he had missed the parry, but without a split second's thought about it, without the hesitation of fear or dismay, Entreri followed with a perfect evasive maneuver, turning his hips toward the left, opposite the incoming axe strike, and thrusting his waist back.

He got clipped—there was no avoiding it—on his right, leading hip, Olwen's fine battle-axe tearing through the assassin's leather padding, through his flesh, and painfully cracking against his bone.

A wince was all Entreri allowed himself, for Olwen came on, sensing the kill.

Entreri cut a wild swing, from far out to his right and across with his mighty sword. Olwen, predictably, put his axe in line to easily defeat it. But the desperation on Entreri's face, and echoed by his seemingly off-balance swing, only heightened the feint, and the assassin dropped his swing short and used the momentum, instead of as a base to strike at Olwen, to spin himself to the side.

He sprinted off, limping indeed from his wound, but refusing to give in to the waves of burning pain emanating from his torn hip.

"You've nowhere to run!" Olwen chided, and he came in fast pursuit as Entreri sprinted for the doorway, where the glaive hung, its pendulum swing played out.

Entreri shoved the glaive out to the left and rushed past—or seemed to, but he pulled up short, spun, and whipped Charon's Claw in a downward strike. He called upon the magic of the blade as he did, releasing a trailing opaque wall of black ash that hung in the air.

Even as he finished the swing, the assassin simply let go of the sword and charged out to his left, opposite the glaive. His footsteps covered by the clanging of Charon's Claw on the stone floor, Entreri rolled around the wall, judging, rightly, that the visual display of glaive and ash would confound Olwen, albeit briefly. Indeed, the ranger sent his left arm out wide to interrupt the recoil of the glaive, and he pulled up short, astonishment on his face, to see the ash wall before him.

But he couldn't stop completely, and certainly didn't want to become entangled with the cumbersome glaive anyway, so he roared and rushed forward, bursting through the ash veil and into the tunnel.

And he froze, for no enemy stood before him.

A fine and sharp dagger came about to rest on Olwen's throat. A free hand tugged at his thick shock of black hair, yanking his head back, opening his throat fully for an easy kill.

"If I were you, I'd keep my arms out wide and drop my weapons to the floor," Entreri whispered in Olwen's ear.

When the ranger hesitated, Entreri tugged his hair again and pressed a bit more with his jeweled dagger, drawing a line of blood, and when Olwen still hesitated, Entreri showed him the truth of his doom, his utter obliteration, by calling upon the vampiric powers of the dagger to steal a bit of Olwen's soul.

The battle-axe hit the floor, followed by the hand axe.

"You multiply your crimes," came a calm voice from behind.

Entreri tugged Olwen around and pressed him through the ash

and past the glaive, back into the room, to face Kane, who stood at the other open exit. The monk appeared quite relaxed, fully at peace with his arms hanging at his sides, his hands empty.

"The only crime I committed was to dare step out of Gareth's gutter," the assassin retorted.

"If that is true, then why are we in battle?"

"I defend myself."

"And your kingdom?"

Entreri narrowed his eyes at that and did not respond.

"You hold your blade at the throat of a goodly man, a hero throughout the Bloodstone Lands," Kane remarked.

"Who tried to kill me, and would have gladly cut me in half had I allowed it."

Kane shrugged as if it didn't really matter. "A misunderstanding. Be reasonable now. Allow your actions to speak clearly for you when you face the justice of King Gareth, as you surely must."

"Or I walk away . . ." Entreri started to say, but he paused as a second figure came into view, ambling down the corridor to stand beside Kane. Emelyn the Gray huffed and puffed and snorted all sorts of halting and sputtering protests at the unseemly sight before him.

"Or I walk away with this man," Entreri reiterated. "Without obstruction, and release him when I am free of the misjudgments of Gareth Dragonsbane and his agitated followers."

The wizard sputtered again and started forward, only to be intercepted by an outstretched arm from Kane. That only slightly deterred Emelyn, though, for he began waving his arms.

"I will reduce you to ash!" the wizard declared.

Entreri gave a crooked grin and willed his dagger to drink, just a bit.

"Stop!" Olwen bellowed, his eyes wide with terror, and indeed, that gave Emelyn and Kane pause. Olwen had faced death many times, of course, had faced a demon lord beside them, but never had they seen their friend so unhinged.

"You will not survive this," Emelyn promised Entreri.

Beside him, Kane lowered his arms and closed his eyes. A blue gemstone on a ring he wore flickered briefly.

"Enough!" Entreri warned, and he ducked aside, pulling Olwen with him, as a spectral hand appeared in the air beside him. "My first pain is his last breath," the assassin promised.

Kane opened his eyes and brought his hands up in a gesture of apparent concession.

The spectral hand swept down, lightly brushing Entreri but feeling as nothing more than a slight breeze as it dissipated to nothingness.

Entreri breathed heavily, a bit confused. He didn't want to play his hand; killing Olwen, of course, left him with no bargaining power. He tugged the man's head for good measure, drawing a pained groan.

"Turn and lead me out," Entreri instructed.

Emelyn did begin to turn, but he paused halfway, his gaze—and subsequently, Entreri's—going to the monk, for Kane stood perfectly still, his eyes closed, his lips moving slightly, as if in incantation.

Entreri was about to issue a warning, but the monk opened his eyes and looked at him directly. "It is over," Kane declared.

The assassin's expression showed his doubt.

But then, a moment later, that expression showed Entreri's confusion, for he felt very strange. His muscles twitched, legs and arms. His eyes blinked rapidly, and he snorted, though he didn't will himself to snort.

"Ah, well done!" Emelyn said, still looking at Kane.

"Wh-wh-what?" Entreri managed to stutter.

"You have within you the intrusion of Kane," the monk explained. "I have attuned our separate energies."

The muscles on Entreri's forearm bulged, knotting and twisting painfully. He thought to slice his prisoner's throat then and there, but it was as if his mind could no longer communicate with his hand!

"Picture your life energy as a cord," Emelyn explained, "stretched taut from your head to your groin. Master Kane now holds that cord before him, and he can thrum it at will."

Entreri stared in disbelief at his forearm, and he winced, nauseous, as he began to recognize the subtle vibrations rolling throughout his body. He watched helplessly as Olwen pushed his dagger-arm out, then reached up and extracted himself from Entreri's grasp all together.

To the side, Kane calmly walked over to the fallen Charon's Claw. Entreri had a distant understanding of some satisfaction as the monk bent to retrieve it, thinking that the sentient, powerful, and malevolent weapon would melt Kane's soul, as it had so many who had foolishly taken it in hand.

Kane picked it up—his eyes widened in shock for just a moment. Then he shrugged, considered the weapon, and set it under the sash that tied his dirty robes.

Confusion mixed with outrage in the swirling thoughts of Artemis Entreri. He closed his eyes and growled, then forced himself against the intrusion. For a moment, a split second, he shook himself free, and he came forward awkwardly, as if to strike.

"Beware, King Artemis," Emelyn said, and there was indeed a hint of mocking in his voice, though Entreri was far too confused to catch the subtlety. "Master Kane can cut that cord. It is a terrible way to die."

As if on cue, and still long before Entreri had neared the pair, Kane spoke but a word, and wracking pains the likes of which Artemis Entreri had never imagined possible coursed through his body. Paralysis gripped him, as if his entire body twitched in the spasm of a single, complete muscle cramp.

He heard his dagger hit the floor.

He was hardly aware of the impact when he followed it down.

CHAPTER

KING OF VAASA

15

With Kane's strong arm supporting him, Entreri managed to get up again, but he had little strength and balance. There was no resistance within him as Olwen pulled his arms back behind him and bound them tightly with a fine elven cord.

"Where is Jarlaxle?" Emelyn asked him, and though the wizard moved very near as he spoke, his voice came to Entreri as if from far, far away. And the words didn't register in any cohesive manner.

"Where is Jarlaxle?" the wizard asked, more insistently, and he moved so close that his hawkish nose brushed against Entreri's.

"Gone," the assassin heard himself whisper, and he was surprised that he had answered. He felt as if his mind had disconnected from his body and was floating around the room like a bunch of puffy clouds, each self-contained with partial thoughts that might have once been connected to, but had come fully removed from, any of the thoughts flitting through the other clouds.

He saw Emelyn turn to Kane, who merely shrugged.

"I'll go check it," the distant voice of Olwen said.

"More carefully this time," said Emelyn.

The ranger snorted and walked past, directly in front of Entreri, and he paused just long enough to offer the beaten assassin a glare.

Kane took Entreri by the arm and led him off, with Emelyn coming close behind. As they entered the ascending corridor and wound their way up, the assassin's coordination, mental and physical, did not return, and on several occasions, the only thing that kept him standing was the support of Kane.

They found King Gareth, Friar Dugald, and many soldiers milling about the audience chamber. Gareth stood by one wall, hands on his hips and staring curiously at one of the tapestries, which had been unfastened to hang to its full length.

"Well, now," Emelyn muttered, walking by Entreri and stroking his beard.

"Ah, you have him," Dugald said, turning to see the trio. "Good."

"It is curious, is it not?" Gareth asked, turning to face his friends. "Can you explain?" he started to ask Entreri, but he paused and considered the man before turning a questioning stare at his two friends.

"Kane touched him in a special way," Emelyn said dryly.

Gareth slowly nodded. "Where is Olwen?" he asked, a sudden urgency coming into his tone.

"Confirming that the drow has departed."

"And he has," came the ranger's voice from the tunnel entrance. "Through a magical gate, I suspect. And if the tracks are any indication, and we all know that they always are, then Jarlaxle wasn't the only elf—probably drow—walking about the place. I'm thinking that our friend here, the King of Vaasa, will have some answering to do."

"He should start with this, then," said Emelyn, and both he and Gareth moved aside from the tapestry, revealing it fully to Entreri and his nearest captors. Behind the assassin, Olwen sputtered. Beside him, Kane offered no words, sounds, or expression.

As he gradually began to focus on the tapestry, Entreri became even more confused. The image seemed double, as if the tapestry was coming alive, its inhabitants stepping from the fabric into the chamber.

But then he realized, far in the recesses of his groggy mind at first, but gradually working its way into his general thoughts, that the people portrayed on the tapestry were the very same ones who stood beside him in the audience chamber. For the tapestry depicted the victory of King Gareth over Zhengyi the Witch-King, and with great and accurate detail.

"Well, King Artemis?" Gareth asked. "Why would you decorate your audience chamber with such depictions as these?

Entreri stared at him, dumbfounded.

Kane pushed him to the side, then, and eased him into one of the mushroom thrones.

"He is not ready to speak yet," Kane explained to Gareth. "The mystery will hold for a bit longer."

"As will this one," Gareth replied, and handed Kane a rolled scroll, the same one Kane had noted on the throne in his passing. He took it from Gareth and unrolled it, and again showed no emotion, though the cryptic words were surprising indeed.

Welcome Gareth, King of Damara.
Welcome Gareth, King of Vaasa.

King of Vaasa, you are most welcome.

"What trick is this?" asked Emelyn, reading over Kane's shoulder.

Outside the audience chamber, a great cheer went up for King Gareth, led by the elated soldiers of Palishchuk.

All looked to Gareth.

"The threat to their fair city is defeated," he said.

Friar Dugald gave a great belly laugh, and several of the others joined in.

"And the drow is nowhere to be found," Emelyn said to Entreri. "Are you the sacrifice, then?"

"A great waste of talent," said Olwen. "He is a fine fighter."

"But not so fleet of foot," Dugald said. "But if we are done here, then let us return to Bloodstone Village. It's a bit too cold up here."

"Bah, you've enough layers of Dugald to fend off the north wind," teased Riordan Parnell, coming in the keep's open door. "Our friends from Palishchuk wish a celebration, of course."

"They always wish a celebration," Dugald replied.

"I do like the place."

"Straightaway, as soon as we are sure the threat here is no more, we turn for home," said Gareth. "We'll leave a contingent to remain in Palishchuk throughout the winter if our half-orc friends so desire, in case the drow has any tricks left to play. But for us, it will be good and wise to be home."

"And him?" Kane asked, indicating Entreri.

"Bring him," Entreri heard Gareth say, and Entreri was disappointed at that, wishing that it would just end.

"Home to Bloodstone Village, where your friend will be executed," Kimmuriel Oblodra said as they watched the exchange in the scrying pool.

"Gareth will not kill him," Jarlaxle insisted.

"He will have no choice," said the psionicist. "You declared Entreri King of Vaasa. If Gareth allows that to stand, he is diminished in the eyes of his subjects—irreparably so. No king would be foolish enough to suffer that sort of challenge to stand. It is once removed from anarchy."

"You underestimate him. You view him through the prism of experience with the matron mothers of our homeland."

"You pray that I do, but your reason tells you otherwise," Kimmuriel replied. "Step away from your friendship with the human, Jarlaxle, for it clouds your common sense."

Jarlaxle shifted back as the wizards ended their quiet chanting and the pool fell silent, its image beginning to blur. Jarlaxle was a drow who usually spoke with certainty, and who backed up that certainty with a generous understanding of others. But he was also one who long ago learned to trust in Kimmuriel's judgment, for never did that one let hope or passion cloud simple logic.

"We cannot allow it," Jarlaxle remarked, speaking as much to himself as to Kimmuriel.

"We cannot prevent it," Kimmuriel replied, and Jarlaxle noted that the wizards to the sides raised their eyebrows at that. Were they expecting a confrontation, a battle for the leadership of Bregan D'aerthe?

"I will not put Bregan D'aerthe against King Gareth," Kimmuriel went on. "I have explained as much to you once already. Nothing that has happened has changed that stance, and certainly not for the sake of a pathetic human who, even if rescued, will be dead of natural causes anyway before the memory of this incident has faded from my consciousness."

Jarlaxle wondered at that last statement, in light of Entreri drawing a bit of the essence of shadow into his blood through the use of his vampiric dagger. He let that thought go for another day, though, and focused on the issue at hand. "I did not ask you to wage war with Gareth," he said. "If I had wanted such a thing, would I have abandoned the power of the castle? Would I not have called forth Urshula to strike hard into Gareth's ranks? Nay, my friend, we will not battle the King of Damara and his formidable army. But he is, by all accounts, a reasonable and wise human. We will barter for Entreri."

A brief flash of expression across Kimmuriel's stone face revealed his doubt. "You have nothing with which to barter."

"You did not see King Gareth's expression when he viewed my gift?"

"Confusion more than gratitude."

"Confusion is the first step to gratitude, if we're clever." Jarlaxle's sly grin brought looks of concern from all around, except from Kimmuriel, of course. "The field of battle is prepared. We need only another point of barter. Help me to attain it."

Kimmuriel stared at him hard, and doubtfully, but Jarlaxle knew that the intelligent drow would easily sort out the still-unspoken proposal.

"It will be entertaining," Jarlaxle promised.

"And worth the cost?" Kimmuriel asked. "Or the time?"

"Sometimes entertainment alone is enough."

"Indeed," replied the psionicist. "And was all of this—the arrival of the troops, the death of the slaves, the magically exhausting withdrawal—worth the trouble for you, a simple game for your amusement merely to run away when the predictable occurred and King Gareth arrived at his door?"

Jarlaxle grinned and shrugged as if it did not matter. He pulled out a curious gem, one shaped as a small dragon's skull, and with a flick of his hand, sent it spinning to Kimmuriel.

"Urshula," Jarlaxle explained. "A powerful ally to Bregan D'aerthe."

"The Jarlaxle I know would not relinquish such a prize."

"I loan it to you as an asset of Bregan D'aerthe. Besides, you will undoubtedly learn more of the dracolich than I can, aided as you will be by priests and wizards, and even illithids, no doubt."

"You offer payment for our assistance in your next endeavor?"

"Payment for that already rendered, and for that which you will still provide."

"When we find your barter for the pathetic human?"

"Of course."

"Again, Jarlaxle, why?"

"For the same reason I took in a refugee from House Oblodra, perhaps."

"To expand the powers of Bregan D'aerthe?" Kimmuriel asked. "Or to expand the experiences of Jarlaxle?"

Kimmuriel considered it for a moment and nodded, and with a laugh, Jarlaxle answered, "Yes."

CHAPTER

16

As he neared the audience chamber in his Bloodstone Village palace, King Gareth heard that the interrogation of Artemis Entreri had already begun. He glanced to his wife, who walked beside him, but Lady Christine stared ahead with that steely gaze Gareth knew so well. Clearly, she was not as conflicted about the prosecution of the would-be king as was he.

"And you claim to know nothing of the tapestries, or of the scroll we found on the fungus-fashioned throne?" he heard Celedon ask.

"Please, be reasonable," the man continued. "This could be exculpatory, to some extent."

"To make my death more pleasant?" Entreri replied, and Gareth winced at the level of venom in the man's voice.

He pushed into the audience chamber then, to see Entreri standing on the carpet before the raised dais that held the thrones. Friar Dugald and Riordan Parnell sat on the step, with Kane standing nearby. Celedon stood nearer to Entreri, pacing a respectfully wide circle around the assassin.

Many guards stood ready on either side of the carpet.

Dugald and Riordan stood up at the approach of the king and queen, and all the men bowed.

Gareth hardly noticed them. He locked stares with Entreri, and within the assassin's gaze he found the most hateful glare he had ever known, a measure of contempt that not even Zhengyi himself had approached. He continued to stare at the man as he assumed his throne.

"He has indicated that the tapestries were not of his doing," Friar Dugald explained to the king.

"And he professes no knowledge of the parchment," added Riordan.

"And he speaks truly?" asked Gareth.

"I have detected no lie," the priest replied.

"Why would I lie?" Entreri said. "That you might uncover it and justify your actions in your own twisted hearts?"

Celedon moved as if to strike the impertinent prisoner, but Gareth held him back with an upraised hand.

"You presume much of what we intend," the king said.

"I have seen far too many King Gareths in my lifetime . . ."

"Doubtful, that," Riordan remarked, but Entreri didn't even look at the man, his gaze locked firmly on the King of Damara.

". . . men who take what they pretend is rightfully theirs," Entreri continued as if Riordan had not spoken at all—and Gareth could see that, as far as the intriguing foreigner was concerned, Riordan had not.

"Take care your words," Lady Christine interjected then, and all eyes, Entreri's included, turned to her. "Gareth Dragonsbane is the rightful King of Damara."

"A claim every king would need make, no doubt."

"Kill the fool and be done with it," came a voice from the doorway, and Gareth looked past Entreri to see Olwen enter the room. The ranger paused and bowed, then came forward, taking a route that brought him within a step of the captured man. He whispered something to Entreri as he passed, and did so with a smirk.

That smug expression lasted about two steps further, until Entreri remarked, "If you are to be so emotionally wounded when you are bested in battle, then perhaps you would do well to hone your skills."

"Olwen, be at ease," Gareth warned as he watched the volatile ranger's eyes go wide.

Olwen spun anyway, and from the way Celedon stepped aside, Gareth thought the man might leap onto Entreri then and there.

But Entreri merely snickered at him.

"We are reasonable men, living in dangerous times," Gareth said to Entreri when Olwen finally stepped aside. "There is much to learn—"

"You doubt my husband's claim to the throne?" Lady Christine interrupted.

Gareth put a hand on her leg to calm her.

"Your god himself would argue with me, no doubt," said Entreri. "As would the chosen god of every king."

"His bloodline is—" Christine started to reply.

"Irrelevant!" Entreri shouted. "The claim of birthright is a method of control and not a surety of justice."

"You impertinent fool!" Christine shouted right back, and she stood tall and came forward a step. "By blood or by deed—you choose! By either standard, Gareth is the rightful king."

"And I have intruded upon his rightful domain?"

"Yes!"

"King of Damara or King of Vaasa?"

"Of both!" Christine insisted.

"Interesting bloodline you have there, Gareth—"

Celedon stepped over and slapped him. "*King* Gareth," the man corrected.

"Does your heritage extend to Palishchuk?" Entreri asked, and Gareth could not believe how fully the man ignored Celedon's rude intrusion. "You are King of Vaasa by blood?"

"By deed," Master Kane said, and he stepped in front of the sputtering Dugald as he did.

"Then strength of arm becomes right of claim," reasoned Entreri. "And so we are back to where we began. I have seen far too many King Gareths in my lifetime."

"Someone fetch me my sword," said the queen.

"Lady, please sit down," Gareth said. Then to Entreri, "You were the one who claimed dominion over Vaasa, King Artemis."

The roll of Entreri's eyes strengthened Gareth's belief that the drow, Jarlaxle, had been the true instigator of that claim.

"I claimed that which I conquered," Entreri replied. "It was I who defeated the dracolich, and so . . ." He turned to Christine and grinned. "Yes, Milady, by deed, I claim a throne that is rightfully mine." He turned back to Gareth and finished, "Is my claim upon the castle and the surrounding region any less valid than your own?"

"Well, you are here in chains, and he is still the king," Riordan said.

"Strength of arms, Master Fool. Strength of arms."

"Oh, would you just let me kill him and be done with it?" Olwen pleaded.

To Gareth, it was as if they weren't even in the room.

"You went to the castle under the banner of Bloodstone," Celedon reminded the prisoner.

"And with agents of the Citadel of Assassins," Entreri spat back.

"And a Commander of the Army of Bl—"

"Who brought along the agents of Timoshenko!" Entreri snapped back before Celedon could even finish the thought. "And who betrayed us within the castle, at an hour most dark." He turned and squared his shoulders to Gareth. "Your niece Ellery was killed by my blade," he declared, drawing a gasp from all around. "Inadvertently and after she attacked Jarlaxle without cause—without cause for her king, but with cause for her masters from the Citadel of Assassins."

"Those are grand claims," Olwen growled.

"And you were there?" Entreri shot right back.

"What of Mariabronne, then?" Olwen demanded. "Was he, too, in league with our enemies? Is that what you're claiming?"

"I claimed nothing in regards to him. He fell to creatures of shadow when he moved ahead of the rest of us."

"Yet we found him in the dracolich's chamber," said Riordan.

"We needed all the help we could garner."

"Are you claiming that he was resurrected, only to die again?" Riordan asked.

"Or animated," Friar Dugald added. "And you know of course that to animate the corpse of a goodly man is a crime against all that is good and right. A crime against the Broken God!"

Entreri stared at Dugald, narrowed his eyes, grinned, and spat on the floor. "Not my god," he explained.

Celedon rushed over and slugged him. He staggered, just a step, but refused to fall over.

"Gareth is king by blood and by deed!" Dugald shouted. "Anointed by Ilmater himself."

"As every drow matron claims to be blessed by Lolth!" the stubborn prisoner cried.

"Lord Ilmater strike you dead!" Lady Christine shouted.

"Fetch your sword and strike for him," Entreri shouted right back.

"Or get your sword and give me my own, and we will learn whose god is the stronger!"

Celedon moved as if to hit him again, but the man stopped fast, for Entreri finished his insult in a gurgle, as vibrations of wracking pain ran the course of his body, sending his muscles into cramps and convulsions.

"Master Kane!" King Gareth scolded.

"He will not speak such to the queen, on pain of death," Kane replied.

"Release him from your grasp," Gareth ordered.

Kane nodded and closed his eyes.

Entreri straightened and sucked in a deep breath. He stumbled and went down to one knee.

"Do give him a sword, then," Christine called out.

"Sit down and be still!" Gareth ordered. He from his chair and walked forward, right toward the stunned expressions of most everyone in the room—except for Entreri, who glanced up at him with that hateful intensity.

"Remove him to a cell on the first dungeon level," Gareth ordered. "Keep it lit and warm, and his food will be ample and sweet."

"But my king . . ." Olwen started to protest.

"And harm him not at all," Gareth went on without hesitation. "Now. Be gone."

Riordan and Celedon moved to flank Entreri, and began pulling him from the chamber. Olwen cast one surprised, angry look at Gareth, and rushed to follow.

"Go and ease his pain," Gareth said to Friar Dugald, who stood staring at him incredulously. When the friar didn't immediately move, he said, "Go! Go!" and waved his hand.

Dugald stared at Gareth over his shoulder for many steps as he exited the room.

"You suffer him at your peril," Christine scolded her husband.

"I had warned you not to engage him so."

"You would accept his insults?"

"I would hear him out."

"You are the king, Gareth Dragonsbane, king of Damara and king of Vaasa. Your patience is a virtue, I do not doubt, but it is misplaced here."

Gareth was too wise a husband to point out the irony of that statement. He didn't blink, though, and didn't nod his agreement in any way, and so with a huff, Lady Christine headed out the side door through which she and Gareth had entered.

"You cannot suffer him to live," Kane said to the king when they were alone. "To do so would invite challenges throughout your realm. Dimian Ree watches us carefully at this time, I am certain."

"Was he so wrong?" Gareth asked.

"Yes," the monk answered without the slightest pause.

But Gareth shook his head. Had Entreri and that strange drow creature done anything different than he? Truly?

You would think them wiser, Kimmuriel Oblodra signaled in the silent drow hand code, and the way he waggled his thumb at the end showed his great contempt for the humans.

They do not understand the world below, Jarlaxle's dexterous hands replied. *The Underdark is a distant thought to the surface dwellers.* As he signed the words, Jarlaxle considered them—the truth of them and the implications. He also wondered why he so often rushed to the defense of the surface dwellers. Knellict was an archmage, brilliant by the standards of any of the common races of Toril, a master of intricate and complicated arts. Yet he had chosen his hideout, no doubt looking east, west, north, and south, but never bothering to look down.

A mere forty feet below the most secretive and protected regions of the citadel's mountain retreat, ran a tunnel wide and deep, a conduit along the upper reaches of the vast network of tunnels and caverns known as the Underdark, a route for caravans.

An approach for enemies.

Do not forget our bargain, Kimmuriel signed to him.

The last time, Jarlaxle promised, and he tapped his belt pouch, which contained the magical item to which Kimmuriel had just referred.

Kimmuriel's return look showed that he didn't believe Jarlaxle for a minute, but then again, neither did Jarlaxle. The demand was akin to telling a shadow mastiff not to bark, or a matron mother not to torture. Controlling one's nature could only be taken so far.

Kimmuriel's expression reflected little beyond that initial doubt, of course, but in it, if there was anything, it was only resignation, even amusement. The psionicist turned to the line of wizards assembled at his side and nodded. The first rushed to Kimmuriel and pointed straight up. He quickly traced an outline, and as soon as Kimmuriel agreed, the wizard launched into spellcasting.

A few moments later, the drow completed his spell with a great flourish, and a square block of the stone ceiling twice a drow's height simply dematerialized, vanished to nothingness.

Without hesitation, for the spell had a finite duration, the second wizard rushed up beside the first, touched his insignia, levitated up into the magical chimney, and similarly cast. Before he had even finished, the third had begun levitating.

Twenty or more feet up from the corridor, the third wizard executed the same powerful spell.

With the next we will be into the complex, Kimmuriel's hands told the Bregan D'aerthe soldiers gathered nearby. *Fast and silent!*

The fourth wizard ascended, and with him went the first contingent, Bregan D'aerthe's finest forward assassins led by an experienced scout named Valas Hune. They were the infiltrators, the trailblazers, and they most often marked their paths with the blood of sentries.

They timed their rise perfectly, of course, and floated past the fourth wizard just as the stone dematerialized, so that without breaking their momentum in the least, the group floated through the last ten feet and into the lower complex of the Citadel of Assassins.

The first three wizards went up right behind them, and as soon as the scouts had gathered the lay of the region and had slipped off into the torchlit tunnels, the wizards cast again.

All through the lower reaches of Knellict's mountain hideaway, a mysterious fog began to rise. More a misty veil than an opaque wall, the wafting fog elicited curiosity, no doubt.

It also rendered the quiet footsteps of drow warriors completely silent.

It also dampened most evocative magic.

It also countered all of the most common magical wards.

More warriors floated through the breach and moved along with practiced skill. Jarlaxle tipped his great hat to enable its magical powers, and he and Kimmuriel came through, accompanied by an elite group of fighters. They swept up two of the wizards in their wake, the other two moving to their predetermined positions.

This was not strange ground to the dark elves. Kimmuriel's spying of the hideaway had been near complete, and at Jarlaxle's insistence, the maps he had drawn had been studied and fully memorized by every raider rising through the floor. Even the two guard contingents left in the Underdark corridor below knew the layout fully.

Bregan D'aerthe left little to chance.

To the head, Jarlaxle's fingers flashed, and his small, elite band slipped away.

Knellict was more angry than afraid. He didn't have time to be afraid.

Screams of alarm and pain chased him and his three guards down the misty hallway and into his private chambers. The guards slammed the door shut and moved to bolt it, but Knellict held them back.

"One lock only," he explained. "Let them try to get through once. The ashes of their leading intruders will warn others away." As he finished, he began casting, uttering the activation words for the many magically explosive glyphs and wards that protected his private abode.

"We should consider leaving," said one of his guards, a young and promising wizard.

"Not yet, but hold the spell on the tip of your tongue." He drew out a slender wand, metal-tipped black shot through with lines of dark blue.

An especially shrill scream rent the air. The sound of men running moved past the door, followed at once by the sound of a couple of small crossbows firing and of one man, at least, tumbling to the floor.

"Be ready now," Knellict said. "If they breach the door, the explosions will destroy them. Those in front, at least, but you must be quick to close it again and drop the locking bars into place."

His guards nodded, knowing well their duties.

They all focused on the door, but nothing happened and the sounds moved away.

Still, they all focused intently on the door.

So much so that when the wall to the next room in line, more than half a dozen feet of solid stone, simply vanished, none of them even noticed at first.

Jarlaxle's five warriors fell to one knee and fired the poison-tipped bolts from their hand crossbows. One of the wizards amplified the shots with a spell that turned each dart into two, so that each of Knellict's two guards was struck five times in rapid succession. For the wizard sentry, there came a missile of another sort: a flying green glob of goo, popping out from the end of a slender wand Jarlaxle held.

It hit the man, engulfed him, and drove him back hard into the wall where he stuck fast, fully engulfed, and he could move nothing beyond the fingers of one hand that was flattened out to the side, could not even draw in air through the gooey mask.

Knellict reacted with typical and practiced efficiency, turning his lightning wand to the side. The trigger phrase was "By Talos!" and so Knellict cried it out, or tried to.

His words hiccupped in his mind and in his larynx, and he said "B-by Thooo."

Nothing happened.

Knellict called to the wand again, and again, his brain blinked in mid-phrase. For as fast as Knellict was with his wand and his words, Kimmuriel Oblodra was faster with his thoughts.

The wizard plastered on the wall continued to helplessly waggle his fingers and feet. The two warriors slumped down to the ground, fast asleep under the spell of the powerful drow poison.

And Knellict could only sputter. He threw the wand down in outrage and launched into spellcasting, a quick dweomer that would get him far enough away to enact a proper teleportation spell and be gone from there.

A burst of psionic energy broke the chant.

The eight dark elves confidently strode into the room, four of the warriors taking up guard positions at either side of the main door and either side of the magically opened wall. The fifth warrior, on a nod from Jarlaxle, crossed the room and cut the goo from in front of the trapped wizard's nose, so that the man could breathe and watch in terror, and little else. One of the drow wizards began casting a series of detection spells, to better loot any hidden treasures.

Jarlaxle, Kimmuriel, and the other wizard calmly walked over to stand before Knellict.

"For all of your preparations, archmage, you simply do not have the understanding of the magic of the mind," Jarlaxle said.

Knellict stubbornly lifted one hand Jarlaxle's way, and with a determined sneer, spat out a quick spell.

Or tried to, but was again mentally flicked by Kimmuriel.

Knellict widened his eyes in outrage.

"I am trying to be reasonable here," Jarlaxle said.

Knellict trembled with rage. But within his boiling anger, he was still the archmage, still the seasoned and powerful leader of a great band of killers. He didn't betray the soldiers who were quietly coming to his aid from the other room.

But his enemies were drow. He didn't have to.

Even as the dark elf warriors flanking the open wall prepped their twin swords to intercede, Jarlaxle spun on his heel to face the soldiers.

They yelled, realizing that they were discovered. A priest and a wizard launched into spellcasting, three warriors howled and charged, and one lightly armored halfling slipped into the shadows.

Jarlaxle's hands worked in a blur, spinning circles over each other before him. And as each came around, the drow's magical bracers deposited into it a throwing knife, which was sent spinning away immediately.

The drow warriors at either side of the opening didn't dare move as the hail of missiles spun between them. A human warrior dropped his sword, his hands clutching a blade planted firmly in his throat, and he stumbled into the room and to the floor. A second fighter came in spinning—and took three daggers in rapid succession in his back, to match the three, including a mortal heart wound, that had taken him in the front.

He, too, fell.

The wizard tumbled away, a knife stuck into the back of his

opened mouth. The priest never even got his hands up as blades drove through both of his eyes successively.

"Damn you!" the remaining warrior managed to growl, forcing himself forward despite several blades protruding from various seams in his armor. Two more hit him, one two, and he fell backward.

Almost as an afterthought, Jarlaxle spun one to the side, and it wasn't until it hit something soft and not the hard wall or floor that Knellict and the others realized that the halfling wasn't quite as good at hiding as he apparently believed.

At least, not in the eyes of Jarlaxle, one of which was covered, as always, by an enchanted eye patch—a covering that enhanced rather than limited his vision.

"Now, are you ready to talk?" Jarlaxle asked.

It had all taken only a matter of a few heartbeats, and Knellict's entire rescue squad lay dead.

Not quite dead, for one at least, as the stubborn fighter regained his feet, growled again, and stepped forward. Without even looking that way, Jarlaxle flicked his wrist.

Right in the eye.

He collapsed in a heap, straight down, and was dead before he hit the floor.

The drow fighters stared at Jarlaxle, reminded, for the first time in a long time, of who he truly was.

"Such a waste," the calm Jarlaxle lamented, never taking his eyes off of Knellict. "And we have come in the spirit of mutually beneficial bargaining."

"You are murdering my soldiers," Knellict said through gritted teeth, but even that determined grimace didn't prevent another mental jolt from Kimmuriel.

"A few," Jarlaxle admitted. "Fewer if you would simply let us be done with this."

"Do you know who I am?" the imperious archmage declared, leaning forward.

But Jarlaxle, too, came forward, and suddenly, whether it was magic or simple inner might, the drow seemed the taller of the two. "I remember all too well your treatment," he said. "If I was not such a merciful soul, I would now hold your heart in my hand—before your eyes that you might see its last beats."

Knellict growled and started a spell—and got about a half a word out before a dagger tip prodded in at his throat, drawing a pinprick of blood. That made Knellict's eyes go wide.

"Your personal wards, your stoneskin, all of them, were long ago stripped from you, fool," said Jarlaxle. "I do not need my master of the mind's magic here to kill you. In fact, it would please me to do it personally."

Jarlaxle glanced at Kimmuriel and chuckled. Then suddenly, almost crazily, he retracted the blade and danced back from Knellict.

"But it does not need to be like this," Jarlaxle said. "I am a businessman, first and foremost. I want something and so I shall have it, but there is no reason that Knellict, too, cannot gain here."

"Am I to trust—"

"Have you a choice?" Jarlaxle interrupted. "Look around you. Or are you one of those wizards who is brilliant with his books but perfectly idiotic when it comes to understanding the simplest truism of the people around him?"

Knellict straightened his robes.

"Ah, yes, you are the second leader of a gang of assassins, so the latter cannot be true," said Jarlaxle. "Then, for your sake, Knellict, prove yourself now."

"You would seem to hold all of the bargaining power."

"Seem?"

Knellict narrowed his gaze.

Jarlaxle turned to one of his wizards, the one who still stood beside Kimmuriel while the other continued to ransack Knellict's desk. The drow leader looked around, then nodded toward the wizard trapped on the wall.

The wizard walked over and began to cast an elaborate and lengthy spell. Soon into it, Kimmuriel focused his psionic powers on the casting drow, heightening his concentration, strengthening his focus.

"What are you . . ." Knellict demanded, but his voice died away when all of the dark elves turned to eye him threateningly.

"I tell you this only once," Jarlaxle warned. "I need something that I can easily get from you. Or . . ." He turned and pointed at the terrified, flailing wizard on the wall. "I can take it from him. Trust me when I tell you that you want me to take it from him."

Knellict fell silent, and Jarlaxle motioned for his wizard and psionicist to resume.

It took some time, but finally the spellcaster completed his enchantment, and the poor trapped wizard glowed with a green light that obscured his features. He grunted and groaned behind that veil of light, and he thrashed even more violently behind the trapping goo.

The light faded and all went calm, and the man hanging on the wall had transformed into an exact likeness of Archmage Knellict.

"Now, there are conditions, of course, for my mercy," said Jarlaxle. "We do not lightly allow other organizations to pledge allegiance to Bregan D'aerthe."

Knellict seemed on the verge of an explosion.

"There is a beauty to the Underdark," Jarlaxle told him. "Our tunnels are all around you, but you never quite know where, or when, we might come calling. Anytime, any place, Knellict. You cannot continually look below you, but we are always looking up."

"What do you want, Jarlaxle?"

"Less than you presume. You will find a benefit if you can but let go of your anger. Oh, yes, and for your sake, I hope the Lady Calihye is still alive."

Knellict shifted, but not uneasily, showing Jarlaxle that she was indeed.

"That is good. We may yet fashion a deal."

"Timoshenko speaks for the Citadel of Assassins, not I."

"We can change that, if you like."

The blood drained from Knellict's face as the enormity of it all finally descended upon him. He watched as one of the drow warriors approached the wizard who bore his exact likeness.

A crossbow clicked and the man who looked exactly like Knellict soon quieted in slumber.

Mercifully.

❧━❦━❧

"All hail the king," Entreri said when the door of his cell opened and Gareth Dragonsbane unexpectedly walked in. The king turned to the guard and motioned for him to move away.

The man hesitated, looked hard at the dangerous assassin, but Gareth was the king and he could not question him.

"You will forgive me if I do not kneel," Entreri said.

"I did not ask you to do so."

"But your monk could make me, I suppose. A word from his mouth and my muscles betray me, yes?"

"Master Kane could have killed you, legally and without inquiry, and yet he did not. For that you should be grateful."

"Saved for the spectacle of the gallows, no doubt."

Gareth didn't answer.

"Why have you come here?" Entreri asked. "To taunt me?" He paused and studied Gareth's face for a moment, and a smile spread upon his own. "No," he said. "I know why you have come. You fear me."

Gareth didn't answer.

"You fear me because you see the truth in me, don't you, King of Damara?" Entreri laughed and paced his cell, a knowing grin splayed across his face, and Gareth followed his every step warily, with eyes that reflected a deep and pervading turmoil.

"Because you know I was right," Entreri continued. "In your audience chamber, when the others grew outraged, you did not. You could not, because my words echoed not just in your ears but in your heart. Your claim is no stronger than was my own."

"I did not say that, nor do I agree."

"Some things need not be spoken. You know the truth of it as well as I do—I wonder how many kings, pashas, or lords know it. I wonder how many could admit it."

"You presume much, King Artemis."

"Don't call me that."

"I did not bestow the title."

"Nor did I. Nor does it suit me. Nor would I want it."

"Are you bargaining?"

Entreri scoffed at him. "I assure you, paladin king, that if I had a sword in hand, I would willingly cut out your heart, here and now. If you expect me to beg, then look elsewhere. The fool monk can bring me to my knees, but if I am not there of my own choosing, then calling it begging would ring as hollow as does your crown, yes?"

"As I said, you presume much. Too much."

"Do I? Then why are you here?"

Gareth's eyes flared with anger, but he said nothing.

"An accident of birth?" Entreri asked. "Had I been born to your mother, would I then be the rightful king? Would your mighty friends rally to my side as they do yours? Would the monk exercise his powers over an enemy of mine at my bidding?"

"It is far more complicated than that."

"Is it?"

"Blood is not enough. Deed—"

"I killed the dracolich, have you forgotten?"

"And all the deeds along your road led you to this point?" Gareth asked, a sharp edge creeping into his voice. "You have lived a life worthy of the throne?"

"I survived, and in a place you could not know," Entreri growled back at him. "How easy for the son of a lord to proclaim the goodness of his road! I am certain that your trials were grand, heir of Dragonsbane. Oh, but the bards could fill a month of merrymaking with the tales of thee."

"Enough," Gareth bade him. "You know nothing."

"I know that you are here. And I know why you are here."

"Indeed?" came the doubtful reply.

"To learn more of me. To study me. Because you must find the differences between us. You must convince yourself that we are not alike."

"Do you believe that we are?"

The incredulity did not impress Entreri. "In more ways than his majesty wishes to admit," he said. "So you come here to learn more in the hope that you will discern where our paths and characters diverge. Because if you cannot find that place, Gareth, then your worst fears are realized."

"And those would be?"

"Rightful. The rightful king. An odd phrase, that, don't you agree? What does it mean to be the rightful king, Gareth Dragonsbane? Does it mean that you are the strongest? The most holy? Does your god Ilmater anoint you?"

"I am the descendant of the former king, long before Damara was split by war."

"And if I had been born to your parents?"

Gareth shook his head. "It could not have been so. I am the product of their loins, of their breeding and of my heritage."

"So it is not just circumstance? There is meaning in bloodlines, you say?"

"Yes."

"You have to believe that, don't you? For the sake of your own sanity. You are king because your father was king?"

"He was a baron, at a time when Damara had no king. The kingdom was not unified until joined in common cause against Zhengyi."

"And that is where, by deed, Gareth rose above the other barons and dukes and their children?"

Gareth's look showed Entreri that he knew he was being mocked, or at least, that he suspected as much.

"A wonderful nexus of circumstance and heritage," Entreri said. "I am truly touched."

"Should I give you your sword and slay you in combat to rightly claim Vaasa?" Gareth asked, and Entreri smiled at every word.

"And if I should slay you?"

"My god would not allow it."

"You have to believe that, don't you? But humor me, I pray you. Let us say that we did battle, and I emerged the victor. By your reasoning, I would thus become the rightful King of Vaa—oh, wait. I see now. That would not serve, since I haven't the proper bloodline. What a cunning system you have there. You and all the other self-proclaimed royalty of Faerûn. By your conditions, you alone are kings and queens and lords and ladies of court. You alone matter, while the peasant grovels and kneels in the mud, and since you are 'rightful' in the eyes of this god or that, then the peasant cannot complain. He must accept his muddy lot in life and revel in his misery, all in the knowledge that he serves the rightful king."

Gareth's jaw tightened, and he ground his teeth as he continued to stare unblinking at Entreri.

"You should have had Kane kill me, back at the castle. Break the mirror, King Gareth. You will fancy yourself prettier in that instance."

Gareth stared at him a short while longer, then moved to the cell door, which was opened by the returned guard. Beside him stood Master Kane, who stared at Entreri.

Entreri saw him and offered an exaggerated bow.

Gareth pushed past the pair and moved along, his hard boots stomping on the stone floor.

"You wish that you had killed me, I expect," Entreri said to Kane. "Of course, you still can. I feel the vibrations of your demonic touch."

"I am not your judge."

"Just my executioner."

Kane bowed and walked off. By the time he caught up to Gareth, the man had departed the dungeons and was nearing his private rooms.

"You heard?" Gareth asked him.

"He is a clever one."

"Is he so wrong?"

"Yes."

The simple answer stopped Gareth and he turned to face the monk.

"In my order, rank is attained through achievement and single combat," Kane explained. "In a kingdom as large as Damara, in a town as large as Bloodstone Village, such a system would invite anarchy and terrible suffering. On that level, it is the way of the orc."

"And so we have bloodlines of royalty?"

"It is one way. But such would be meaningless absent heroic deeds. In the darkest hours of Damara, when Zhengyi ruled, Gareth Dragonsbane stepped forward."

"Many did," said Gareth. "You did."

"I followed King Gareth."

Gareth smiled in gratitude and put a hand on Kane's shoulder.

"The title holds you as tightly as you hold the title," Kane said. "It is no easy task, bearing the responsibility of an entire kingdom on your shoulders."

"There are times I fear I will bend to breaking."

"One ill decision and people die," said Kane. "And you alone are the protector of justice. If you are overwhelmed, men will suffer. Your guilt stems from a feeling that you are not worthy, of course, but only if you view your position as one of luxury. People need a leader, and an orderly manner in which to choose one."

"And that leader is surrounded by finery," said Gareth, sweeping his hands at the tapestries and sculptures that decorated the corridor. "By fine food and soft bedding."

"A necessary elevation of status and wealth," said Kane, "to incite hope in the common folk that there is a better life for them; if not here then in the afterworld. You are the representative of their dreams and fantasies."

"And it is necessary?"

Kane didn't immediately answer, and Gareth looked closely at the man, great by any measure, yet standing in dirty, road-worn robes. Gareth laughed at that image, thinking that perhaps it was time for the Bloodstone Lands to see a bit more charity from the top.

"Damara is blessed, so her people say, and the goodly folk of Vaasa hold hope that they, too, will be swept under your protection," said Kane. "You heard their cheers at the castle. Wingham and all of Palishchuk call to Gareth to accept their fealty."

"You are a good friend."

"I am an honest observer."

Gareth patted his shoulder again.

"What of Entreri?" Kane asked.

"You should have left that dog dead on the muddy lands of Vaasa," said Lady Christine, coming out of her bedchamber.

Gareth looked at her, shook his head, and asked, "Does his foolish game warrant such a penalty?"

"He slew Lady Ellery, by his own admission," said Kane.

Gareth winced at that, as Christine barked, "What? I will kill the dog myself!"

"You will not," said Gareth. "There are circumstances yet to be determined."

"By his own admission," Christine said.

"I am protector of justice, am I not, Master Kane?"

"You are."

"Then let us hold an inquiry into this matter, to see where the truth lies."

"Then kill the dog," said Christine.

"If it is warranted," Gareth replied. "Only if it is warranted."

Gareth didn't say it, and he knew that Kane understood, but he hoped that it would not come to that.

◅═╫═▻

He had just heard the report from Vaasa, where his soldiers held forth at Palishchuk, and motioned to the majordomo to bring forth the Commander of the Heliogabalus garrison, where promising reports had been filtering in for a tenday. But to Gareth's astonishment, and to that of Lady Christine and Friar Dugald who sat with him in chambers, it was not a soldier of the Bloodstone Army who entered through the doors.

It was an outrageous dark elf, his bald head shining in the glow of the morning light filtering in through the many windows of the palace. Hat in hand, giant feather bobbing with every step, Jarlaxle smiled widely as he approached.

The guards at either side bristled and leaned forward, ready to leap upon the dark elf at but a word from their king.

But that word did not come.

Jarlaxle's boots clicked loudly as he made his way along the thickly-carpeted aisle. "King Gareth," he said as he neared the dais that held the thrones, and he swept into a low, exaggerated bow. "Truly Damara is warmer now that you have returned to your home."

"What fool are you?" cried Lady Christine, obviously no less surprised than were Gareth and Dugald.

"A grand one, if the rumors are to be believed," Jarlaxle replied. The three exchanged looks, ever so briefly.

"Yes, I know," Jarlaxle added. "You believe them. 'Tis my lot in life, I fear."

Behind the drow, at the far end of the carpet, the majordomo entered along with the couriers from Heliogabalus. The attendant stopped short and glanced around in confusion when he noticed the drow.

Gareth nodded, understanding that Jarlaxle had used a bit of magic to get by the anteroom—a room that was supposedly dampened to such spells. Gareth's hand went to his side, to his sheathed long sword, Crusader, a holy blade that held within its blessed

256

metal a powerful dweomer of disenchantment.

A look from the king to the sputtering majordomo sent the attendant scrambling out of the room.

"I am surprised that I am surprising," Jarlaxle said, and he glanced back to let them know that he had caught on to all of the signaling. "I would have thought that I was expected."

"You have come to surrender?" Lady Christine asked.

Jarlaxle looked at her as if he did not understand.

"Have you a twin, then?" asked Dugald. "One who traveled to Palishchuk and beyond to the castle beside Artemis Entreri?"

"Yes, of course, that was me."

"You traveled with King Artemis the First?"

Jarlaxle laughed. "An interesting title, don't you agree? I thought it necessary to ensure that you would venture forth. One cannot miss such opportunities as Castle D'aerthe presented."

"Do tell," said Lady Christine.

A commotion at the back of the room turned Jarlaxle to glance over his shoulder, to see Master Kane cautiously but deliberately approaching. Behind him, staying near the door, the majordomo peered in. Then Emelyn the Gray appeared, pushing past the man and quick-stepping into the great room, casting as he went. He looked every which way—and with magical vision as well, they all realized.

Jarlaxle offered a bow to Kane as the man neared, stepping off to the side and standing calmly, and very ready, of course.

"You were saying," Lady Christine prompted as soon as the drow turned back to face the dais.

"I was indeed," Jarlaxle replied. "Though I had expected to be congratulated, honestly, and perhaps even thanked."

"Thanked?" Christine echoed. "For challenging the throne?"

"For helping me to secure the allegiance of Vaasa," Gareth said, and Christine turned a doubting expression his way. "That was your point, I suppose."

"That, and ridding the region immediately surrounding Palishchuk of a couple of hundred goblin and kobold vermin, who, no doubt, would have caused much mischief with the good half-orcs during the wintry months."

At the back of the room, Emelyn the Gray began to chuckle.

"Preposterous!" Friar Dugald interjected. "You were overwhelmed, your plans destroyed, and so now . . ." He stopped when Gareth held his hand up before him, bidding patience.

"I trust that none of your fine knights were seriously injured by the outpouring of vermin," Jarlaxle went on as if the friar hadn't uttered a word. "I timed the charge so that few, if any, would even reach your ranks before being cut down."

"And you expect gratitude for inciting battle?" Lady Christine asked.

"A slaughter, Milady, and not a battle. It was necessary that King Gareth show himself in battle in deposing King Artemis. The contrast could not have been more clear to the half-orcs—they saw Artemis hoarding monstrous minions, while King Gareth utterly destroyed them. Their cheering was genuine, and the tales they tell of the conquest of Castle D'aerthe will only heighten in heroic proportions, of course. And with Wingham's troupe in town at the time of the battle, those tales will quickly spread across all of Vaasa."

"And you planned for all of this?" Gareth asked, sarcasm and doubt evident in his tone—but not too much so.

Jarlaxle put a hand on one hip and cocked his head, as if wounded by the accusation. "I had to make it all authentic, of course," the drow explained. "The proclamation of King Artemis, the forced march of King Gareth and his army. It could not have been known a ruse to any, even among your court, else your own integrity might have been compromised, and your complicity in the ruse might have been revealed."

"I say foul," Lady Christine answered a few moments later, breaking the stunned silence.

"Aye, foul and now fear," Dugald agreed.

Gareth motioned for Kane and Emelyn to join him at the dais. Then he instructed Jarlaxle to leave and wait in the anteroom—and several guards accompanied the drow.

"Why do we bother wasting time with this obvious lie?" Christine said as soon as they had gathered. "His plans to rule Vaasa crumbled and now he tries to salvage something from the wreckage of ill-designed dreams."

"It is a pity that he chose the route he did," said Gareth. "He and his companion might have made fine interim barons of Vaasa."

All eyes turned to Gareth, and Christine seemed as if she would explode, so violently did she tremble at the thought.

"If Olwen were here, he would have struck you for such a remark," Emelyn said.

"You believe the drow?" Kane asked.

Gareth considered the question, but began shaking his head almost immediately, for his instinct on this was clear enough, whatever he wanted to believe. "I know not whether it was a ruse from the beginning or a convenient escape at the end," he said.

"He is a dangerous character, this Jarlaxle," said Emelyn.

"And his friend has no doubt committed countless crimes worthy of the gallows," Christine added. "His eyes are full of murder and malice, and those weapons he carries . . ."

"We do not know that," Gareth said. "Am I to convict and condemn a man on your instinct?"

"We could investigate," said Emelyn.

"On what basis?" Gareth snapped right back.

The others, except for Kane, exchanged concerned glances, for they had seen their friend dig in his heels in similar situations and they knew well that Gareth Dragonsbane was not a malleable man. He was the king, after all, and a paladin king, as well, sanctioned by the state and by the god Ilmater.

"We have no basis whatsoever," said Kane, and Christine gasped. "The only crime for which we now hold Artemis Entreri is one of treason."

"A crime calling for the gallows," said Christine.

"But Jarlaxle's explanation is at least plausible," said Kane. "You cannot deny that the actions of these two, whatever their intent, solidified your hold in Vaasa and reminded the half-orcs of Palishchuk of heroic deeds past and the clearest road for their future."

"You cannot believe that this . . . this . . . this drow, went to Vaasa and arranged all of that which transpired simply for the good of the Kingdom of Bloodstone," said Christine.

"Nor can I say with any confidence that what has transpired was anything different than exactly that," said Kane.

"They sent an army of monsters against us," Dugald reminded them all, but his description drew an unexpected burst of dismissive laughter from Emelyn.

"They called a bunch of goblins and kobolds to their side, then put them before us for the slaughter," said Gareth. "I know not the depths of Jarlaxle's foolishness or his wisdom, but I am certain that he knew his monstrous army would not even reach our ranks when he sent them forth from the gates. Much more formidable would have been the gargoyles and other monsters of the castle itself, which he did not animate."

"Because he could not," Dugald insisted.

"That is not what Wingham, Arrayan, and Olgerkhan reported," reminded Kane. "The gargoyles were aloft when first they went to see what mischief was about the castle."

"And so we are left with no more than the crime of inconvenience," said Gareth. "These impetuous two circumvented all protocol and stepped far beyond their province in forcing me north, even if it was for the good of the kingdom. We have no proof that what they did was anything more than that."

"They tried to usurp your title," Christine said. "If you are to let that stand, then you condone lawlessness of a level that will bring down Bloodstone."

"There are darker matters at hand," Emelyn added. "Let us not forget the warnings we were given by Ilnezhara and Tazmikella. This Jarlaxle creature is much more than he appears."

The sobering remark left them all quiet for some time, before Gareth finally responded, "They are guilty of nothing more than hubris, and such is a reflection of our own actions those years ago when we determined the fate of Damara. It is possible, even logical, that Jarlaxle's ruse was exactly as he portrayed it, perhaps in a clever—overly clever, for he wound himself into a trap—attempt to gain favor and power in the wilds of the north. Maybe he was trying to secure a comfortable title. I do not know. But I have no desire to hold Artemis Entreri in my dungeon any longer, and he has not proven himself worthy of the noose. I will not hang a man on suspicion and my own fears.

"They will be banished, both of them, to leave the Blood-stone Lands within the tenday, and never to return, on pain of imprisonment."

"On pain of death," Christine insisted, and when Gareth turned to the queen, he saw no room for debate in her stern expression.

"As you will," he conceded. "We will get them far from here."

"You would do well to warn your neighbors," said Emelyn, and Gareth nodded.

The king pointed to Emelyn's robe, and the wizard huffed and pulled it open. He produced from a deep, extra-dimensional pocket the scroll they had found in the Zhengyian castle.

Gareth waved his friends back from the dais and motioned to the back of the room. A few moments later, Jarlaxle, his great hat still in his hands, again stood before the king.

Gareth tossed the scroll to the drow. "I know not whether you are clever by one, or by two," he said.

"I lived in the Underdark," the drow replied with a wry grin. "I am clever by multiples, I assure you."

"You need not, for it is exactly that suspicion that has led me to conclude that you and Artemis Entreri are guilty for your actions north of Palishchuk."

Jarlaxle didn't seem impressed, which put all of Gareth's friends on their guard.

"Exactly what that crime is, however, cannot be deduced," Gareth went on. "And so I take the only course left open to me, for the good of the kingdom. You are to remove yourself from the region, from all the Bloodstone Lands, within the tenday."

Jarlaxle considered the verdict for just a moment, and shrugged. "And my friend?"

"Artemis Entreri or the dwarf?" Gareth asked.

"Ah, you have Athrogate, then?" Jarlaxle replied. "Good! I feared for the poor fool, entangled as circumstance had made him with the Citadel of Assassins."

It was Gareth's turn to pause and consider.

"I was speaking of Artemis Entreri, of course," said Jarlaxle. "Is he under similar penalty?"

"We considered much worse," Christine warned.

"He is," said Gareth. "Although he was the one who assumed the title of king, I note that the castle was named for Jarlaxle. Similar crimes, similar fate."

"Whatever those crimes may be," said the drow.

"Whatever that fate may be," said Gareth. "So long as it is not a fate you discover here."

"Fair enough," Jarlaxle said with a bow.

"And if it were not?" said Christine. "Do you think your acceptance of the judgment of the king an important thing?"

Jarlaxle looked at her and smiled, and so serene was that look that Christine shifted uneasily in her chair.

"One more piece of business then," said Jarlaxle. "I would like to take the dwarf. Though he was entangled with the Citadel of Assassins, as you discerned, he is not a bad sort."

"You presume to bargain?" Christine asked indignantly.

"If I do, it is not without barter." Jarlaxle slowly pulled open his waistcoat and slid a parchment from its pocket. Kane shifted near as he did, and the drow willingly handed it over.

"A map to the hideout of the Citadel of Assassins," the drow explained.

"And how might you have fashioned or found such a thing?" Gareth asked suspiciously as his friends bristled.

"Clever by more ways than a human king could ever count," the drow explained. As he did, Jarlaxle shifted his great hat, turning it opening up. "Clever and with allies unseen." He reached into the hat and produced his trophy, then set it at the foot of the dais.

The head of Knellict.

After the gasps had quieted, Jarlaxle bowed to the king. "I accept your judgment, indeed," he said. "And would pray you to accept my trade, the map and the archmage for the dwarf, though I have already turned them over, of course. I trust in your sense of fair play. It is time for me to go, I agree. But do note, Gareth Dragonsbane, King of Damara, and now King of Vaasa, that you are stronger and your enemies weaker for the work of Jarlaxle. I expect no gratitude, and accept no gifts—other than one annoying dwarf for whom you have little use anyway. You wish us gone, and so we will go, with a good tale, a fine adventure, and an outcome well served."

He finished with a great and sweeping bow, and spun his feathered hat back up to his bald head as he came up straight.

Gareth stared at the head, his mouth hanging open in disbelief that the drow, that anyone, had brought down the archmage of the Citadel of Assassins so efficiently.

"Who are you?" Christine asked.

"I am he who rules the world, don't you know?" Jarlaxle replied with a grin. "One little piece at a time. I am the stuff of Riordan Parnell's most outrageous songs, and I am a confused memory for those whose lives I've entered and departed. I wish you no ill—I never did. Nor have I worked against you in any way. Nor shall I. You wish us gone, and so we go. But I pray you entrust the dwarf to my care, and do tell Riordan to sing of me well."

Neither Gareth nor Christine nor any of the others could begin to fashion a reply to that.

Which only confirmed to Jarlaxle that it was indeed time to go.

CHAPTER

17

Entreri looked up as his cell door swung open and Master Kane entered, bearing a large canvas sack. "Your possessions," the monk explained, swinging the sack off his shoulder and dropping it on the floor at the man's feet.

Entreri looked down at it then back up at Kane, and said not a word.

"You are being released," Kane explained. "All of your possessions are in there. Your unusual steed, your dagger, your fine sword . . . everything you had with you when you were captured."

Still eyeing the man suspiciously, Entreri crouched down and pulled back the top of the sack, revealing the decorated pommel of Charon's Claw. As soon as he gripped the hilt and felt the sentient weapon come alive in his thoughts, he knew that this was no bluff.

"My respect for you multiplied many times over when I lifted your blade," Kane said. "Few men could wield such a sword without being consumed by it."

"You seemed to have little trouble picking it up," Entreri said.

"I am far beyond such concerns," Kane replied. Entreri pulled the *piwafwi* out and slung it around his shoulders in one fluid motion. "Your cloak is of drow make, is it not?" Kane asked. "Have you spent time with the drow, in their lands?"

"I am far beyond such questions," the assassin replied, mocking the monk's tone.

Kane nodded in acceptance.

"Unless you plan to compel me to answer," Entreri said, "with this sickness you have inserted into my being."

Kane stepped back, his hands folded causally at his waist before him. Entreri watched him for a few moments, seeking a sign, any sign. But then, with a dismissive snicker, he went back to the bag and began collecting his items, and kept a mental inventory all the way through.

"Are you going to tell me more about this sudden change of mind?" he asked when he was fully outfitted. "Or am I to suffer the explanations of King Gareth?"

"Your crime is not proven," said Kane, "since there is an alternative explanation of intent."

"And that would be?"

"Come along," Kane said. "You have far to go in a short amount of time. You are freed of your dungeon, but your road will be out of Damara and Vaasa."

"Who would wish to stay?"

Kane ignored the flippant remark and began walking up the corridor, Entreri in tow. "In a tenday's time, Artemis Entreri will enter the Bloodstone Lands only on pain of death. For the next few days, you are here at the sufferance of King Gareth and Queen Christine, and theirs is a patience that is not limitless. One tenday alone."

"I've a fast horse that doesn't tire," Entreri replied. "A tenday is nine too long."

"Good, then we are in agreement."

They walked in silence for a short while, past the curious and alert stares of many guards. Entreri returned those stares with his own, silent but overt threats that had the sentries, to a man, tightly clutching their weapons. Even the presence of Grandmaster Kane did not free them from the dangerous glare of Artemis Entreri, the look that so many had suffered, a foretelling of death.

Artemis Entreri was not in a generous mood. He felt the vibrations of Kane's indecent intrusion into his body, a swirling and tingling sensation that seemed like strange ocean waves caught within the uneven contours of his corporeal being, rolling and breaking and re-gathering as they swept about. Emelyn's explanation of an elven cord of energy pulled taut seemed very on the mark to the assassin. What he knew beyond that description was that this intrusion seemed in many ways as awful as the life-draining properties of his own prized dagger.

Entreri's hand subconsciously slipped to the jeweled hilt of that trusted weapon, and he considered the possibilities.

"Pause," Entreri said as the pair neared the king's audience chamber.

Kane obeyed and turned back to regard the man. The guards flanking the door leaned forward, hands wringing tightly around their adamantine-tipped halberds.

"How am I to trust in this?" Entreri asked. "In you?"

"There is an alternative?"

"You would have me walk out of here, judgment passed and rendered, and that judgment being banishment and not death, and yet you hold the cord of my life in the single puff of your breath?"

"The effects of Quivering Palm will wear away in a short enough time," Kane assured him. "They are not permanent."

"But while they last, you can kill me, and easily?"

"Yes."

As the monk spoke the word, Entreri swept into motion, drawing forth his dagger and closing the ground between them. Kane was not caught unawares, as Entreri had not expected him to be, and the monk executed a perfect block.

But Entreri wasn't trying for a kill, or for the monk's heart. He got what he wanted and managed to prick Kane's palm with his vampiric blade. He held the dagger against the monk's torn flesh.

He stared at Kane and smiled, to keep the monk curious.

"Am I to facilitate your suicide, then?" the monk asked.

In response, Entreri called upon the life draining abilities of his jeweled dagger. Kane's eyes went wide; apparently the monk wasn't beyond all such concerns.

Behind Kane, one guard lowered his halberd, though he wisely held back—if Grandmaster Kane couldn't handle the assassin, then what might he do, after all? The other turned to the door and shoved it open, shouting for King Gareth.

"An interesting dilemma, wouldn't you agree?" Entreri said to the monk. "You hold my life in your thoughts, and can paralyze me, as I have seen, with a simple utterance. But I need only will the dagger to feed and it will feed to me, in replacement, your own life energy.

Where does that leave us, Master Kane? Will your Quivering Palm be quick enough to slay me before my blade can drink enough to save me? Will we both succumb? Are you willing to take the chance?"

Kane stared at him, and matched his unnerving smile.

"What is the meaning of this?" King Gareth said, coming to the door.

Beside him, Friar Dugald sputtered something indecipherable, and Queen Christine growled, "Treachery!"

"No more so than that shown to me," Entreri answered, his stare never leaving the gaze of Kane.

"We should have expected as much from a dog like you," Christine said.

Would that your throat had been in my reach, Entreri thought, but wisely did not say. Gareth was a reasonable man, he believed, but likely not where that queen of his was concerned.

"You were granted your possessions and your freedom," Gareth said. "Did Kane not tell you?"

"He told me," Entreri replied. He heard the shuffling of mail-clad feet coming up the corridor behind him, but he paid it no heed.

"Then why have you done this?" asked Gareth.

"I will not leave here under the immoral hold of Master Kane," Entreri replied. "He will relinquish his grip on my physical being, or one of us, perhaps both, will die here and now."

"Fool," said Christine, but Gareth hushed her.

"Your life is worth so little to you, 'tis apparent," Gareth began, but Kane held up his free hand to intervene.

The monk stared hard at Entreri the whole time. "Pride is considered the deadliest of the sins," he said.

"Then dismiss your own," Entreri countered.

Kane's smile was one of acceptance, and he slowly nodded, then closed his eyes.

Entreri rolled his fingers on the dagger hilt, ready to call fully on its powers if it came to that. He really didn't believe that he had a chance, though, even if it had been just him and Kane alone in the palace. The monk's insidious grasp was too strong and too quickly debilitating. If Kane called upon the Quivering Palm, Entreri suspected that he would be incapacitated, perhaps even killed, before the dagger could do any substantial work.

But only serenity showed on Master Kane's face as he opened his eyes once more, and almost immediately, Entreri felt his inner tide fall still.

"You are released," Kane informed him, and within the blink of an eye, the monk's hand was simply removed, gone, from the tip of the dagger. Too fast for Entreri to even have begun drawing forth with its vampiric powers had he so desired.

"You give in to such demands?" Queen Christine railed.

"Only because they were justly demanded," said Kane. "Artemis Entreri has been told of the conditions and granted his release. If we are not to trust that he will accept his sentence, then perhaps we should not be releasing him at all."

"Perhaps not," said Christine.

"His release was justly secured," said Gareth. "And we cannot diminish the importance of the rationale for such a judgment. But now this assault . . ."

"Was justified, and in the end, meaningless to us," Kane assured him.

Entreri slipped his dagger away, and Gareth turned and drove Christine and Dugald before him back into the audience chamber.

"Have I missed all the excitement?" came a voice from within, one that Artemis Entreri knew all too well.

"The bargainer, I presume," he said to Kane.

"Your drow friend is quite persuasive, and comes prepared."

"If only you knew."

Walking down the cobblestone road beside Jarlaxle a short while later, Entreri did not feel as if he was free. True, he was out of Gareth's dungeon, but the drow walking beside him reminded him that there were many dungeons, and not all were made of wood and stone and iron bars. As he considered that, his hand slid back to brush the flute he had tucked inside the back of his belt, and it occurred to him that he was not yet certain whether the instrument was, in and of itself, a prison or a key.

Entreri and Jarlaxle cast long shadows before them, for the sun was fast setting behind the mountains across the small lake.

Already the cold night wind had begun to blow.

"So ye're to be walkin', and whistlin' and talkin', and thinkin' yer world's all the grand," a voice rang out behind them.

Jarlaxle turned, but Entreri just closed his eyes.

"While I'm to be sittin', and grumblin' and spittin', and wiggling me toes in the sand?" Athrogate finished. "I'd rather, I'm thinkin', be drinkin' and stinkin'"—he paused, lifted one leg, and let fly a tremendous fart—"and holdin' a wench in each hand! *Bwahaha!* Hold up, then, ye hairless hunk o' coal, and let me little legs catch ye. I won't be hugging ye, but I'm grateful enough that ye bargained me way out o' that place!"

"You didn't," Entreri muttered.

"A fine ally," Jarlaxle replied. "Strong of arm and indomitable of spirit."

"And boundless in annoyance."

"He has been sad of late, for the trouble with the Citadel. I owe him this much at least."

"And here I was, hoping that you had bargained for my freedom by turning him over instead," Entreri said, and Athrogate was close enough to hear.

"*Bwahaha!*" the dwarf boomed.

Entreri figured it was impossible to offend the wretched creature.

"Why, but I am hurt, Artemis," Jarlaxle said, and he feigned a wound, throwing his forearm dramatically across his brow. "Never would I abandon an ally."

Entreri offered a doubting smirk.

"Indeed, when I had heard that Calihye had been grabbed from her room at the Vaasan Gate by Knellict and the Citadel . . ." Jarlaxle began, but he stopped short and let the weight of the proclamation hang there for a few moments, let Entreri's eyes go wide with alarm.

"Traveling to Knellict's lair was no minor expedition, of course," Jarlaxle went on.

"Where is she?" the assassin asked.

"Safe and roomed at the tavern down the road, of course," Jarlaxle replied. "Never would I abandon an ally."

"Knellict took her?"

"Yup yup," said Athrogate. "And yer bald hunk o' coal friend took

Knellict's head and put it on Gareth's dais, he did. *Bwahaha!* Bet I'd've liked to see Lady Christine's nose go all crinkly at that!"

Entreri stared hard at Jarlaxle, who swept a low bow. "Your lady awaits," he said. "The three of us are bound to be gone from the Bloodstone Lands within the tenday, on pain of death, but we can spare a day, I expect. Perhaps you can persuade Lady Calihye that her road runs with ours."

Entreri continued to stare. He had no answers. When he had forced Jarlaxle through Kimmuriel's magical gate in the bowels of the castle, he had expected that he would never see the drow again, and all of what followed, his release, the dwarf, the news about Calihye, rushed over him like a breaking ocean wave. And as it receded, pulling back, it dragged him inexorably along with it.

"Go to her," Jarlaxle said quietly, seriously. "She will be pleased to see you."

"And while ye're stayin' and gots to be playin', meself is thinkin' I got to be drinkin'!" Athrogate roared with another great burst of foolish laughter.

Entreri's eyes shot daggers at Jarlaxle. The drow just motioned toward the tavern.

Jarlaxle and Athrogate watched Entreri disappear up the stairs of the Last Respite, the most prominent inn of Bloodstone Village, which boasted of clean rooms, fine elven wine, and an unobstructed view of the White Tree from every balcony.

Both the dwarf and the drow were known in the village, of course, for Athrogate's morningstars had made quite an impression on the folk at the Vaasan Gate, just to the north, and Jarlaxle was, after all, a drow!

The glances that came their way that day, however, were ones full of suspicion, something that didn't escape the notice of either of the companions.

"Word of Gareth's pardon has not yet reached them, it seems," Jarlaxle remarked, sliding into a chair against the far wall of the common room.

" 'Tween't no pardon," Athrogate said. "Though I'm not for

thinking that a banishing from the Bloodstone Lands is a bad thing. Not with the Citadel lookin' to pay ye back for Knellict and all."

"Yes, there is that," said the drow. He hid his smile in a motion to the barmaid.

The two had barely ordered their first round—wine for the drow and honey mead for the dwarf—when a couple of Jarlaxle's acquaintances unexpectedly walked in through the Last Respite's front door.

"Ain't many times I seen ye lookin' surprised," Athrogate remarked.

"It is not a common occurrence, I assure you," Jarlaxle replied, his eyes never leaving the new arrivals, a pair of sisters who, he knew, were much more than they seemed.

"Ye got a fancy, do ye?" Athrogate said, following that gaze, and he gave a great laugh that only intensified as the two women moved to join them.

"Lady Ilnezhara and dear Tazmikella," Jarlaxle said, rising politely. "I meant to speak with you in Heliogabalus on my road south out of the realm."

There were only three chairs around the small table, and Tazmikella took the empty one, motioning for Jarlaxle to sit down. Ilnezhara looked at Athrogate.

"We must speak with Jarlaxle," she told the dwarf.

"*Bwahaha!*" Athrogate bellowed back. "Well, I'm for listening! Ain't like he can make the both of ye grin, now can—?"

He almost finished the question before Ilnezhara grabbed him by the front of the tunic, and with just one hand, hoisted him easily into the air and held him there.

Athrogate sputtered and wriggled about. "Here now, drow!" he said. "She's got an arm on her! *Bwahaha!*"

Ilnezhara glared at him, and the fact that almost everyone in the tavern stared at the spectacle of a lithe woman holding a heavily armored, two-hundred-pound dwarf up in the air at the end of one slender arm seemed not to disturb her in the least.

"Now, pretty girl, I'm guessin' ye got yerself a potion or a spell, mighten even a girdle like me own," Athrogate said. "But I'm also thinking that ye'd be a smart wench to know yer place and put me down."

Jarlaxle winced.

"As you wish," Ilnezhara replied. She glanced around, seeking a clear path, and with a flick of her wrist, launched the dwarf across the common room where he crashed through an empty table and took it and a couple of chairs hard into the wall with him.

He leaped up, enraged, but his eyes rolled and he tumbled down in a heap.

Ilnezhara took his seat without a second look at him.

"Please don't break him," said Jarlaxle. "He cost me greatly."

"You are leaving our employ," Tazmikella said.

"There is no choice in the matter," replied the drow. "At least not for me. Your King Gareth made it quite clear that his hospitality has reached its limit."

"Through no fault of your own, no doubt."

"Your sarcasm is well placed," Jarlaxle admitted.

"You have something we want," Ilnezhara said.

Jarlaxle put on his wounded expression. "My lady, I have given it to you many times." He was glad when that brought a smile to Ilnezhara's face, for Jarlaxle knew that he was treading on dangerous ground, and with extremely dangerous characters.

"We know what you have," Tazmikella cut in before her sister and the drow could get sidetracked. "Both items—one from Herminicle's tower, and one from the castle."

"The more valuable one from the castle," Ilnezhara agreed.

"Urshula would agree," Jarlaxle admitted. "This Witch-King who once ruled here was a clever sort, indeed."

"Then you admit possession?"

"Skull gems," said Jarlaxle. "A human one from the tower, that of a dragon from the castle, of course. But then, you knew as much when you dispatched me to Vaasa."

"And you acquired them?" reasoned Ilnezhara.

"Both, yes."

"Then give them over."

"There is no room for bargaining in this," Tazmikella warned.

"I don't have them."

The dragon sisters exchanged concerned glances, and turned their doubtful stares at Jarlaxle.

Across the room, Athrogate pulled himself up to his knees and shook his hairy head. Still wobbly, he gained his feet, and staggered a step back toward the table.

"To escape King Gareth, I had to call upon old friends," said Jarlaxle. He paused and looked at Ilnezhara. "You are well versed in divine magic, are you not?" he asked. "Cast upon me an enchantment to discern whether I am speaking the truth, for I would have you believe my every word."

"The Jarlaxle I know would not readily part with such powerful artifacts," Ilnezhara replied. Still, she did launch into spellcasting, as he had requested.

"That is only because you do not know of Bregan D'aerthe."

"D'aerthe? Is that not what you named your castle?" Tazmikella asked as soon as her sister finished and indicated that her dweomer was complete.

"It is, and it was named after a band of independent . . . entrepreneurs from my homeland of Menzoberranzan. I called upon them, of course, to escape King Gareth's army, and to facilitate the release of Lady Calihye from the Citadel of Assassins."

"We heard that you delivered Knellict's head to Gareth," said Tazmikella.

Behind Ilnezhara, Athrogate lowered his head, and fell forward as much as charged. He ran into the woman's upraised hand, and stopped as surely as if he had hit a rocky mountain wall. He bounced back just a bit, standing dazed, and Ilnezhara faced him squarely and blew upon him, sending him into a backward roll that left him on his belly in the middle of the floor. He propped himself up on his elbows, staring incredulously at the woman, unaware of her real nature, of course.

"Got to get meself a girdle like hers, I'm thinking," he said, and collapsed.

"It was an expensive proposition," Jarlaxle said when the excitement was over. "But I could not let Lady Calihye die and I needed the bargaining chip to facilitate the release of my friend . . ." He paused and considered Athrogate. "My friends," he corrected, "from King Gareth's dungeon."

"You gave the skull gems to your drow associates from the Underdark?" Tazmikella asked.

"I had no further use for them," said Jarlaxle. "And the Underdark is a good place for such artifacts. They cause nothing but mischief here in the sunlit world."

"They will cause nothing but mischief in the Underdark," said Ilnezhara.

"All the better," said Jarlaxle, and he lifted his glass in toast.

Tazmikella looked to her sister, who spent a few moments staring at Jarlaxle, before slowly nodding.

"We will study this further," Tazmikella said to the drow, turning back.

Jarlaxle hardly heard her, though, for another call had come to him suddenly, in his thoughts.

"Indeed, I would be disappointed if you did not," he said after he sorted through her words. "But pray excuse me, for I have business to attend."

He stood up and tipped his hat.

"We did not dismiss you," Tazmikella said.

"Dear lady, I pray you allow me to go."

"We are tasked by Master Kane to fly you from these lands," said Ilnezhara. "At sunrise."

"Sunrise, then," said Jarlaxle and he stepped forward.

Tazmikella's arm came out and blocked his way, and Jarlaxle cast a plaintive look at Ilnezhara.

"Let him go, sister," Ilnezhara bade.

Tazmikella locked Jarlaxle with her gaze, the stare of an angry dragon, but she did drop her arm to allow him to pass.

"Do see to him," Jarlaxle bade the waitress, indicating Athrogate. "Put him in a chair when he awakens and dull his pain with all the drink he desires." He tossed a small bag of coins to her as he finished, and she nodded.

"He spoke truthfully?" Tazmikella asked as soon as she and her sister were alone.

"If incompletely, and I am not so sure about Knellict's fate."

"A wise choice by King Gareth to send that one on his way," Tazmikella said. "He remains in contact with the creatures of the Underdark?" She gave a derisive snort. "The fool, to be sure, but we are all better off if the skull gems are indeed removed from the lands. Perhaps good consequence can come from evil dealings, for that one is naught but trouble."

"I will miss him," was all that the obviously distracted Ilnezhara would reply, and she stared wistfully at the departing drow.

She swayed in the smoky candlelight, her hair rolling behind her, shoulder to shoulder. Sweat glistened on her naked form, and she arched her back and looked up at the ceiling of the inn room, breathing and moaning softly.

Beneath her, Artemis Entreri clutched that beautiful image in his thoughts, found respite from the frustration and anger. He was angry at being used by Jarlaxle, and more so at being rescued by the drow—the last thing he wanted was to be indebted in any way to that one. And the road beckoned again, a road he would walk with Jarlaxle and the annoying Athrogate, apparently.

And with Calihye, he reminded himself as he reached up and ran his hand gently from the underside of the woman's chin all the way down to her belly. She would be his anchor, he hoped, his solid foundation, and with that firm footing, perhaps he could find a way to be rid of Jarlaxle.

But did he really want that?

It was all too confusing for the poor man. He glanced to the side, to where he had piled his clothes and other gear, and he saw Idalia's flute among that pile. The flute had done things to him, he knew, had pried open his heart and had forced him to ask for more out of his life than simple existence.

He hated it and appreciated it all at once.

Everything seemed like that to Artemis Entreri. Everything was a jumble, a confusing paradox of love and hate, of stoicism and desperate need, of friendship and the desire for solitude. Nothing seemed clear, nothing consistent.

He looked up at his lover and changed his mind on those last points. It was real, and warm. For the first time in his life, he had given himself fully to a woman.

Calihye rolled her head forward and looked at him, her eyes full of intensity and determination. She chewed her bottom lip a bit; her breath came in short puffs. Then she threw her head back and arched her spine, and Entreri felt her tighten like a drawn bowstring.

He closed his eyes and let the moment wash over him and take him with it, and he felt Calihye relax. He opened his eyes, expecting to see her crumbling atop him.

He saw instead the woman staring down at him, a dagger in her hand.

A dagger aimed for his heart.

And he had no defense, had no way to stop its deadly plunge. He could have brought his hand across to accept the stab there, perhaps, but he did not.

For in the split second of the dagger's plunge, Entreri understood that all of his hope had flown, that all of it, the entire foundation that held his sanity, was just another lie. He didn't try to block it. He didn't try to dodge aside.

The dagger could not hurt him more than the betrayal already had.

PART  3

T H E R O A D H O M E

The point of self-reflection is, foremost, to clarify and to find honesty. Self-reflection is the way to throw self-lies out and face the truth—however painful it might be to admit that you were wrong. We seek consistency in ourselves, and so when we are faced with inconsistency, we struggle to deny.

Denial has no place in self-reflection, and so it is incumbent upon a person to admit his errors, to embrace them and to move along in a more positive direction.

We can fool ourselves for all sorts of reasons. Mostly for the sake of our ego, of course, but sometimes, I now understand, because we are afraid.

For sometimes we are afraid to hope, because hope breeds expectation, and expectation can lead to disappointment.

And so I ask myself again, without the protective wall—or at least, conscious of it and determined to climb over it—why do I feel kinship to this man, Artemis Entreri, who has betrayed almost everything that I have come to hold dear? Why do I think about him—ever? Why did I not kill him when I had the chance? What instinct halted the thrust of a scimitar?

I have often wondered, even recently and even as I ponder this new direction, if Artemis Entreri is who I might have been had I not escaped Menzoberranzan. Would my increasing anger have led me down the road he chose, that of passionless killer? It seems a logical thing to me that I might have lost myself in the demands of perfectionism, and would have found refuge in the banality of a life lived without passion.

A lack of passion is perhaps a lack of introspection, and it is that very nature of self-evaluation that would have utterly destroyed my soul had I remained in the city of my birth.

It is only now, in these days when I have at last shed the weight of guilt that for so long burdened my shoulders, that I can say without hesitation that no, had I remained in Menzoberranzan, I would not have become the image of Artemis Entreri. More like Zaknafein, I expect, turning my anger outward instead of inward, wearing rage as armor and not garmenting my frame in the fears of what is in my heart. Zaknafein's was not an existence I desire, nor is it one in which I would have long survived, I am sure, but neither is it the way of Entreri.

So the worries are shed, and we, Entreri and I, are not akin in the ways that I had feared. And yet, I think of him still, and often. It is, I know now, because I suspect that we are indeed akin in some ways, and they are not my fears, but my hopes.

Reality is a curious thing. Truth is not as solid and universal as any of us would like it to be; selfishness guides perception, and perception invites justification. The physical image in the mirror, if not pleasing, can be altered by the mere brush of fingers through hair.

And so it is true that we can manipulate our own reality. We can persuade, even deceive. We can make others view us in dishonest ways. We can hide selfishness with charity, make a craving for acceptance into magnanimity, and amplify our smile to coerce a hesitant lover. The world is illusion, and often delusion, as victors write the histories and the children who die quietly under the stamp of a triumphant army never really existed. The robber baron becomes philanthropist in the final analysis, by bequeathing only that for which he had no more use. The king who sends young men and women to die becomes beneficent with the kiss of a baby. Every problem becomes a problem of perception to those who understand that reality, in reality, is what you make reality to be.

This is the way of the world, but it is not the only way. It is not the way of the truly goodly king, of Gareth Dragonsbane who rules in Damara, of Lady Alustriel of Silverymoon, or of Bruenor Battlehammer of Mithral Hall. Theirs is not a manner of masquerading reality to alter perception, but a determination to better reality, to follow a vision, and to trust their course is true, and it therefore follows, that perception of them will be just and kind.

For a more difficult alteration than the physical is the image that appears in the glass of introspection, the pureness or rot of the heart and the soul.

For many, sadly, this is not an issue, for the illusion of their lives becomes self-delusion, a masquerade that revels in the applause and sees in a pittance to charity a stain remover for the soul. How many conquerors, I wonder, who crushed out the lives of tens of thousands, could not hear those cries of inflicted despair beyond the applause of those who believed the wars would make the world a better place? How many thieves, I wonder, hear not the laments of victims and willingly blind themselves to the misery wrought of their violation under a blanket of their own suffered injustices?

When does theft become entitlement?

There are those who cannot see the stains on their souls. Some lack the capacity to look in the glass of introspection, perhaps, and others alter reality without and within.

It is, then, the outward misery of Artemis Entreri that has long offered me hope. He doesn't lack passion; he hides from it. He becomes an instrument, a weapon, because otherwise he must be human. He knows the glass all too well, I see clearly now, and he cannot talk himself around the obvious stain. His justifications for his actions ring hollow—to him most of all.

Only there, in that place, is the road of redemption, for any of us. Only in facing honestly that image in the glass can we change the reality of who we are. Only in seeing the scars and the stains and the rot can we begin to heal.

I think of Artemis Entreri because that is my hope for the man. It is a fleeting and distant hope to be sure, and perhaps in the end, it is nothing more than my own selfish need to believe that there is redemption and that there can be change. For Entreri? If so, then for anyone.

For Menzoberranzan?

—Drizzt Do'Urden

CHAPTER

18

The end of the assault was no less brutal than the beginning. The man, past middle age, gyrated fiercely and growled and grunted with primordial savagery, and even slapped the young woman across the face once in his climactic delirium.

Then it ended, like the snap of fingers, and the man pulled himself off the young girl and lowered his many-layered red, gold, and white robes as he calmly walked away with not a look back at the deflowered creature. For Principal Cleric Yozumian Dudui Yinochek, the Blessed Voice Proper of the Protector's House, the most powerful man in at least one entire ward of the port city of Memnon, had not the time to consider the rabble.

His pursuits were intellectual, his obstacles physical, and his "flock" often more an inconvenience than a source of strength.

He walked stiff-legged and swayed a bit as he crossed the cluttered room, his energy spent. He considered the carts and the crates, the canvas sacks and piled tools. Rarely did he or any of the clerics of Selûne, who controlled the all-important tides, go to that room for purposes other than that one. The place was dirty and smelled of brine; it was a chamber for the servants and not the blessed clerics. The place had only a single redeeming quality: a fairly secretive door heading out to the street, through which "visitors" could readily be smuggled.

That thought turned the principal cleric back to the young woman, barely more than a girl. She cried, but was apparently wise enough not to whine too loudly and insult his performance. She was in pain of course, but it would pass. Her confusion and inner tumult would be more damaging than the sting of a punctured hymen, Yinochek knew.

"You performed a valuable service to Selûne this night," he said to her. "Free of my earthly desires, I can better contemplate the mysteries of paradise, and as they are revealed to me, the road to redemption will be better shown to you and to your failing father. Here."

He lifted a loaf of stale bread he had set on a cart by the hall door when he had entered, and gave it a shake to dislodge a few of the crawling creatures, then tossed it to her. She caught it and clutched it tightly, desperately to her breast. That brought a condescending chuckle from Yinochek.

"You treasure it, of course," he said. "Because you do not understand that your greater reward will be the result of my contemplations. You are so rooted in the needs of the physical that you cannot begin to comprehend the divine."

With a derisive snort at the blank, tear-streaked expression that came back at him, Yinochek turned to the door and pulled it open, startling a handsome young cleric.

"Devout Gositek," he greeted.

"My apologies, Principal," Papan Gositek said, crossing his arms at his belt and bending stiffly in supplication. "I heard . . ."

"Yes, I am finished," Yinochek explained, glancing back and leading Gositek's gaze to the woman, who slowly rocked and clutched at the bread. The principal cleric turned back to the younger priest.

"Your treatise on the Promise of Ibrandul awaits me in my quarters," he said, and the young priest beamed. "I have been told that your insights are nothing short of brilliant, and from what I have perused, I am finding that the rumors are credible. So misunderstood is that god, whose domain is death itself."

Gositek's teeth showed, despite his strenuous attempt at humility.

"Your work proceeds?" Yinochek asked, and he knew he had caught the young man in a prideful gloat.

"Y-yes, yes, Principal," Gositek stammered, respectfully lowering his gaze.

Yinochek hid his amusement. Pride was considered a weakness of course, even a sin, but Yinochek understood the truth of the matter:

absent pride, no young man would undertake the rigors of such contemplation. He shifted aside just a bit as Gositek began to lift his head, allowing the man a view of the shivering girl.

Gositek's eyes, and even a little lick of his lips, betrayed his lust.

"Take her," Yinochek offered. "She is pained, if you care, but your work is more important than her comfort. Release your earthly passions and find a state of contemplation. I am beyond curious to view your thesis regarding the godly propaganda ploys of the Fugue Plane. The thought of the gods themselves vying for the souls of the uncommitted dead fascinates me, and presents opportunities for us to recruit for the worship of Selûne."

Yinochek turned to the girl. "Your dead mother has not yet attained paradise," he said, and he didn't even try to hide his contemptuous snicker. "Devout Gositek here," he stepped aside so that she could better see the man, "prays for her. Your attention to his needs will allow him to better assure her ascent."

He turned back to Gositek and shrugged. "It will be better this way," he said, and walked out of the room.

The girl was all but forgotten by Yinochek by the time he arrived at his chamber on the temple's third and highest floor. He moved past his wooden desk—polished and rich in hue, unlike the gray and grainy driftwood that was most often used in the desert port. The wood had been imported, as was the case with most of the implements, furniture, and decorations of the fabulous temple, by far the largest and most grand structure in the southwestern quarter of the sprawling city.

Divine contemplations required inspirational surroundings.

Yinochek moved to the western door, the one that led to the private balcony, in the great temple known as the Protector's House. There resided the priests of Selûne, the Moon Goddess, and their sister faiths of Valkur and Shaundakul. The single encompassing structure was the center of prayer and contemplation, with a growing library that was fast becoming the envy of the Sword Coast. That library had expanded considerably—and ironically—only a few years earlier, soon after the Time of Troubles, when a cult of the death god Ibrandul had been discovered in the catacombs of that very building. Flushed from their secrecy, not all of those rogue priests had been killed. Under the daring and bold command of

Yinochek, many had been assimilated. "Expand the knowledge," he had told his doubting lessers.

Of course, they had done it secretly.

The balcony was shielded from the ever-prying eyes of idiot peasants who continually gathered in the square below, begging indulgences or healing spells when they had not the coin to pay. His other balcony didn't have the angled high railing to prevent those spiritual beggars from viewing him. Yinochek could view the harbor in full, a round moon setting beyond the watery horizon, silhouetting the tall masts of the great trading ships moored off the coast as they swayed with the rhythmic, gentle waves. That natural harmony reminded the principal cleric of his lovemaking that night, creating in him a connectedness to the universe and lifting him to thoughts of eternity and oneness with Selûne. He sighed and basked in the moment. Physically sated of base and corrupting urges, he soared among the stars and the gods, and more than an hour passed, the moon disappearing from sight, before he turned his thoughts to Gositek's brilliant thesis.

He had found inner peace and so he could find Selûne.

He couldn't even remember what his shivering vessel had looked like that night, nor did he care to try.

CHAPTER

19

Lady Christine, Queen of Damara, sat on the white, iron-backed stool before the grand, platinum-decorated mirror of her vanity. Before her rested an assortment of beauty treatments, jars, and perfumes she had been given as gifts from all over the kingdom, and from Impiltur as well. Her appearance was important, the ladies-in-waiting continually reminded her, for with her stature and with her magnificent husband, she held the hopes and dreams of women across the Bloodstone Lands.

She was an illusion, built to sustain the facade necessary for effective leadership.

Though she had been raised as a noblewoman, Christine was not comfortable with such things. In her heart she was an adventurer, a fighter, and a determined voice.

How thin her voice had seemed that day, when Artemis Entreri had been let go. She heard Gareth moving around the bedroom behind her, and saw him flitter across the image at the corner of her mirror. He was on edge, she knew, for her lack of conversation after the release of the assassin had told him clearly that she did not approve.

It was such a coy little game, she thought, the relationship called marriage. They both knew the issue at hand, but they would dance around it for hours, even days, rather than face the volatility head on.

At least, that was the usual way for most couples, but never had demurring been a staple of Lady Christine's emotional repetoire.

"If you would prefer a less opinionated queen, I'm sure one can be easily found," she said. She regretted the sarcasm as soon as the words had left her mouth, but at least she had started the dialogue.

She saw the image of Gareth behind her, and felt his strong and comforting hands come to rest upon her shoulders. She liked the touch of his fingers against her bare flesh, interrupted only by the thin straps of her nightgown.

"What a fool I would be if I desired to be rid of the closest friend and advisor I have ever known," he said, and he bent and kissed her on top of her head.

"I didn't suggest that you be rid of Master Kane," she replied, and she let Gareth see her smile in the mirror.

He joined in her laugh and gently squeezed her shoulders.

Christine turned in her seat and looked at him. "Yet you were quick to dismiss my advice throughout this ordeal with Artemis Entreri and that devilish drow."

Gareth's nodding sigh was one of both agreement and resignation.

"Why?" Christine asked. "What is it you know of them that the rest of us—other than Kane, it seems—do not?"

"I know little of either of them," Gareth admitted. "And I suspect that the world would be a better place with both of them removed from it. Certainly I find few redeeming qualities in the likes of Artemis Entreri or that confounding drow. But neither have I the right to pass such judgment. By all accounts they are innocent of any heinous actions."

"They committed treason to the throne."

"By claiming a land over which no man has rightful dominion?" Gareth asked.

"Yet you went to dethrone them, posthaste."

Gareth nodded again. "I would not let it stand. Vaasa will become a barony of Damara. Of that I am determined. And I am certain it will be done with the blessing and support of every city within our northern neighbor. Surely Palishchuk desires such a union."

"Then which is it? Treason? Or are you a conqueror?"

"A little of both, I suspect."

"And you believe the drow and his wild tale that this was all prearranged?" Christine did not hide her skepticism in the least. "That he planned for you to come so that you could be seen as a hero yet again to the folk of Palishchuk? He is an opportunist in the extreme, and only your quick action prevented him from securing his kingdom!"

"I do not doubt that," said Gareth. "Nor do I underestimate the threat from that one. For him to successfully infiltrate the Citadel of Assassins is no small feat, nor is retrieving the head of Archmage Knellict an action of one who should be easily dismissed. Spysong is watching them, and carefully, I assure you. They will be gone from the land within the tenday, as demanded."

"Or they will be killed?"

"Efficiently," Gareth promised. "Indeed, the dragon sisters have agreed to fly them far from our borders."

"Where they may wreak havoc somewhere else."

"Perhaps."

"And in that admission, do you believe that you serve Ilmater?"

"I often do not know," the man said. He turned away and paced back to the side of the bed.

Christine shifted her chair so that she could face him directly, and earnestly asked, "What is it, my love? What hold has this man upon you?"

Gareth stared at her and let a long moment pass silently, then said, "The experience with Artemis Entreri will make me a better king."

That proclamation made Lady Christine raise her eyebrows. "In that you are determined that you will not become akin to him?" she asked, and her inflection revealed doubt and confusion with every word.

"No, that is not the point," Gareth replied. "But in my private conversation with Artemis Entreri, he was correct in that neither blood nor a disconnected deed is the true measure of leadership. My actions now, and now alone, can justify this title I hold dear . . . and it is an empty title unless it is one that truly represents the hopes, dreams, and betterment of the people of the kingdom—of *all* the people of the kingdom."

"Artemis Entreri told you that?" Christine asked, not attempting to mask the doubt in her voice.

"I'm uncertain that he understood what he was asking," said Gareth. "But in essence, yes, that is exactly what he told—what he taught—to me. I rule Damara, and wish to bring Vaasa under my fold in the single Kingdom of Bloodstone. But that decision must be one that serves the betterment of the folk of Vaasa, else I am no more worthy to claim this title than—"

"Than Entreri, Jarlaxle, or Zhengyi?"

"Yes," said Gareth, and he nodded as he looked at her, his eyes set with determination, his lips showing that optimistic and hopeful grin that so endeared him to almost everyone who had ever looked upon him. Against that sincere expression, Lady Christine could not maintain her resentment.

"Then let the image of Artemis Entreri linger in your thoughts, my love, for the good of Damara and Vaasa," she said. "And let the man be far gone from here, his dark elf friend beside him."

"For the good of Damara and Vaasa," said Gareth.

Christine went to her husband, the man she loved.

<hr/>

She barely felt the dagger tip connect with his skin before she retracted her arm and stabbed him again, and again. In a wild, crying frenzy, Calihye struck at the helpless man. She felt the warmth of blood under her thigh and pumped her arm even more furiously, her eyes closed, tears streaming down her cheeks and crying for Parissus all the while.

Her anger, her frustration, her sadness, her remorse, and her explosion of desperation all played out, leaving her in a great physical weariness, and she looked down at the man who had been her lover.

He lay on his back, arms out wide and making no move to defend against her. He stared at her, his jaw clenched, his expression a mask of disappointment.

He didn't have a scratch on him. The blood on her thigh was her own, caused by a cut she had inflicted on one retraction of the blade.

<hr/>

"So predictable, these weak human creatures," Kimmuriel Oblodra remarked as he and Jarlaxle watched the spectacle playing out on Entreri's bed from an extra-dimensional pocket from which had opened a gate to the side of the room.

"She was so convincing," Jarlaxle said. "I never would have believed . . ."

"Then you have been around these fools too long," Kimmuriel said. "Are your judgments so impaired that I should not welcome you back to Bregan D'aerthe when you at last abandon this folly and return to Menzoberranzan?"

Jarlaxle glanced at the psionicist, a frozen look, a murderer's look, that reminded Kimmuriel in no uncertain terms who he was addressing.

But Jarlaxle didn't hold to the threatening stare, as he was drawn back to the spectacle on the bed. Calihye's expression had turned more to terror by that point, and she struck again, at Entreri's eye, as if she wanted so desperately to stop him from looking at her with his accusing gaze.

Entreri did flinch, but so remotely that Jarlaxle marveled at the sheer discipline of the man. He had ordered Kimmuriel to enact the psionic kinetic barrier, of course, for the psionicist had learned of Calihye's desperate plan. But Entreri could not have known that he was so protected, and yet he had not in any way tried to fend off the attacks.

Had Calihye coaxed him to a point of such vulnerability? Had her actions and soothing words so put Artemis Entreri off his guard?

Or did he simply not care?

"Fascinating," Jarlaxle whispered.

"It reminds you of your own birth, no doubt," said Kimmuriel, catching him off balance. He looked at his companion.

"No doubt," Jarlaxle replied, and since his companion had mentioned it, he could indeed picture a terrified and frustrated Matron Baenre plunging her spider-shaped dagger at his newborn breast. He imagined that her look must have been somewhat similar to Calihye's at that very moment, such a delicious mixture of a dozen conflicting emotions.

"You never did get the opportunity to thank my House's matron mother," Kimmuriel remarked.

"Oh, but I did," Jarlaxle assured him.

"When Baenre's Secondboy scooped you from the altar and all

of the kinetic energy bound within your infant frame exploded into him and tore his chest apart," Kimmuriel agreed, recalling the stories of that distant time, tales that had been told and retold in House Oblodra over the centuries. "My grandmatron did have a way of removing her sworn enemies."

"Few could so fluster Matron Baenre as the matron mothers of House Oblodra," said Jarlaxle. "I am certain that Baenre keenly considered such insults as the power of Lolth flowed through her and offered her the power to tumble House Oblodra into the Clawrift."

Kimmuriel, ever so in control, did wince at that, and Jarlaxle smiled. For only a few short years before, Jarlaxle's mother had obliterated Kimmuriel's House in one devastating burst of power.

The two exchanged looks of mutual surrender, then turned their attention back to the room, where the stubborn and terrified Calihye lifted the dagger before her in both hands, clutched it tightly, and drove it at Entreri's heart yet again. He reached up and stopped her, and as she struggled to push through his powerful grasp, his other hand came up and slapped her hard. As he did that, he turned his hips and sent her tumbling off the far side of the bed.

"He knows what happened," Kimmuriel remarked. He led Jarlaxle's gaze behind them, to the brutish orc warrior patiently awaiting its orders.

"End the dweomer," Jarlaxle instructed, and he grabbed the orc's tether and pulled the creature behind him into the room. As Entreri jumped up from the bed to face them, Jarlaxle tugged the orc close and whispered, "Kill him," into its ear, then shoved it forward at Entreri.

The sight of a naked human, his right side red with blood from chest to hip, was all the encouragement the brutish beast needed. It charged Entreri and leaped for him.

With hardly an effort, only simple instinct, Entreri's hand came out hard to grasp the orc by the throat, and all of the energy that had been bound up kinetically within his frame, every one of Calihye's vicious strokes and stabs, flowed through that connection.

The orc's chest exploded with garish wounds; its left eye drove into its brain, blood spurting from the wound.

It spasmed and jerked, and tried to cry out in stunned horror.

But all it could do was gurgle on its own blood, and Entreri unceremoniously dropped the dead thing down to the ground.

He stood there on the edge of disaster, covered in blood, breathing deeply as if fighting for control.

Jarlaxle knew that the furious man wanted nothing more than to spring forward and strike at him, then. He also held faith that Artemis Entreri was too disciplined to do such a stupid thing.

Behind Entreri, Calihye rose and gasped at the sight of the dead orc and the two dark elves. Her arms went limp at her sides and the dagger fell to the floor.

"I am sorry," Jarlaxle said to Entreri.

The assassin didn't blink.

"It is not the way I wanted it to be," Jarlaxle said.

Entreri's look told him clearly that the man considered it none of Jarlaxle's business.

"I could not let her kill you, even if you seemed resigned to that fate," Jarlaxle explained.

Kimmuriel's fingers flashed disapproval in the air. *You spend too much time justifying yourself to your inferiors,* the psionicist scolded.

"And you spend too much time breathing," Entreri said to Kimmuriel, reminding the drow that he had learned to interpret that silent drow language during his stay in Menzoberranzan, even though his less delicate human fingers could not "speak" it well.

Jarlaxle put his hand on Kimmuriel's arm, a silent reminder to the psionicist that he did not have permission to kill Entreri.

Never blinking, never taking his awful stare off of Artemis Entreri, Kimmuriel obediently stepped back, prepared, Jarlaxle knew all too well, to cripple or even kill the human with a wave of psionic energy.

As Kimmuriel retreated, Calihye stumbled forward to Entreri's side. Her sobs genuine, she grabbed his arm and lowered her head to his shoulder in supplication, whispering that she was sorry over and over again.

"The poor thing has wound herself into an emotional collapse," Kimmuriel remarked.

"Shut up," said Entreri. He turned to Calihye and roughly pulled her back.

"It was Parissus," she blabbered. "And you were leaving. You can't leave . . . I can't let you . . . I'm sorry."

Entreri's responding expression was, perhaps, the most profound look of disappointment and dismay Jarlaxle Baenre had ever seen. Entreri let out a long sigh and seemed to relax, and apparently bolstered by that, taking confidence that the moment of crisis had passed, Calihye dared to look up and say, "You will never hurt me." She even managed to put a weak, hopeful smile on her face.

She was trying to be cute, to be coy, to be playful, Jarlaxle recognized, but he saw, too, that to Entreri, she appeared as nothing but mocking.

He ran his hand down her cheek softly, then changed in a blink, his expression going hard, his hand grabbing at her chin. Her eyes went wide and she clutched and clawed at his unyielding wrist with both hands.

He drove her before him with two powerful strides and with frightening strength shoved her backward. She crashed through the shutters, she smashed through the glass of the window, and she shrieked only once as she tumbled over the pane to fall a dozen feet to the street below.

Entreri turned back to Jarlaxle.

"You should have killed her," the drow said, and in a voice dripping with sympathy and regret. "She is dangerous."

"Shut up."

Jarlaxle sighed.

"And if you slay her, I promise you that you will join her in death," Entreri added.

Jarlaxle sighed again. But of course, he could only blame himself for using the flute to manipulate the assassin, for prying open the heart of Artemis Entreri, which for so long had been shielded from the agony of love.

The cold began to overtake her. Blood flowed from a hundred cuts and when she tried to extract herself from the planking and broken glass, Calihye found that her leg would not support her.

She was dying, she knew. Miserable and alone in the biting cold, naked and bleeding before the world. She held no hope, and didn't want to live, anyway. She had failed, in all ways.

She had fallen in love with the man who had killed her dear Parissus, and that discordant reality had broken her. When faced with the thought of leaving her home, or of saying farewell to Entreri, she had found the options untenable.

So she had made her own course, reverting to her fierce desire for revenge, using her despair at the loss of her dearest love Parissus as armor against the heartbreak Entreri was about to inflict upon her by leaving her.

And she had failed.

So she was dying, and she was glad of it. She crawled through the glass in search of a suitable shard, agony burning, cold wind biting. She found a sizable chunk, elongated like a dagger's blade, and with it clutched in hand, she crawled around the side of the inn, into the alleyway where she could die, free from the intrusion of any curious eyes.

She barely made it in, and fell back into a sitting position against the wall. Her breathing came in rasps, and she coughed up some blood. She realized she didn't even have to put the shard to her throat to end it all; the fall had done the work.

But death from her wounds would be too slow, and it hurt too much.

Calihye lifted the point of the shard to her throat. She thought of Entreri, of their lovemaking, but she brushed it away. She pictured Parissus instead, and imagined her waiting in death, arms wide to embrace her dear Calihye again.

Calihye closed her eyes and stabbed.

Or tried to, but a stronger hand clasped her wrist and held it steady. Calihye opened her eyes, and they went all the wider when she realized that a dark elf held her wrist, and that other drow were about, all leering at her. In that instant of terror, the fog and the pain abandoned her.

"We are not finished with you quite yet," she heard from the back of the group, and the dark elves parted to reveal one of the drow she had just seen in the room above, the one Entreri had spoken of before and had named as Kimmuriel.

"Perhaps in time we will allow you to take your life," Kimmuriel said to her. "Perhaps we will even do it for you, though I doubt you will enjoy our technique."

A pair of dark elves forced her to her feet and a twist of her wrist made her drop the glass shard.

"But then, perhaps you will enjoy the Underdark even less," said Kimmuriel. "Fail in your duties, and we will be happy to determine which is the worst fate for Lady Calihye."

"Duties?" the stunned woman managed to whisper.

The drow dragged her away.

CHAPTER

DREAMS AND MEMORIES

20

"He went looking for her," Jarlaxle said to Kimmuriel when the pair met up the next day in a shaded glen near the appointed rendezvous with the dragon sisters. Not far away, Entreri and Athrogate sat about a tumble of boulders in the middle of a rocky lea.

Kimmuriel had joined them, intending to prevent the conversation from veering toward Calihye. Jarlaxle, as if reading his mind, had led with a reference to the wretched human woman.

"It is typical of humans, is it not?" the psionicist answered. "To throw a lover through a glass window, then seek her out in remorse? Our way is much more straightforward and honest, I think. No drow matron would expel a male and let him live."

"With notable exception."

"Notable," Kimmuriel agreed. "Of course, in the instance to which you refer, Matron Baenre had little choice in the matter. Is it true that the Secondboy of House Baenre was the one commanded to rid the House of the cursed Jarlaxle, who lay on the altar without a mark despite the repeated stabbing of the mighty matron mother herself?"

"You know the tale," Jarlaxle replied.

"Yes, but I would like to hear it as often as you would deign to tell it. To see your mother's face twisted in exquisite frustration and horror when her blade would not bite into the infant! And then to see her expression of the sheerest terror, and that of Triel as well, when Secondboy Doquaio whisked you from the slab! He must have looked much like that bloody creature in Artemis's room when the infant Jarlaxle unwittingly released the captured energy into him."

Kimmuriel took hope at Jarlaxle's chuckle, an indication, perhaps, that he had deflected the conversation from Calihye.

"And of course, then Jarlaxle was no longer the third son, and no longer a fitting sacrifice," he rambled on.

"I haven't seen Kimmuriel bantering this much since you wagged your hands in trying to alleviate a cramp in your forearm," Jarlaxle said, and the psionicist's lips went tight.

"She was gone from the alley," Jarlaxle said. "She didn't crawl far, for the blood trail ended—and rather abruptly, and right near a place where the blood had pooled. She was sitting there, against the wall, of course, before she was taken away."

"Lady Calihye has made powerful enemies, and powerful friends," said Kimmuriel. "Perhaps it is a good thing that Artemis Entreri is leaving the realm, and quickly."

"And she has made friends of convenience," Jarlaxle remarked, staring his associate right in the eye. "Who will turn on her, no doubt, at the slightest hint of betrayal."

Kimmuriel didn't deny it.

"This place is worth the trouble of Bregan D'aerthe," Jarlaxle went on. "There is much to be found here, such as the bloodstone, a mineral we cannot easily procure in the Underdark. With Knellict serving our . . . *your* cause, you will find easy access to it and other valuables."

"You have explained it all, many times."

Jarlaxle clapped Kimmuriel on the shoulder, and the stiff psionicist just stared at him with awkward curiosity. Kimmuriel did intend to use Calihye and Knellict to create a network in the Bloodstone Lands, but in truth it was more for the preservation of Jarlaxle's reputation than for any monetary gains or increase of power the psionicist expected to make. Jarlaxle's reputation couldn't withstand another disaster like the one in Calimport, so close on the heels of that debacle, Kimmuriel believed, and the last thing he wanted was for Bregan D'aerthe to turn away from Jarlaxle. For Jarlaxle would one day return to Menzoberranzan and resume his mantle of leadership. Bregan D'aerthe needed that in order to keep Matron Mother Triel Baenre at proper distance and in proper humor, and more than that, Kimmuriel needed it. His pursuits of the purely intellectual were not served well by the responsibilities of maintaining Jarlaxle's band. He longed for the day when Jarlaxle returned and he could turn his attention more fully to the illithids and the mysteries of their expansive mental powers.

And turn his attention away from the concerns of the mercenary band, and away from protecting the increasingly renegade Jarlaxle.

"I know that you doubt," Jarlaxle said, again as if reading his mind, which the psionicist knew to be impossible. Kimmuriel was far too mentally shielded for any such intrusions. "And I am glad that you do, for else who would force me to question my every twist and turn?"

"Your own common sense?"

Jarlaxle laughed aloud. "My vision is correct," he insisted.

"Menzoberranzan demands our attention at all times."

Jarlaxle nodded. "But the day will come when the contacts we—the contacts *you* secure on the surface will prove invaluable to the matron mothers."

"What do you know?"

"I know that the world is in flux," said Jarlaxle. "Entreri and I were attacked by a Netherese shade, and he made it quite clear that he was not alone. If the shadows fall across the World Above, the matron mothers will not wish to remain oblivious.

"Furthermore, my friend, there is growing here on the surface a following of Eilistraee. Drizzt Do'Urden is hardly unique among surface drow, and he is finding more acceptance among the surface dwellers."

"Your former House—"

"I was never of their House," Jarlaxle corrected.

"House Baenre," said Kimmuriel, "will not go against Drizzt again, nor would they find any followers if they so decided. There are even priestesses postulating that Drizzt is secretly in the favor of Lolth."

"They said the same of me after the failed sacrifice."

"The evidence was strong."

"And I have never bended knee for the spider bitch. Nor has Drizzt Do'Urden. I am certain that if he learned that he was in Lady

Lolth's favor, it would torment him more than a festering wound ever could."

"More the reason for the goddess to so favor him, then."

Jarlaxle merely shrugged at the inescapable logic. Such was the irony of following a deity dedicated to chaos.

"But I do not speak of Drizzt in any case," said Jarlaxle. "I find it unlikely that the Spider Queen will tolerate the worshipers of Eilistraee much longer, and when that day of reckoning befalls the dancing fools, their judgment may well be served by the Houses of Menzoberranzan. Bregan D'aerthe will prove invaluable at that time, of course."

"Even if it is centuries hence."

"Patience has sustained me," said Jarlaxle. "And our endeavors will be profitable in the meantime. In human parlance, that is known as a win-win."

"Humans often think they are winning until the moment they are thrown through the glass window."

Jarlaxle surrendered with another laugh and with the full understanding, Kimmuriel knew, that Bregan D'aerthe would indeed exploit the contacts made here in this rugged land of Damara and Vaasa.

Kimmuriel looked past Jarlaxle to the open field and nodded, and the other drow turned around.

"Your dragons approach," said Kimmuriel.

Jarlaxle turned back to him and extended his hand. "Then farewell."

Kimmuriel didn't shake the hand, and so Jarlaxle moved it to his belt pouch to show his lieutenant that he was carrying the item, as they had agreed. Kimmuriel nodded at that, and one hand came out from under his dark robes, bearing a small coffer that held three small vials.

Jarlaxle's eyes gleamed when he viewed them. "I have opened his heart, and now I will open his mind," he said.

"For reasons that no sane drow could ever fathom."

"Sane is boring."

Kimmuriel snorted derisively as Jarlaxle took the potions. "His mother, his childhood . . . these are the questions that will open Entreri's mind to you," the psionicist said, and as he retracted the empty coffer, he brought forth his other hand from under the folds of his robes, bearing Idalia's flute.

"The residual memories lingering within the flute showed you this?" asked Jarlaxle.

"You asked me to inspect it, and so I did. You asked me for the potions, and so they are yours."

Jarlaxle, smiling widely, took the flute.

"And now we are gone, Jarlaxle," said Kimmuriel. "I'll not heed your call again until our next arranged meeting."

"A long time hence."

"Rightly so—I've grown far too weary of this blinding surface world, and spent not enough energy heeding the needs of Bregan D'aerthe in Menzoberranzan. It is a city of chaos and constant change, and my former master taught me well that Bregan D'aerthe must change with it, or before it, even."

"Your former master was brilliant, I am told."

"So he often says."

Jarlaxle had rarely laughed as much in the presence of the dry-witted psionicist. "I am certain that I will find the band well tended when I return to Menzoberranzan," he said.

"Of course. And when will that be?"

Jarlaxle glanced back toward Entreri, who stood with Athrogate before Ilnezhara and Tazmikella. "A human's lifetime, perhaps."

"Or the remainder of this one's?"

"Or that. But recall that he was infused with the stuff of shadow. It could be a longer time than you believe." He looked back at Kimmuriel and offered a wink. "But I will indeed return."

"Don't bring the dwarf."

Yet another burst of laughter escaped Jarlaxle's lips, and Kimmuriel tightened his expression even more. Jarlaxle seemed almost giddy to him, and it was not a sight he enjoyed.

"Why, Kimmuriel, you lack imagination!" Jarlaxle declared dramatically. "Do you not see that Athrogate would be a fine gift for my sister, whichever one rules House Baenre, when I return?"

Kimmuriel didn't smile at all, and at that, Jarlaxle only laughed even louder.

"Well, I ain't much for wizard teleportin'," Athrogate was grumbling when Jarlaxle joined the foursome at the boulder tumble in the small field. The dwarf blew a stray strand of black hair from his mouth and crossed his burly arms over his chest. For added effect, he stomped one foot, which set his morningstar heads bouncing at the ends of their respective chains, one over each shoulder as the weapons were crossed on his back. "Knew a halfling once joined a mage such. A skinny old wizard in need of a crutch. And his eyes weren't so good to the price o' their bones, for he shot a bit low and landed both in the stones! *Bwahaha!*"

Athrogate snapped off his knee-slapping laughter almost as soon as it began, re-crossed his arms and returned a scowl at Jarlaxle. "And I'm meanin' *in* the stones."

The drow looked to Entreri, who just stood there shaking his head and showing no interest in tipping the dwarf off to the reality of their impending journey. He turned to the dragon sisters, who seemed quite amused by it all.

"You think they have come to teleport us?" Jarlaxle asked. "You forget your flight across the tavern's common room."

"Ain't forgetting nothing," said the dwarf. "Wizard tricks . . . bah! They ain't to throw us across the damn sea. Though hell of a landing that might be!"

"Wizard?" the oblivious Entreri asked, for he had not witnessed the flying dwarf. "You think they mean to teleport us?"

"Well they ain't about to carry me, with skinny girl arms and skinny girl knees! *Bwahaha!*"

"Well maybe instead they'll tie you to a tree," rhymed Entreri, drawing curious, surprised stares from all the others. "Bend it to the ground and let it fly free. Launching you high to the clouds in the sky, and when you come falling we all hope you'll die."

Athrogate's lips moved as he digested the words by repeating them, and Entreri, his brow furrowed, for he was far from joking, wisely moved a hand to his sword hilt as if expecting the dwarf to launch himself forward.

But Athrogate exploded into laughter instead of into action. *"Bwahaha!* Hey, I'm stealin' that!"

"An appropriate price," Ilnezhara said. "Can we be on with this? I've a shop to attend in the morning."

"Of course, milady," Jarlaxle said with one of his characteristic, hat-sweeping bows. "But we must prepare our oblivious friend—"

"No, I don't think we shall," said Ilnezhara, and her voice changed abruptly in timbre and volume, cutting Jarlaxle short and sending Athrogate's jaw to his chest.

"I care not what he might say, and less that he runs away!" Ilnezhara roared, and the boulders shook from the strength of her voice.

Her jaws elongated, as if the sheer power of the words had pulled it forward, and a pair of copper-colored horns prodded through her golden hair and stretched upward. As she half-turned, a heavy tail thumped onto the ground and began to lengthen, as her torso stretched and twisted, bones popping into place.

"You thought we'd ride in a wagon," Entreri teased the mercifully speechless dwarf. "But instead we're flying a . . ." He paused and waved his hand to prompt the poet dwarf. "Yes, as I expected," Entreri remarked when no words came forth.

"Uh-uh," said Athrogate, his hands out in front of him and waving, and he began backing away.

Hardly noticed at the side, Jarlaxle produced a thin wand and pointed it at Entreri, then Athrogate, then himself, each time speaking the command word to enact its magic.

"Ah, but to soar to the clouds!" Jarlaxle said, and he moved around Ilnezhara. "May I mount you, good lady?" he teased, and Ilnezhara, her transformation continuing, her body elongating, roared in reply. Jarlaxle scrambled astride her scaly back just before two great leathery wings erupted from behind her shoulders, snapping out mightily to their full extension.

"Dragon," Athrogate muttered.

"You missed the cue, sorry," Entreri said to him, his voice mirthless though he enjoyed the spectacle of a befuddled Athrogate.

"Dragon," sputtered Athrogate. "It's a dragon. She's a wyrm . . . a dragon . . . a dragon."

"May I eat the dwarf?" Ilnezhara asked Jarlaxle as soon as her transformation was complete. She stood on four legs, a mighty copper dragon. "I will need sustenance for the journey."

Jarlaxle leaned forward and whispered into her ear, and her serpentine neck snapped her head out toward Athrogate, who blanched and nearly fainted. Ilnezhara hit him with a burst of her windy breath, a magical cone of "heavy" air. Suddenly Athrogate seemed to be moving much more slowly, and he turned as if running through deep mud.

But Ilnezhara had no such bonds on her, and she reared and leaped forward, a single snapping beat of her wings lifting her and her rider drow from the ground. They shot past Entreri, who fell away, and Tazmikella, who seemed to take pleasure in the sudden buffet of wind.

Athrogate dived aside—or was beginning to—when Ilnezhara passed over him, and her claw grabbed him hard and yanked him along. In a blink of the stunned and terrified dwarf's eye, he found himself fifty feet off the ground and climbing fast.

"I will miss you, Artemis Entreri," Tazmikella said when the two were alone on the field. "I grew fond of you, though I never came to trust you." She gave a little grin as her face started to twist and distort. "Perhaps there is something to this element of danger that my sister so enjoys."

Entreri wanted to remind her that she was a dragon, but it occurred to him that insulting such a creature might not be the smartest thing he ever did. As Tazmikella moved more fully into her transformation, he slipped around her side and onto her back, thinking to emulate Jarlaxle instead of Athrogate.

In a few moments, they were airborne, the wind whipping around them, the world spinning below in a dizzying blur. Entreri and Athrogate didn't know it, but Jarlaxle's use of the wand saved them from the killing bite of the winter wind. As the dragons climbed higher into the cold sky, the trio of lesser creatures would have frozen to death had it not been for the protective enchantment.

Artemis Entreri didn't notice any of that. His cape buffeted out behind him and the world below moved past at dizzying speed. Shortly into the flight, he could see the northern shore of the Moonsea.

Still the dragons climbed, so that any observers on the ground would think them nothing more than a bird. A short while later, to Entreri's surprise, they went out over the sea, and the sisters executed a right turn, veering west-southwest. They flew through the night and landed on a small island just before the break of dawn.

Entreri scrambled down from Tazmikella.

"Rest," the dragon instructed. "We will be up again at nightfall, to finish crossing the sea. We will set you down north of Cormyr, and there your road is your own."

Entreri noted the approach of Jarlaxle and Athrogate—mostly from the sputtering and grumbling of the obviously thoroughly shaken dwarf.

"Ought to hit 'em both," he mumbled. "Treatin' a dwarf like that. Just ain't polite."

Entreri could only hope that his threat was more than mere words. The spectacle of Tazmikella's giant maw closing over Athrogate was one the assassin surely would enjoy, but he let the pleasant image go and kept his attention on the dragon.

"I have coin," he said. "Some, at least." He gave a look to Jarlaxle. "I would ask that you take me farther along that course, to the southwest."

Jarlaxle came up beside him then, and offered him a curious glance. "Cormyr is a fine diversion," he said.

"I wish you well there, in that case," said Entreri, and Jarlaxle backed a step and blinked as if he had been slapped. "I've neither the time nor the desire."

"How far would you wish to go?" Tazmikella asked, keeping her dragon voice as quiet as she could so that it did not carry across the open water.

"As far as you will take me. My road is to Memnon, on the southern Sword Coast."

"That is a long way," remarked Ilnezhara.

Entreri looked to Jarlaxle. "Whatever my share is, give it to them."

"Share of what?" the drow replied. "We lost."

Entreri narrowed his eyes.

"I can arrange some payment," Jarlaxle said to the dragons. "How much will you require? Or perhaps there are other things for which you would barter. We can discuss it later."

The dragons exchanged wary looks, which struck Entreri as very strange, since they were, after all, dragons.

Except at that moment, Ilnezhara reverted to her human form, and bade her sister to do likewise. "In case the island has visitors," the blond-haired woman explained, though Tazmikella's look as she came out of her natural form showed that she understood Ilnezhara's ulterior motives all too well, particularly when Ilnezhara shot Jarlaxle a rather lewd wink.

"That, too, of course," said Jarlaxle. "Though I feel as if I should pay you even more."

"You should," said Ilnezhara.

Entreri's sigh showed that he had heard about enough of that nonsense. "Will you fly me?"

"Not all the way to Memnon, no," Tazmikella replied. "I've made enemies in the southern deserts that I do not wish to encounter. But we will see how far the winds will carry us."

"And what of you?" Ilnezhara asked Jarlaxle.

"And meself?" Athrogate asked hopefully.

Jarlaxle and the dragon looked at the dwarf.

"Well, ye taked me from the place I've known as home for many a year," Athrogate protested. "Ye can't be expecting me to just swim to Cormyr, now can ye?"

"We will stay together, we three," Jarlaxle answered both the dragon and the dwarf. "I would be grateful if you would fly me in the wake of your sister and Artemis."

If he was trying to gauge the reaction of the surprising Entreri as he declared his intentions, the drow was sorely disappointed, for Entreri, who simply did not care, had already started away.

Ilnezhara grabbed Jarlaxle by the hand and pulled him along. "Come and show me your gratitude," she bade him.

Jarlaxle followed without complaint, but he kept looking back at Entreri, who sat with his back against a rock, staring out at the dark and empty waters to the west.

⊷══⊶

"I remain surprised that you would provide such information," Ilnezhara said to Jarlaxle around noon the next day, when she awoke beside him. "Why would you trust me with such information after I sided with King Gareth against you? Or is it that you wish harm to befall this Kimmuriel creature and your former associates?"

"You will not see Kimmuriel, nor any of my Underdark brethren," a sleepy Jarlaxle replied. He yawned and stretched, and considered his surroundings. Waves lapped rhythmically at the rocky shores of the small island, drowned out intermittently by Athrogate's snoring. "They will work from the shadows below."

"Then why tell me?"

"They pose no threat to King Gareth," said Jarlaxle. "And now I know your loyalty there. Indeed, Kimmuriel will force Knellict to behave himself, so consider the efforts of Bregan D'aerthe to be a welcomed leash on the Citadel of Assassins. And an opportunity for you and your sister. Items we consider commonplace and cheap in Menzoberranzan will no doubt interest you greatly for your collections, and will bring a fine price on the surface. Similarly, you can barter goods that hold little value here but will light the red eyes of matron mothers in the city of drow."

"Bregan D'aerthe is a merchant operation, then?"

"First, foremost, and whenever the choice is before us."

Ilnezhara slowly nodded, though her expression remained doubtful. "We will watch them carefully."

"You will never see them," said Jarlaxle, and he pulled himself to his feet and gathered his clothing. "Kimmuriel is not skilled in the ways of polite society. Ever has that been my role, and of course your beloved King Gareth is too small a man to understand the worth of my company. Now, if you will excuse me, good lady. The day grows long already and I must go and speak with my associate." He finished with a bow, and pulled on his shirt.

"He surprised you with his request," Ilnezhara said as Jarlaxle started away. The drow paused and glanced back.

"Or are you simply not used to him leading?" Ilnezhara teased.

Jarlaxle grinned, shrugged, and walked off. He spotted Entreri, dozing against the same rock, shaded from the rising sun and with the western waters before him.

The drow looked all around, then quickly quaffed one of the potions Kimmuriel had given him. He waited a moment for the magic to settle in, then focused his attention on Entreri, considering the questions he might ask to spur the man's thoughts.

Jarlaxle blinked in surprise, for Entreri's thoughts began to crystallize in his intruding mind. The potions facilitated mind-reading, and as images of a great seaport began to flit through his thoughts,

306

Jarlaxle realized that Entreri was already there, in Memnon, the city of his birth.

So clear were those images that Jarlaxle could almost smell the salty air, and hear the seabirds. Entreri's dream—was it a dream or a memory, the drow wondered—showed him a plain-looking woman, one who might have once been somewhat attractive, though the soil and dust, and hard living had taken a great toll on her. Her few remaining teeth were crooked and yellow, and her eyes, perhaps once shining black orbs, showed the listlessness of despair, the empty and weary eyes of a person who had suffered prolonged poverty. The world had broken that once-pretty woman.

Jarlaxle felt a tenderness emanating from Entreri as the man's dream lingered on her.

Then a cart, a priest, a young boy's screams . . .

Jarlaxle fell back a step as a wave of rage rolled out from Entreri to nearly overwhelm him. Such anger! Passionate, feral outrage!

He saw the woman again, receding into the dust, and sensed that he was on a cart rolling away from her. The tenderness was gone, replaced by a sense of betrayal that filled Jarlaxle with trepidation.

The drow came out of it, shaken, a short while later. He stood staring at Entreri, and he knew that what he had seen when he had insinuated himself into the assassin's dreams were indeed memories.

"Your mother," the drow whispered under his breath as he considered the image of the black-haired, black-eyed woman.

The drow snorted at the irony. Perhaps the kinship he felt toward Artemis Entreri was more rooted in common experiences than he had consciously known.

CHAPTER

21

Entreri stood staring at the west, at a cluster of palm trees rising from the rolling dunes of sand. He nodded as he realized where they were, for he was quite familiar with the mountains south of their position. Not much of this region north of the divide was rolling white sand, though south of those mountains, closer to Calimport, the desert extended for miles and miles. The land was almost equally barren, but was more a matter of mesas and long-dead river valleys, but one stretch was the exception. They were along the trade route, and since the mountains stretched out, impassable, southeast of their position, Entreri realized that they were no more than a few days from Memnon. He looked back at the dragon sisters, who were preparing to depart, and offered Tazmikella, when she caught his glance, as close to an expression of gratitude as he'd ever offered anyone.

Off to the side of Entreri, Athrogate sat, spitting curses and pulling off his boots. "Rotten stuff," he said, pouring a generous amount of sand from one shoe. When they came in, Ilnezhara had skimmed low, and the rut the claw-riding Athrogate had cut in the coarse sand could be traced back many yards.

While the dwarf's discomfort pleased Entreri, he shifted his gaze to his other companion. Jarlaxle stood near the dragons with his back to Entreri, his hat far back on his head, completely obscuring the assassin's view of him. Something in the expressions of the two gigantic creatures clued him in that Jarlaxle had somehow caught them off guard. With a cursory glance at the complaining Athrogate, Entreri moved beside his long-time companion.

And saw a handsome elf, with golden skin and hair the color of the morning sun.

Entreri fell back a step.

"Although the hair suits you well, I prefer the drow image," Ilnezhara said. "Exotic, mysterious, enticing . . ."

"Dangerous," said her sister. "That is always the lure for you, dear sister, which is why we are farther into Dojomentikus's domain than I had desired. Come now, it is time for us to be gone."

"Dojo would not strike out at the both of us, sister," said Ilnezhara. She turned back to Entreri and Jarlaxle. "Such a petty beast, like most males. Imagine that just a few trinkets could invoke such wrath."

"A few trinkets and your refusal to breed with him."

"He bored me."

"Perhaps he should have donned a drow disguise," Tazmikella said, and Entreri realized that that should have been his line—except that he was hardly listening to the conversation, for he remained transfixed on Jarlaxle.

"You should close your mouth," Ilnezhara said, and it took Entreri a moment to understand that she had directed the comment at him. "The sand will blow in. It is most uncomfortable."

Entreri shot her a quick look, but turned back to his companion.

"Kimmuriel is often difficult in his dealings," Jarlaxle explained. "He conceded quite a bit, but demanded of me that I wear this mantle beyond the Bloodstone Lands, for all the rest of my days on the surface."

"Agatha's mask," Entreri realized, for he had once worn the magical item, many years before. With it, he had assumed the mien of Regis, the troublesome halfling, and had used the disguise to infiltrate Mithral Hall before the drow invasion. He shook that memory from his mind, for from that failed invasion had come his servitude in the city of drow, a place he did not like to think about.

"The same," Jarlaxle confirmed.

"I had thought it lost, or destroyed."

"Little gets lost that cannot be found, and no magic is ever truly destroyed for those who know how to put it back together." He smiled as he spoke, reached behind him, and brought forth a familiar gauntlet, the complimentary piece to Entreri's mighty sword.

"Kimmuriel managed to piece it back together; he is no fonder of magic-users than are you, my friend." He tossed the gauntlet to Entreri, who studied it for a moment, noting the red lines shot through the black material. He slipped it on his hand and clutched the hilt of Charon's Claw. The gauntlet minimized the magical connection. Kimmuriel, as always, had done well.

"Well now, I'd say that's better, but it'd be a lie," Athrogate said, walking up to join the group and taking a long look at the transformed Jarlaxle. "Any elf's but a girl making ready to cry. *Bwahaha!*" The dwarf waggled his bare toes in the hot sand as he laughed.

"And if you keep rhyming, you're going to die," Entreri said, and Athrogate laughed all the louder.

"No," Entreri said, his voice deadly even. Athrogate stopped and stared at the man and his undeniably grim tone. "There is no joke in my words," Entreri promised. "And the rhyme was coincidental."

Athrogate winced, but at the burn on the soles of his feet, not at the threat, and he hopped about. "Well, tell that one to quit inspiring me, then," he blustered, waving his arms at Jarlaxle. "Ye can't be expectin' me to behave when he's springin' such surprises on me!" He walked around Jarlaxle, inspecting him more closely, and even reached up with his stubby fingers and pinched the drow's cheek, then fiddled with the golden hair. "Bah, but that's a good one," he decided. "Good for getting into places ye don't belong. Ye got more o' that magic? Might be that if we find some orcs, ye can make me look like 'em so I can walk in before bashing?"

"That wouldn't take magic," said Entreri. "Just trim your beard."

Athrogate shot him a dangerous look. "Now ye're crossing a line, boy."

"I should have eaten him," said Ilnezhara.

"No, and all is quite well," said Jarlaxle. "Well met and well left, good ladies. I . . . *we* are most grateful for your assistance, and I speak truly when I say that I will miss your company. In all of my travels across the wide world, never before have I encountered such beauty and grace, such power and intelligence." He bowed low, his outrageous hat sweeping the desert sands.

"So you believe the tales that proclaim that dragons are weak for flattery?" said Ilnezhara, but her grin showed that she really was quite pleased with the drow's proclamation.

"I speak truly," Jarlaxle insisted. "In all things. You will find the Bloodstone Lands an interesting and profitable place upon your return, I believe."

"And we will see you again," said Tazmikella. "And I warn you, your disguises do not fool dragon eyes."

"But I cannot return, I fear," the drow replied.

"Dragons and drow live longer than humans, longer even than the memories of humans," said Ilnezhara. "Until we meet again, Jarlaxle."

As she finished, she leaped and turned, her great wings going wide and catching the rising heat of the desert sands. Her sister leaped after her, and though it only took one great beat of their tremendous wings to spirit them swiftly away, the downdraft of that action sent a storm of sand flying over the three companions.

"Durned wyrms!" Athrogate complained.

By the time the three got the sand out of their eyes and managed to look back, the sisters were no more than small spots in the distant east.

"Well, I won't be missing them two, but I'm not for walking on this ground," Athrogate muttered. He plopped back down on his butt and began pulling on his boots. "Too soft and unsure for me liking."

"I don't walk," Jarlaxle assured him. The drow-turned-elf reached into his belt pouch and pulled out a curious red figurine. He offered a wink at Entreri and tossed it to Athrogate.

The dwarf caught it and sat staring at the item: a small red boar. "Sculptor forget to put the skin on the damned thing?"

"It's an infernal boar," Jarlaxle explained. "A creature of the lower planes, fierce and untiring—a suitable mount for Athrogate."

"Suitable?" the dwarf asked, obviously perplexed. "Why, if I sat on it, I'd lose it up me bum! *Bwahaha!*"

"The figurine is a conduit," Jarlaxle explained, and he pulled out his own obsidian statuette and dropped it on the ground beside him. He called to the hellish nightmare, and in moments, the fiery steed pawed the soft ground beside him.

Athrogate gave him a crooked smile, then likewise dropped the red boar to the ground. "What do I call it?" he eagerly asked.

"Snort," Jarlaxle said.

Athrogate snorted.

"No, that is its name. Call to 'Snort,' and 'Snort' will come to your call, if you see what I mean."

Watching with little amusement and no surprise, Entreri brought his own mount, Blackfire, to his side. At the same time, Athrogate did as instructed, and sure enough, a large red-skinned boar appeared beside the dwarf. Steam rose from its back, and when it snorted, as it often did, little bursts of red flame erupted from its nostrils.

"Snort," Athrogate said approvingly. He moved beside the creature, which, like the nightmares, appeared with full saddle, but he hesitated before lifting his leg over it. "Seems a bit hot," he explained to his companions.

Entreri just shook his head and turned his nightmare around, starting off toward a distant oasis at a gallop.

Jarlaxle and Athrogate came soon after, and the smaller mount had no trouble pacing the nightmares, its little legs stepping furiously.

Entreri stayed in front of the others all the way to the last high dune overlooking the oasis. He stopped his mount and waited there, not out of any desire for companionship, but rather, because the sight below gave him cautious pause. He knew the ways of the desert, knew the various peoples who roamed the shifting sands. That particular stop along the trade route was classified as "*everni*," which translated, literally, as lawless. An oasis such as that was under no formal control, with no governing militia in place, and by edict of the pashas of both Memnon and Calimport to the south, "unavailable to claim." Anyone who tried to set up a residence or fortress in such an oasis would find himself at war with both powerful city-states.

The obvious benefit to such an arrangement was that it prevented any tolls from being forced on the frequent merchant caravans traveling between the cities. The downside, of course, was that caravans often had to defend themselves from competing interests and bandits.

The wreckage of a trio of wagons beside the small pond in the shadow of the palms showed that one recent caravan had not done so successfully.

"Perhaps we should have bid the dragons stay beside us just a bit longer," Jarlaxle remarked when he and Athrogate came up on the bluff and looked down at the many white-robed forms milling about the place.

"Desert nomads," Entreri explained. "They hold no allegiance to elves or to dwarves, or even to humans who are not of their tribe."

"They sacked them wagons?" Athrogate asked.

"Or found them destroyed," said Jarlaxle.

"They did it," Entreri insisted. "That caravan was destroyed within the tenday, or else the wood would have already been scavenged. The night gets cold here, as you will learn soon enough, and wood is greatly treasured." He nodded to the south of the small oasis pond, where buzzards hopped about. "The carrion birds haven't even finished their feast. This caravan was sacked within the last couple of days, and there are your highwaymen, enjoying their respite."

"How long will they remain?" Jarlaxle asked.

"As long as they choose. There is no pattern to the nomads' wandering. They roam, they fight, they steal, and they eat."

"Sounds like a good life to me," Athrogate remarked. "Though I'd be looking for a bit o' the drink to top it all off!"

Entreri scowled at him.

"At least he's not rhyming anymore," Jarlaxle whispered. "Though his words tear no less."

"So if we go down there, we're looking at a fight?" Athrogate asked.

"Perhaps. Perhaps not," said Entreri. "Desert nomads fight for gain and gain alone. If they saw us as a threat, or as worthy victims, they would fight. Else, they would ask of us stories, and perhaps even share their spoils. They are an unpredictable lot."

"That makes them dangerous," said Athrogate.

"That makes them intriguing," Jarlaxle corrected. He slid down from his hell horse and dismissed it, pocketing the figurine.

"Ah well, if it's a fight, all the better," Athrogate said and began to dismount.

Jarlaxle stopped him, though. "Stay here and stay astride," the drow instructed.

"Yerself's going down there?"

"Us?" Entreri asked.

Jarlaxle considered the oasis and began a quick count. "There can't be more than twenty of the creatures. And I find that I am thirsty."

Entreri knew well that Jarlaxle could summon some drink if that were the case, or could create an entire extra-dimensional chamber full of food and fine wine if he so desired. "I did not come here to engage in random fights in the desert," he said, his expression sour.

"But you came here for information, or at least, you will need information to find that which you seek. Who better to tell us of the road to Memnon, or the current disposition within the city? Let us learn what we might."

Entreri stared at his troublesome companion for a long while, but he did indeed draw his foot over his horse and drop to the sand. He dismissed the nightmare and placed the figurine in his belt pouch, within easy reach.

"If we need you, charge in hard and fast," Jarlaxle said to Athrogate.

"Don't know any other way," the dwarf replied.

"Which is why I value your companionship," the drow said. "And you will find, I do believe, that your mount is possessed of the same fighting spirit—and a few tricks of its own."

Entreri looked to the dwarf as he sat astride that strange-looking, fierce war boar. He glanced back at the oasis and the white headgear of the nomads. He could well imagine where events were leading, but he found himself walking beside Jarlaxle down the western face of the high dune nonetheless.

"The nomads have been known to fill uninvited guests with arrows, then seek their answers in the items on the corpses," Entreri said as they neared the oasis—and already several sets of eyes turned their way.

Jarlaxle whispered something that the assassin could not make out, and Entreri felt a surge of warmth within him, rolling from his core to tickle all of his being, arms, legs, and head.

"If they let fly with their bows, they'll find only more questions," Jarlaxle replied.

"Questions in the arrows that will be lying at our feet?" Entreri rightly surmised.

"It will take a mighty bolt to get through that enchantment, I assure you."

Just before the duo stepped onto the sudden transformation of sand to grass, a pair of men rushed over to block their way. Both held wide-bladed weapons—khopesh blades, they were called—and with an ease that showed them to be quite skilled with them.

"You tink to joost walk trooh our camp?" one asked in the common language of the land, one that neither Entreri or Jarlaxle had heard in many months, and spoken with so severe an accent that it took both of them a moment to decipher the words.

"Show us the boundary, and we will walk around," said Entreri.

"De boundary? Why de boundary is de oasis, silly man."

"Ah, but if that is the case, then how are we to fill our skins from the pond?" Jarlaxle asked.

"Dat ees a problem," the nomad agreed. "But for you and not for me." Beside him, the other put his second hand to the long hilt of the great khopesh sword.

"We are not here to fight," said Entreri. "Nor do we care about your dealings with the caravan."

"Caravan?" the man echoed. "Dese wagons? But we found dem here. Poor men. Dey should take more care. Bandits, you know."

"Indeed," said Entreri. "And their ill luck is not my concern. We have come for some water, that we might be on our way. Nothing more"—he eyed the second nomad, who seemed quite eager to put his great sword into action—"and nothing less. By edict of the pashas of both Memnon and Calimport, these oases are open and free."

A dangerous grin creased the face of the first man.

"But we will pay anyway," said Entreri, similarly grinning. "We will take the water we need and in exchange we will entertain you with tales of our exploits beside Pasha Basadoni in Calimport."

The nomad's grin disappeared in the blink of an eye. "Basadoni?"

"Ah, Artemis, they know the name!" said Jarlaxle.

Both bandits blanched at the mention of Entreri's name, and the second one actually fell back a step, his hands loosening on the hilt of the khopesh.

"Well . . . yes," the first stammered. "We would not be friends of de desert if we did not accept barter, of course."

Entreri snorted and walked right past him, brushing him with his shoulder and pushing him aside. Jarlaxle kept close beside him the thirty feet to the pond's edge.

"Your reputation precedes you," the drow mentioned quietly.

Entreri snorted again as if he did not care, and bent low to put his waterskin in the cool waters. By the time he stood straight again, several other desert nomads approached, including an enormously fat man dressed in richer robes of white and red. Instead of the simple cloth hoods the others wore, he wore a white and red turban, stitched with golden thread, and he carried a jeweled scepter wrought of solid gold. His gold-colored shoes were no less ornate, with their toes stretching forward and rolling up into an almost complete circle.

He moved to stand a few feet from the pair, while his bodyguards fanned out in a semicircle about them.

"There is a saying in the desert that bold is once removed from foolish," he said in a dialect far more cultured and reminiscent of Calimport than the open sands.

"Your sentries appeared to have dropped their protestations," Jarlaxle replied. "We had thought a deal struck. Water for stories."

"I have no need of your stories."

"Ah, but they are grand, and the water will not be missed."

"I know a story of a man named Artemis Entreri," the boss said. "A man who served with Pasha Basadoni."

"He is dead," said Entreri.

The boss eyed him curiously. "Did he not name you as . . . ?"

"Artemis," Entreri confirmed. "Just Artemis."

"Of Pasha Basadoni's guild?"

"No," Entreri said, at the same time Jarlaxle replied, "Yes." The pair turned and looked at each other.

"I claim no allegiance to any guild," Entreri said to the boss.

"And yet you dare to walk into my oasis—"

"It is not yours."

"Your diplomacy skills are amazing," Jarlaxle muttered to Entreri.

The fat man held his scepter out before him horizontally. "Bold," he said and he tipped one end up slightly. "Foolish," he added, and he more than reversed the angle, as if weighing his words with a scale.

"My friend is weary from many days on the road, and in the hot sun," said Jarlaxle. "We are traveling adventurers."

"Blades for hire?"

Jarlaxle smiled.

"So you would offer your services in exchange for my water?"

"That would be quite a bargain for . . . ?"

"I am Sultan Alhabara."

"Quite a bargain for Sultan Alhabara, then," said Jarlaxle. "I assure you that our services are quite formidable."

"Indeed," said the fat man, and he gave a slight chuckle, which brought a response of laughter from the six men fanned out about him. "And what fee would be deemed appropriate for the services of Artemis and . . . ?"

"I am Drizzt Do'Urden," said the drow-turned-elf.

"By the balls of a castrated orc," muttered Entreri and he heaved a great sigh.

"What?" Jarlaxle asked, feigning innocence as he turned to him.

"We could not have just ridden by, could we?" Entreri replied. "Very well, then."

"Easy, Artemis," Jarlaxle bade him.

"Our fee is more than fat Alhabara can afford," Entreri said to the man. "More than stupid Alhabara can imagine. The water is free, in any case, by edict of Memnon and of Calimport. Can the criminal Alhabara understand that?"

Alhabara flashed a fierce scowl and the men around him sputtered with outrage, but Entreri didn't relent.

"And so I take what is free, without asking the permission of a common thief," he said and he swept his gaze out at the others as he finished, "And the first of you to lift blade against me will be the first to die this day."

The man in the middle of the trio to Entreri's left did draw on him, tearing a khopesh from his belt and waving it menacingly in Entreri's direction. The man even came forward a step, or started to, but a look from Entreri held him in place.

Alhabara, meanwhile, fell back several steps and lifted his scepter defensively before him.

"Rulership," Jarlaxle whispered to Entreri, correctly identifying the magical rod the sultan held, for it was one he had seen before, many times, among chieftains and tribal leaders. If it was akin to any of the similar rods Jarlaxle had known, such an item could enable its wielder to impose his will on his would-be subjects—those of weak mind, at least.

A moment later, both the drow and the assassin felt a wave of compulsion wash over them, a telepathic call from Sultan Alhabara to fall to their knees.

The pair looked to each other, then back at the man. "Hardly," Entreri said.

To either side of the companions, weapons came forth. Jarlaxle responded by plucking the feather from his cap and tossing it to the ground him. The item transformed into a gigantic, twelve-foot-tall creature known as a diatryma, a great flightless bird with short wings tucked in close to its sides, and a thick, strong neck and powerful triangular beak.

The six closest men screamed and fell back. Alhabara scrambled away and cried out, "Kill them!"

The man nearest the bird on the right tried to rush past it to get at the man and the elf, but the diatryma's powerful neck snapped as he passed, driving the beak into his shoulder with such force that it snapped bone and dislocated his shoulder so badly that it left his arm swinging numbly several inches down from its previous position, and far to the back. The man yelped and tumbled to the grass, howling pitifully.

Charon's Claw and his jeweled dagger in hand, Entreri leaped at the trio on the left. Back-to-back with him, Jarlaxle snapped his wrist, bringing a magical dagger into his hand from his enchanted bracer. A second snap elongated that dagger into a slender sword, which the drow flipped to his left hand and used to parry the nearest khopesh in the same movement.

His right hand snapped again and the bracer answered. While working his sword brilliantly and fluidly to keep that troublesome khopesh at bay, he retracted and flung the dagger at the last in line. Hardly slowing, he wrist-snapped, retracted, and threw again, and again.

The man was good with his blade and quite agile. After five throws, he only had one dagger-wound in one thigh, and that had been no more than a glancing blow. His friend tried to press the attack on Jarlaxle, but the agile drow easily held him at bay, even working his sword around the khopesh to stick him lightly in the ribs.

And all the while, Jarlaxle kept up the flow of daggers, spinning end over end and coming at the man high, low, and center with no discernable, thus no defensible pattern. The man couldn't anticipate, he could only react, and in that state, another blade got through, grazing the side of his face, then a third—a solid strike into the shoulder of his sword arm.

Worse for him, and for his friend, Jarlaxle's pet bird intervened, trampling the man as he pressed in on Jarlaxle. The man managed to bang his khopesh off the giant creature's leg, but the bird stomped him, then jabbed down with three hard pecks.

Jarlaxle sent it off after Sultan Alhabara, as he turned his attention to the remaining man. His next dagger came forth and he did not throw it, but snapped his hand to elongate it into a second, sister blade.

He stalked at his wounded opponent.

A trio of arrows soared in from the side, shot from a tree across the oasis.

Jarlaxle saw them too late to avoid them.

Entreri turned left, then went that direction and forward, moving to the flank of the trio so that they all couldn't get at him at once. He led with an underhanded sweep of his dagger, one that, because of his bold stride forward, caught the swinging sword up near the hilt and allowed him the leverage to turn it out with just that small blade. Without room to maneuver his own sword, he came across with a right-hand punch instead, cracking Charon's Claw's pommel into the man's cheek.

He followed through with the punch past the man's broken face, extended his left arm, taking both the khopesh and the man's arm out wide with him, and rolled his sword arm over that extension then down and under.

Feeling pressure from a second attacker coming in behind him, Entreri rolled right over the arm, a complete flip that left him on his feet, and he came up strong, lifting his sword arm high, gashing the bandit's arm in the process. A twist had the man rolling over Entreri's hip, flailing helplessly.

"You are dead," Entreri promised, for the man had no defense at all. "Except . . ."

Entreri reversed his grip as he dropped his sword arm, and he stabbed out behind him as he did a sudden reverse pivot.

The blade drove into the gut of a second bandit, the one who had been in the middle of the trio, the one who had drawn first.

"I promised him that he would die first," Entreri explained. He kicked the prone man—who had dropped his khopesh to hold his badly torn arm—in the face and leaped past him, dagger and sword working in complimentary circles to foil the attack of the third man.

It was all going so smoothly and easily, he thought, but then he noted that dozens of others were closing in, hooting and raising swords and bows. A quick glance back showed him arrows diving for Jarlaxle. Beyond the drow, he saw his other companion, one better forgotten, roaring down the side of the dune on his war pig, holding tight with his powerful legs, his arms out wide and swinging morningstars left and right.

"Wahoo!" Athrogate yelled, the clear and steady tone of his shout defying the jolting, stiff-legged romp down the side of the dune. Despite those stiff legs and their shortness, Athrogate learned that his magical boar could cover tremendous ground.

The dwarf clamped his legs tight and sent his morningstars swinging wide left and right. He crossed from sand to grass, and the nearest bandits moved to intercept, a couple leveling spears.

Athrogate just howled louder and kept straight his course, thinking to pick off the prodding spears with his weapons. As he bore in, however, he found that his mount was more than a beast of burden. The boar had been summoned from the fiery pits of the Nine Hells, where battle was constant. Both its temperament and its armament were well suited to that harsh environment. It broke its stride only briefly, so it could snort and stomp a hoof, and as it did, a burst of orange flames rushed out from its body, a complete ring of wispy fire rolling away as it dissipated.

"Bwahaha!" Athrogate howled in gleeful surprise, and as the boar drove on, the dwarf clamped his legs tighter around it and adjusted the angle of his spinning weapons.

The bandits fell back and curled, shocked by the fiery burst. A bit of residual flame burned on one's robes, while the other had wisps of smoke rising from his singed hair. And both showed bright red skin where the flames had touched them.

Neither was really harmed by the burst, but as Athrogate rushed between them, the weight of his already heavy blows was only enhanced by the momentum of the boar. One man took a hit in the chest and went into a nearly complete backward somersault, except that he landed on his face instead of his feet. The other somehow maintained his footing after the strike.

But the morningstar had taken him across the side of his head, and though he was standing, he was far, far from consciousness. Athrogate was many strides away before he crumbled to the ground.

"Wahoo!" the dwarf roared wildly, thoroughly enjoying it all.

The arrows hit Jarlaxle's magical barrier barely an inch from the drow. They just stopped, in mid-air, and fell to the ground. The enchantment wasn't going to last, though, the drow knew, and so he looked out at the tree and the archers and used his innate magic to summon a globe of darkness over them.

"I'm blinded!" he heard one man cry, and he smiled, for he had indeed heard that false claim before.

The man before him was a stubborn one, he found, who came on yet again. With a sigh, Jarlaxle met his slashing khopesh, executing a downward diagonal, with a double-sword block. A turn to face the three locked blades gave him all the leverage he needed, and he easily drove the sword down.

He retracted suddenly, and the man nearly overbalanced. The drow began a "rattling parry," where both his swords rolled out a tapping drum roll on the blade. As his opponent finally began to compensate against the almost continual push, Jarlaxle side-stepped and with a sudden flourish rushed his sword downward, reversing the tip to point at the ground and taking the khopesh down with it.

The bandit pushed back, and found his blade climbing freely, but only because Jarlaxle had disengaged. The drow rolled his arms out wide, right blade closest to his opponent and angled out and down, left blade angled out and up. He tilted his body accordingly to provide maximum balance to the pose.

But it was a pose he held only briefly, for he drove his blades back in with sudden fury, the right blade coming up and under the khopesh down near the hilt, the left slamming down near the thicker end of the blade.

The bandit couldn't negotiate the alteration of pressure, and the drow's swipes tore the blade from his hands completely and sent it into a spin. Jarlaxle held that spin, the khopesh rotating around its hilt and the drow's right-hand sword.

The bandit stared at it as if mesmerized.

"Here," the gracious Jarlaxle offered, and he released the sword from its twirl, sending it up into the air back toward the bandit. The man looked up, his hands went up, and just before the khopesh landed in his grasp, the sole of the drow's boot landed against his face.

He hit the ground before the khopesh bounced atop him.

Jarlaxle glanced at Entreri. "Summon your . . ." he started to cry, but before he had even finished, Entreri's nightmare arrived on the scene, snorting fire and pawing the ground.

The poor remaining bandit on that side had already been stripped of his weapons, and the sight of the hellish horse stripped him of his sensibilities as well, apparently, for he blubbered something undecipherable and half-ran, half-crawled away, crying and screaming all the way.

Entreri leaped astride the powerful nightmare, and kicked the steed into a gallop that drove back the nearest group of approaching bandits. A pair of spears and an arrow came at him, but Jarlaxle's magical shield held them back.

Then Jarlaxle was up on his own black steed behind Entreri, who kicked his nightmare into a run. The two were swept up in

Athrogate's wake, then thundered past the dwarf and his war pig. A battery of archers rose from behind one wagon, but almost as they stood, they, too, began screaming about blindness, as Jarlaxle's magical darkness engulfed them.

Behind the riding trio, Jarlaxle's diatryma continued its rampage, and the bandits had to settle for that fight.

Out the far side of the oasis, running free across desert sands once more, the three covered nearly a mile before Jarlaxle pulled up and bid his friend do likewise.

"Bwahaha!" Athrogate roared. "I can't ever be thankin' ye enough for me new pet! *Bwahaha!* Snort! *Bwahaha!"*

Jarlaxle offered him a smile, but turned on Entreri. "That went well," the drow said dryly. "All of my lessons in diplomacy were wasted on you, it seems."

Entreri started to respond, but he noticed then that a new feather was already growing inside the band on Jarlaxle's magnificent hat. He just shook his head and spurred his steed forward.

"We should be going back," said Athrogate. "More to hit!"

Jarlaxle never turned from the departing Entreri, and without a response, he kicked his nightmare into a run behind his departing companion.

"Bah," Athrogate snorted in disappointment.

He gave a wistful glance back toward the oasis, and reluctantly followed.

CHAPTER

INDULGING THE GODS

22

"Well, now we're knowing why the last fool died," Athrogate said when he and his two companions entered the house that had been offered to them in the southwestern quarter of Memnon.

They had come into the city earlier that morning, and on Entreri's insistence—at least for himself—had eschewed the better sections of the port, where all the taverns were located, and had gone straight to a ramshackle district where the houses were no more than flimsy walls and floors of stone and dirt—and that was for the people fortunate enough to even have a shelter at all. Many of their neighbors, the poorest citizens by far in the city, slept on the side of the sandy avenues, often without even lean-tos to protect them from the occasional rains. A flash of gold from Jarlaxle had spared the trio that fate, at least, and the man, one of the clerks from the Protector's House, the temple of Selûne, had told them of their good fortune, for the owner of the house had recently departed the mortal world, leaving it open for the taking.

Jarlaxle groaned when he entered behind the dwarf, and knew he had greatly over-bribed the clerk. The place was no more than four walls, a roof that showed as much sky as reed, a floor of dirt, and a single table of piled stones so covered by crawling bugs—evil-looking reddish-brown critters with long pincers and an upward-curling tail—that it seemed obvious to the drow that the creatures had called the place home for a long, long time.

Athrogate walked over to the table and snorted, seeming amused. "Back home, we had a name for this," he said, and he extended one fat thumb and squished a crawler flat with a crunching sound. "Buffet."

"Do not dare eat that," said Jarlaxle, and Athrogate gave one of his characteristic *"bwahahas"* in reply.

Entreri walked in last. He glanced around and gave it all hardly a thought.

"Seemin' a bit too familiar to ye, by me own thinkin'," Athrogate teased.

Entreri looked at him out of the corner of his eye, but just shook his head and turned away. "They have midday services in the square overlooking the docks," he said to Jarlaxle. "I will be there, south side of the Protector's House." He turned and started back out the ill-fitting door.

"You are leaving us?" the drow asked.

"I never invited you here to begin with," Entreri reminded him as he walked away.

"Bwahaha!" roared Athrogate.

"Enough, good dwarf," Jarlaxle said, though he never took his eyes off the door. "This is difficult for our friend."

"Place didn't seem to bother him all that much," said Athrogate.

Jarlaxle turned to face him. "This?" he asked. "I suspect that Artemis Entreri is well acquainted with similar accommodations. But returning to this city, the place of his birth and early life, brings with it some painful memories, I would expect, which is why he needed to come here."

To Jarlaxle's surprise, Athrogate winced at that, and nodded but didn't otherwise reply, a very uncharacteristic response that revealed quite a bit to the perceptive, worldly drow.

"So are ye thinking the time's come to do some drinking?" the dwarf blurted. "I a'weighin' to go hear the prayin', or to make me a treat with these critters to eat! *Bwahaha!*"

"Is that all there is to Athrogate?" Jarlaxle asked in all seriousness, cutting short the dwarf's outburst. Athrogate stared at him hard, suddenly sobered.

"You are free of all feelings, it seems, other than your own humor," Jarlaxle pressed, and Athrogate's face tightened with every word. "Such as it is. Is there nothing but your pleasure?"

"I might be saying the same to yerself."

"You might, but my answer would involve a long history of explanation."

"Or ye might be telling me to mind me own business."

"Indeed, and which will you do, my hairy friend?"

"Ye're going to a place where ye don't belong."

"Your level of carefree is not attained without cause," said the drow. "Something to drink, something to hit, and a joke to make them groan—is that all there is to Athrogate?"

"Ye don't know nothing."

Indeed, Jarlaxle thought and smirked and decided to keep the irony of that double negative to himself. "So tell me."

Athrogate ground his teeth and slowly shook his head.

"Should I fill you with potent drink before I ask such things?" Jarlaxle asked.

"Ye do and ye'll find the ball end of a morningstar crunched into the side o' yer head."

Jarlaxle took the threat with a laugh, and let it drop. In discussion, at least, for in his thoughts he played it through over and over again. Something had created Athrogate as he was; something had broken the dwarf to that base level, where he had no emotional defense other than a wall of ridicule and self-ridicule, fastened by the occasional rap of a mighty morningstar and hidden by the more-than-occasional drink.

Jarlaxle nodded, thinking that he had just found something interesting, something he meant to explore, despite the dwarf's very serious threat.

The scene was all too familiar to Artemis Entreri and sent his thoughts careening back across the years. Before him, in the wide square that fronted the gigantic Protector's House, by far the largest structure in that part of the city, stood, sat, and lay the rabble of southwestern Memnon. They were the dispossessed, the poorest of the poor in the city, nearly all of them suffering the maladies so common among those who could not find enough to eat or drink, who could not keep clean, and who could not find shelter from the rain.

But they were not hopeless. No, the men on the eastern side of the square, richly dressed and bejeweled, would not allow for such a state of despair. They called out in melodic voices of the glories of Selûne and of the wonders that awaited her servants. Their pages went among the crowd, offering good news and good cheer, speaking of salvation and promises of an eternity free of all pain.

But there was more to this than cheerleading, Entreri knew all too well. There were promises of immediate relief from ailments, and even suggestions—normally reserved for grieving parents— that the afterlife for their dearly departed could be made even more accommodating than the promises of their god.

"Would you have your child suffer on the Fugue Plane a moment longer than he must?" one young acolyte said to a tearful woman not far from Entreri. "Of course not! Come along, good woman. Every moment we tarry is another moment your dear Toyjo will suffer."

It wasn't the first time the acolyte had pulled that same woman forward, Entreri could tell, and he watched as the pair shuffled through the crowd, the acolyte tugging her along.

"By Moradin, but yerselfs are calling me kin heartless," Athrogate muttered as he and Jarlaxle walked up beside Entreri. "Such a brotherhood ye got here. Makes me want to be findin' a wizard that'd polymorph me into a human." He ended with a fake sniffle, and wiped his eye.

Entreri flashed him a sour look, but as he was no more enamored with his fellow humans than was Athrogate, he really had no practical response. He looked to Jarlaxle instead—and did a double-take, still not used to seeing the drow with golden hair and tanned skin.

"You know this scene?" Jarlaxle asked.

"They are selling indulgences," Entreri explained.

"Selling?" Athrogate snorted. "These dirty fools got coin for spending?"

"What little they have, they spend."

Athrogate snorted as one particularly skinny man ambled by. "Ye might be better off in buying a cookie, if ye're asking me."

"The priests will heal their wounds for a fee?" Jarlaxle asked.

"Minor healing, and temporary at best," said Entreri. "Most who wish for physical heals are wasting their time. They are selling the indulgence of the god Selûne. For a few silver pieces, a grieving mother can spare her dead child a tenday in the Fugue, or can facilitate her own way when she dies, if that is her choice."

"They are paying for a priest's promise of such a thing?"

Entreri looked at him and shrugged.

Jarlaxle looked back over the throng—and it was indeed a throng of poor souls—then focused on the activity near the temple doors. Lines of dirty peasants waited their turn at the desks that had been set up. One by one, they walked forward and handed over a pittance, and one of the two men at the desk scribbled down a name.

"What a marvelous business," the drow said. "For a few comforting words and a line of text . . ." He gave an envious laugh, but to the side, Athrogate spat.

Both Entreri and Jarlaxle regarded the dwarf.

"They're telling them women that turning over their coins'll help dead kids?"

"Some," said Entreri.

"Orcs," muttered the dwarf. "Worse than orcs." He spat again and stormed off.

Entreri and Jarlaxle exchanged a confused glance, and Jarlaxle set off after the dwarf. Entreri watched them go, but didn't follow.

He remained at the square for quite a while, and every so often found his eyes drawn to a street entrance across the way, an avenue that wound down toward the docks.

A place he knew well.

"The Fugue Plane is a place of torment," Devout Gositek assured the nervous little man who stood before his desk. The man's hands worked feverishly about a tiny coin purse, rolling the dirty bag incessantly.

"I've not much," he said through his two remaining teeth, crooked and yellow.

"The charity given by the poor is more greatly appreciated, of course," Gositek recited, and the devout brothers standing guard behind him both smirked. One even winked at the other, for Gositek had done nothing but complain to them all morning, as soon as the listing had been pegged in the foyer, naming Gositek as one of the indulgence agents every day for the next tenday. He would spend his mornings, collecting coin, and his afternoons offering prayers for the paupers at the smelly graveyard. It was not an envied duty at the Protector's House.

"It is not the amount of coin," Gositek lied, "but rather the amount of *sacrifice* that is important for Selûne. So the poor are blessed, don't you see? Your opportunities for freeing your loved ones from the Fugue, and shortening your own visit, are far greater than those of the rich man."

The dirty old peasant rolled his tiny purse yet again. He licked his lips repeatedly as he fumbled about and extracted a single coin. Then, with a nearly toothless grin that spoke of lechery and deceit, he handed the coin to Devout Gositek's assistant, who sat beside him to watch over the heavy metal box, a slot in the top to accept the donations.

The peasant seemed quite pleased with himself, of course, but Gositek's glare was uncompromising. "You hold a purse," the devout said. "It bulges with coin, and you offer a single piece?"

"My only silver," the old peasant wheezed. "The rest're but copper, and just a score."

Gositek just stared at him.

"But my belly's growling bad," the man whined.

"For food or for drink?"

The peasant stammered and sputtered, but couldn't quite seem to find the words to deny the charge—and indeed, the stench that wafted from him would have made any such denial seem rather foolish.

Gositek sat back in his wooden chair and folded his arms in front of him. "I am disappointed," he said.

"But my belly . . ."

"I am not disappointed in your lack of charity, good brother," Gositek interrupted. "But in your continuing lack of common sense."

The peasant stared at him blankly.

"Twice the chance!" Gositek derided him. "Twice the opportunity to impress your devotion upon sacred Selûne! You can sacrifice greatly, for a pittance, and at the same time better your earthly standing by controlling your impure thoughts. Forsake your coin to Selûne, and forego your drink for yourself. Do you not understand?"

The man stuttered and shook his head.

"Each coin buys you double the indulgence and more," said Gositek, extending his hand.

The peasant slapped the purse into it.

Gositek smiled at the man, but it was a cold grin indeed, the smug grin of the cat dominating the mouse before feasting. Slowly and deliberately, Gositek pulled open the purse and dumped the meager contents into his free hand. His eyes flashed as he noted a silver piece among the two dozen coppers, and he looked up from it to the lying peasant, who squirmed and withered under that gaze.

"Record the name," Gositek instructed his assistant.

"Bullium," the peasant said, and he bobbed his head in a pathetic attempt to bow, and started away. He paused, though, and licked his lips again, staring at the pile of coins in Gositek's hand.

Devout Gositek pulled a few coppers from the pile, staring at the man all the while. He handed the rest to his assistant for the collection box, and started to put the others in the purse. He paused again, however, still staring at the man, and gave half of that pile to his assistant as well. Three coppers went into the purse, which Gositek handed back to the man.

But when the peasant grabbed it, Gositek didn't immediately let go.

"These are a loan, Bullium," he said, his tone grave and even. "Your indulgences are bought—a full year removed from your time on the Fugue Plane. But they are bought for the full contents of your purse, due to your reluctance and your lie about the second piece of silver. You have back three. I expect five returned to Selûne to complete the purchase of the indulgence."

Still stupidly bobbing his head, the peasant grabbed the purse and shuffled away.

Beside the wooden chair, Gositek's assistant chuckled.

"You believe that Knellict and his band haven't done worse?" Jarlaxle asked when he at last caught up to the dwarf. They were almost back at their bug-filled shack by then.

"Knellict's a fool, and an ugly one, too," Athrogate grumbled. "Not much I'm liking there."

"But you served him, and the Citadel of Assassins."

"Better that than fight the dogs."

"So it is all pragmatism with you."

"If I knew what the word meant, I'd agree or not," said the dwarf. "What's that, a religion?"

"Practicality," Jarlaxle explained. "You do what serves your needs as you see fit."

"Don't everyone?"

Jarlaxle laughed at that. "To a degree, I expect. But few use that as the guiding principle of their lives."

"Maybe that's all I got left."

"Again you speak in riddles," said the drow, and when Athrogate scowled at him, Jarlaxle held up his hands defensively. "I know, I know. You do not wish to speak of it."

Athrogate snorted. "Ye ever hear o' Felbarr, elf?"

"Was he a dwarf?"

"Not a he, but a place. Citadel Felbarr."

Jarlaxle considered the name for a bit, then nodded. "Dwarven stronghold . . . east of Mithral Hall."

"South o' Adbar," Athrogate confirmed with a nod of his own. "Was me home and me place, and ne'er did me thoughts expect I'd ever be living anywhere but."

"But . . . ?"

"An orc clan," Athrogate explained. "They come in hard and fast—I'm not even knowin' how many years ago it's been. Not enough and too many, if ye get me meaning."

"So the orcs sacked your home and now you cannot but wander?" asked Jarlaxle. "Surely your clan is about. Scattered perhaps, but . . ."

"Nah, me kin're back in Felbarr. Drove them orcs out, and none too long ago."

Athrogate's face grew tight as he said that, Jarlaxle noted, and he decided to pause there and let Athrogate digest it all. He had started the dwarf down a painful road, he knew, but he did not want to press Athrogate too much.

To his surprise, and his delight, the dwarf went on without

prodding, running his mouth as if he were a river and the drow had just crashed through the beaver dam.

"Ye got young ones?" Athrogate asked.

"Children?" Jarlaxle chuckled. "None that I am aware of."

"Bah, but ye're missing, then," said the dwarf.

To Jarlaxle's surprise, there was moistness about Athrogate's eyes—something he never thought he'd see.

"You had children," Jarlaxle surmised, gauging Athrogate's reaction to his every word before speaking the next. "They were slain when the orcs invaded."

"Good sprites, one and all," Athrogate said, and he looked away, past Jarlaxle, as if his eyes were staring into a distant place and distant time. "And me Gerthalie—what dwarf could ever be thinking he'd be so blessed by Sharindlar to find himself a woman o' such charms?"

He paused and closed his eyes, and Jarlaxle swallowed hard and wondered if he had been wise in leading Athrogate back to that place.

"Yep, ye got it," the dwarf said, eyes popping wide. All hint of tears were gone, replaced by the wildness Jarlaxle had grown used to. "Orcs took 'em all. Watched me littlest one, Drenthro, die. In me arms, he went. Bah, but curse Moradin and all the rest for letting that happen!

"So we were chased out, but them orcs was too stupid to hold the place, and soon enough, they started fighting betwixt themselves. Me king called for a fight, and a fight he got, but meself didn't go. Surprised them all, don't ye doubt."

"Athrogate doesn't seem one to shy from a fight."

"And never's he been one. But not that time, elf. Couldn't go back there." He stood with his hands on hips, shaking his head. "Nothing there for me. They got their Felbarr back, but Felbarr's not me home no more."

"Perhaps now, after all these years. . . ."

"Nah! Ain't one o' them who was alive when the orcs come is still alive now. I'm old, elf, older than ye'd believe, but a dwarf's memory is older than the dwarf himself. Them boys in Felbarr now wouldn't have me, and I wouldn't be wanting them to have me. Dolts. In the first try on getting the place back, more than three hunnerd years ago, Athrogate said no. They called me a coward, elf. Yep, can ye be believing that? Me own kin. Thinkin' me afraid o' orcs. I ain't afraid o' undead dragons! But to them, Athrogate's the coward."

"Because you would not partake of the retribution?" Not wanting to break the dwarf's momentum, Jarlaxle didn't speak the other part of his question, regarding Athrogate's recounting of time. Few dwarves lived three centuries, and none, to Jarlaxle's knowledge, could survive for so long and still retain the vigor and power of one such as Athrogate. Either he was confused with his dates, or there was even more to the creature than Jarlaxle had assumed.

"Because I wouldn't be going back into that cursed hole," Athrogate answered. "Seen too much o' me dead kin in every corner and every shadow."

"Athrogate died that day the orcs came," said Jarlaxle, and the dwarf's look was one of appreciation, telling the drow that he had spoken the truth. "But if that was centuries ago, perhaps now. . . ."

"No!" the dwarf blurted. "Ain't nothing there for me. Ain't been nothing there for me in a dwarf's lifetime and more."

"So you set out to the east?"

"East, west, south—didn't much matter to meself," explained Athrogate. "Just anywhere but there."

"You have heard of Mithral Hall, then?"

"Sure, them Battlehammer boys. Good enough folk. They lost their place a hunnerd years after we lost Felbarr, but I'm hearing they got it back."

"Good enough folk?" asked Jarlaxle, and he filed away the confirmation of the timeline in his thoughts, for indeed, Mithral Hall had been lost to the duergar and the shadow dragon some two centuries before. "Or too good for Athrogate? Does Athrogate think himself unworthy? Were the barbs of your kin striking true?"

"Bah!" the dwarf snorted convincingly. "But what's good and what's bad? And what's mattering, elf? It's all a game with them gods laughing at us, ye're knowing as well as meself's knowing!"

"And so you laugh at everything, and hit whatever appears to need a hit."

"Hitting it good, too, but ain't I?"

"Better than almost any I've ever seen."

Athrogate snorted again. "Better'n any."

Jarlaxle received more than a few curious stares as he walked through the streets of the human-dominated city. They were not like the suspicious glares to which he had grown accustomed when he had walked as a drow, however, for there was no hatred, just curiosity, and more than a passing interest in his garments, which appeared far too rich for that poor section of Memnon.

In truth, the sum value of Jarlaxle's garments, just those he wore as he walked across the city, would have made a Waterdhavian lady of court jealous.

The drow shook all the distractions from his thoughts, reminding himself that the man he secretly followed was no novice to the ways of the thief. He knew that in all likelihood, Artemis Entreri had already detected the covert pursuit, but the man didn't show it.

Which of course meant nothing.

Entreri crossed the square before the temple with determined strides, making a beeline for an avenue on the southern side, a dusty way that sloped down and overlooked the southern harbor. With no cover available, Jarlaxle skirted the edge, and he feared that he'd lose the swift-moving Entreri because of his longer route. As he came around the southern edge of the square, though, he found that Entreri had slowed considerably. As the assassin made his way, Jarlaxle paralleled him, moving with all speed behind the row of shacks.

Within a few yards onto the avenue, Jarlaxle noted the visible change that had come over his friend, and never had he seen the sure and confident Entreri looking such. He seemed as if he could barely muster the strength to put one foot in front of the other. The blood had drained from his face, giving him a chalky visage, and made his lips seem even thinner.

With hardly an effort, the graceful drow climbed up to the roof of a shack, and shimmied across on his belly to overlook the avenue.

A few feet down the road, Entreri had stopped, and stood staring. His hands were by his sides, but they weren't at the ready near his weapon hilts.

Jarlaxle knew it beyond any doubt: Artemis Entreri, as he stood there, was helpless. A novice assassin could have walked up behind him and dispatched him easily.

That unsettling thought made Jarlaxle glance around, though he had no reason to suspect that any killers might be nearby.

He silently laughed at himself and his irrational fit of nerves, and when he looked back at Entreri, he only then fathomed the absolute strangeness of it all. He rolled over the edge of the roof, dropped lightly to his feet and walked over to stand beside Entreri—who didn't notice him until the very last moment.

Even then, Entreri never bothered to cast a glance Jarlaxle's way. His eyes remained fixed on a shack down the way, an unremarkable structure of clay and wood, and with the skeleton of a long-rotted awning jutting out in front. Beneath that, a ruined wicker chair was nestled against the shack, beside the open entrance.

"You know this place?"

Entreri didn't look at him and didn't answer. His breathing became more labored, however, telling Jarlaxle the truth of it.

This had been Entreri's home, the place of his earliest days.

CHAPTER

23

I f I am to help you, then I need to know," Jarlaxle argued, but Entreri's expression alone showed that the drow's logic was falling on deaf ears. They were back at the house with Athrogate, and Entreri had said not a word in the hour since they had rejoined their hairy companion.

"I'm getting the feelin' that he's not wanting yer help, elf," Athrogate said.

"He allowed us to come along on his adventure."

"I did not stop you from following me," Entreri clarified. "My business here is my own."

"And what, then, am I to do?" asked the drow with exaggerated drama.

"Live here in luxury, o' course!" said Athrogate, and he accentuated his point by slamming his hand down on the table, crushing a beetle beneath it. "Good huntin' and good food," he said, lifting the crushed bug before his face as if he meant to eat it. "Who could be asking for anything more? *Bwahaha!*" To Jarlaxle's relief, though Entreri hardly cared either way, the dwarf flicked the crushed beetle across the room instead of depositing it in his mouth.

"I care not at all," Entreri answered. "Go and find more comfortable lodgings. Leave Memnon all together."

"Why have you come here?" Jarlaxle asked, and Entreri showed the slightest wince. "And how long will you stay?"

"I don't know."

"To which."

336

Entreri didn't answer. He turned on his heel and stalked out of the house into the early morning sun.

"He's an angry one, ain't he?" Athrogate asked.

"With good reason, I presume."

"Well, ye said he growed up here," said the dwarf. "That'd put a pinch in me own butt, to be sure."

Jarlaxle looked from the open door to the dwarf, and gave a little laugh, and for the first time he realized that he was truly glad Athrogate had decided to come along. He considered his own role in this ordeal, as well, and he began to doubt the wisdom of entangling Entreri with Idalia's flute. Kimmuriel had warned him against that very thing, explaining to him that prying open a person's heart could bring many unexpected consequences.

No, Jarlaxle decided after some reflection. He was correct in giving Entreri the flute. In the end, it would be a good thing for his friend.

If it didn't kill him.

The compulsion that took him back to the sandy avenue that morning was so overpowering that Entreri didn't even realize he was returning to stand before the shack until he was there. The street was far from deserted, with many people sitting in the meager shade of the other buildings, and all of them eyeing the unusual stranger, with his high black leather boots, so finely stitched, and two weapons of great value strapped at his waist.

Clearly, Entreri didn't belong there, and the trepidation he saw in the gazes that came his way, and the background sensation of pure disgust, brought recognition and recollection indeed.

Artemis Entreri had seen those same stares during his days in Calimport serving Pasha Basadoni. The peasants of Memnon thought him a mercenary, sent by one of the more prosperous lords to collect a debt or settle a score, no doubt.

He relegated them to the back of his mind, reminding himself that if they all charged him together, he would leave them all dead in the dirt, then reminding himself further that those peasants would never find the courage to attack him in the first place. It wasn't in their humor—anyone with such gumption and willpower would have long ago left such a place.

It was even easier to dismiss them—in fact, it wasn't even a choice—when Entreri looked back to the ill-fitting door on the shack that had been his home for the first twelve years of his life. As soon as he focused on that place again, nothing else seemed to matter, as he fell into the same state of reflection that had allowed Jarlaxle to walk up right beside him unnoticed the night before.

Hardly aware of his movements, Entreri found himself approaching the door. He paused when he got there and lifted his fist to knock. He held it there, however, and reminded himself of who he was and of who these inconsequential, pathetic peasants were, and he just pushed through the door.

The room was quiet and still cool, as the morning sun hadn't yet come high enough over the hill to chase away the nighttime chill. No candles burned within, and no one was home, but a piece of stale bread on the table and a ruffled and tattered blanket in the corner told Entreri that someone had indeed been in the house recently. The bread wasn't covered in hungry beetles, even, and to Entreri, who knew the climate and the ways of Memnon, that was as telling as a warm campfire.

Someone lived in the house that had been his. His mother? Was it possible? She would be in her early sixties now, he knew. Was it possible that she still lived in the same place where she and his father, Belrigger, had made their home?

The smell told him otherwise, for whoever was living there took no care whatsoever in hygiene. He saw no chamber pot, but it wasn't hard for him to tell that one should have been in use.

That wasn't how he remembered his mother. She had barely a copper to her name, but she had always worked hard to keep herself, and her child, clean.

The thought came over him that the years might have broken that relic of pride from her. He grimaced, and hoped that it was not Shanali's home. But if that were the case, then she must have died. She could not have found her way out, he knew, for she was past twenty when he left. No one got out of that neighborhood past the age of twenty.

And if she was still there, then it must still have been her house.

The walls began to close in on him suddenly. The stench of feces assailed his nostrils and drove him back. He shoved through the door more forcefully than he'd entered, and staggered out into the street.

He found his breath coming in gasps. He looked around, as near to panic as he had been throughout his adult life. He saw the faces leering at him, glaring at him, hating him, and felt in that moment of uncertainty that the most frail among the onlookers could easily run up and dispatch him.

He tried to steady himself, but couldn't help but glance back over his shoulder at the swaying door. Memories of his childhood flooded his thoughts, of cold nights huddled on that very floor, brushing away the biting insects. He thought of his mother and her near-constant pain, and of his surly father and the pain he too often inflicted. He remembered those years in a way he hadn't in decades, and even thought of the few friends he had run the streets with.

There was a measure of freedom in poverty, he figured, and found some composure in that ridiculous irony.

He turned away again, thinking to plot his course, to find some way to move forward from there.

He found a faceful of wrinkled old woman instead.

"Byah, but ain't you the pretty one, with your shiny swords and fine boots," she cackled at him.

Entreri stared at the bent little creature, at her leathery face and dull eyes—a face he had seen a million times and not at all before.

"Ain't you the superior one?" she scolded. "Where you can just come down here and do as you please, when you please, no doubting."

Entreri looked past her, to the many eyes upon him, and understood that she spoke for them all. Even there, there was a collective pride.

"Well, you should be thinking your steps more carefully," the woman said more assertively, growing bolder with every word. She moved to poke Entreri in the chest.

That, Entreri could not allow, for he had known clever wizards to assume just such a guise as a pretense for touching an enemy, whereupon they could loose some prepared enchantment that would jolt their opponent right out of his boots. With uncanny reflexes and precision, and using his sword hand and the gauntlet Jarlaxle had reconstituted, he caught the thrust before it got near to him, and none-too-gently turned the woman's hand out.

"You know nothing of me," he said quietly. "And nothing of my reason for being here. It is not your affair, and do not interfere again." As he spoke, he looked past her to the many people rising in the shadows, all of them unsure but outraged.

"On pain of death," he assured the old wretch as he released her, shoved her aside, and walked past. The first one who came after him, he decided, would be put down in blood. If they kept on coming, the second one, he decided, he would cripple at his feet, and use the man to feed his health back to him through the dagger, if necessary. Two steps from the woman, however, he knew his planning unnecessary, for none would move on him.

But neither would the stubborn old woman let it drop. "Ah, but you're the dangerous one, ain't you?" she yelled. "We'll see how proud you puff your chest when Belrigger learns that you been in his house!"

At that proclamation, Entreri nearly fell over, his legs going weak beneath him.

He fought the urge to turn on the woman and demand more information. It was not the time, not with so many watching, and already angry at him. He studied the people around him more carefully as he made his way back to the square, in light of the knowledge that one of the old crowd, Belrigger, at least, was indeed still alive and about. Indeed, he started to notice more in-depth things about some—a tilt of the head, a look, the way one woman sat on her chair. A sense of familiarity came at him from many corners. So many people were the same ones Artemis Entreri had known as a child. Older now, but the same. And others, he thought, particularly one group of younger men and women, were people he had not known, but who showed enough similarities for him to guess that they might be the children of people he had.

Or maybe there was just a commonality of habit, and a shared manner of expression among all the peasants, he told himself.

It didn't matter, though, since in the end, Belrigger, his father, was alive.

That thought stayed with Entreri throughout the day. It followed him down the streets of Memnon, and all the way to the port. It haunted him under the bright, hot sun, and followed him, wraith-like, into the shadows.

Artemis Entreri had willingly, eagerly, stepped into mortal battle with the likes of Drizzt Do'Urden, but returning to his old home soon after sundown proved to be the most difficult challenge he had ever accepted. He used every trick he knew to get around to the back of the shack unnoticed, then quietly pried off a few planks of the back wall and slipped inside.

No one was home, so he replaced the planks and moved to the darkness of the back corner and sat down, staring at the door.

Hours passed, but Entreri remained on alert. He did not start, did not move at all, when at last the door swung in.

An old man shuffled in. Small and bent, his steps were so tiny that it took him a dozen to reach the table that was only three feet in.

Entreri heard flint hit steel and a single candle flared to life, affording the assassin a clear look at the old man's face. He was thin, so thin, emaciated, even, and with a bald head so reddened by the unrelenting Memnon sun that it seemed to glow in the faint light. He sported a wild gray beard and kept his face continually squinting, which jutted out his chin and made the facial hair seem even more pronounced.

He pulled out a small pouch with his dirty, trembling hands, and managed to dump its contents on the table. Muttering to himself the whole time, he began sorting through copper, silver, and other shiny pieces that Entreri recognized as the polished stones that could be found among the rocks south of the docks. The assassin understood, for he remembered well that some of the people of the neighborhood would venture there and collect pretty stones then sell them to the folk of Memnon, who paid for them as much to get rid of the annoying vagabonds as anything else.

Entreri couldn't be sure of the man's identity, but he knew that it certainly wasn't Belrigger. Age could not have bent his father so.

The man began giggling, and Entreri's eyes opened wide at the sound—one he had heard before. He rose without a whisper and moved to the table. Still unnoticed by the wretch, he slammed his hand down on the coins and stones.

"What?" the old man asked, falling back and turning on Entreri.

That wild-eyed look . . . the smell of his breath . . .

Entreri knew.

"Who are you?"

Entreri smiled. "You don't remember your own nephew?"

"Damn yourself, Tosso-posh," the man said as he entered the house an hour later. "If you're to shit yourself, then stay out of . . ." He was carrying a lit candle, and moved right for the table, but stopped just short as the door was pushed closed behind him—obviously by someone who had been standing behind it as it opened.

Belrigger took a step forward and spun. "You're not Tosso," he said as he took the measure of Entreri.

Entreri stared at the man for a few moments, for he surely recognized Belrigger. The years had not been kind to him. He looked drawn and stretched, as if he had been getting no nourishment other than the potent liquor he no doubt poured regularly down his throat.

Entreri looked past the man, to the far back corner, and Belrigger followed his lead and glanced back that way, bringing his candle around to illuminate the space. There lay Tosso-posh, face down, a small pool of blood around his midsection.

Belrigger spun back, his face a mask of rage and fear, but if he meant to lash out at the intruder, the sight of a long red blade leveled his way seemed to dissuade him more than a little.

"Who are you?" he breathed.

"Someone who just settled a score," Entreri answered.

"You murdered Tosso?"

"He's probably not dead yet. Belly wounds take their time."

Belrigger sputtered as if he simply couldn't find the words.

"You know what he did to me," Entreri stated.

Belrigger began shaking his head, and finally managed to say, "Did to you? Who are *you*?"

Entreri laughed at him. "I see that you hold no familial loyalty. I am hardly surprised."

"Familial?" Belrigger mouthed, and then his eyes went wider still as he asked again, "Who are you?"

"You know."

"I grow tired of your games," Belrigger said, and started as if he meant to leave. But the red sword flashed, tip coming in under his chin and stopping him in his tracks. With a slight twist of his wrist, Entreri forced the man back to the table, and then Entreri came forward and turned the blade again, angling Belrigger for a chair, where he fell back into a sitting position.

"Words I have heard before," Entreri said, and he pulled the other chair over and sat closer to the door. "Usually followed by the back of your hand. I would almost invite that slap now."

Belrigger seemed as if he could hardly breathe. "Artemis?" he asked, his voice barely a whisper.

"Have I changed so much, Father?"

After another few moments of gasping, Belrigger finally seemed to find his composure. "What are you doing here?" He glanced over the side of the table, at Entreri's fine sword and dress. "You escaped this place. Why would you come back?"

"Escaped? I was sold into slavery."

Belrigger snorted and looked away.

Entreri slammed his hand upon the table, demanding the man's full attention. "That notion amuses you?"

"It does nothing for me. It was not my decision, nor my care!"

"My loving father," came Entreri's sarcastic reply. To his surprise, and outrage, Belrigger laughed at him.

"Even Tosso didn't find such nerve as that," said Entreri, and his mention of Belrigger's dying friend sobered the man.

"What do you want?"

"I want to know of my mother," said Entreri. "Is she alive?"

Belrigger's mocking expression answered before the man ever spoke. "You went to Calimport, yes?"

Entreri nodded.

"Shanali was dead before you arrived there, even if the merchants drove their horses furiously," said Belrigger. "She knew she was dying, you fool. Why do you think she sold off her precious Artemis?"

Entreri's thoughts began spinning. He tried to recall that last meeting, and saw the frailty in his mother in an entirely new light.

"I actually pitied the whore," Belrigger said, and even as the word left his mouth, Entreri came forward with frightening speed and smashed him hard across the face.

Entreri fell back into his own seat, and Belrigger stared at him threateningly, and spat blood on the floor.

"She had no choice," Belrigger went on. "She needed coin to pay the priests to save her miserable life, and they wouldn't even take her diseased body in trade for their spells. So she sold you, and they took her coin. And still she died. I doubt they did anything to try to stop it."

Belrigger fell quiet, and Entreri sat there for a long while, digesting the surprising words, trying to find some way to deny them.

"Have you found what you sought, murderer?" said Belrigger.

"She sold me?" Entreri asked.

"I just told you so."

"And my dear father protected me," Entreri replied.

"Your dear father?" asked Belrigger. "And you know who that is?"

Entreri's face went very tight.

"Are you stupid enough to think me your father?" Belrigger asked with a laugh. "I'm not your father, you fool. If I was, I'd've beaten more sense into you."

"You lie."

"Shanali was fat with you when I met her. Fat in the womb from whoring herself out to those priests. Like all the rest of the girls. Might that you left too young to know the truth of it, but most of the brats you see running the dirty streets come from priest seed." He stopped and snorted, then laughed again. "I just gave her a place to live, and she gave me some pleasures in exchange."

Entreri hardly heard him. He considered again the scenes of his youth, when men came in and paid Belrigger, then went to Shanali's bed. The assassin closed his eyes, almost hoping that Belrigger would move fast in his moment of vulnerability. If Belrigger had come forward and taken Entreri's dagger, he wouldn't stop him, and would invite the blade into his heart.

But the man didn't move, Entreri knew, because he continued to laugh.

Until, that is, Entreri opened his eyes again and gave him that tell-tale stare.

Belrigger cleared his throat, obviously uncomfortable.

Entreri rose and sheathed his sword. One step brought him towering over the seated man. "Get up."

Belrigger stared at him defiantly. "What do you want?"

Entreri's fist crushed his nose. "Get up."

Bleeding, Belrigger rose, with one arm raised defensively before him. "What do you want? I told you everything. I'm not your father!"

Entreri's left hand snapped up and caught Belrigger's blocking hand. With the simplest of moves, the assassin bent Belrigger's hand over backward and wrenched the arm painfully to the side.

"But you beat me," Entreri said.

"You needed it," Belrigger gasped, trying to raise his other arm.

Entreri's free hand snapped out, slamming him in his already-bloody face.

"A tough life!" Belrigger protested. "You needed sense! You needed to know!"

"Say again that my mother was a whore," said Entreri. He twisted the bent arm a bit more, driving Belrigger to one knee.

"What would you have me say?" the man pleaded. "She did what she had to do to survive. It's what we all do. I don't blame her, and never did. I took her in when none would."

"To your own gain."

"Some," Belrigger admitted. "You cannot blame me for the way things are."

"I can blame you for every fist you laid upon me," Entreri calmly replied. "I can blame you for letting that filth"—he nodded his chin at Tosso-posh—"near me. Or did he pay you, too? A bit of coin for your boy, Belrigger?"

Gasping in pain, Belrigger furiously shook his head. "No . . . I didn't . . ."

Entreri's knee drove into Belrigger's face, knocking him to the floor on his back. Out came the jeweled dagger, and Entreri moved over the groaning man.

But Entreri shook his head. He put the dagger away, and walked out the door.

The old woman was out there again, having apparently heard the scuffle. Heard that and more, Entreri realized, as, instead of scolding him yet again, she said, "I knew Shanali, and I'm remembering yerself, Artemis."

Entreri stared at her hard.

"Did you kill Belrigger?"

"No," Entreri replied. "You heard our conversation?"

The woman shrank back. "Some," she admitted.

"If he lied to me, I will return and cut him apart."

The woman shook her head, a resigned look coming over her wrinkled old face. She nodded toward the chair set in front of her house, and Entreri followed her there.

"Your mother was a pretty one," she said as soon as she sat down. "I knew her mother, too, just as pretty, and just as young when she bore Shanali as Shanali was when she gave birth to you. Only a girl, doing th'only thing a girl down here can do."

"With the priests?"

"With whoe'er's the coin," the old one said with obvious disgust.

"And she really is dead?"

"Not long after you left," said the woman. "She was dying, and it got all the worse when she let her son go. Like she had no reason to keep fighting, not when them priests took her coins and cast their spells and said they couldn't do anything more for her."

Entreri took a deep, steadying breath, reminding himself that he expected from the beginning that he would not find Shanali alive.

"She's with the rest of them," the old woman said, surprising him, as his expression revealed. "On the hill, behind the rock, where they bury them that got no names worth remembering."

Like everyone who had spent his childhood in that part of Memnon, Entreri knew well the pauper's graveyard, a patch of dirt behind a large rocky outcropping that overlooked the southwestern most point of Memnon Harbor. Despite himself, he looked that way, and without another word to the old woman, and with only a final glance at the shack that had been his home, a place to which he knew he would never return, he walked away.

CHAPTER

24

Jarlaxle had his back to Entreri, pretending to look out the shack's front door at the early morning street. Athrogate snored contentedly in the corner of the room, his breathing interrupted at irregular intervals—Jarlaxle amused himself by imagining spiders climbing into the dwarf's open mouth.

Entreri sat at the table, his face tight and angry—the expression he had worn for most of the years he and Jarlaxle had spent together, one that Jarlaxle had hoped to replace forever with the use of Idalia's flute.

So much progress they had made, the drow silently lamented, but then that foolish woman had betrayed Entreri and torn a hole in his opened heart. And worst of all, what the drow knew but Entreri did not was that Calihye hadn't even wanted to attack him. Emotionally torn, confused by her loyalties and frightened of leaving the Bloodstone Lands, the woman had acted purely on impulse. Her strike was not wrought of malice toward Artemis Entreri, as it would have been in the early days of their relationship, but rather, was propelled by terror and grief and an anguish she could not overcome.

Jarlaxle hoped that someday Artemis Entreri might know that, but he doubted it strongly. Still, with Calihye safely under the control of Bregan D'aerthe, the drow knew better than to say "never."

The more pressing problem, of course, surrounded them in the hellish city of Memnon. Entreri had come home, though what that meant, Jarlaxle could not be sure. He glanced back at the grim man, who seemed not to notice him at all, not to notice anything. Entreri sat upright and his eyes were open, but he was no more aware, Jarlaxle reasoned, than was the sputtering dwarf in the corner.

His hands moving slowly and surely, Jarlaxle retrieved one of the small potion vials from his belt pouch. He stared at it for a long while, hating himself for having to so manipulate his friend yet again.

That thought surprised the drow; when in his entire life had he ever felt such a twang? In his betrayal of Zaknafein those centuries before, perhaps?

He looked at Entreri again, and he felt as if he was staring at his old drow companion.

I needed to do this, he reminded himself, and for Entreri most of all.

He quaffed the potion.

Jarlaxle closed his eyes as the magic settled in his body and in his mind, as he began to "hear" the thoughts of the other people in the room. He considered the life of Kimmuriel, who was always in such a state of heightened perception, and for an instant, he truly pitied the psionicist.

He shook his head and gave a great sigh, reminding himself that he had no time for such distractions. The potion wouldn't last long.

"So are you going to tell me where you went yesterday?" he said, turning to face the human.

Entreri looked up at him. "No."

But he was already telling Jarlaxle much more, for the question had elicited memories of the previous day's events: images of the street they had visited, of an old man lying on the floor holding in his spilling guts, of another man.

His father! No, the man he had thought his father, had known as his father for all his life.

"You have come here to find your mother. That much I know," Jarlaxle dared to say, though Entreri's expression grew more threatening from the moment he mentioned the lost woman.

An image flashed in Jarlaxle's mind, not of a woman, but of a view.

"You know, too, that I have told you that none of this is your affair," Entreri said.

"Why would you push an ally away?" Jarlaxle asked.

"You cannot help me in this."

"Of course I can."

"No!"

Jarlaxle straightened, assailed suddenly by a wall of red. He felt Entreri's anger more keenly than ever before, a razor edge that bordered on murderous rage. Images flashed too quickly for him to sort them and grasp them. He noted many of priests, of the great Protector's House, of the lines for indulgences playing out in the square.

Then just hatred.

Jarlaxle held up his hand defensively without even realizing it, though Entreri had made no move from the table.

The drow shook his head, to see the man staring at him curiously.

"What are you about?" the obviously suspicious Entreri asked.

"About tall enough to put me face between a woman's bosoms!" came a roar from the side, and Jarlaxle was truly relieved for the interruption at that particular moment.

Entreri cast a glance at Athrogate, then stood up quickly, his chair sliding out behind him. He stalked around the table, and never taking his stare off Jarlaxle, left the house.

"What's tyin' that one's armpit hair in knots?" Athrogate asked.

Jarlaxle merely smiled, glad that the potion's effects were already fading. The last thing he wanted was to be bombarded by the images that flitted through the mind of Athrogate!

Little life showed on the facings of the wind-swept brown rocks footing the mountains south of Memnon. There were a few lizards, though, sunning themselves or scampering from ledge to ledge, and so Jarlaxle knew that beneath the surface, deep in cracks or in caves formed by the incongruity of stone on stone, life found a way.

It always did—under the desert sun, or in the pits of the Underdark, where no stars shone.

A crude stone stair wound up the hundred feet or so around a large jut of rock, but Jarlaxle didn't use it. He moved off to the side, where the jag would keep him covered from view, and tipped his great hat to enact its levitation properties. He half-walked and half-floated up the sheer face. As he neared the top, he paused and glanced back behind him to view the distant harbor, and nodded with recognition in confirming that it was the same view he had seen in Entreri's thoughts when he had used the mind-reading potion.

Certain that Entreri was on the other side of the stone, Jarlaxle crept low as he went to the top.

Behind it was a flat patch of sandy ground, wider than the drow had expected. Many small and weathered stones littered the place—ancient gravestones, Jarlaxle realized. Across the sandy field directly south of his position, the drow noted a tarp-covered mound.

Bodies awaiting burial.

Entreri was indeed up there, walking among the stones, looking down at the sand and apparently lost in contemplation. Only one other man was about, a priest of Selûne, who stood at the westernmost edge, looking down at the harbor through a break in the brown stones.

It was a paupers' graveyard, where Entreri's mother was likely buried, Jarlaxle surmised. He retreated a bit over the far side of the rock and rested his back against it, considering it all. His friend was in turmoil, clearly. In breaking through Entreri's emotional wall, Jarlaxle had opened him to those painful memories.

He crawled back up and took one last look at Entreri, wondering what might result.

He floated back down carrying more than a little guilt on his slender shoulders.

⊷═══⊶

"You'll not find any names on those stones," the priest said to Entreri as the assassin puttered about, coincidentally moving nearer to the man.

Entreri looked up and noticed the priest—the same one who had been collecting indulgences in the square that day—for the first time, really, so absorbed had he been in pondering the dirt and the many souls buried beneath it. He noted the man's defensive posture, and understood that the priest felt threatened.

He offered a helpless shrug and walked off a bit.

"It's not often that a man of your obvious means would come here," the priest persisted.

Entreri turned and regarded him again.

"I mean, these wretches don't get much in the manner of visitors," the priest went on. "Mostly unknown, unloved, and unwanted . . ." He ended with a condescending chuckle, which disappeared abruptly in light of Entreri's ensuing scowl.

"Yet you write their names on your scrolls when they give you their coins in the square," the assassin remarked. "Are you up here to pray for them, then? To fulfill the indulgences they purchased at your table?"

The priest cleared his throat and said, "I am Devout Gositek."

"You've confused me with someone who cares."

"I am a priest of Selûne," the man protested.

"You are a charlatan who sells false hope."

Gositek steadied himself and straightened his robes. "Beware your words . . ." he said, inquiring of Entreri's name with his expression and inflection.

Entreri didn't blink, and at first didn't respond at all. It was all he could do to keep from leaping across the ten feet that separated him from Gositek and throwing the fool from the cliff.

Entreri reminded himself to do nothing so rash. The young man was barely half his age and could not have been involved with his mother in any way.

"As I said, I am Devout Gositek," the man said again, apparently drawing strength from Entreri's snub. "A favored scribe of Principal Cleric Yozumian Dudui Yinochek, the Blessed Voice Proper, himself. Speak ill to me at your peril. We rule the Protector's House. We are the hope and prayers of Memnon."

He babbled on for a bit, but Entreri hardly heard him, for that name, Yinochek, sparked memory in him.

"How old is he?" Entreri asked, interrupting the fool.

"What? Who?"

"This man, this Blessed Voice Proper?"

"Yinochek?"

"How old is he?"

"Why, I don't know his exact—"

"How old is he?"

"Sixty years, perhaps?" Gositek asked as much as answered.

Entreri nodded as memories came back to him of a young and fiery priest, an oratory prodigy, a blessed voice proper, who had often delivered powerful homilies from the balcony of the Protector's House. He remembered viewing some of those beside his young mother, her eyes upturned, her heart uplifted.

"And this man has been at the Protector's House for many years?" Entreri asked. "And he has been known as Blessed Voice Proper . . ."

"From the beginning," Gositek confirmed. "And yes, he was a young man when first he came to join the priests of Selûne. Why? Do you know of him?"

Entreri turned and walked away.

"You used to live here," Gositek called after him, but Entreri didn't stop.

"What was her name?" the perceptive priest asked.

Entreri stopped, and turned to regard the man.

"The woman you seek here," Gositek explained. "It was a woman, yes? What was her name?"

"She had no name," Entreri replied. "None that you would remember. Look around you for your answers. Look at all their names, for they are etched on every stone."

Gositek straightened.

Entreri walked out of the graveyard.

Entreri hardly glanced at Jarlaxle as he took the bag of gold.

"You are welcome," the drow said, with more amusement than sarcasm.

"I know," was all he got in return.

The man's mood hardly surprised Jarlaxle. "I see that you are wearing your hat this day," he said, trying to lighten the mood, and referring to a thin-brimmed black top hat he had provided to Entreri, one with many magical properties—though not as many as Jarlaxle's great hat, of course! "I have not seen it on your head in many days."

Entreri stared at him. The hat was tightly form-fitted, owing to a thin wire beneath its band. Entreri reached up and found the magical-mechanical clip, set just above his left temple. With a flick of his fingers, he disengaged it, and with a turn of his wrist, he removed the hat, tossing it to Jarlaxle, as if the reminder of where he had gotten the hat somehow sullied his desire to wear it.

That wasn't it at all, of course, as Jarlaxle clearly understood. Entreri had gotten exactly what he wanted from the hat, for it held much less rigidity, absent the wire. The idea of snubbing Jarlaxle had simply been an added bonus.

Entreri held stares with him for a moment longer, then hoisted the small sack of gold and walked out of the house.

"Must've had a bug crawl up his bum last night," said Athrogate, pulling himself up from the floor and stretching the aches from his knotty old muscles.

Still watching the departing man, and rolling the discarded hat in his hands, Jarlaxle answered, "No, my hirsute friend, it goes far deeper than that. Artemis has been forced to remember his past, and so now he has to confront the truth of who he is. Witness your own mood when speaking of Citadel Felbarr."

"I told ye I don't want to be talkin' about that."

"Exactly. Only Artemis isn't talking about anything. He's living it, in his heart. We did that to him, I fear, when he was given the flute." Finally, the drow turned to regard the dwarf. "And now we have to help him through this."

"We? Ye're pretty good with throwing around that word, elf. Course, if I knew what ye was talking about, I might be inclined to agree. Then again, I'm thinking that agreeing with ye is just going to get meself in trouble."

"Probably."

"*Bwahaha!*"

Jarlaxle knew that he could depend upon that one.

The scene at the square that morning was much as it had been when Entreri and Jarlaxle had first looked upon it, as it was almost every morning. The cobblestones could hardly be seen beneath the hordes of squatting peasants, and the long lines leading to the two tables flanking the Protector's House's great doors.

When they arrived, Jarlaxle and Athrogate had little trouble picking Artemis Entreri out from that ragamuffin crowd. He stood in the line at the farthest table, which struck Jarlaxle as odd until he noted the priest seated there, the same one he had seen in the pauper's graveyard the previous day. Entreri wondered if he had made a connection with the man.

Athrogate in tow, the drow cut through the first line of peasants and weaved across the way to move beside his companion. Those immediately behind Entreri protested the cut—or started to, until Athrogate barked at them. With his morningstars so prevalent, and a face scarred by a hundred years of battle, Athrogate had little trouble suppressing the protests of the paupers.

"Go away," Entreri said to Jarlaxle.

"I would be remiss—"

"Go away," the assassin said again, turning his head to look the elf in the eye. Jarlaxle held that stare for a few moments, long enough so that the line had time to thin ahead of them and when he disengaged the stare, Entreri was practically at the table. Entreri snorted at him dismissively, but Jarlaxle did not back off more than a couple of steps.

"First at a graveyard and now here," the priest, Gositek, said when Entreri's turn arrived. "You are truly a man of surprises."

"More than you can imagine," Entreri replied and he hoisted the sack of gold onto the table, which shook under its weight. As the bag settled, the top slipped open a bit, revealing the shiny yellow metal, and a collective gasp erupted from the peasants behind Entreri, and before, from the priest whose eyes widened so much that they seemed as if they might roll out onto the pile.

The guards behind Gositek came forward to hold back the pressing crowd, and Gositek finally sputtered, "Are you trying to incite a riot?" And it seemed as if he could hardly find breath for his voice.

"I am buying an indulgence," Entreri replied.

"The graveyard—"

"For a name long-forgotten by the priests of Selûne, their promises be damned."

"Wh-what do you mean?" Gositek stammered, and he worked to tighten the drawstring and hide away the gold before it could cause a stampede. As he moved to pull the sack toward him, though, Entreri's hand clamped hard and fast around his wrist, an iron grip that halted the man.

"Yes, the n-n-name . . ." Gositek stuttered, turning to his scribe, who sat with his mouth agape, staring stupidly. "Record the name—and a great indulgence it will—"

"Not from you," Entreri instructed.

Gositek stared at him blankly.

"I will purchase this indulgence from the blessed voice proper alone," Entreri explained. "He will receive the gold personally, will record the name personally, and recite the prayers personally."

"But that is not—"

"It is that, or it is nothing," said Entreri. "Would you go to your blessed voice proper after I have left with my gold, and explain to him why you could not allow me to see him?"

Gositek shifted nervously, rubbed a hand across his face, and licked his thin lips.

"I haven't the authority," the priest managed to say.

"Then go and find it."

The priest looked to his scribe and to the guards, all of them shaking their heads helplessly. Finally, Gositek managed to tell one of the guards to go, and the man ran off.

The line grew restless behind Entreri, but he wasn't moving for the short while it took before the guard returned. He pulled Gositek aside and whispered to him, and the devout came back to the table and sat down.

"You are fortunate," he said, "for the blessed voice proper is in his audience hall at this very time, and with a calendar that is not full. For the sake of an extreme indulgence—"

"For a sack of gold coins," Entreri corrected, and Gositek cleared his throat and did not argue the point.

"He will see you."

Entreri lifted the bag and stepped beyond the table, moving for the door, but the guards blocked his way.

"You cannot bring weapons inside the Protector's House," Gositek explained, rising again and moving to the side of Entreri. "Nor any magical items. I am sorry, but the safety of . . ."

Entreri unhitched his weapon belt and handed it back to Jarlaxle, who moved over, Athrogate still in tow—and with the dwarf still facing the crowd, holding them back with his snarling visage.

"Shall I strip naked here?" Entreri asked, pulling his *piwafwi* from his shoulders.

Gositek fumbled on that one. "Just inside," he said, motioning for the guard to open the door. Entreri went in with the priest, Jarlaxle, and Athrogate close behind.

"Your belt," Gositek instructed. "And your boots."

Entreri untied his belt and handed it to the drow, then pulled off his boots while Gositek began casting a spell. When finished, the priest scanned Entreri head to toe, and bade him to open his shirt. A nod from the priest to a burly guard had the man up close to Entreri, patting him down.

A few moments later, wearing nothing but his pants and shirt and holding a sack of gold, Entreri was escorted by yet another pair of armored soldiers through the next set of doors, disappearing into the Protector's House. In the anteroom, Jarlaxle bagged his belongings.

Gositek motioned for the elf and the dwarf to head back outside.

"There are many more bags of gold where that one came from," Jarlaxle said to the poor, stuttering priest. Noting Gositek's obvious interest, Jarlaxle gingerly reached back and pushed the door closed. "Let me explain," he said sweetly.

Some moments later, the crowd shifted uneasily as Devout Gositek walked out of the building. "Take care of their needs," he instructed the scribe and the two guards.

A flurry of protests erupted from the peasants, but the man held up his hand and cast a stern look at them to silence them. Then he disappeared back into the structure.

As the two sentries, their heavy armor clanking noisily, led him through the palace known as the Protector's House, Artemis Entreri's thoughts kept going back to his days in Calimport, serving the notorious Pasha Basadoni. For only there had Entreri seen so much gold and silver lining, and platinum artifacts and tapestries woven by the day's greatest artists. Only there had Entreri witnessed such grandeur, and hoarding of wealth. He was hardly surprised by the ostentatious decorations. Fabulous paintings and sculptures were each individually worth more coin than half the people gathered in the square could make in their lifetimes, even if they pooled all their wealth together.

Entreri knew the scene all too well. The wealth always flowed uphill and into the hands of a few. It was the way of the world, and whether it was facilitated by the threats and intimidation of the pashas of Calimport, or priests with their more subtle and insidious extortions, he had long ago ceased being surprised by it. Nor did he really care, except . . .

Except that part of the wealth that particular sect had taken from his mother had involved the most personal property of all. And she had since lay forgotten, in an unremarkable patch of sandy ground, hidden from the view of the city.

He looked at the sentries flanking him. It would would be his last walk, he knew, his last day.

So be it.

He came into a grand hall, with a ceiling that stretched up two score feet, and gigantic columns all carved and decorated with gold leaf standing in two rows, front to back. Between them lay a long and narrow bright red carpet, flanked every few feet by a soldier of the church in shining plate mail and with a halberd planted solidly at his side, its tip twice his height from the floor and tied with the banners of the principal cleric and his god, Selûne.

At the end of the carpet, perhaps thirty strides away, sat Principal Cleric Yinochek, the Blessed Voice Proper of Selûne, in a throne of polished hardwood, fashioned with white pillows shot with lines of pink and red. He wore voluminous robes, stitched with gold, and a crown of fabulous jewels rested on his head. He was indeed sixty or more, Entreri saw, though his eyes were still bright and his physique still hard and muscular. He even imagined that he saw a bit of his own features in the man, but he quickly dismissed that uncomfortable notion.

Before the throne stood three priests, two to the right and one to the left, and all half-turned to regard the approach of the man with his sack of gold.

Entreri felt the weight of their stares, their suspicions clear upon their faces, and for the flash of an instant, he believed himself too obvious, his intentions too clear. The wire of the hat band pressed in on him, and he nearly forgot himself and reached up to adjust it under his black hair.

But he stopped himself, then laughed at himself as he shook his head and glanced around, remembering who he was. He was not the bastard pauper child from the dirty streets—that was who he had been.

"I have come to purchase an indulgence," he said.

"We were told as much by Devout Gositek," one of the priests before the throne replied, but Entreri dismissed him with a wave of his hand.

"I have come to purchase an indulgence," he said again, his eyes set on, and his finger pointing at, the principal cleric, the blessed voice proper, who sat on the throne.

The four priests exchanged glances—more than one seemed out of sorts and seething.

"So we have been informed," Principal Cleric Yinochek replied. "And so we have welcomed you into our home, a place few people outside of the clergy ever see. And you speak directly to me, Principal Cleric Yinochek, as you requested." He motioned to the bag of gold. "Devout Tyre here will record the name of the person for whom you desire prayer."

"You will pray for her personally?" Entreri asked.

"Your indulgence is worthy of such, so I have been told," Yinochek replied. "Pray you leave the bag and offer the name. Then be gone in the comfort of knowing that the Blessed Voice Proper of Selûne prays for this woman."

Entreri shook his head and held the bag of gold close to his chest. "It is more than that."

"More?"

"Her name is—was, Shanali," said Entreri, and he paused and stared hard at the man, seeking a flash of recognition.

Yinochek wouldn't give him that satisfaction. If the principal cleric knew the name at all, he hid it completely, and when Entreri rationally considered the passage of thirty years and the reality of it all, he could only silently berate himself. Did the man even ask the names of the women he bedded? Even if he had, Yinochek couldn't likely remember them, the multitudes, if what the old woman had told Entreri was indeed the truth of it—and he knew in his heart that it was.

"She was my mother," Entreri said.

The looks that came back at him were of boredom, not interest.

"And she is deceased?" Yinochek asked. "As is my own mother, I assure you. That is the way of—"

"She has been dead for thirty years," Entreri interrupted, and Yinochek flashed a scowl and the other three priests and several of the guards bristled that the man would dare cut short the Blessed Voice Proper of Selûne.

But Entreri persisted. "She was a young girl—less than half my current age."

"It was a long time ago," Yinochek stated.

"I have been gone a long time," said Entreri. "Shanali—do you know the name?"

The man held his hands out helplessly and looked around at his similarly confused fellow priests. "Should I?"

"She was known among the priests of the Protector's House, so I am told."

"A noblewoman?" asked Yinochek. "But I was informed that you were at the cemetery on the rise—"

"Nobler than any in this room today," Entreri again interrupted. "She did what she had to do to survive, and to provide for me, her only child. I consider that noble."

"Of course," Yinochek replied, and he did well—better, at least—than the other three priests at hiding his amusement at the proclamation.

"Even if that meant whoring herself to priests in the Protector's House," Entreri said, and their mirth disappeared in the blink of an eye. "But you don't remember her, of course, though you were surely here at the time."

Yinochek didn't answer, other than to stare hard at the man, for a long, long time. "She has been dead for many, many years," he said finally. "Likely she has passed through the Fugue Plane in any case. Spare your indulgence for yourself, impertinent child, I pray you."

Entreri snorted. "Prayers to a god who would allow priests, even a blessed voice proper, to steal the dignity of the women of their flock?" he asked. "Prayers to Selûne, whose priests fornicate with starving young girls? Do you believe that I would wish such prayers? Better to pray to Lady Lolth, who at least admits the truth of her vile clergy."

Yinochek trembled with rage. At either side of Entreri, the guards stepped forward, weapons coming ready.

"Leave your gold and begone!" the blessed voice proper demanded. "It will purchase your life, and nothing more. And be glad that I am in a generous mood!"

"Go to your balcony," Entreri retorted. "Look out over them, Foul Voice Improper. How many are of your seed? Like myself, perhaps?"

"Remove him!" one of the priests before the throne yelled, but Yinochek stood up suddenly and shouted above them all, *"Enough!*

"You have tried my patience to its limits," he went on. "What is your . . ."

Entreri's scalp itched. He glanced around, measuring his strides, calculating the time his movements might bring. He stopped, as did Yinochek, as the door behind him banged open, forcefully, as if it had been kicked from up high.

"Wait! Your pardon and one moment, Blessed Voice Proper," said Devout Gositek, scrambling into the room. He held a wide-brimmed, feathered hat—Jarlaxle's hat.

"There is much more to this than our friend here, who consorts with elves who are much more than they seem," the man went on. As he finished he pulled something—a black fabric disk—from out of the great hat. "Much more than they seem," he said again.

Entreri's jaw dropped open at the reference, at the clue. He had his distraction.

Yinochek sat back down. "How dare you intrude, Devout Gositek?" he asked.

Gositek held up the disk of fabric, eliciting many curious stares.

Entreri leaped out to the side and smashed the guard across the face plate of his helmet with the sack of gold, launching the man to the floor. As he fell away, Entreri yanked the guard's halberd free, half turned, and launched it into the gut of the guard opposite, bending him double. His feet already moving, the assassin charged the throne, and when one of the three priests managed to react quickly enough to block his way, he threw the bag of gold into the man's face. Coins flew, and blood, and the priest fell back—even harder as Entreri planted a bare foot on his chest and leaped across.

He covered the distance to the throne in one stride, reaching up and pulling the slip-knot in the wire set under his hair. He swung it around as he went, catching the free end with his other hand, and with his fists outstretched before him, bore down on his prey. Yinochek lifted both hands defensively, but Entreri leaped headlong above the attempt to block him, snapped his hands down when they were behind the priest's defenses, then rolled over Yinochek's shoulder. Somersaulting and twisting as he went, Entreri brought his arm up and over his head so that as he descended he was back-to-back with the priest, the wire—the garrote—tight across Yinochek's throat.

Entreri used his momentum to yank the man away from the throne, hoping to snap his neck cleanly and be done with it.

But Yinochek was more stubborn and quicker than that, and he managed to come around with the flow of momentum. When it untangled, he remained very much alive, though Entreri was right behind him, tugging hard on the vicious wire, digging it into Yinochek's throat.

It would take too long, Entreri feared, expecting the guards and the priests to rush over him.

When he looked back, however, he pressed on with determination and hope that it would end then and there.

Even as Entreri had first started his move, even as he had lunged to the right at the guard, the man on the carpet behind him, Devout Gositek by all appearances, flicked the oblong piece of fabric through the air. It elongated as it twirled, widening to several feet in diameter, and slapped against the side of one of the immense pillars lining the hall.

And it was no longer a piece of fabric at all, but a magical, portable hole, a dimensional pocket. From within it, almost as soon as it hit the wall, there came a tumult and a shout.

"Snort!"

The guards nearest the hole fell back as flames erupted from the blackness, and out leaped a red war pig, snorting fire, and with a hairy and no less fiery dwarf astride it. He passed between the nearest guards, morningstars whirling left and right, and landed a solid hit on both, launching them aside.

All across the room, guards and priests finally moved to respond, and yet another surprise caught them and held them momentarily, as Devout Gositek reached a hand under his chin and tore off the magical mask, revealing himself in all of his ebon-skinned glory.

Jarlaxle threw his hat to the floor, plucking free and tossing the magical feather as he did. His hands went into a rolling spin, summoning daggers into them from his enchanted bracers and launching them out in a steady line at the nearest guard. Even with those movements, the drow kept his wits about him enough to glance across the way, where Entreri knelt behind the blessed voice proper, who sat on the floor and clawed furiously at the assassin and at the wire that dug into his throat.

With but a thought, Jarlaxle summoned his innate drow magical abilities and brought a globe of darkness over the pair.

The armor worn by soldiers of the Protector's House was beautifully crafted and with few vulnerable areas, and so Jarlaxle's barrage did little real damage to the man. As that finally dawned on the sentry, he roared and lowered his halberd.

Jarlaxle snapped his wrists alternately, elongated daggers into swords, and even as one came into being, he parried across, turning the halberd, and leaped forward and to the side, right past the stumbling man.

The drow executed a perfect spin, and launched a backhanded uppercut that brought his fine blade under the rim of the guard's great helm, driving up into his skull.

Jarlaxle retracted it almost immediately and leaped away, gaining some time by finding Athrogate's swath of destruction, as the sentry went to the floor, flailing furiously and grabbing at the vicious wound.

Artemis Entreri understood Jarlaxle's tactical meaning in summoning the globe of darkness, of course, but it didn't suit him. Not then.

He wanted to see Yinochek's face.

He rolled his legs under him and heaved backward, dragging the man out of the globe. As he came through the back limit of the darkness, he saw one of the priests, Devout Tyre, following his every move, the man's hands waving in spellcasting. Very familiar with clerical magic, Entreri knew what was coming, and he was not caught the least bit off guard as waves of compelling magical energy washed over him, an enchantment that could hold a man fast in place as surely as any paralysis.

Indeed, Entreri felt his arms go rigid, felt his body begin to deceive him.

But he conjured an image of Shanali, that last sight he had of her, and he imagined the man before him atop her, rutting like an animal, and thinking her no more than that.

His arms crossed more powerfully and Yinochek gave a pathetic wheeze.

But on came the other three priests and a pair of guards, and behind them lumbered . . . a gigantic bird?

Snort stomped and flames rolled out in a perfect circle, distracting the sentries, who were then swatted away by the wild Athrogate. His mighty legs clamping and twisting, he turned the boar at the next bunch to repeat the maneuver.

But the guards, well-trained men all, accepted the burst of flames and held their lowered halberds steady. Athrogate managed to drive one aside, but the other jabbed in at him, catching him just above the side seam in his metal breastplate. The fine tip drove through the leather under-padding and into the dwarf's armpit, and he had to throw himself back, letting Snort run right out from under him.

He fell hard to the floor, snapping the shaft of the halberd, but arched his small back and jerked his muscles in a single sudden spasm that propelled him back to his feet to meet the charge. Athrogate took some hope in the fact that the man's halberd had snapped, but it was short lived as the sentry, in one fluid motion, pulled a sword and slid a shield from his back. The man closed as if to run the dwarf right over.

From the other side came the second sentry, who similarly dropped his long weapon for sword and shield.

And Athrogate found he could hardly lift his right arm, blood running freely down his side.

Metal rang against metal as one long note across the way, closer to the door, as a pair of guards engaged the drow, and two more rushed in to join. Fighting defensively, diving into sudden rolls and using his lighter armor and better agility to keep ahead of the lunging men, Jarlaxle had little hope of scoring any solid hits against four skilled opponents. His swords whipped about every which way, seemingly randomly, but almost always deflecting a strike or forcing an attacker back.

Out in the hall behind him came many shouts, and the guards took heart.

So did the drow. And he rolled again, making sure that the approaching reinforcements could properly view the battle from the outside hall, and that they could see him, a drow, clearly. He wanted to hold their attention. He didn't want them to notice what was above the door jamb.

The release of fire, the breath of a red dragon, shook the structure with its sheer intensity as the leading guard passed under the archway. That man avoided most of the flames, but still came into the audience hall on fire, flailing. Behind him, for Jarlaxle had been sure to set the silver statuette with its little maw facing backward, the dozen men charging after him were not so fortunate, and were not about to rush through the tremendous force of that conflagration.

Fire rolled on for what seemed like many heartbeats, immolating the screaming sentries, ending any hopes of reinforcements and igniting tapestries, benches, carpeting, and the wooden beams of the structure.

Around Jarlaxle, the four sentries stared in disbelief—and though the distraction lasted for no more than perhaps two seconds, that was a second longer than Jarlaxle needed.

The drow came up from his roll, planted his feet, and propelled himself back the other way, into their midst. Out to the left slashed one blade, chopping hard on a sword arm and driving the weapon from the man's grasp. Out to the right stabbed the second sword, through a seam in armor and into the side of a man.

Out to the left leaped the drow, planting his feet on the chest of one guard and shoving off, launching the man to the floor and himself back and to the right, where he got up and over the blade of the fourth, turning as he went so that he was almost sitting on the man's shoulders. Jarlaxle dropped his bloody blades in a cross before the man's throat and slashed them out to their respective sides as he back-rolled over that shoulder, gracefully gaining his feet and spinning away.

The sentry grasped at his throat and sank to his knees.

"For Selûne!" the guard cried, thinking his victory at hand.

And under the cover of his shout, Athrogate called to his right-hand morningstar, enabling its magic, bringing forth explosive oil from its prongs. The dwarf snapped himself around, launching the head of the weapon at the guard's blocking shield. His arm was a limp thing, and there was no weight behind the strike, but when it connected with that shield, the oil exploded, shattering both the shield and the arm that held it and throwing the man back to the floor.

Athrogate fell off to the left, swiping across with his second weapon, one coated with the magically-duplicated ooze of a creature known to strike fear in the hearts of the greatest warriors: a rust monster. The initial contact of morningstar against shield did little to dissuade the oblivious attacker, who shield-rushed the dwarf and crashed his sword down hard on Athrogate's shoulder.

Roaring in pain, the dwarf sent his left arm in furious pumps, spinning the morningstar head in horizontal twirls, each connecting with the shield. So furious was his attack that the guard had to backtrack.

But the man seemed unconcerned, was even mocking the dwarf,

as, bloody and battered, Athrogate turned to square up with him.

On he charged, and the dwarf spun left, his right arm swinging, his morningstar coming at the shield with little power behind it.

It needed none, however, for the shield had turned to rust, and the impact blew it apart, red dust flying all over them both.

The guard paused in surprise, and Athrogate roared and spun the rest of the way around more furiously, his left coming across in a mighty backhand. His shield ruined, the guard had no choice but to spin away from the blow.

And Athrogate, leaping in that final turn, planted his leading left foot solidly and stepped into perfect balance with his right, halting his momentum with brutal efficiency. He stepped forward with his left foot, swinging his weapon, smashing the guard in the back in mid-turn, and sending him staggering forward.

Athrogate was with him, every stride, his left arm working left-to-right and down, then reversing right-to-left and over, the ball smashing against the man's back repeatedly, driving him forward in a stumbling run. Again and again the pursuing dwarf hit him, as if guiding him with the morningstar.

Headlong, face-first, into a stone pillar.

The guard's arms reflexively went around the thing as he slid down, though he was hardly conscious of the movement.

Athrogate whacked him again, just because.

Entreri snapped his arms left and right as he drove up to his feet, dragging the poor Yinochek with him. He tried to break the man's neck, but had no leverage to do so, nor did he have the time to complete the strangulation. Reluctantly, angrily, he released the priest and shoved him forward at the nearest man, another priest, then rushed in hard behind and shoulder-blocked another aside. He spun out to the right in a dead run, hoping to get ahead of the stab of another man.

He wouldn't have made it, except that suddenly, instead of stabbing, the man was flying forward, launched by the powerful peck of Jarlaxle's diatryma. Entreri ran right by the giant bird as it plowed forward, trampling the fallen defender.

On Entreri sprinted, his bare feet slapping the stone floor. He cut and veered as guards closed in on him from both sides, but with a sudden burst, he got beyond them, diving into a headlong roll over the fallen chair. He came back to his feet with three men in close pursuit.

He noted Jarlaxle's sudden flurry, saw men falling every which way, and marked the fires raging out beyond the room, thick smoke starting to come in the door. None of it would help him, he knew.

He had to anticipate Jarlaxle, had to think like his drow companion.

He went straight for the extra-dimensional hole hanging on the side of the pillar.

With halberds reaching out just behind him, Entreri dived in and disappeared from sight.

He felt a body in there, one that moved and groaned, and he slugged the man across the face, laying him low. As he scrambled around, his hand closed on a pommel.

Kill them! came a message in his mind, one of eagerness.

Entreri wasn't about to disappoint the blade.

The three guards stood before the hole, rightly hesitating and tentative. Out came Entreri in a great leap, red-bladed sword in one hand, jeweled dagger in the other. He smashed Charon's Claw down atop the nearest halberd, to his right and before him, and drove the weapon down, but then rolled his sword underneath it as he landed and quick-stepped forward. He swung his arm back up and over his shoulder, taking the long, spearlike weapon with it, and swinging it out to intercept the thrusting sword of the next man in line.

At the same time, the assassin executed a reverse backhand parry with his dagger, driving the sword on his left out behind him. He turned as he did to face the man holding the sword, and lifted his left arm high, taking the sword with it, then thrust across with Charon's Claw, stabbing the man in the chest. As that one fell away, freeing up his dagger hand, Entreri threw himself backward and under the swipe of the cumbersome halberd. He fell into a sitting position, but kept turning, driving his jeweled dagger into the spearman's knee then rolling around as the man howled, tearing his dagger free. He slashed across with Charon's Claw, taking the man's legs out and toppling him to the ground. Entreri used the falling man as a shield, leaping back to his feet, but he needn't have, he realized, for the third had turned to run off.

Entreri leaped into pursuit, but pulled up short, his attention drawn across the room, where the three priests escorted the blessed voice proper out a back door.

"No!" Entreri yelled charging that way, though he knew he'd never get there in time to stop the escape. It couldn't happen like this! Not after all his effort, not after all the memories of Shanali had assaulted him.

Devout Tyre, in the lead, pulled open the door; Entreri did the only thing he could and launched his sword like a great spear.

"Ah, but ye're a good pig," Athrogate said to Snort. He leaned heavily on the boar, nearly collapsing from loss of blood, and directed the creature to the extra-dimensional pocket. As he neared the black hole, the dwarf noted a man crawling out.

Devout Gositek turned to him pitifully.

Athrogate slugged him hard, knocking him out, so that he was hanging by the waist over the lip of the hole, the fingers of his extended arms just brushing the floor.

On a word from the dwarf, Snort leaped back into the hole. Athrogate looked to Jarlaxle and saluted, though the drow hardly seemed to notice. Then the dwarf hopped into a sitting position on the rim of the dimensional pocket, grabbed Gositek by the scruff of his neck, and rolled back out of sight, taking the battered priest with him.

Out of the corner of his eye, Devout Tyre saw the missile coming. He fell back with a yelp, knocking his fellows into a stumble, with Blessed Voice Proper Yinochek, still gasping for breath, falling back against the wall. The red-bladed sword rushed past Tyre and hit the wood, the weight of the missile closing the door hard, and leaving the sword stuck there, quivering.

"Get him out!" Tyre commanded the other two, turning toward the charging Entreri. "I will finish this one."

With a snarl of defiance, the priest grabbed Charon's Claw and yanked it from the door.

Everything seemed to move in slow motion for Devout Tyre. He stumbled away from the door as one of his companions, Devout Premmy, tugged the portal back open. He saw the man Entreri, screaming in protest, still thirty feet or more away. He watched the man change hands with his remaining weapon, saw him leap high and far, planting his left foot as he came down.

Entreri's hips rotated to square with the door. His left arm swung out wide as he rolled his right shoulder forward, arm coming up and over in a mighty throw.

Tyre hardly registered the movement, the silver flickers of the missile, but he knew somehow exactly where it was heading. He tried to scream a warning, but his voice came out as a high-pitched shriek.

He hardly heard that, but instead heard Entreri's seemingly elongated cry of *"Shanali!"*

And as though with the snap of some unseen wizard's fingers, time sped up and the silver missile flashed past him. Devout Tyre turned and saw his Blessed Voice Proper, the Principal Cleric of the Protector's House, with his arms out before him, quivering, his face a mask of exquisite pain, the jeweled hilt of a dagger protruding from his chest.

And Tyre saw . . . white. Just hot white, as his sensibilities finally registered the excruciating pain that burned throughout his body and soul. He screamed again—or tried to, but his lips curled up over his teeth, and rolled back even farther as if melting away. Somewhere deep inside him, Tyre knew that he should drop the evil sword.

But his sensibilities were long gone by then, his thoughts no longer connecting to his body. Pain controlled him, and nothing more, as he felt a million stinging needles, a million burning bites, a fire within him as profound and devastating as the one that had exploded in the corridor across the way.

He fell to the floor but never knew it. He lay there trembling, his skin smoldering and crackling into charred bits as Charon's Claw ate him.

The throw—both of them—had come from somewhere so deep inside of him that Artemis Entreri had hardly even realized his actions. He had seen nothing but Shanali, frail and dying in the dust. He had felt nothing but his rage, his absolute fury that the vile priest would escape him.

The moment his dagger thudded into Principal Cleric Yinochek's heart, the spell was broken, and Entreri, running at the four priests, felt a flood of angry satisfaction.

He slowed his pace, noting movement from the side, then watched as two of the priests deserted Yinochek and rushed out the door, Jarlaxle's diatryma in close pursuit. There were soldiers coming toward the room down the hall beyond, he saw, but how they changed their attitude and their direction when that giant bird crashed out through the doorway.

Entreri rushed up and pushed the door closed. He glanced at the dying Tyre but paid him no more heed than that, moving instead to stand before the principal cleric.

"Do you know how many lives you have ruined?" he asked the man.

Trembling, sputtering, his eyes wide with horror, Yinochek's lips moved but no words came forth.

"Yes," Entreri noted. "You know. You understand it all. You know the wretchedness of your actions as you steal the coin of the peasants and the innocence of the girls. You know, and so you are afraid." He reached up and grabbed the dagger hilt, and Yinochek stiffened.

Entreri thought to obliterate the man's soul with his magical weapon, but he shook his head and dismissed the notion.

"Selûne is a goodly god, so I've heard," he said, "and thus will have nothing to do with the likes of you. I call you a fraud, and there is nowhere left for you to hide."

The man's eyes rolled back into his head, and he slumped to the floor.

"A better way to go than that one," Jarlaxle said, and only then did Entreri realize that the drow had come to his side. Jarlaxle's gaze led Entreri's to what remained of Devout Tyre, who lay on his back shaking wildly, his robes smoking and his face showing more bone than flesh.

With a growl, Entreri stomped hard on the man's forearm,

crushing the burnt skin and bone, and the recoil lifted Charon's Claw into the air, where Entreri easily caught it.

He looked back at Jarlaxle as the drow settled the fabric patch back into his great hat.

The building shook violently, and across the room, a gout of flames rushed in.

"Come," Jarlaxle bade him, putting on his magical mask. "We must be away."

Entreri looked back at the blessed voice proper, sitting against the wall, his chest covered in blood, his eyes white.

He thought of Shanali one last time. He took a brief moment to consider the long and dirty road of his miserable life, which had ultimately brought him to that awful place.

EPILOGUE

The commotion behind him did little to take Entreri's gaze from the city below him. He stood on the jag of rock at the paupers' graveyard, staring down at the plume of smoke that hung lazily over the ruins of the Protector's House.

His vengeance had been sated, obviously so, but there was little left in the man. Finally he turned back to Jarlaxle, who had opened his portable hole against another stone, and stood with Athrogate beside him, staring into the darkness.

"Well, ye might as well be coming here," the dwarf recited. "Afore I find me way in there. In that case, yerself should fear, me pulling ye out by the tip o' yer ears!"

Entreri rubbed a hand over his weary face, and moved down from the perch as Devout Gositek, his face all bruised, crawled out of the hole.

"I am not afraid to die," he said, trembling so badly he seemed as if he was about to soil himself.

Jarlaxle turned deferentially to Entreri.

"Then get out of here," the assassin said.

Gositek's jaw dropped open.

"Generous," Jarlaxle remarked.

"Surprised," said Athrogate.

Gositek looked at the elf and dwarf, then scrambled for the stair. But Entreri intercepted him, and with frightening strength yanked him aside and ran him to the very edge of the hundred-foot drop.

"No, please!" the priest who was not afraid to die desperately pleaded.

"If you wish to remain alive, then look down there," Entreri growled in his ear. "Mark well the destruction of the Protector's House. You will rebuild it—you and your fellow priests?"

When Gositek didn't immediately answer, Entreri shifted him forward, almost off the ledge.

The terrified man yelped and blurted, "Yes!"

Entreri tugged him back. "And you will never forget their names again," he instructed. "Any of them. And you and your brethren will come up here, every day, and pray for the souls of those who have gone before."

"Yes, yes, yes," Gositek stammered.

"Do you understand me?" Entreri roared, shaking him near the edge again.

"I do! We will!"

"I don't believe you," Entreri said, and the man began to cry.

Entreri threw him back from the cliff and to the ground. "Remember that view," he warned. "For if you forget your promise, you will see it again, with smoke once more rising from the ruins of your rebuilt temple. And on that next occasion, I will throw you from the cliff."

The man nodded stupidly as he crawled away. Finally, near the edge of the graveyard, he managed to put his feet under him, and he scrambled down the long stair.

Entreri moved to the top of that stair and watched him run away.

"Are you satisfied now, my friend?" Jarlaxle asked.

Entreri put his head down and forced himself to remain calm then turned around, his expression revealing his emptiness.

Jarlaxle offered a shrug. "It is often the way," he said. "We've all demons needing to be put to rest, but the experience is not as rewardi—"

"Shut up," Entreri interrupted.

Athrogate laughed.

"We must be gone from this place," Jarlaxle said.

"I don't care where you go," Entreri answered. He reached into his pouch and pulled forth Idalia's flute, which he had broken into two pieces. He locked stares with the drow and tossed it to Jarlaxle's feet.

Jarlaxle gave a helpless chuckle, but there was no real mirth in it. Finally breaking Entreri's imposing stare, he bent and retrieved the flute. "A valuable item," he said.

"Cursed," came Entreri's reply.

"Ah, Artemis," said the drow. "I understand your wounds and your anger, but in the end, you will see that this was all for the best."

"You might be right, but that changes little."

"How so?" asked the drow.

Entreri pulled his pack around. He fished out the obsidian figurine and dropped it to the ground, calling forth his nightmare mount. As the creature materialized, Entreri pulled forth another object and sent it spinning at Jarlaxle.

A black, small-brimmed hat.

"I am finished with you," Entreri said. "Your road is your own, and I care not if it takes you to the gates of the Nine Hells."

Jarlaxle caught the hat and rolled it over in his slender hands. "But Artemis, be reasonable."

"I have never been more so," Entreri replied, and he put one foot in a stirrup and hoisted himself astride the tall black horse. "Farewell, Jarlaxle. Or fare ill. It matters not to me."

"But I am your muse."

"I don't like the songs you inspire."

Entreri turned his mount around, stepping to the stair.

"Where will you go?"

The assassin paused and looked back sourly.

"I can find out, in any case," Jarlaxle reminded him.

"To Calimport," Entreri answered, and he gave a helpless laugh at the truth of the drow's statement—and Jarlaxle took heart in that, at least. "To Dwahvel, and to a place I might call home."

"Ah, Mistress Tiggerwillies!" Jarlaxle said with sudden animation. "And will you seek to regain your status among the streets of that fair city?"

Entreri chortled and nodded toward the distant plume of smoke. "Artemis Entreri is dead," he said. "He died in the Protector's House in Memnon, chasing ghosts."

He turned his horse away, down the stairs and out of sight.

"Might that we should follow him," Athrogate said to Jarlaxle. "He'll be gettin' hisself into trouble, no doubt. It's the way his blood's flowing."

But Jarlaxle, staring at the empty stair, shook his head with every word. "No," he said. "And no. I suspect that Artemis Entreri really is dead, my friend."

"Looked living to me."

Jarlaxle laughed, not willing to explain it, and not expecting that Athrogate, who had his own emotional barriers defining him, would begin to understand.

But Athrogate remarked, "Ah, he died the way meself died when them orcs come to Felbarr."

"More than three centuries ago?" Jarlaxle asked.

"Three and a half, elf."

"And yet you look so young."

"Might be that livin' long's a curse more than a blessing."

"A curse imposed by . . . ?"

"Ever twist the bum hairs of a wizard, elf?"

Jarlaxle rolled his eyes and laughed.

" 'Ill-argued and ill-met,' he told me. 'A pox on me bones for not payin' me debt. To grab the sun and not let it set, ye'll not die young, and ye'll never forget.' "

"That was his curse?"

"And after three hunnerd years, I'm tellin' ye it worked."

Jarlaxle nodded and considered the tale for a short while. Then, on a sudden impulse, he reached over and plopped the hat atop the dwarf's hairy head.

"Hey, now!"

"Yes," Jarlaxle said, nodding with admiration. "It suits you well."

As he spoke, the drow dropped a hand into his pouch, feeling the broken pieces of Idalia's flute and wondering how much it would cost him to get it repaired.

He winced just a bit, because he realized that Athrogate couldn't likely blow a note.

But he looked back to the empty stair, where Artemis Entreri had gone, and he reminded himself that sometimes you just had to play the hand you were dealt.

During the Last War, Gaven was an
adventurer, searching the darkest reaches
of the underworld. But an encounter with
a powerful artifact forever changed him,
breaking his mind and landing him in the
deepest cell of the darkest prison in
all the world.

THE DRACONIC PROPHECIES

BOOK I

When war looms on the horizon, some see it as more
than renewed hostilities between nations. Some see the
fulfillment of an ancient prophecy—one that promises
both the doom and salvation of the world. And Gaven may
be the key to it all.

THE STORM DRAGON

The first EBERRON® hardcover by veteran game designer
and the author of *In the Claws of the Tiger*:

James Wyatt

SEPTEMBER 2007

MARGARET WEIS
&
TRACY HICKMAN

The co-creators of the DRAGONLANCE® world return to the
epic tale that introduced Krynn to a generation of fans!

THE LOST CHRONICLES

VOLUME ONE
DRAGONS OF THE DWARVEN DEPTHS

As Tanis and Flint bargain for refuge in Thorbardin, Raistlin
and Caramon go to Neraka to search for one of the spellbooks of
Fistandantilus. The refugees in Thorbardin are trapped when the
draconian army marches, and Flint undertakes a quest to find the
Hammer of Kharas to free them all, while Sturm becomes a key of a
different sort.
Now Available in Paperback!

VOLUME TWO
DRAGONS OF THE HIGHLORD SKIES

Dragon Highlord Ariakas assigns the recovery of the dragon orb taken to
Ice Wall to Kitiara Uth-Matar, who is rising up the ranks of both the dark
forces and of Ariakas's esteem. Finding the orb proves easy, but getting
it from Laurana proves more difficult. Difficult enough to attract the
attention of Lord Soth.
Now Available in Hardcover!

VOLUME THREE
DRAGONS OF THE HOURGLASS MAGE

The wizard Raistlin Majere takes the black robes and travels to the
capital city of the evil empire, Neraka, to serve the Queen of Darkness.
July 2008

RAVENLOFT
the covenant

RAVENLOFT'S LORDS OF DARKNESS HAVE ALWAYS WAITED FOR THE UNWARY TO FIND THEM.

Six classic tales of horror set in the RAVENLOFT™ world have returned to print in all-new editions.

From the autocratic vampire who wrote the memoirs found in *I, Strahd* to the demon lord and his son whose story is told in *Tapestry of Dark Souls*, some of the finest horror characters created by some of the most influential authors of horror and dark fantasy have found their way to RAVENLOFT, to be trapped there forever.

LAURELL K. HAMILTON
Death of a Darklord

CHRISTIE GOLDEN
Vampire of the Mists

P.N. ELROD
I, Strahd: The Memoirs of a Vampire

ANDRIA CARDARELLE
To Sleep With Evil

ELAINE BERGSTROM
Tapestry of Dark Souls

TANYA HUFF
Scholar of Decay
October 2007